The Woman Who Was Poor

Other Works of Note from St. Augustine's Press

Raïssa Maritain, *We Have Been Friends Together* and *Adventures in Grace*

Jacques Maritain, *Natural Law: Reflections on Theory and Practice*

Robert Hugh Benson, *Lord of the World*

Gabriel Marcel, *The Mystery of Being* (in two volumes)

Gabriel Marcel, *Man Against Mass Society*

Gabriel Marcel, *Homo Viator*

Gabriel Marcel, *Thou Shall Not Die*

Gabriel Marcel, *A Gabriel Marcel Reader*

Yves R. Simon, *The Great Dialogues of Nature and Space*

Richard Peddicord, o.p., *The Sacred Monster of Thomism: An Introduction to the Life and Legacy of Reginald Garrigou-Lagrange*, o.p.

Josef Pieper and Heinz Raskop, *What Catholics Believe*

Josef Pieper, *Scholasticism: Personalities and Problems*

Josef Pieper, *The Silence of St. Thomas*

Josef Pieper, *The Concept of Sin*

Josef Pieper, *Death and Immortality*

C.S. Lewis and Don Giovanni Calabria, *The Latin Letters of C.S. Lewis*

Henrik Syse, *Natural Law, Religion, and Rights*

Fulvio di Blasi, *God and Natural Law: A Rereading of Thomas Aquinas*

Rémi Brague, *On the God of the Christians*

Philippe Bénéton, *The Kingdom Suffereth Violence: The Machiavelli / Erasmus / More Correspondence and Other Unpublished Documents*

The Woman Who Was Poor

A Contemporary Novel of the French 'Eighties

Leon Bloy

Translated by I. J. Collins

St. Augustine's Press
South Bend, Indiana

Manufactured in the United States of America.

1 2 3 4 5 6   21 20 19 18 17 16 15

Library of Congress Cataloging in Publication Data
Bloy, Léon, 1846–1917.
[Femme pauvre. English]
The woman who was poor: a contemporary novel of the French 'Eighties / Leon Bloy; translated by I. J. Collins.
pages cm
Originally published: New York: Sheed & Ward, 1939.
First published 1897 in France as La femme pauvre.
ISBN 978-1-890318-92-5 (paperback)
1. Poor women – Fiction. 2. France – Fiction.
I. Collins, I. J., translator. II. Title.
PQ2198.B18F413 2015
843'.8 – dc23   2015005665

∞ The paper used in this publication meets the minimum requirements of the American National Standard for Information Sciences – Permanence of Paper for Printed Materials, ANSI Z39.48-1984.

ST. AUGUSTINE'S PRESS
www.staugustine.net

Contents

To
G. M. S. W.

This English edition (of a book whose author reached
a lesson which your own life—with its years of
grimmest poverty invited and embraced quite volun-
tarily, in lonely heroism, for the sake of others, so long
as their need lasted and made you indifferent to your
own–could have well illustrated) is dedicated to you,
in reverent humility, by the translator.

England, 1937   I. J. C.

To Pierre Antide Edmond
BRIGAND-KAIRE
OCEAN CAPTAIN

And so, now, here is THE WOMAN WHO WAS POOR—the one you desired so long, and did not know—and I, as it seemly, invoke for her the patronage of these for whom is said the Office for the Dead.

I know of no man more amazing than yourself, my dear Bigan; and, one day, I shall expound this in writing as fine as I can achieve.

Your friendship—that came to me unlooked for and, as I must needs believe, Heaven-sent—ranks, indeed, as one of those rare marvels which it has been vouchsafed to me to see while on earth.

For who buy you, with the exception of our great painter, Henry de Groux, has penetrated to each a depft, and with such a galland heart, into my gloomy grave? Remember, how you were my host when I lodged in the nameless house, the house of decay and despair, which I have attempted to depict, and whose horror must, I think, have accompanied you into the midst of the splendars and bloodshed of Asia.

To you, then, I dedicate this unhappy work, imposed on me by the vigour of your personality—a work that would be, probably, a masterpiece, were I not its author.

God keep you safe from fire and steel and contemporary literature and the malevolence of the evil dead.

Grand Montrouge,   Leon Bloy
Ash Wednesday, 1897

To Pierre Antide Edmond

BRIGAND-KAIRE
OCEAN CAPTAIN

And so, now, here is THE WOMAN WHO WAS POOR—the one you desired so long, and did not know—and I, as is seemly, invoke for her the patronage of those for whom is said the Office for the Dead.

I know of no man more amazing than yourself, my dear Bigan; and, one day, I shall expound this in writing as fine as I can achieve.

Your friendship—that came to me unlooked for and, as I must needs believe, Heaven-sent—ranks, indeed, as one of those rare marvels which it has been vouchsafed to me to see while on earth.

For who but you, with the exception of our great painter, Henry de Groux, has penetrated to such a depth, and with such a gallant heart, into my gloomy grave? Remember, how you were my host when I lodged in the nameless house, the house of decay and despair, which I have attempted to depict, and whose horror must, I think, have accompanied you into the midst of the splendours and bloodshed of Asia.

To you, then, I dedicate this unhappy work, imposed on me by the vigour of your personality—a work that would be, probably, a masterpiece, were I not its author.

God keep you safe from fire and steel and contemporary literature and the malevolence of the evil dead.

Grand Montrouge,   Leon Bloy
Ash Wednesday, 1897.

PART ONE

FLOTSAM OF THE SHADOWS

Qui erant in poenis tenebrarum,
clamantes et discentes: Advenisti
Redemptor noster.

Officium Defunctorum.

CHAPTER I

" This place stinks of God "

This bit of gutter-snipe's impudence was belched forth
like a vomit on the very humble threshold of the Lazarist
Missionaries' chapel in the Rue de Sèvres, in 1879.

It was the first Sunday in Advent, and the population of
Paris was making its toilsome way along to the Great
Winter Circus.

Like so many other years, that year had not turned out
to be the Year of the End of the World—and it never
occurred to anybody to be surprised. Least of all to old
Isidore Chapuis, scale-maker and weighing-machine
mechanic by profession, and one of the most highly
respected tipplers of the Gros Caillou.

By temperament and training he belonged to that world
of perfect squalid vice that is to be found nowhere but in
Paris, unparalleled by the vulgar dissipation of any other
nation under the sun.

A most unproductive sterile scoundrelism, indeed,
despite any amount of assiduous political tillage and un-
remitting " literary " watering. Even showers of blood
would not raise a crop of noteworthy individuals from such
a soil.

The elderly scale-maker who had just opened the cesspool
of his soul as he passed a holy place, was a worthy and not
unduly modest representative of all the loud-mouthed and
foul-mouthed oratorical skill of that social group into which

the dirty slops of middle-class intellectualism, and the reeking filth of the working man, are everlastingly emptied, as into a common sewage sump.

Thoroughly pleased with his own snappy wit, and the consternation it had caused in a few devout souls who were eyeing him in horror, he swayed along with zig-zag steps to some vague destination, like a sleep-walker feeling seasick.

A sort of forewarning of perilous giddiness seemed to impend over the addled head of this unit of the common rabble, blotchy with liquor, and broken on the wheel of the uncleaner lusts.

A surly, haughty waggishness played over his gallows mask, making his lower lip curl outwards, below the rotting crenellations of his foul teeth, so that both corners of his mouth turned down to the lowest of the muddy or scaly ruts, dug into his face by the ravages of grog and chemical adulterants.

In the middle there had grown for sixty years a nose of Jewish, money-lending, sharp exactitude of aspect, beneath which sprouted the stubble of a rebellious moustache, that might profitably have served for currying mangy nags.

His mean little eyes, improbably small, quick and active as a flitter-mouse's or rat's eyes, had a lustreless glitter that made one think of some habitual church robber breaking the poor-box open at night.

The broken-down ruffian's whole aspect gave the general impression of some ruthless monstrosity, exacting and ready-witted even in his cups, depleted of all ardour in adventures of long ago, and, ever since, keeping up his bully's heart only by attacks on the feeble and unarmed.

But the worthy old Chapuis was not altogether un-lettered. He habitually read certain trenchant and dog-matic newspapers, such as *La Lanterne*, or the *Cri du Peuple*, with a firm faith in the inevitable advent of the Social Revolution, and was very fond of babbling oracular wisdom, in the pot-houses, on Politics and Religion—those two delightful sciences, so marvellously easy (as everybody knows) that any fool can master them like a specialist.

Love, of course, as distinct from lust, he scorned, treating it as a lot of nonsense. If any other learned doctor made any serious allusion to love, Chapuis burst into loud guffaws, and clowned and burlesqued it with vim.

Consequently, the charming Isidore claimed the respect of an amazing number of saloon keepers.

Nobody knew much about his antecedents, though he professed to be of respectable middle-class extraction, from Perigord. That was some way back, obviously, because the old fellow, by his own showing, was born in the Fauborg du Temple, where his people had been compelled to practise various peculiarly Parisian trades of a vague nature on which he did not dwell in any detail.

He claimed, accordingly, a provincial descent worthy of the utmost respect, and an incalculable number of family connections scattered far and wide, and he boasted of their wealth, administering good vigorous snubbings to the snobbery of landed proprietors who despised the proud smock of a labouring citizen, which he himself wore. Actually, however, nobody had ever seen one of these relations. So their problematical existence was at the same time a means of glorification and a pretext for generous invective.

Even more energetically, however, would he inveigh against the injustice of his own lot, narrating, with all the eloquence of a native of the glowing south, the accursed ill-luck that had frustrated all his ventures, and the sickening dishonesty of the unscrupulous rivals who had forced him to doff the frock coat of an employer and don the overalls of the proletariat.

For he had actually been a capitalist, and run his own workshop, working on his own account—or, rather, making some half a dozen workmen work for him. And to them he had seemed the Commander of the Faithful of drinking-bouts and endless debaucheries.

The Glacière neighbourhood could still remember those gay, rollicking weighing-machine mechanics, so uncertain of their own balance when one ran into them in the wine-shops, where the "boss", drunk as a lord, was always expounding his lore to them.

The crash, not long in coming, and easy enough to fore-see from such omens, surprised nobody but Chapuis him-self. At first he stormed imprecations against the heavens and the earth ; but eventually, with the touching faith of a toper, confessed that he had committed the folly of " being too honest in business ".

As to the source of this short-lived prosperity—a source long exhausted—no one knew a thing. "A little legacy he came into, from the provinces," was the scale-maker's vague explanation. But it was rendered a little doubtful by certain odd rumours that had at one time been current.

People remembered distinctly how before the two sieges they had known him as a ruffian without any bloated luxury about him, just a bad lot lugging his carcase about from one workshop to another.

Then, after the Commune, he was suddenly seen as a rich man with a few score thousand francs, with which he had bought his business.

If the hushed murmurs of the neighbourhood were to be believed, this money, collected in some ghastly hole reeking with bloodshed, had been the ransom of a merchant prince who had inexplicably been preserved from shot and fire, the heroic Chapuis having been a Commandant, or even a Lieutenant-Colonel, in the insurgent forces.[1]

The extremely mysterious and arbitrary clemency, which spared a certain number of the mutineers after the insurrection, had sheltered him as it had sheltered many more famous rebels who were known or supposed to be the repositories of sordid secrets, and liable to make unwelcome revelations.

So he was left alone to soak himself in drink on his wrecker's loot, in peace and undisturbed, having taken care to be completely invisible during such time as the summary executions were taking place.

A little later on, a few half-hearted attempts to interview him were made by the representatives of Public Order and Morals, but they found the habitual drunkard really or ostensibly so stupefied and befuddled that they gave it up, and old Chapuis, after being for a brief moment almost a celebrity, settled down again for good into complete obscurity.

In this way the man moved in a cloud of confused events

[1] The Prussian siege of Paris, March 18th, 1871, and the second siege by the Thiers government forces, May 28th, 1871, which overthrew the Commune set up by the insurrection accompanying the Prussian siege.

that made him an important oracle to the poor wretches
with whom he condescended to resort, their puerile minds
ready to be mastered by anybody with a loud voice and a
cheap reputation for " knowing a thing or two ". Have
not the Sovereign Commons themselves become the
Sacred Geese of ancient superstition, for those wine-house
augurs whose astuteness the police are sometimes glad to
use ?

In short, the elderly Isidore had the general reputation
of being a " tough ", a generic classification beyond all
dispute.

He certainly belonged to that race of worthless
scum originally created by Providence to off-set the
Seraphim.

Does not the great stream of humanity need such a
receptacle to give warning, by its splash and stench, when
aught is dropped from Heaven ? And how could any
heart achieve greatness without the wonderful educational
value of the nausea such a vessel must beget ?

Without Barabbas the Redemption would not have
been. God would not have been *worthy* to create the
world had He forgotten to evoke from the void that
host of riff-raff who crucified Him.

CHAPTER II

DESPITE his erratic gait, it would seem that the some-time
Master Scale-Maker had that on hand which would suffer
no delay, for he did not stop at the *Rendez-vous Des Ennemis*

Du Phyloxéra, and he deigned no reply to the ebony-skinned chucker-out who hailed him from the threshold of the *Cocher Fidèle*.

Possibly, too, he had already had enough, for, although it was barely noon, he refused to let himself be tempted by any of those bars amidst whose delights he was wont to make innumerable breaks in his journeyings. Moreover, he was muttering to himself, and spitting on his boots, a well-known symptom of sullen preoccupation that was always respected by those who knew him best.

Having thus rebuffed every offer of comfort, he arrived at last at his own door, midway along a gloomy Grenelle street, where he had lived since his failure in business.

Reaching the fourth floor with some difficulty, a floor reeking with the noisome effluvia of plumbing and " sanitation ", he banged with his elbow, like a paralytic, against a peeling door that looked like the most horrid of Hell's entrances.

The door opened to his knock, and an old woman made her appearance, gazing at him with a question in her eyes.

" Well! " he answered. " It's all settled. Only depends on the Princess now."

He dropped into the first chair to hand, at the same time aiming at the grate a jet of muddy saliva whose trajectory, calculated with insufficient exactitude, ended in the fringed trimming of a tattered rug that adorned the floor in front of the hearth.

While the old woman hastened to efface with her foot the unpleasant evidence of this inaccurate spitting, he cleared his throat generously of some preliminary grievances.

" Oh, Lord, it's a way, that damned Faubourg Honoré—

and not a copper for a bus—and then having to cool my heels and wait for his lordship. A painter, if you please, who works for the aristos! Ten o'clock, and he wasn't up yet! I'd a good mind to tell him off. But I says to myself, it's for your daughter. High time she worked us a bit of dough, going on for six months and her not doing a stroke —Look here, you old pest, haven't you got anything to drink in the place?"

The woman addressed flung two skinny arms up towards the heavens, drawing a deep, long sigh.

"Alas, dear, sweet Christ, what shall I say to this poor darling, who has gone through so much for his poor family? Holy Virgin, bear me witness, there's nothing left in the place! Everything worth a penny has gone to the pawnshop. Everything they gave us has gone on food. Oh, dear Saviour, why don't you take me away from this world, where I've suffered so much, so long?"

The word "suffered", obviously rehearsed for years, was strangled with a sob.

Isidore stretched out one hand and grasped hold of her skirt.

"Enough of that, d'you hear? You know I don't like your damned Jesuit cant. If you want a dance, you've only got to say so. I'll see that you have one, free gratis. And come to that, where *is* your drab of a daughter?"

"Why, Zizi, you *know* she had to go to Cousin Amédée's, in the Boulevard de Vaugirard, to try and see if she could borrow five francs or so. She said she wouldn't be more than an hour gone. When you knocked I thought it was her coming back."

"You never told me, you old crow. Her cousin's a bitch. *She* won't give her a bean ; refused *me*, she did, the other day, and said she had no money for boozing. I shan't forget that in a hurry! Oh, my God, my God, this is Hell," he added, almost under his breath. "There's a duck to go and make her disgorge her lousy charity for another girl! Oh, all right, then, we'll wait and sit sucking our thumbs, and see if Mademoiselle Gentility will do her old folks the honour of listening to them!"

"No, tell me all about how you got on this morning," said the snivelling old termagant, sitting down. "You say it's all fixed up with Monsieur Gacougnol?"

"Yes, yes. Two francs an hour, and three or four hours a day—if her person suits him, of course! It's a cushy job ; no hard work to break her back, you bet. Your little chick's got to be there at eleven to-morrow, then he'll decide on the spot.

"The swine doesn't seem easy to get on with. He asked me a whole heap of questions. Wanted to know if she had any lovers, if she could be depended on, if she never got tight now and then. How do I know? I had a good mind to tell him to—— Seems as if he wouldn't have seen me, but for the boss's letter. It's a bit thick, you know, to have to be patronised by these dudes who're afraid to let a working man go near them, as if you were dung.

"On the way back I looked in at the Croix-Rouge to touch a chap who gets fifteen francs a day allowance. Another mean worm for you! He handed out three francs—and then I had to pay for the second round! High time Clotilde did do something for us. I've made sacrifices enough. Besides, I'm one for politics, and a bit of fun. The workshop's beginning to be bad for my inside, damn it!"

At this point the old lady gave utterance to another sigh, like a sepulchral dove, and said :

"Four hours, at two francs an hour, that's eight francs. We can live on that. But aren't you afraid of this gentleman asking her to do anything too difficult? I only mention it, Zidore dear, because I *am* the poor child's own mother. We must make her understand it's for her own good. I spoke to her about it this morning. Told her, I did, that it was to have her portrait painted by a Great Artist. That frightened the life out of her."

"Grr! Blasted chit! She going to come the empress over us again? You wait a bit, I'll knock the dignity out of her. When you haven't got money, you've got to work and earn it, and provide for your family, that's all *I* know!"

The dialogue was cut short by a sudden gust of silence. It was as if these two creatures dreaded seeing their reflections in each other if they unmasked the unclean mirrors of their hearts.

Chapuis began filling his pipe with oratorical gestures, while his worthy mate, still seated, arms folded, head leaning a little sideways over her left shoulder, in the sanctimonious pose of a resigned hostage, beat a Devil's tattoo with her finger-tips on her bony elbows, her eyes gazing soulfully upwards.

CHAPTER III

A GRIMLY gloomy shrine it was, in the livid light of that roofing of congealed late autumn sky. We may assume, however, that under dazzling Indian suns it would have looked even more ghastly.

Just black, bleak, Parisian poverty, bedizened with all its tawdry make-pretend; the repulsive ornamental oddments of a by-gone respectable working-class prosperity, that still remained from a slow erosion by feast and famine.

First, an enormous Napoleonic bed that must have been handsome in 1810—its brass-work tarnished, all its golden glitter gone, since the Hundred Days of Napoleon's last brief régime—polish and varnish gone—castors crippled —its very legs piteously tinkered and mended, while countless surface scars bore witness to its decrepitude. This unluxurious bed, scantily equipped with a dubious mattress and a pair of dirty sheets, inadequately veiled by a greasily decaying counterpane, must have broken the backs of three generations of flitting tenants.

This ancient monument filled a third of the attic—and in its shadow could be discerned another mattress, spread out with all simplicity on the floor, crawling with vermin and black with filth. Across the room an old arm-chair, that might well have been loot from a sacked city, was discharging its entrails of flock and wire, in spite of the almost pathetic coyness of a tattered cover of childish embroidery. Beside this piece, which all the old-clothes and second-hand furniture dealers had steadfastly refused to purchase, stood one of those tiny, disreputable " furnished room " wash-tables, topped with its ewer and basin, that make one think of the Day of Judgment.

And, finally, in front of the room's solitary window was another table, a round walnut table without either charm or steadiness, one to which no amount of the most industrious elbow-grease would ever have restored polish or lustre ; and three cane-seated chairs—two of them almost seatless. House-linen, if any were still extant, must have had its hiding-place in an old, shaggy, padlocked trunk, sometimes used by visitors as a seat.

Such was the furniture, typical enough of many a home in the City of Joy and Frolic, Light and Laughter, Licence, Riot, and Revelry.

But the room's peculiar and horrible feature was its assertion of a haughty dignity, of highly respectable " distinction ", smeared like an unguent all over the mouldering ruin of that ghastly hovel by Chapuis's romantic companion.

The fire-place, fireless and cinderless, might have struck a note of pathos, despite its ugliness, had it not been for the grotesque clutter of " souvenirs " and revolting " ornaments " crowded over it.

There were to be observed little cylindrical glass covers sheltering little nosegays of dried flowers ; another glass cover, this one globular, mounted on a rockery of shell-encrusted concrete, displayed to beholders a nebulously suspended scene of German-Swiss landscape. And there was a collection of those univalvular shells in which a poetically inclined ear can readily distinguish the murmurous music of the distant sea ; and a couple of those loving Florian shepherds, male and female, turned out for the masses, in coloured porcelain, at some obscure and ignominious factory.

Alongside these works of art were displayed devotional images—Doves drinking from a golden chalice—angels carrying armfuls of wheat, the " sheaves of the elect "—much-titivated children making their First Communion, bearing candles adorned with paper fringes—and then a few " questions of the day " such as "*Where is the Cat?* " "*Where is the Park Keeper?* " framed for some inconceivable reason in passe-partout.

And, finally, photographs of workmen, of soldiers, of respectable tradesmen and tradeswomen. There was an incredible number of these likenesses, and they rose in pyramidal tiers to the very ceiling.

Here and there on the walls, alternating with tattered rags hung a few framed pictures. Obviously, it would be disgraceful not to have that famous print, so dear to all feminine hearts, "At Last We Are Alone!" in which nobody could ever tire of admiring how a rich gentleman is clasping his tremulously thrilling bride in his arms, with some emphasis, in the sight of their Creator.

This Marriage-Registrar's—or Licensed Woman's—picture was the Chapuis couple's pride. They had once brought home a Charenton cobbler purposely to look at it.

The others—atrocious chromolithographs, bought in fairs or given away at popular bazaars—may not have soared to quite the same height of aesthetic grandeur, but they all had a certain " spice " about them, and, what mattered even more, that even more certain touch of the " distinguished " for which Old Mother Chapuis was such a fanatic.

This craze for titivation was one of the most depressing

manifestations of the idiotic vanity of the woman, and the contagious decay of that " spare bone " (as Bossuet called it) would have scared away Plague himself.

She was, so she used to say with an air of mystery, the natural child of a " prince ", a very high-born prince, who died before he had time to acknowledge her. She had always refused to name this august personage, declaring her resolve to keep that secret buried in the most inward depths of her heart. But that was the source of all her mincing airs of superiority.

Naturally, nobody had ever attempted to check up on this pedigree. But still there must have been something in it, for the bedizened woman of fifty who was concubine to the unsavoury Chapuis had once been a woman of rather aristocratic beauty, a cut above the working-class environment in which she had always lived.

The daughter of an obscure repairing tailoress and an unknown father, she had suddenly become possessed of a little fortune at the age of eighteen, and almost immediately married a respectable trader, in the Rue St. Antoine.

Admittedly her elementary education was inexpressibly deficient. She had barely known her mother, who was cut off in the prime of her life of clandestine prostitution, and had been taken in and adopted by a Montrouge mattress-maker.

This woman, on becoming her foster-mother, subsidised in all probability by the famous " prince ", gave her a most careful up-bringing—in the gutter. In fact, the only education she could possibly have imparted to her, with daily cuffings, was that derived from the mattress-maker's personal experience of fibre horse-hair substitutes and combed flock, a course of technical instruction that presumably

did not appear in the official curriculum for primary
schools.

So she sent the child to school, where her youthful
intellect never got much beyond the art, acquired during
many years, of writing without being able to spell, and of
doing sums without getting them right. But the manifold
filth of the gutters had no secrets from her. Her arith-
metical organs were only to develop later, namely, when
money entered into her life.

When this new factor was introduced, subject to the
condition of her acceptance of a certain husband, this
affecting Spartan maid, stoically heedless of any foxes that
might be gnawing at her bosom, suddenly gave evidence
of a hitherto unsuspected grim virtue, and the worthy
tradesman who was marrying her, glad to have a lawful
cashier to bring prosperity into his business, asked for
nothing better.

Thenceforward she became a Refined Woman, for ever
and ever.

Her idiom, luckily, remained that of the streets. But,
simultaneously with the change in her station of life, her ego
became miraculously cleansed of the scars and scabs of her
slum childhood. A complete cure and obliteration.

She became, in fine, an irreproachable wife. Oh, dear,
yes! One who could not fail to draw down Heaven's
choicest blessings on the fortunate husband, even if he was
incapable of realising his good fortune.

Of course, she " got religion ", because that is a thing
that it is indispensable to have when you belong to " decent
society "—a rational degree of religion, needless to say,
with nothing exaggerated or fanatical about it.

This was in the flourishing days of the reign of Louis

Philippe, the Citizen-King, and not all the calves of university and philosophical circles were equal to supplying all the lymph with which the French intellect was being vaccinated against the infection of the superstitions of the bygone order.

Nevertheless, young Madame Maréchale—such was this Christian woman's name—would not tolerate jokes against piety, and her husband, who loved the flippant wit of Béranger, had to be constantly and severely recalled to a due sense of what was becoming to his position.

For it is time to declare the truth about this inexpressibly worthy lady—she had essentially a *poetic soul*. The wealth of poetry latent within her had been revealed to her by certain " Meditations " of Lamartine, whom she called " her divine Alphonse ", and by two or three mealy elegies of Jean Reboul's, like " The Angel and the Child " :—

> "*Sweet child, who art so like myself . . .*
> *The earth is unworthy of thee.*"

When she had a little girl, two years after her marriage, her prudishness became so inflamed that it produced a very paragon of ferocious, crabbed, repellent dullness. Consequently, the whole neighbourhood was unanimous in proclaiming as with a single voice the impeccable rigidity of her morals.

On one occasion, however, the much envied husband surprised Mme. Maréchale in the company of a very scantily clad gentleman. The situation was one in which a man would have had to be not only blind but as deaf as a corpse, as well, to entertain the slightest vestige of doubt.

The austere matron, engaged in betraying his marital honour with an ardour obviously shared by her visitor, had not sufficient literary culture to make use of Ninon's inspired words, "Ah! You have ceased to love me! You believe what you see, instead of believing what I tell you!" But she achieved almost as fine a line.

She strode up to her husband, bosom bare, and in very quiet tones, very grave, deep, gentle tones, addressed the thunder-struck man with these words :

"My dear good man, I am importantly engaged with *Monsieur le Comte.* So don't you think you had better attend to your customers ? "

And with that she closed her door.

And that was all. A couple of hours later she intimated to her husband that he was not in future to speak to her, except in the case of any matter of absolutely urgent necessity, as she was tired of demeaning herself to his shopkeeper's spiritual level ; indeed, she was deeply to be pitied, to think she had sacrificed all her girlish hopes for an ill-bred lout, utterly without ideals, who had the indelicacy to spy upon her. She did not, on that occasion, omit to remind him of her illustrious birth.

From that day onwards the exemplary wife carried the martyr's palm about with her everywhere, and life became a hell on earth, an unplumbable abyss of misery, for the poor betrayed husband whom she had tamed. He took to drink and neglected his business.

Life is too short, and romance too precarious, for the epic of this commercial downfall to be narrated in detail. The culmination must suffice.

In four years, with bankruptcy complete, and her husband an inmate of a pauper institution, the wife who had shared his ruin took her child to lodge as best they might in a back-street of the Faubourg St. Jacques, where a creditor's clemency permitted her to take a few odds and ends of her former furniture.

The martyr lived there till 1872, at which memorable epoch she made the acquaintance of Chapuis. Although entirely without means, she managed to live, in fair comfort, on her alleged needlework, which it would seem evident that she executed to people's satisfaction, since she declared herself overwhelmed with orders, though it was very seldom that anybody saw her sewing in her room. But it seems equally evident that she accomplished an appalling amount of work out, since she usually came home very late, and sometimes did not come home at all.

The poor child grew up as best she could, horribly terrified of her mother, who would sometimes make her sit up all night for her, because, she said, she needed some proofs of affection and devotion at home, after a whole day piously spent in hard work.

So the little girl gradually grew up into a big girl, and then into a young woman, ill-fed and worse clad, but still with a tremulous admiration, retained for years, for her mother, who did not beat her *too* much, who even kissed her occasionally, on the rare days when she had acute attacks of maternal emotion, and whose stylish dress, disturbing for a working woman, amazed the girl.

She had a simple-minded belief in the genuineness of those unfathomable depths of suffering of the sacrilegious humbug who used to take her once a year to her father's grave—" He died impenitent "—and tell her (in the accents of the Holy Widows in their agony) of the implacable punishment of that impious man who had scorned and broken the heart of the wife he never understood.

The truth dawned later, much later, when the girl was

working herself, working very genuinely and very hard, and practically keeping her mother (who had probably begun to be a little too unattractive for the street), and saw her suddenly abandon all her patrician airs and become the mate and " regular " concubine of a repulsive blackguard whose very look gave her a shuddering horror.

The Widow Maréchale, thus transformed into " Mme. Chapuis ", sometimes, in fact, called by the more euphonious appellation of Mother Isidore, had aged rapidly, from that moment, under the heel of this sot, who loved knocking her about.

This vile woman, who had never loved anyone, worshipped him for some unaccountable reason ; was his, body and soul, delighted in being struck and bullied by him, and would have had her daughter burned alive to please him. Her humility was reserved for him alone ; with others, she still adopted her old strutting poses, as of an ostrich.

Physically, she had become hideous—to the despair of the bankrupt Chapuis, who would not at all have minded marketing his loving partner, but could not see his way to offering her services now, except as a mop for cleaning mortuary slabs in a leper hospital.

CHAPTER IV

At last the door opened, and Clotilde appeared—like April coming into the hold of a galley.

Clotilde Maréchale, " Isidore's girl ", as she was called in Grenelle, was of that order of wistful, appealing beings, the vision of whom revives the flagging fortitude of tortured men.

Pretty rather than beautiful, she had a certain air of dignity, due to her tall figure, with its slight stoop from the shoulders produced by the burden of hard days. That air was her only inheritance from her mother, her opposite in infinite contrasts, whose angelic foil she was.

Her glorious hair, vividly black, and lustrous great captive-gypsy eyes, " pools whence shadows seemed to well ", but in which there floated the beaten army of Resignations—the grievous pallor of her child-like face, its lines grown almost austere under the influence of misery all-knowing—the voluptuous suppleness of her gait and movements—all had earned her a reputation for what the burghers of Paris, talking among themselves, call a " Spanish type ".

Poor " Spaniard ", a peculiarly timid one! Something about her smile made one want to cry if one looked at her. A host of yearnings for tenderness—like little birds in the woods—fluttered about her innocent mild lips, lips crimson as if with paint, by reason of the heart's blood that surged into them to be kissed.

It was a heart-breaking, divine smile, supplicating and gently anxious to please, which nobody could forget who had ever earned it by the most common-place politeness.

In 1879 she was about thirty—thirty years of poverty, cruelty, despair!

The trampled roses of her garret adolescence had been brutally stripped of their petals by the tempests in that great black cavern that was the garden of her dreams, and yet a whole Orient of youth still shone about her, as if it were a light radiated by her own soul, her soul that nothing had succeeded in ageing.

It was so clear to see that a little happiness would have made her dazzlingly lovely, and that in default of earthly joys this humble creature might have kindled to flame, like the adoring torch of the Gospels, at the vision of Christ passing bare-foot along His way!

But the Saviour, nailed to His Cross for nineteen centuries, does not come down from it now just for poor girls, and the ill-starred Clotilde's personal experiences were hardly such as to give her any great confidence in hopes of human consolations.

As she entered the room, the sight of Chapuis made her instinctively recoil. Her pretty lips trembled—she seemed on the point of flight. This man was actually the only human being she felt she had a sound right to hate, having suffered at his hands atrociously.

However, she closed the door, and, flinging a half-franc piece on the table, said to her mother :—

" That is all Godmother could do for us! She was just sitting down to lunch, and it smelled very appetising. But I knew you were waiting for me, mother dear, and I daren't tell her I was so hungry."

Isidore began bellowing.

" The old cow! And you didn't shove it back in her face, the old turnip-field drab, with a hundred thousand francs she's earned, laying her filthy body down, the old sow? Bah! You're mad, my girl! "

He had risen to his feet to declaim his denunciation ; and the pathetic whine at the end was accompanied by a gesture as of a decrepit clown, calculated to depress the very Muse of Ignominy.

Clotilde's pale cheeks were scarlet, the dark tarns of mild eyes aflame.

"First," she cried, "I'm not your girl—thank God! And I will not allow you to speak as if you were my father! Next, my godmother is a respectable woman, and you have no right to insult her. She's done us favours enough, long enough. If she is not more generous nowadays, that's because you've got her sick to death with your hypocrisy and your lazy drunken ways. And I've had enough of it all, too—your impudence and your spite, and if you don't like what I say, I'll soon leave this wretched hole, if I have to starve in the gutter!"

The old woman, in her turn, rushed in between the two disputants, and took advantage of the opportunity to perform her great Pathetic Act, her own invention, which consisted in groaning in various keys, with her hands clasped together, and, still clasped, sawing upwards and downwards, and from east to west.

"My child, my child! Is that the way you let yourself speak to the man Heaven has sent us, to assuage the declining days of the mother who has always sacrificed herself for you? I, too, was beautiful in my youth, and could have had my fun like other girls, and gone gadding about like a hussy, if I had hearkened to the voice of the Tempter. But I knew how to settle down to do my duty, and made myself a martyr to your father. May dear God and all His Saints preserve me from accusing the unhappy man before his child! But I call Heaven to witness to the agonies that man of blood made me endure, wallowing in my tears and feasting on my torments. What my heart suffered is a secret that I shall carry with me to my grave. Oh, Clotilde! Spare your sainted mother's bruised heart! Add not to her

martyrdom. And respect the grey hairs of this noble friend
who is to close my dying eyes. And you, my consoler, my
last love, forgive this child who does not really know you.
Show yourself magnanimous, so that she will learn to love
you and cherish you. My Zizi, my darling Clo-Clo, you are
giving me gall and wormwood for my thirst, you are ripping
all my old wounds open again, your quarrels make me
yearn two-fold for my eternal home, where angels are
plaiting my crown! Kill me, rather! See, I offer myself, a
willing holocaust! I am here, between you! "

And the canting scarecrow hung her despoiled head in
the presumable general direction of that famous heart of
hers, and, standing immobile before an invisible cross,
spread her huge arms out to the two ends of the horizon,
with a supreme, conclusive gesture, that suggested some
twin gibbet at an ancient crossroads.

Chapuis, obviously annoyed, had no desire just at the
moment to kill anybody. If Clotilde had not been there,
and certain other circumstances had been different, a box on
the ears would certainly have put a stop to the tragic mono-
logue as soon as it began. But he was relying on being able
to exploit the goodwill of the younger woman, whom any
fresh act of brutality might render intractable, and who
would definitely have defended her mother against him, in
spite of her boundless shame at that mother's exhibition of
lying and absurdity. So he decided, all things considered,
on a pose of conciliatory and persuasive good humour.

" There, there! That's all right, old woman, you just go
and sit down. Nobody wants to do you in. Plenty of time
to think about that between now and Christmas, if you can
manage to put a bit of fat on your bones meanwhile! And
you, Miss Clotilde," he added, with a note of irony that he

immediately suppressed, " have the kindness to take a seat.
You know there's no charge! You went for me just now,
but I don't bear you any grudge for it. Must bawl each
other out now and then, eh, Ma ? Makes one all the pallier.
You called me a drunkard. Heavens! I don't say I want to
make myself any better than anybody else ; but a chap has
to do himself justice, in little courtesies between friends, if
you're civilised people, and an odd glass here and there
doesn't hurt anybody. Your Ma here doesn't spit at a glass,
when it comes her way. But that's not what I wanted to
talk to you about. Look here, I've found you a job,
good work and good pay. It won't kill you to show your
hide to a painter, and do a bit of posing, sweet little virgin
stuff, for pictures. Two francs an hour. That's worth
thinking of, when one's on the rocks. And mind you, you
needn't be afraid of any monkey-tricks. Your old woman
wouldn't like that, for one thing. And I'm not a ponce,
myself, I *don't* think! A man may be a bit fond of lifting
his elbow, but that doesn't mean he's got no sense of honour!
If this individual was to get disrespectful with you, he'd
have me to reckon with—Isidore Chapuis! And you can
tell him so, with my compliments."

With these words, throwing out his insect-like chest with
a gallant air, and thumping on his hollow ribs with his
hand, he paused to spit in the fire-place again, and, pointing
round the wretched garret, went on :—

" Have a squint at the moated grange! Here's a dainty
little nest for lords and ladies! Can we ask anybody in
here ? I don't ask for the House of Lords, but, just the
same, I shouldn't mind being somewhere different to this
hole. But there's no need to make a face like ' The Lady In
Black '. Nobody's going to eat you. Only want you to

be a good girl and help us a bit in your turn. That's fair,
isn't it? We haven't let you go short of necessities since
you came out of hospital; all this time you've been sitting
with your arms folded all the blessed day——"

The trembling Clotilde was like a swallow in the grasp
of a tramp's fist. Her mother's grotesque "act" had
quenched the feeble flame of her anger and chilled her soul.
A vast disgust, an illimitable humiliation, held her motionless beneath the now triumphant gaze of the wretch, while
his words terrified and outraged her.

She had too long been trained to accept the bitterness of
things for any revolt of hers now to be more than a pallid,
transient flash.

And those final words broke her down. She accused
herself of having been idle and useless for long months, of
having lain whole days, prostrate and helplessly weak, and
eaten the bread of that abominable man.

So she must—Merciful Heavens!—swallow one more
ignominy; become a studio model, palette flesh, have her
body scanned from morning to night by painters or
sculptors!

Not, perhaps, as discreditable as prostitution; but she
wondered if it were not even more humiliating. She
remembered so well those women she had seen in
the morning going past the School of Fine Arts before
the studios opened.

They had seemed to her ghastly creatures, the scum
of professional immodesty, of vile, crawling insensibility,
and she had thought the last depth of wretchedness would
have been to become like those cattle of the figure-studios
and the easel, beings whom old Dante would have scrutinised
pensively when returning from his Inferno.

It was inevitable, of course, since she had had to give up her work as a gilder, which had almost cost her her life, and, all strength and courage lost, was now fit to do nothing except suffer and let herself be dragged by the feet and hair into foulness.

She made no reply, surprised, herself, to find she had not a word to say by way of protest. Weighed down with utter weariness, it was as if she bowed her head.

Then her mother, regarding the battle as won, came and took her head between her arms, clasping her hands on the knot of hair at the nape of her neck, while, in that pose, she breathed forth to the Heavens energetic Acts of Thanksgiving in gratitude, as was fitting, for the softening of her daughter's heart.

At this sight, Chapuis suddenly remembered an important engagement of the utmost urgency, and disappeared, leaving a few coppers behind, to return only about three in the morning, and completely drunk.

CHAPTER V

As the reader will have guessed, the mattress spread on the floor, spoken of above, was Clotilde's.

It would be easy to pose as an extremely credible narrator, by imagining a softer and less romantic bed. But such are the ways of a certain section of the people, and this unhappy story is all too literally realistic in its details.

She had slept there for two years—that is to say, ever since Chapuis's ruin. Before that, they had lived in a fairly comfortable flat near the Parc Montsouris, and Clotilde had had her own room.

But the sudden and complete collapse of the scale-maker had rendered it impossible to stay there longer than the time needed to find a new shelter that would be a trifle less inclement than the open air.

Except for six weeks spent in hospital (which, by comparison, had seemed happy weeks to her) the poor girl had, accordingly, slept for two years there, in the foul miasma of the two senile horrors who slept alongside, rolled up in her rags, a prey to the shudders of a disgust that custom had not been able to allay.

This particular night she slept little. Her thoughts were too painful. She was cold, too, and shivering under the tattered vestige of her coverings, for the ghastly winter of that year, so fatal to the poor, had already set in. She mused, as she stared into the blackness, that it was peculiarly cruel, above all, not to have the right to weep in a wretched corner. For, even if the horror of fouling her tears had not inhibited her from shedding them now and then in the reeking filth of that pigsty, such a dismal indulgence would have been condemned out of hand as an evidence of selfishness and criminal cowardice.

Chapuis would not have missed the opportunity to overwhelm her with the irony of his filthy consolations, and the Martyr Mother would have started giving her an exhibition of Draining the Dregs of her Cup once more, imploring her, in the name of Heaven, to compare *her* sufferings to her own.

From her childhood she had been rigorously taught by that purgatorial bore, her mother, that she must never complain, on the ground that a child should be the mother's recompense and " crown ". The latter even had a stock of tearful apophthegms on the subject borrowed from the ejaculatory eloquence of the little devotional books she idolised.

The unhappy little girl's heart, held rigidly compressed as in a vice, had therefore re-absorbed all its bitterness in silence, yet never succeeding in arming or hardening itself. Whatever people might do to her, she agonised with the famine for love, and, having nobody on whom to lavish tenderness, she sometimes went into the dusky churches during the middle of the day to weep there in peace in some dark unnoticed chapel. . . .

Poor deserted creature! It was hard to think she had known no other joy throughout her childhood and the freshest years of her youth! True, she had never made a real effort to mix with the apprentices she had known at the gilding shop. But her almost morbid shyness had jarred on them. Her extreme gentleness and the simple dignity and refinement of her deportment had disgusted those gutter brats; they said she " gave herself airs "; while, at the same time, an instinctive modesty had preserved her from the putrifying influence of their example.

Oh, yes! She had learned everything—her ears had scarcely given her much chance of missing any of the most intimate dirt of the underworld of humanity! But the vicious prattle of those adolescents had not taken any roots in her character, which remained as chaste as a Visitationist Sister's rosary.

That was why she used to go and offer up her tears to the God Who was in the churches, unaware that thus she was presenting the great sacrifice, the beatific and tremendous Oblation which has beyond doubt much more than the power to displace the constellations, since Christ our Lord found no better draught for His solace and refreshment in the Sweat of Blood and the Agony. All the same, she was not what the worthy hangers-on of the sacristies would call a " pious child ". She had received such semblance of religious instruction as is commonly conferred in Parisian parishes by catechists.

Her mother, who indulged in no devotional practices except the parodied invocation of a patchwork Heaven, and who thought, like every good bourgeois ape, that " affectation was an offence against Him Who made us ", was not exactly the model needed to mould her into a pattern of Christian perfection.

She had " made her do " her First Communion, following the example of all the shopkeepers' wanton wives, because it was an opportunity for an exceptional display of maternal sentiment. But she would have denounced the superstitious exaggerations of praying, and especially of shedding useless tears in corners where nobody could see one.

She always kept scrupulously to the observance of the profound liturgy of the small shopkeeper of orthodox beliefs—" drawing the Kings " on Twelfth Day, eating stock-fish on Good Friday, and sucking-pigs at Christmas ; above all, taking flowers to the " Dear Departed " on All Souls' Day. It would have been sheer delirious raving to ask more than that of her!

Yes, those hours of sentimental tenderness had been the best moments in Clotilde's life, and the simulacrum of passion that came to her later was nothing by comparison.

At all events, they had left no bitter aftermath, those dear moments, with the deeps of her heart silently calling to the deeps of Heaven. She could remember having known the very self of Love's Tenderness, and when she would burst into tears it was as if she felt the distant, far-off echo, the unfathomable, mysterious dim impression, the veiled, anonymous intuition, of assuaging an unknown thirst, of giving consolation to One Unknown, Ineffable—— There came a day, a day that was for ever unforgettable, when a Personage had spoken to her, a priest with a patriarchal beard, wearing a pectoral cross and amethyst ring, who seemed to have come from the solitary outposts of distant lands, where the evangelical lions of the episcopate roam beneath dread skies. Seeing such a young girl weeping, he had drawn near, contemplated her with a kindly eye, and given her his blessing very, very slowly, with gently moving lips, and then laid his hand on her head, in the manner of one accustomed to the governance of souls.

"My child," he had said, "why are you crying?"

She could still hear that voice, serene, impressive, like the voice of a being, it seemed to her, of another world. But what reply could she have given, just then, except that she was dying of the longing to live? She simply gazed back at him, with her big, lost faun's eyes, that made her anguish so visible.

It was then that the stranger spoke those amazing words, words she was never to forget :—

"You must have heard of Eve, the first Mother of the human race. She is a great Saint in the eyes of the Church, though in the West little honour is paid to her, and her name is often used in connection with profane ideas. But she is still invoked in our Christian communities of the ancient East, where the traditions of antiquity are preserved. Her name signifies, 'Mother Of All Living'. . . . God, maker of all our thoughts, must have willed me to think of her when I saw you. Address yourself, therefore, to this mother, who is closer to you than she who bore you. She alone can help you, you who are like nobody, poor child athirst for Life! . . . It may be, too, that the Holy Spirit has marked you with His great and terrible Sign, for the paths are inscrutable and unknown. . . . Farewell, gentle child, I leave again, in a few minutes, for distant lands, whence I shall probably not return, in view of my great age. . . . But I shall not forget you. . . . *When you are in the midst of the flames* remember the old missionary who will be praying for you in the heart of the desert."

And he had, in fact, gone, leaving a twenty-franc piece on the ledge of the prie-dieu, where Clotilde, rooted to her knees, remained stupefied with amaze and a wholly unutterable reverence.

With no way of finding out about him there and then, she never learned anything of this old man who she fancied had been sent to her direct by the Father of unhappy children. For her, he was simply " The Missionary ".

In memory of him, she often called with a simple-minded affection on that Mother of us all of whom no other priest would ever have been likely to speak to her in that way. And she often wondered what he had meant by those " flames " in whose midst she was one day to remember him who had come to her. . . .

As a matter of course, she let the twenty francs be stolen from her by her mother, *who asked for no explanation*—who, in fact, actually left her a little more free than hitherto, until at last, seeing no sign of any more treasure flowing in, she became once more the fierce duenna, declaring her daughter to be " too big a fool " to be running the risks of seductions and escapades. The innocent girl did not at that time really know the vile old woman, as has been pointed out, and it was only later that she was to realise the abominable nature of her calculating ideas.

The whole of her past life came back thus to her mind, during this wretched, sleepless night. She had been barely sixteen at the time of the Missionary episode, and— Heavens, the things that had happened since!

She, who had fancied herself weeping in the arms of the angels, to whom the Lord Himself had sent a Messenger, to what depths of profanation had she not descended! She could never understand this ghastly fall. Clinging to the power of prayer, of the Sacraments, to every pillar of the sacred places where the Saviour hangs in His agony, could she not have escaped that foul hope of earthly happiness which had so appallingly failed her?

For facts are inexorable. They know no pity. Forgetfulness itself, even if one can achieve it, is powerless to obliterate their crushing testimony. . . . "Not all the power of Heaven itself can alter it, that I let that man possess me, of my own free will, and that I am defiled by him till I die! Oh, God! Oh, God!"

CHAPTER VI

SHE groaned and sat up in the darkness. She was going out of her mind with the agony of her thoughts, as this realisation came back in all its clarity.

Her "adventure" had been pitifully commonplace. She had succumbed, as have a million others, to the everlasting trap of the most sordidly ordinary seduction. She had gone astray simply, sillily, with a certain Faublas in the civil service who had promised her nothing and given her nothing—not even an hour of fleeting pleasure—and from whom she herself had never hoped or expected anything.

The torturing truth was that she had just surrendered herself to the first male animal who happened to come along, because he happened to cross her path, because he cried, because she was suffering in nerves and heart, because she was sick to death of the monotony of misery, and, too, probably from curiosity. Looking back, she herself did not know why. It was a thing that had become utterly incomprehensible.

It had all been such a hatefully platitudinous intrigue—those appointments at bus stops, at table-d'hôte restaurants. Her best excuse perhaps had been—as always, alas!—the glamour a girl in such penurious wretchedness finds so easily in a well-dressed, exquisitely well-mannered man—that mirage of a finer life which, for a moment, overwhelms and dazzles.

The relationship had lasted some little time ; and, from a certain natural sense of noble dignity, of pride, to avoid feeling herself a prostitute (though he barely gave her any material help), she had conscientiously forced herself to love him, this young man whose selfishness and pretentious mediocrity she perceived so clearly.

It was not easy, but she thought she had succeeded, doubtless by that impelling instinct, a more mysterious one than is commonly thought, which so often leads an abandoned or fugitive woman back to the first man who took her. Now, however—now, indeed, after years had passed—that was all finished with. She no longer felt anything but an unbearable disgust for the wretched lover whose pettiness of soul she might have endured, but whose incredible poltroonery had made her whole being writhe with contempt and revulsion.

The unhappy romance had ended thus. Chapuis, whose ruin was not then complete, and not caring one way or the other himself, but egged on by the old woman, who had suddenly become aware of her child's unprofitable contamination, went one day to call on the young man at his office, and, in very gentle tones, informed him that he, Chapuis, would be reluctantly compelled to injure his chances of promotion by creating a tremendous scandal, unless the other could offer " compensation " to the respectable family " into whose bosom he had brought shame and dishonour ".

They did not exactly insist on marriage, because they had loftier views than an alliance with a clerk who had neither means nor prospects, but the old fox had brought with him stamped forms for notes of hand.

The seducer, in all his inexperience and terror, signed some mysterious bills payable at monthly intervals, for a fantastic amount—" for value of goods received "—which were regularly honoured till, one day, the young man's family intervened and threatened the scale-maker with unpleasant criminal proceedings.

Clotilde's shame and despair were overwhelming; for Chapuis, doubtless looking forward to a more profitable ruin of the pretty girl whose protector he deemed himself to be, had insisted on an immediate break in the form of an insulting letter which this bold courtier, this Lauzun of Sandaraque, had generously written at his dictation.

Betrayed, sold, outraged, and basely pelted with filth by the very man to whom she had sacrificed her only jewel,

how fierce a punishment for one day's madness! And her
mother, whose hand she perceived in all this, her horrible
mother, pretending to know nothing that took place, so
long as she had remained unaware of the *commercial* futility
of that deplorable love affair, why was Clotilde compelled
by diabolical necessity to go on living with her?

There had been a ghastly scene, in which the abominable
hag, cornered till she had to admit her infamy, had bethought
herself to take refuge in terrifying screams of agony,
leading the neighbours to think the scale-maker was
thrashing his wife.

That rascal, on the contrary, was threatening to kill
Clotilde, who was venting her anger more particularly on
him—an anger that, if it was not the first anger in her life,
was certainly the fiercest she had ever felt.

Then it was all over. The girl's deep inner self continued
to subsist, below the surface of the stranded monotony and
stagnant swamp of her visible earthly life, and below the
dire buried torrent of her repentance—like those marvellous
crypts hidden in the centre of the grove, where a single
spark of light would kindle a resplendence equal to that of
the basilica of Heaven.

Outwardly, she seemed to have forgotten everything.
Her gentleness became more touching, especially when she
spoke to her mother, with eyes lowered so as not to see
her, which earned her, from that worthy old drab, the
appellation of " little hypocrite ".

Only, by dint of suffering, her abounding vigour deterio-
rated. The ravages of anæmia destroyed her delightful
colouring, and she grew as pale as humility itself. Soon,
she had not the strength to stand up to the exhausting
fatigue of a saleswoman's work in a large store, which

had taken the place of the daily poisoning of the gilding.

Eventually she had to be taken into hospital, where the house surgeon found her interesting, and one day spoke severely to Chapuis, who had come to see her, telling him that the girl was ill, seriously ill, as a result of what she suffered from her treatment at home, and advised him for the future to beware—for his own sake—of the formidable consequences of any more brutality.

This warning had the Heaven-sent effect of sparing her, later on, during her convalescence, such scenes and outrageous insults as could not have failed to bring on a recrudescence of her weakness and collapse. Thus it came about that she was able to linger on for so many months in that verminous hovel.

CHAPTER VII

BUT now, what was to become of her? Was there really no way of escaping the hateful thing of which that blackguard had spoken?

A studio model! Could it be possible? And yet she had vowed that henceforth no man should *see* her. But the poor are not even the owners of their own bodies, and when they lie in the hospitals, after their despairing souls have fled, their pitiful, precious bodies, promised for the eternal Resurrection—Oh, Man of Sorrows!—are carted off without cross or prayer far from your Church and your altars, far from the stained glass windows in which your Friends are depicted, to serve like the carcases of beasts for the futile profanations of the vultures of human science.

Truly the wretched poor are subject to a law too hard! So it is quite impossible for a poverty-stricken girl to escape, one way or another, from prostitution.

For, after all, to sell her body, the intimate nakedness of her body, for this or that purpose, still amounts to prostituting it. Men's eyes are as devouring as their impure hands, and what an artist transfers to canvas is that same modesty itself that has had to be sacrificed to pose for the picture.

Yes, assuredly, *modesty itself.* For a little money the girl must give that to those artists. What she sells them is just the very thing which has the exact weight of a ransom in the scale in which the Creator weighs His unknown daughters. . . . Can't people understand that this is something even lower than what is commonly called prostitution ?

Whether it glitter with pearls or with filthy slime, a woman's raiment is no ordinary veil. It is a most mystic symbol of that unfathomable *sapientia,* that " prudence " which is both Wisdom and Goodness, in which future Love is locked away.

Love alone is privileged to strip itself bare, and any nudity that Love has not sanctioned is necessarily a betrayal. Nevertheless, the vilest prostitute can always plead in the face of the most rigorous Justice that after all she has not perverted her own essential nature, and that the sacred Pictures have not been displaced by her, in so much as she was but a simulacrum of woman, paying her devotion to a simulacrum of love. The very nature of the *illusion* she offers to men may, in a desperate effort to defend a hopeless case, wring some pardon from God.

The model's profession, on the other hand, leaves femininity utterly destitute, and sends it exiled from the woman's person, to be relegated to the darkest limbo of unconsciousness.

Clotilde certainly did not reason all this out, but her living soul gave her a very clear intuitive realisation of what it meant. If this surrender of her own flesh might be a sinless thing, even then how was she to stomach the disgust inspired by an innocence more degrading, as it seemed to her, than sin itself?

What would the "Missionary" say? What would he say, that dear aged man who had seen so clearly that she was passing through the throes of the agonising thirst for life? . . . The memory of that stranger set her weeping silently in the darkness.

" Alas! " ran her thought. " He would be so sorry for his child, he would save me, he *would!* But is he still alive, even? After all these years! And what part of the world is he in, alive or dead? "

Then she started dreaming, as the wretched will, of all the possible rescuers that a despairing creature *might* find —and that nobody ever, ever, does find!

She remembered a picture she had once admired in the gilder's shop, and would have loved to possess. It was a picture of a scene in a bad house, a few men with evil-looking faces sitting drinking with degraded loose women. On the right, one of the walls of that den had disappeared to show a radiant vision—the gentle Christ of Galilee, surrounded by His glory, as He had appeared to the Magdalen in the garden of the Resurrection, standing

immobile in the light, His sorrowful countenance expressing
a Divine compassion, and His hands outstretched, filled with
pardon, towards one of the women, quite a young girl,
who had drawn away from the rest of the group, and was
crawling on her knees towards Him with an imploring
fervour.

How often, when the memory of that frame-maker's
lithograph came back to her, had she longed to meet once
more that miraculous Friend who is not to be met with
nowadays in town or country, who used to speak familiarly
of old with the happy women who had been sinners in
Jerusalem!

For she thought herself no better than the most utterly
lost. Her fault having been committed without intoxication, there was nothing that could extenuate its bitterness
and its humiliation. This constant recollection hypnotised
her, paralysed her, sometimes made her seem witless and
dazed, with the panic-filled eyes of a Cassandra of Penitence,
open and fixed.

She had given, beyond recall, for all endless time and
eternity, her only treasure. Had given it—to whom?
Why? ...

And now the Blessed Trinity might do what They would
—erase creation, congeal all time and space, reconstruct
the primeval Void, confound all the infinities into one—
but it would not alter that one fact by the slightest iota :
that at one moment she had been virgin, and at the next
moment she was so no longer. In vain to command that
the transformation be reversed.

When Jesus should at last come down from His Cross,
He might find her immediately, her who was defiled, as He
followed the easy downward path from Calvary, leading as

it surely did to the dwellings of the unbelievers and the unfaithful. She, for her part, might bathe and perfume His feet, like that great Magdalen who had been called the splendid Bride. But it would not be within her power —not with diamond claws!—to draw out a single thorn from His tortured brow!

He, the fasting Bridegroom, would have to make do with the remnants of the unclean banquet where no one had preserved the wedding robe, and to breathe the scent of the withered lilies of His disloyal loves.

"What can I offer now," she murmured. " How am I any better than any of the creatures men trample on in their filth? When I was good, I thought I was tending white lambs on a mountain filled with perfumes and the song of nightingales. It did not matter how unhappy I was, I felt that there was within me a well of courage to defend the precious thing entrusted to me—and now when the Lord has need of it, He will never find it. Now my well-spring is dried up. The beautiful clear water has become mud, and loathsome creatures crawl in it. . . . I who might have become a Saint as radiant as the day, and prayed with the angels looking down from the floor of Heaven, now I haven't even the right to be loved by a decent man who might be so charitable as to want me! . . ."

At that moment the young woman's thoughts became clotted like a dead man's blood. The drunkard was tip-toeing back into the room, colliding with everything, belching blasphemies and obscenities, and eventually sprawled, grunting like a hog, beside his malignant feminine counterpart, who uttered a few sleepy, hoarse breaths.

The vicinity of this brute was an unbearable torture for Clotilde. It often surprised her that she had not died of

disgust and despair in all the long months she had been
compelled to endure it.

There was not only the horror of that revolting promis-
cuity, with all the unclean lyricism of its episodes and their
attendant comings and goings, but another memory, even
more atrocious and constantly evoked, obsessed her like an
endless nightmare.

One day, some years earlier, when they were still living
at Montsouris, before Chapuis's magnificence had been
extinguished, the foul creature, taking advantage of an
unusually prolonged—and perhaps *collusive*—absence on
the part of her mother, had tried to violate her.

At that time Clotilde was very innocent, but very far
from ignorant. It was a grim, and very nearly a fatal, fight
between the maddened drunkard and the vigorous girl,
her strength as the strength of ten from indignation.
Having contrived, by dint of a ferocious bite, to make him
relax his grasp an instant, she had got hold of a flat-iron,
and inflicted such a terrible wound on his head with it that
Chapuis, three-quarters killed, kept his bed for a month.

This incident passed off quite amicably, and the com-
munal life continued. Clotilde lacked any means for flight,
and the old pander's imagination, on which as forcible an
impression had been made as on his skull, was quite
definitely sufficient to dissuade him from any fresh enter-
prise. In fact he retained a vague awe of that gentle-eyed
virgin, whom he would never have thought capable of
such tempestuous intrepidity.

For her part, she never dreamed for an instant of suspecting her mother, to whom the invalid seemed to have
explained his wound by a story of some commonplace
accident, which the hazards of drunkenness rendered

perfectly plausible. But the picture of that sordid scene
was forever before her mind's eye, and the psychological
disturbance it created in her was not the least of the
contributory factors in her own fall, which occurred a
little later.

"Well!" she resolved finally, "I shall go there, since
I can't do anything else. One shame more or less, what
does it matter? I can never despise myself more than I
do now. And anyhow my work—lovely ' work ', that!—
will no doubt provide the money for Monsieur Chapuis's
rounds of drinks, and for Mama's ' little comforts '. That's
worth bearing in mind! So stop thinking of anything, and
go to sleep, poor little stray dog that nobody wants back.
Your lot is to suffer, you see. That's practically what
the Missionary told me—that old, good missionary of
mine, who ought to have taken me with him into the
deserts! Perhaps he is watching me now, and weeping
from the depths of his grave!"

CHAPTER VIII

THE poor are punctual. At eleven in the morning Clotilde
was at the top of the Faubourg St. Honoré and ringing at
the door of Monsieur Pélopidas Anacharsis Gacougnol.

He was the creator of the famous group entitled " Victory
of a Husband ", in which a commonplace little man of the
present day is feeding a dozen or more little fauns, his
wife's offspring but obviously not his. That was a typical
specimen of this artist's imagination.

Painter, sculptor, poet, and musician alike, and even critic, the universally talented Gacougnol seemed to have undertaken a contract for the illustration of all the proverbs and sententious metaphors known. He would get quite worked up over such maxims as *"castigat ridendo mores"*, and claimed the distinction of being a trenchant satirist.

La Fontaine's fables alone were responsible for no fewer than fifteen pictures of his, and provided the subject-matter for half a dozen bas-reliefs.

He it was, and none other, who invented the " Milesian Bust "—that is to say, a sculptural portrait in marble or bronze of some famous man, from the top of the head down to the navel inclusive—but with the arms carefully cut off— which, in his opinion, gave the effigy the imposing charm of a formidable impassivity.

It was he, too, who, in an illustrated paper, published that series of graduated caricatures that Paris raved over. These consisted, it will be remembered, of showing an evolution from a primitive pig, for instance, through a number of presumed intermediate animals, to Callipygean views of Ernest Renan, or Francisque Sarcey, regarded as the ultimate peaks of natural selection.

In poetry, and still more in music, he was inclined to be sentimental, and liked to make his piano weep, singing ineptitudes in a very fine voice.

A gascon from Toulouse, and a great talker, with a flavouring of garlic and æstheticism, an artist at the roots and a duffer by his fruits, with a beard like Jupiter Pogonatus, and hair tempest-tossed, he habitually affected the sublime brutality of a ravaged Enceladus.

Nobody ever managed to hate this genial fellow, as incapable of spitefulness as of modesty, whose real talent, stultified by the perpetual divagations of his freakish fancy, could never offend anyone. The most tortuously inspired and twisted minds among his comrades, as a matter of fact, were touched and disarmed by the more than human whimsicality of some of his conceptions.

When the bell rang, he opened the door himself.

"And what do *you* want?" he exclaimed, seeing a bareheaded woman standing at the entrance to his studio. "Another of 'em—same old story, I suppose? Your husband's still suffering from his good old rheumatoid arthritis, which he caught repairing the Obelisk, and you've smashed your latest little'un's feeding bottle. That'll be the fourteenth I've paid for within a month! Lord bless us, you aren't over-burdened with imagination or originality all of you! Anyhow, come inside, come inside—I'll see if I've got any change. Well, fair sir, *you* can congratulate yourself on being the sort of dirty dog who never gives a bean to a soul—you don't get bothered!"

This last congratulation was addressed to an odd-looking personage who simply bowed without saying a word.

"This is the sort of thing I get all day long," Pélopidas went on. "Once give these beggars twopence, and they leave me no peace—send their whole damned family. Oh, well! Where the blazes have I shoved my purse? Good Lord, shut that door, you—it's cold enough in this hole!"

Greatly disconcerted by this reception, Clotilde obeyed automatically, then summoned up her courage and succeeded in saying,

"Oh but Sir, I'm not begging. I'm the young woman you were told of. You were expecting me at eleven this morning," and she tendered her card.

Poor solitary card, cut out for the occasion with her scissors from a scrap of yellow paper, and inscribed in her own hand with the name, *Clotilde Maréchal.*

"Ah, you're the model! Splendid! All right, get undressed then."

And as if that were the simplest matter possible, he took up the thread of his conversation again where it had been broken for a moment by the arrival of this " accessory ".

"As to your ghastly tripe about great art, young Zéphyrin, we'll take that up again when you've got something new to tell me. Till then, you just bore me—and I don't charge you anything for the information! Everything you've been gassing at me for the last hour was taught me with the most loving care by certain venerable greybeards when you were nuzzling your wet-nurse. *I* stand for Personal Art—whatever name it's given! The only ' school ' I belong to is *my* school. And that's that! My ambition is to be Pélopidas Gacougnol, not somebody else. A putrid name, if you like—but it was wished on me by my worthy old man, and I'm sticking to it. As to your 'Androgynos' and your ' Young of the Angels ', they represent the aesthetic school of the Gentleman's Lavatory, and I don't want any, thank you! The Masters don't need a lot of doggy tricks like that to carve or paint marvels ; the great Leonardo would have been fed up with his life's work if he could have foreseen your rotten way of admiring it. Look here! I'll tell you what's the matter. You're just slaves, all you ' Younger School ', with your pose of being the inventors of everything—You'd go on all fours beautifully in front of any fellow who had the vim to give you a shove. You just aren't men, that's all! I'll be everlastingly damned if there's one single idea anywhere in all the literary

work of all the pretentious gas-bags with their finicky
fine-writing. You're the real clever little fellow—you.
You've invented the third sex, neither male nor female nor
even eunuch! People were getting bored. You've found
a vein of filth that will make the fortunes of a few dirty
old men of letters, starting with yourself, the initiator and
Grand Prophet of the movement! Only, don't you see,
that doesn't qualify you to be a critic—and you've written
some prime tripe about painting——"

At this point in his speech—a speech emphasised with all
the eloquent gesticulation of the South—Pélopidas's glance
fell upon Clotilde, who had apparently been frozen into
marble, and stood there staring in stupefaction at the
waving mane that billowed round the head of that voluble
and redoubtable figure which had bidden her get undressed.
Worked up already, he thundered—

" What the——! What in blazes are you doing there,
with your eyes gaping like the gates of a carriage drive?
Get stripped, you, and quickly—I've got work to do.
There! There you are, over there—behind that screen!
And do please get a move on."

The poor girl, in a paroxysm of terror, disappeared
immediately.

"And you, bambino of the angels, my own dear little
Delumière, you might do me a little favour—just slip
outside and see if I'm there. Your conversation is as
delicious as it is nutritious, but just for the present I have
had sufficient. Come and see me some time when I've
nothing to do. That's it! Take your hat, and good night
to your birds—I won't see you out."

Zéphyrin Delumière, the celebrated hierophant novelist,
recently raised to the eminence of certain obscure dignities

in the self-appointed councils of Occultism, took up his hat
as suggested, laid one hand on the bronze door-knob, and
—in one of those voices, dead to the world, which always
seem to come from the depths of a bottle—let fall these
few adamantine words by way of farewell :—

"Good-bye for the present, then, or for ever, as you
prefer, graceless painter. It would be all too easy to
punish you by erasing you from my memory. But you
are still a fœtus in the embryonic membrane of irresponsible
sexuality. You are still—How long, O Lord, how long!
—in the welter of the gestational hesitances of formative
evolution, under the yoke of primitive ignorance of the
radiant Norm in which is manifested the perfection of the
seven-months' child. Hence you toil in the dim burrowings
of terrestrial virility inculcated by the Egregorians. Hence,
also, do I give you my pardon and my blessing. One day
you will understand."

Posing there in his oratory, the mystagogue was about
the most fantastic figure of grotesque stateliness that could
well be conceived, with his greasy shock of hair, like a
Kaffir sorcerer or a fakir, his mitre-shaped beard as of a reticent astrologer, and seal-like eyes, dilated with conventional reserves of prudence, set at the roots of a jutting
protuberant nose, calculated one might fancy to sniff out
the most remote scandals.

Adorned with a jacket of violet velvet, and a bag-like
blouse of linen embroidered in silver, draped over with a
burnous of black-dyed camel hair picked out with gold
thread, and shod with deer-hide—but in all probability
shabby enough, under the surface splendours of his attire
—he might have been some conjuring vassal from some
chimeric Poland.

Suddenly a burst of laughter, Homeric, crashing, roared out, as if it must shatter all like an earthquake.

In the worthy Gacougnol the caricaturist was never long dormant—and he had suddenly got the full force of that element of the absurd which emanated day and night from the personality of Delumière.

Pélopidas flung himself down on the divan, and writhed in convulsions of delirious, gasping mirth.

When the paroxysm ended, the fantastic figure, immobilised a moment by surprise had departed, pale and disdainful.

" That creature! " gasped the laughing man finally, with a noisy sigh of repletion, talking to himself as his way was, " he'll be the death of me one of these days! All very well my suspecting him of the filthiest things, I can scarcely bring myself even to hoof him out—he's unique! The old blackguard! With his Franconi top-boots, and his face like a Circassian pimp—all nebulous in the twilight—how I had to laugh! When I knew his father as an assistant master at Toulouse he was nothing like so quaint. He was just known as a good, common-place fellow with a little bee of royalist prophecies in his bonnet, and looked on rather askance by the clergy he claimed to enlighten. But he never got beyond the ordinary limits of a droll provincial crank. The son must take more after his cook-house grandmother—the ' Mother of the Comrades ' as they called her—who doesn't seem to have come from the ' Elohim ' exactly—as he calls his ancestors before the flood! Well, don't let's think any more about that jacka-napes—he's wasted a good hour of my time this morning! Let's have a look at that model. I say, Mademoiselle, it would be frightfully good of you just to get a move on with that undressing——"

At that moment something happened. It was not a noise. It was not a light. It was nothing that seemed like a phenomenon of any sort. Possibly, nothing happened at all.

But Gacougnol felt his skin prickle—and, intensely affected, though he could not have said how, he stood a moment in silence, his mouth half open, his eyes fixed on that screen.

"Well! What's up with me? Is that idiot infectious by any chance?" he muttered.

Approaching the screen, and bending one ear close, he caught a faint moan, very muffled, very remote, like the sound of those apocryphal dead whom the poet of terrors heard writhing in their agonies beneath the ground.

Flinging the flimsy piece of furniture aside with an abrupt movement, he discovered the wretched girl on her knees, her shoulders bare, her face buried in a ragged old blue woollen neckerchief, the only article of her attire that she had managed to get off.

Obviously, her courage had suddenly failed her—she had collapsed in despair, and for a quarter of an hour had been stifling with both hands the convulsive sobs that were shaking her to pieces.

Gacougnol, surprised and touched, suddenly conceived the thought that his burst of laughter just now had been an accompaniment to those extraordinary tears, and, bending over the weeping girl with some emotion, said :—

"*My child—why are you crying?*"

CHAPTER IX

THOSE simple words had the effect of a magnetic shock. With a swift, animal movement Clotilde raised her head and gazed madly at this man from whose lips she had just heard the same question that the Missionary had long ago addressed to her in a similar moment of distress.

In the confusion of her amazement she could almost have thought she recognised the very voice that represented to her the only earthly solace that had ever been vouchsafed to her.

And in that moment she felt an overwhelming sudden hope, which flashed into reflected visibility in her face—her whole beautiful face, a-glitter with tears, the focus of the painter's silent admiration.

Having scarcely glanced at her when she first came, in the middle of an irritating argument that was exasperating him, he now discovered she was very pathetic, almost sublime, beautified by her grief.

To remain indifferent would have been hard enough, anyhow. From that countenance there emanated a gentle sweetness that gripped and drew out the soul from its wrappings, and confined it in a transparent setting of crystal.

This was no conventional Sinful Woman of the Gospels, so much abused by the sacrilegious paganism of the Renaissance. But on the other hand, it was no sister of those fragile Saints, who have been burning themselves out for two thousand years in the endless procession of the Blessed, like the intangible tapers of some eternal candelabrum.

In this prostrated girl there was little but a pitiful loving morsel of flesh, modelled by the Seraphim of Poverty, and decked only with the palest myosotis blooms of sorrow. A submissive sacrifice of commonplace existence, lit by no halo, transfixed by no bolts of Divine torment!

But the paradoxical glory of her disordered hair, the pallor of her face washed over, as it were, by the hot shower of her weeping—the whole picture held something dream-like——

Gacougnol was all the more impressed because for some time past he had been racking his brain to try and compose a St. Philomena threatened by a number of lions, which he contemplated offering to a dear old Toulousian ecclesiastical dignitary who had introduced him to a number of commissions.

All the same, just at the moment it was uncalculating admiration and disinterested pity that were working in him. Seeing how overwhelmed and speechless Clotilde was, and that she was quite incapable of answering, he held out both hands to help her to her feet, and there was something like loving tenderness in his tone as he spoke.

" Cover up your shoulders, little girl," he said, " and come and sit down here by the fire. Let's just have a quiet little chat, like old friends. Don't try to speak yet, but do please just try and wipe your eyes dry. I may be a bit of a brute, but I can't quite bear to see you crying. I just can't help it. Look here! You're scared of posing for the ' altogether ', isn't that it ? I understand. If I had taken a better look at you when you came, I should have spoken to you differently. You mustn't be hurt with me. It's one's work makes one like that. If you only knew the drabs that come along to pose or do whatever else one likes! *They*

don't cry, give you my word, at taking off their chemises!
—and it isn't always very lovely or very stimulating when
they've got 'em off! Besides, one was a bit put out over
something else. You saw me talking to that conceited
idiot just now? Well, there you are! One gets into the
way of riding the high horse, mixing with those asses—
and sometimes one puts one's foot in it. Anyhow, you're
not cross, are you?"

Ah, indeed no! She was not cross now, poor girl, even
if she ever had been! She was so vividly aware of the
compassion in this good man, blaming himself for the sake
of reassuring her! But he gave her no time to express her
gratitude.

"And, besides, if you must know, your introduction by
that person who came here yesterday was anything but a
good one. He isn't your father, is he?"

"My father!" she exclaimed, starting. "Oh! The
beast! Did he dare to say——"

"No, no—take it easy! He didn't say so—but on the
other hand he said nothing to the contrary. Ah, I see!
He's your lady mother's consoler! You poor child! The
gentleman was very drunk, and I should certainly not have
asked him in except for the letter he brought from your
landlord, who happens to be an old friend of mine. The
beggar talked about you as if you were goods for sale.
I even fancied I could read between the lines certain dim
ulterior ideas that did not seem to me to be quite the fine
flower of delicate purity. He finished up by trying to touch
me for some money, and I am rather proud of myself for
not having chucked him out more roughly than I did.
You can see, little girl, the way this inauspicious preliminary
did not quite prepare me beforehand to hand out exaggerated

reverential salutations to you. But don't let's talk about it.
Here is my idea. Will you pose for the head only ? You've
got a saint's face that I've been looking for for months.
I'll give you three francs an hour. That suit you ? Mind,
I'm asking it as a favour—"

Clotilde felt as if she were emerging from the caverns of
the stone age. Without the good kind face of this amazing
Gacougnol, who would still pass for the Churchwarden of
Notre Dame des Paternités, she could hardly have helped,
at first, suspecting some hideous practical joke.

"Monsieur," she said at last, "I am a very poor girl.
I don't know how to express myself properly. If you could
see into my heart—above all, if you knew my life—you
would realise what I am feeling. I was so afraid of you!
I came like the damned come, to Hell. Forgive me for
having bothered you with my silly crying, and if you
can be satisfied with my unhappy face, I shall be, oh, so
happy! Just fancy—nobody ever speaks to me kindly,
not a word! "

And suddenly, before Gacougnol could see what was
coming or prevent it, she caught hold of his hand and
kissed it.

The gesture was so spontaneous, so graceful, so touch-
ingly sincere, that the worthy Pélopidas, completely taken
aback, found it his turn to be afraid he would give an
exhibition of emotion hardly in keeping with a Master of
Self-Domination, and took his big hand away rather
abruptly.

"Come, come! That's all right! No sentiment, please,
young lady! And now to work. Come here, into the light,
and let me study your pose. Lift your eyes, and gaze up at
that joist there, over your head. M'm, yes. That's not

bad. In fact, it's rather good. And what a platitude, my lads! The unbridled clichéness of it! I suppose in paintings there are about five hundred thousand pairs of eyes like that gazing up at the abode of the elect! What the Devil am I going to make this St. Philomena of mine look at? That trick of celestial visions really won't hold water. 'Pon my word, a subject like this is pretty hard to paint when you've never *seen* a martyrdom. Make her look out at the crowd, as if she were imploring mercy? Nonsensical! Besides, one couldn't *do* it, since all the Christians given to the lions are supposed to have been ardently longing to serve as meals for the beasts! Of course, if she is incapable of fear, I *could* have her seem to be exhorting the populace—but that s not very original, either, apart from the fact that people who preach sermons in pictures don't often look exactly irresistible. Well, then, we can't get away from that eyes-up-to-the-sky idea. Obviously it's the most suitable plan for consideration. And then, what? She's standing up, of course. They didn't bring them a chair. That's all very well, but what am I to make her do with her arms? Both her arms? Oh, just Judge! Can't cut 'em off. People would want to know if it was the Martyrdom of the Venus of Milo. Tied? Folded? Stretched out, cross-fashion? Lifted up to Heaven? That everlasting Heavenward idea! Oh, rats! Look here, child—what *is* your name, by the way?"

" Clotilde, Monsieur."

" Good! Well, Mademoiselle Clotilde, or just Clotilde if you will permit the liberty, perhaps you can suggest something. I've got to paint a little martyr being eaten up by lions. Now just put yourself in her place. What would you do if you were *precisely* in her place? Now be very careful to note that this is a real Saint, already as much eaten up as she could possibly be by the longing to enter Paradise, with a beautiful Palm of Martyrdom, and she isn't at all afraid of the animals. Well, once more, what would you do while you were waiting for the first mauling ? "

Clotilde could hardly help smiling at the thought of her mother's celebrated " martyrdom " that had filled the whole background of her childhood. Unknown to herself, a lasting horror of that utilitarian hypocrisy-technique, displayed as setting to every scene in her life, had filled her with a deep-seated longing for simplicity and sincerity, an instinctive need. So her unaffected answer came readily enough.

" Good heavens, Monsieur Gacougnol, I have never had to think along those lines. Even when I was better than I am now, I never thought God would call on me to do Him glory in that way. Still, what you want to know seems simple enough, I think. If I were a saint, like you said, one of those generous girls who loved their Saviour more than anything else in the world, and I had to die by the death of wild animals, I fancy I should still be very frightened, just the same. Only, being so sure of entering into the glory of the Beloved, immediately afterwards, I should remind myself that it isn't very difficult and doesn't take very long to give myself to death, and I should beg the lions, in Jesus' name, not to keep me in pain too long. I imagine those ferocious creatures would understand me, because I would speak to them with an intense faith. Don't you think so ? "

Pélopidas's delight was unbounded, and found spontaneous expression in wild whoops and gambols.

" My dear little Clotilde," he roared, " you're just lovely, and I adore you ! I'm an idiot, that's what I am, do you hear ? A triple idiot. I should never have thought of that. Thanks to you, I'm going to be able to do a pretty decent job. You see, you little black crow, we are such morons, we chaps in oils, we never manage to put ourselves where we'd get the right point of view. We don't know how to be simple, as we should be, because we're so bent on being witty and getting our twopenny halfpenny clever ideas into God's money-box, and carrying our pigs' heads, as if they were the Blessed Sacrament of brutish silliness, forty paces in front of us, in the processions of half-wits! And that applies to the smart ones, as well as to me. Your idea fascinates me. Look here—I'm going to get it roughed out straight away."

With these words he flung himself on a big cardboard box, and feverishly grabbed a huge sheet of paper, pinned it to a drawing-board, and started drawing in bold sweeps, without interrupting his soliloquy.

" You'll see. Just stop where you are, little girl. I don't need you to pose. I've got to try and work up the composition of the thing a bit, first. We'll talk to those lions, never you fear! Naturally, we're right in the middle of a Roman Circus. Over here, the crowd, in the distance. Not worth talking about for the little they'll be seen. Here, you, Philomena that is to say—with God, Who won't be visible, but one must sense His presence, just the same, if I'm not a bungler.—Yes, and how many lions do we want ? Suppose I put in forty ? An *Academy* of lions ?—Certainly not, much too ' clever '. Let's make do with four. That'll suggest the Cardinal Virtues—Justice, Prudence, Temperance, and Fortitude. And, by the way, when you are saying

your little piece, I should advise you to address Fortitude.
I wouldn't rely on the other three too much—and talking
of your little piece, it's always a pretty clumsy business,
making a painted figure speak, with that deuce of a mouth
to be gaping open in everlasting silence—which will be
the despair of noble souls to the end of the centuries.
Can't be helped! I shall have to shut your mouth. Naturally, the spectator will imagine that the conversation is
ended; and, besides, lions aren't particular about you
speaking to them like you do to humans. They listen chiefly
with their eyes, a thing the human brute is almost always
incapable of.—We painters know that!—Very well, then.
We want huge big ones, don't we? The Lions of Daniel,
by Victor Hugo—No? You don't know it? Those lions
chatting among themselves, child. There is even one who
talks like a donkey. Never mind! They have their charm.
There! See that one? He looks quite a nice chap. If
you were to stroke his mane with your hand, perhaps, he'd
be flattered. Try it! There—there—I bet that little
gesture will startle our Vestals. Anyhow, I don't care
a fig for those priestesses; yes, but what about the
Varnishing Day ladies, those vestals who hang round my
lobbies—suppose they were to think that a ' pretty '
touch, now? Good Lord, no! We mustn't fall into the
quagmire of sentimentality. Let's think of something
else——"

Suddenly he jumped up with his hair flying as he shook
his head free of all the Olympia of his thoughts.

" But, man alive—I've never done lions! " he cried. " I
haven't got those carnivora in my mind's eye. Look at
that one with his back to us, in the foreground. You'd
know him for a cow, with your eyes shut! I must go and

study them at the Zoo. I've got an idea! Suppose I took you with me this very day? I love doing things on the spur of the moment. It's not gone twelve yet. That's settled then, eh? You'll come? Right, we'll be off."

CHAPTER X

FIVE minutes later they were in the street, with Gacougnol calling a cab.

" To the *Bon Bazar*," he shouted, " and make it quick ! "

Then, having helped Clotilde in, he sat down beside her, and went on talking volubly while the vehicle trundled along.

" First of all, my dear, you must promise that you'll just let me do as I like without any fuss. I'm one of those creatures who have to be humoured. You came to my place with a view to taking orders from me, I suppose. Consequently, you must just obey me and be very nice about it. You'll understand, I can't take you along with me in that costume.—So we're going to look in at that store we pass on the way, and let you change. Oh, don't worry— it's not a present. I have no right to make you presents. Just a little something on account for our sittings. For one thing, I don't like the poor, you know; can't bear them; my inspiration is too decorative for that. I couldn't do a thing with a dressed model who was not nicely dressed. Then we'll get some lunch somewhere. I'm simply starving, and I expect you are too. We'll try and not bore each other.—Oh, and by the way, it would be awfully good of you if you could manage not to take a couple of hours getting dressed. I've come out to see some distinguished animals, and I should like to avoid getting there too late. I need a whole lot of sketch-book notes——"

Clotilde would have found it highly embarrassing if she had had to reply. Gacougnol was reeling off his liveliest verbosity and speaking mostly to himself. Besides which, the poor girl was scarcely able to formulate a single coherent thought. She seemed to herself to be fast asleep and dreaming, and she hadn't mustered up a word since once this incredible man started taking command of her flexible will, trumpeting like a barbaric chieftain.

With a child-like simplicity, she just *obeyed*, acting on the instinct of the submerged. Her conscious mind bade her accept this amazing Godsend, just as she would have accepted insults, with the same mild submission.

Like all the unhappy who imagine they have caught a fleeting smile on the bronze lips of their fate, she was just giving herself up deliciously to the illusion of having won fate's favour.

Moreover, the idea thus suggested to her, of actually being *dressed*, brought a suffocating lump into her throat, constricted her heart. To get rid of these ghastly rags once for all, rags that beggars would have scorned! No longer to feel on her body that revolting dress whose touch defiled her, branded her—that dress near which all flowers would wither!—the dress of sorrow and ignominy that her wretched lover had given her once, and that she only wore because it had never been within her power to replace it.

Oh! That dress—its faded, nauseous red, washed out with a score of season's rains, corroded by every sun,

engrained with every mud, threadbare to the very annihila-
tion of its texture, and ravaged and rent as by the slashing
knife of a Jack the Ripper or an autopsy surgeon! To be
rid of it—freed from it—never to see it again—to throw it
into some gutter where the very rag-pickers would disdain
it, and then fly!

Could it be possible that there were men so generous!
She certainly would pose for him with all her heart, just
as much as ever he liked, and it should not be *her* fault if
this artist did not produce a masterpiece, for she would
pose as surely nobody ever posed before. She would be like
stone under his eyes——

Oh, yes—— But shoes, she needed them too, for she
was reduced to walking in slippers. And linen, too!
How could she do without that, being, as she was,
completely nude under her tatters? And corsets! And
a shawl! And a hat! A woman needed all these
things, to be seen " decently ", as he had put it. What it
would all cost! But he had money, that was certain,
plenty of money; and he would not want to do things
by halves.

"Dear God! And in a little while I shall look like
that! " she thought, looking out at the modest housewives
hurrying along in the Rue du Bac, " I shall go off my
head! "

It seemed to her as if she could not have allowed herself
to speak for any consideration on earth, for fear of letting
slip something of her joy.

Gacougnol, in despair of securing his companion's
attention, had given up soliloquising aloud. With his
hand thrust into his abundant beard, he smiled to himself
as he watched her.

"Poor creature!" he mused. "To her, at this moment,
I am God—God the Father! If happiness had luminous
properties, our cab would be the chariot of the prophet
Elijah, for it's just exuding jubilation. What poverty the
girl must have known, for it to be so easy to give her such
ecstasy! I jolly well knew I'd succeed in drawing out the
woman in my little Saint of a few minutes ago! And this
miracle will cost me five or six louis, at the most. And well
worth it, too! Funny, though, when you come to think
of it, the power of money. Still, you don't want to dwell
on *that* too much, old fellow. This young woman of mine
may be poor, but she's obviously not just *anybody*. She's
a chrysalis, overjoyed at its coming metamorphosis. And
where's the harm? She is obeying her instinct. Well,
and what about it? Why should her face belie her? A girl
who was a bad lot, even in anticipation, could never rejoice
with such complete abandon. She would take good care
to make me realise it was only her due, and proceed to show
her appreciation of my zeal by a charming smile, like a
plaster cast, stamped with dignity. Whereas, the sheer
child-like reactions of this grown-up young woman just
fascinate me. It is quite possible, after all, that she may
have a really lovable heart. 'The more of a saint a woman is,'
Marchenoir once assured me, ' the more of a woman she is.'
He must have been right, as usual. This one may not be
altogether a saint, and certainly she is not fresh. She's
probably let herself be taken and then basely dropped by
some gallant Knight of the Brilliantined Hair, or some fly-
by-night commercial troubadour. The old, old story of
these pitiable infatuated females! But it may be that the
snail has just crawled over her without her being tainted by
the unclean slime of its memory. Anyhow, I'll entertain

myself by making her talk during lunch, and I'll soon see the colour of her thoughts."

As he reached this point in his reflexions, the cab stopped before the monumental entrance of the Temple of our *real* national cult.

"Ah, my dear!" he exclaimed at once, in a very loud and distinct voice. "Here we are—you get out first; and do please let's be quick!"

CHAPTER XI

WHATEVER doubts the worthy painter might still have entertained, were speedily dissipated at lunch.

The metamorphosis had been as rapid as it was wonderful. Pélopidas, who seemed to be well up in such things, had furnished a fitter at the shop with very precise instructions, and then a tremulously happy Clotilde had vanished into its inner purlieus.

Fifty minutes later the caricaturist, who was never bored in that place of pilgrimage, saw advancing towards him a very well-dressed young lady whom at first he did not recognise, and she had pressed both his hands in silence.

Clotilde was so naturally, so *simply*, superior to her station, that the acutest Parisian observer, even if he had been given a hint beforehand, would never have discovered the slightest discrepant note to reveal the occurrence of so sudden a transformation.

Gacougnol, who had been somewhat cattily prepared to look for the flaws and the little points that were not quite in keeping, found his search futile and became a prey to a really extraordinary bewilderment.

And now, in that café-restaurant of the Boulevard St.-Michel, where their cabman had just dropped them, he was still groping for some explanation of the miracle of that innate air of distinction of which the unsuspected germ, carried down the mysterious currents of heredity (after passing through so many foul mixtures!), had at last developed into this exquisite creature.

There was certainly nothing pretentious about Clotilde's appearance. It was just the most commonplace attire of any one of those three hundred thousand middle-class Parisiennes who have conquered the world without going any farther afield than the Boulevards of Greater Paris. The ruthlessly commonplace black costume of the ordinary industrious young woman, that has been described in thousands of novels, and would cost less than would be needed to furnish the luncheon of some sluttish Indian Empress.

But she wore this panoply of civil war with as much natural grace as the dragon-flies wearing their gold and turquoise corselets. She carried herself upright. In the feminine armour of dress, she threw out her chest and raised again her care-bowed head, so long bent beneath the penitential hands of poverty.

The painter-critic, more and more amazed, strained all his analytical powers in vain, without succeeding in discovering the slightest venial fault, discordant or jarring note, in her deportment or manners.

Even the formidable test of lunch did not produce any disillusioning results. He wondered if she would raise the little finger of her right hand when she took up her glass to drink. She did not. Neither did he observe in her any tendency to hide about half her face with her table-napkin when she spoke to the waiter who served them, nor utter a melodious little cough when she broke her bread. She did not exclaim over the novelty of everything, just contenting herself with the simplest, briefest inquiry when explanation of anything was necessary, and made no apologies about being frankly hungry and thirsty, as became a robust young woman whose present weakness was mainly the result of years of privations and grim want.

In fact, everything about her suggested the idea of a vital young eagle, growing up hitherto in dark places, and recognising in a flash its *own* open sky. In speech and face, she gave exactly that idea of repatriation after exile, of restoration.

She said the same things that she might have said a few hours earlier, being a prisoner within the same circle of pale ideas, circumscribed by a polygon of shadows. But she said them in a stronger voice, which fools would certainly have called vain, precisely because its tone was coloured with the most fundamental humility.

Her countenance was no less touching and sweet, her eyes had still their untranslatable expression of " after the storm ", but her smile was the slightest shade less pathetic.

It was obvious that a vast oppression still lurked behind a delight that might not perhaps last more than a day—that might be built on the illusion of an illusion, like the cloud-castles of the children of the poor.

Nevertheless, the excellent meal that Gacougnol was giving her, and especially the excellent Burgundy he had ordered were dissipating the volatile cloud of her torment, or at least driving it back to somewhere beneath the black crest of her hair.

"My dear Clotilde," Gacougnol was saying, "the ancient Jews had a different name for each of the two twilights. Morning twilight was called the Twilight of the Dove, and evening twilight the Twilight of the Crow. Your melancholy countenance makes me think of the latter.—I want to try a great experiment on you. Just suppose for a moment that I were a very old friend whom you had given up all hope of ever seeing again, and to your delight had rediscovered, two hours ago. Tell yourself, if you like, that I may possibly be the old fellow sent by Providence as an instrument to transform your existence, just as I've transformed your dress—and I'm sure I don't know how—and tell me your whole story, simply. I am convinced that it is an unhappy one, but I conjecture that it is neither very complicated nor very lengthy, and we shall still have time to get to the Zoo. Am I asking too much? You can quite understand, child, that I need to know you better. All I know about you is your name, and I have only just a glimmering of how you are situated. Now and then, like lots of other men, I have amused myself by asking some poor devil of a woman to tell me her life-story, and they have treated me to some tremendous fabrications, accepting me in all good faith as the typical ' mug ', and never suspecting that it was their particular technique in lying that I was actually studying. But it's quite another matter with you, Clotilde. I feel you won't tell me any lies, and that I can believe you. If there is some incident that you would rather not tell me, or cannot tell me, I beg of you not to substitute something else in its place—just two lines of dots, and pass on to the next item. Will you?"

And his eager gaze concentrated on that feminine pheno-menon who had so contradicted his experience.

Clotilde had heard his words with an emotion that set all her veins throbbing. At first a sharp breath had parted her lips, as if some vision were passing before her eyes, then a pink mist had seemed to float for a moment across her face, and now she was gazing at Gacougnol with a look of such utter candour and sincerity that one might have fancied a beam of moonlight had found its way down into her heart.

" I was thinking of telling you," she replied simply.

Then, draining at one draught her little glass of old Corlon, wiping her lips and laying her napkin down on the table, she rose and went across and sat down on a red divan, next to the artist, who had sat her in front of him, full in the light, with a view to studying her at his ease.

" Monsieur," she said, gravely, " I think, really, you have been placed in my path by the will of God. I believe that, in deep earnest. And I am very sure that nobody *ever* knows what he does or why he does it, and I don't even know if anybody could say, without any mistake about it, just what he *is*. You said something about a friend, an ' old friend ', whom I might have lost sight of, and might fancy I was meeting again in you. To me, that was a very amazing thing for you to say, I assure you. You shall judge for yourself, for I am going to talk to you as you wish me to talk—just as I should speak to that absent friend you re-minded me of so much this morning when you took com-passion on my distress. I will tell you everything—if there is shame," she added, her voice breaking, " so much the worse for me! "

Then, without further preamble, without any poetic

trimmings, without skirting round anything, and without any extenuations or excuses, she related her wilted life, so like a million other lives.

" My existence is like a dreary countryside where it's always raining——"

Her companion no longer thought to watch her. Vanquished by a simplicity new to him, he was relishing, down in the depths least known to himself of his mind, the magical and paradoxical limpidity of that ingenuous candour which was not innocence.

For the first time, perhaps, he was wondering what was the use of being so sophisticatedly clever, muddling one's life away, as he had done, in experiments and deep borings, when here, on the level of the footway, under a flagstone of the commonplace pavement of the street of every day, there gushed that crystal spring singing so unaffectedly her pure and plaintive lay.

"—That Missionary's words," she was saying, " became to me like birds from Paradise making their nest in my heart——"

Without willing or witting of it, she bubbled up with that familiar imagery so frequent in the writings of the mystical saints. The frail web of her diction, such a transparent veil for the undistorted shapes of her thoughts, were little but the constant recollection of such humble things of nature as she might have seen.

She was a Primitive, in the artist's sense, painting herself ingenuously with the very limited palette at her disposal, with no regard for laws of perspective or different values, never hesitating to bring an horizon monstrously into the foreground, or to shine a vivid high-light into some dark corner. But she herself always remained a tiny, distant, shadowy figure, as of a character exiled from its proper scene,—wandering lost in the black valleys, carrying a little lamp.

And yet, now and then, she would use strange words, that, like flashes of lightning, would rend apart the veil of her innermost soul—"I was just searching for love like beggars search for adders!—When I struck Monsieur Chapuis, I felt as if I had an oak-tree growing in my heart!" That was all. The clear stream flowed transparently on through the manchineel thickets and perilous glades of her story.

Nothing was omitted. Her sordidly common fall was told without excuse, with all the details that might make it more loathsome. She showed her mother as she was, without bitterness or resentment, even recalling a few long-ago occasions when that old witch seemed to show a disinterested affection for her.

In the end she overwhelmed her hearer with the most unheard-of poetry, seeming to him like some incredible prodigy of Christian renunciation.

"Now," she said, in conclusion, "you know everything you wished to know. I could not be more frank if I were being examined by God Himself—To make sure of leaving nothing out of my confession, I will add this : In the cab, when you said I was to be dressed, after you had frightened me to death by saying the very reverse half an hour earlier, I assure you I completely lost my head with joy. I had a sort of seizure of madness and cruelty. We were going very fast. All the same, I should have liked the driver to thrash his poor horse so as to go faster still. But since that dream has come true, I am more composed ; I hope you will find me quite reasonable now."

Gacougnol signalled to have the bill brought him, then, having dismissed the man, with the money on a small plate, he turned towards Clotilde, and offering her his hand in frank friendship, which she clasped without hesitation, he said :

" Now, my dear or, rather, Mademoiselle, by all means —I'm beginning to feel rather a fool, adopting such a paternal, or else familiar, pose—I have known some very exalted ladies to whom I should greatly like to send the clothes you were wearing this morning. What you have confided in me has given me an immense admiration for you, as well as giving me a tremendous amount of pleasure of a kind you would hardly understand—for I was listening to you as an *artist* and I am supposed to be a pretty critical audience. So it would be very difficult for me to be sorry for my curiosity. All the same, it must have been rather painful to you, and I do want you to forgive me. Now, not another word—we shall be too late for the lions."

As he drove, the indefatigable talker had become a silent man. He kept looking at Clotilde with a kind of vague respect, mingled with an obvious perplexity. Two or three times he opened his mouth—then closed it again, as if it were the entrance to some evil place, without uttering a syllable.

The young woman, attentive to the bustle of the streets, complied with the rule of strict silence, and thus they arrived, full of their thoughts, at the gates of the Jardin des Plantes, the Zoo of Paris.

CHAPTER XII

WHEN Gacougnol had got rid of their driver, they walked in the direction, as he presumed, of the Greater Carnivora house. But neither of them was well acquainted with the Gardens, frequented as they are only by Parisians living in their vicinity and by foreigners, and, naturally, they lost themselves.

As they went, Clotilde admired the zebras and the antelopes, which she stopped to study lovingly.

"Are you very fond of those animals?" the artist asked her, seeing her caressing one of the charming creatures whose eyes were so like her own.

" I love them with all my heart," she replied. " I wish I were allowed to look after them and live with them, really with them, in one of those little lovely houses somebody has built for them. Their company would be a lot pleasanter than that of Monsieur Chapuis."

This remark seemed to have a certain effect on Gacougnol and he was obviously preparing to say something of importance, when a hand was laid familiarly on his shoulder.

"Well, so it's you, Marchenoir!" he cried, turning round. " I was thinking about you a moment ago. How the deuce do you come to be here?"

" I'm here nearly every day," answered the new arrival. " But how is it you're here yourself? I assure you, your presence is amazing——"

Just then his eyes fell on Clotilde, and became mildly interrogatory. Gacougnol immediately took his cue.

"My dear Clotilde, allow me to present one of our most redoubtable authors, Cain Marchenoir. Among ourselves we call him the Grand Inquisitor of France. Cain, I commend to your admiration Mademoiselle Clotilde—er—Maréchal, a friend I met this morning, but whom I must have known away back in the year one thousand in some previous pilgrimage. She is the Poetess of Humility."

Marchenoir made a deep bow and, addressing Clotilde, said :

"Mademoiselle, if my friend is not jesting, you are the greatest thing in the world."

"Then you may be quite sure that he *is* jesting," she retorted, laughing. "And I am surprised at that, for you have a terrifying name. Cain ? " she added, with a sort of musing terror. " That can't possibly be your real name."

"My mother had me baptised under the name of Marie Joseph, but the name Cain genuinely appears in the municipal register of my birth, by the express will of my father. I sign ' Cain ' when I am at war with the fratricides, and reserve Marie Joseph for when I am talking with God. My dear Gacougnol, will you explain this meeting in the Zoo ? "

" I am here for the lions," the man addressed replied in his turn. " I have some sketches to make. We are at this moment in search of their lair."

" If that's the case, it's as well that you have run into me, for you don't seem to know your way about any too well, and you'd certainly have missed the half hour of daylight that you have left. At this moment those fearsome beasts are not on view for the populace. But I will get you into their house. I am rather at home here, you know."

A few minutes later Marchenoir knocked three Masonic raps on the door of the " palace ", and, with his two companions, entered the inner gallery where the carnivores were finishing their evening meal.

" There are your lions, sketch them to your heart's content," he remarked to Gacougnol. " The Keeper of the Beasts, that chap dressed like an office boy over there, will pretend to forget you're here for half an hour. I've just arranged that. Naturally, he relies on *your* not forgetting *him* when you leave. I will have a chat with Mademoiselle."

Turning away from Pélopidas, who had already taken out his sketch-book, he led Clotilde to some distance away and stood her opposite a superb tiger, recently sent by the Governor of Cochin-China.

They were only a couple of paces away from the beast, separated from it only by a chain stretched across in front of the formidable cage.

" Don't be afraid," he told his companion, who was trembling a little, " you are out of its reach. And anyhow this tiger is a friend of mine. He's been here about three weeks, and not a day passes without my coming to see him and console him. Oh! Our conversation is just what we can manage to make it. I don't flatter myself that I can talk fluent tiger without any mistakes, but we manage to make ourselves understood. Just look what a nice welcome! "

The tiger, which at first had reared itself up to its full length against the bars, did in fact seem to have calmed at the sound of the visitor's voice. It dropped back onto its fore-paws, stilled the mighty rumble of its vocal cords, and started bounding from one end of its cage to the other, each time turning about on the visitors' side, so as not to lose sight of Marchenoir for a single instant in turning, on whom it kept fixed those defiant miser's eyes peculiar to that species of felines—the eyes to which it largely owes its special reputation for cruelty.

Finally, in response to a more concentrated gaze from the tamer, it turned back and lay down at full length, its back against the foot of the bars. Then, to Clotilde's unspeakable terror, for she had not even the strength to utter a cry, Marchenoir leaned over the flexible barrier and with his hand ruffled the back of the formidable brute, which just thrilled voluptuously beneath his caress, purring with a sustained deep-throated note that made all the partitions tremble.

" You see, Mademoiselle," he said, after performing this small courtesy, " these admirable creatures are grossly maligned, though I should excuse them for being furious at their ignominious prisons. Do you imagine this poor tiger is so terrifying ? Only a few months ago he was in his beautiful Indian forest, and now—he is dying of cold and distress beneath the eyes of the rabble. That is why we are so fond of one another—there must be something that tells him that I am no less unhappy, no less an exile, than he is. But we have still other points in common. He is of a race whose name has been made infamous, like the name of Cain, with which, as you know, I am equipped ; and my other name, Joseph—does it not imply the beautiful parti-coloured garment of the child-patriarch, with which you see *this* captive is arrayed ? Oh, you don't know what a sense of solidarity I feel with most of the animals that are here—they really seem to have much more affinity with me than many men have. I don't think there is one of them that has not been a help to me in distress of heart or mind. People don't notice that animals are as mysterious as man is, and that their history is a pictorial edition of the Scriptures that enfolds the Divine Secret. But for six thousand years there has appeared no genius to decipher the symbolic alphabet of creation——"

The odd personality of Marchenoir has been described at length in another book,[1] so it would be superfluous to limn him over again in these pages. But Clotilde, in her ignorance, seeing and hearing him now for the first time, was amazed at a man who seemed to speak from the depths of a volcano, and who brought in the Infinite as a matter of course, in the most casual conversations.

The young woman's very elementary education, and especially the ghastly intellectual sterility of her environment, had scarcely been a preparation for the often unique divagations of this nostalgic contemplative, some of whose flashes of perception of " what lay behind " were uncannily disconcerting.

All the same, the directness of her mind told her that here was an intellect not to be despised. Instinctively she guessed at depths and greatnesses in him, and, although she hardly understood a word, she suddenly felt the joy that a starving beggar would feel as he leaned against the walls of a feudal castle where bread for the destitute was a-baking.

" Creation! " she said. " I know the human mind can never comprehend it. In fact, I've heard it said that there is no man who can understand anything perfectly. But, Monsieur, among so many mysteries, there is one that especially confuses and discourages me. Here, for instance, is a creature beautiful and innocent, in spite of its ferocity—

[1] *Le Désesperé* (*Edition Soirat*, the only edition authorised by the author).

for it lacks the use of reason—why should it lack the use
of liberty as well ? Why do animals suffer ? I have often
seen animals ill-treated, and I have wondered how it is that
God can bear such injustice against those poor creatures
who have not deserved punishment as we have."

"Ah, Mademoiselle! First, one would have to inquire
where the *boundaries* of ' man ' really lie. The zoologists,
writing out their little labels a few yards away, will undertake to teach you the exact peculiarities that distinguish the
human animal from all the lower species. They'll tell you
it is absolutely essential to be born with two feet and two
hands, and not to possess, at birth, any feathers or scales.
But that doesn't help to explain why that unhappy tiger
is a prisoner. We should have to know what God has not
revealed to anybody—that is to say, the position that
feline occupies in the universal redistribution of the collective responsibilities and consequences of the Fall. You
must have been taught, if it was only in your catechism,
that when God created man He gave him the sovereignty
over the animals. Are you aware that Adam, in his turn,
gave to each of them a name, and thus the lower animals
have been created in the image of his faculty of reason,
just as he himself was formed in the likeness of God ?
Because that *name* of a creature is the creature itself. Our
first ancestor, when he named the beasts, made them *his*
in a special, ineffable manner. He did not merely subjugate
them like a sovereign. His own essence permeated them.
He attached them, bound them, to himself, for evermore,
affiliating them to his own equilibrium, and involving them
in his own fate. Why should you be surprised to find these
animals round us are captives, when the human race is a
captive race seven times over ? It was inevitable that *all*

should fall, then and there, when Man fell. It has been said that the animals rebelled against man at the same time that man rebelled against God. That's pious rhetoric, without any depth. These cages are in gloom only because they are placed beneath the human Cage, propping it up and crushed by it. But, in captivity or not, wild or domesticated, close to their wretched Sultan or at a distance from him, the animals are compelled to be under him, because of him, and, in consequence, *for* him. Even far away from where man is, they undergo the invincible law and prey on one another, as we do, in the uninhabited places, under the pretext of being carnivorous. The immense volume of their suffering forms part of our ransom, and, right along the whole linked line of animal life, from humanity down to the lowest of the beasts, universal Pain is one identical propitiation."

"If I understand you, Monsieur Marchenoir," said Clotilde, hesitantly, "the sufferings of animals are just, and willed by God, because He has condemned them to bear a very heavy portion of our burden. How can that be, since they die without hope?"

"Why would they exist, then, and how could we say that they suffer, if they did not suffer *in us*? We know nothing, absolutely nothing, Mademoiselle, if it be not this: that no creatures, reasoning or unreasoning, can suffer, except by the Will of God, and, consequently, by His Justice. Have you noticed that a suffering animal is usually the reflection of the suffering man whom it accompanies? In every part of the world you may be sure of seeing an unhappy slave leading a miserable animal. That angelic dog of the poor man's, for instance, so much misused by romantic lyricists—can't you see that it is a representation of that poor man's soul, a grievous picture of his thoughts, in fact something like an external mirage of that wretched man's consciousness ? When we see a beast suffering, the compassion that we feel is only so keen because it impinges in us on our prescience of Redemption. We feel somehow aware, as you put it just now, that such a creature is suffering without having deserved it, without any kind of compensation, since it has no hope beyond this present life, and that thus it is a terrible injustice. So it must follow that they suffer *for* Us, us the Immortals, unless God is to be absurd. It is He who gives pain, since there is none but He who can give anything, and Pain is so holy that it idealises and magnifies the most wretchedly ignoble beings ! But we are so superficial and so callous that we need the most frightful admonitions of misfortune before we can realise them. The human race seems to have forgotten that everything capable of experiencing suffering, since the world began, has humanity alone to thank for sixty centuries of anguish, and that man's disobedience, in virtue of his arrogance as the Divine Animal, was what destroyed the precarious happiness of these despised creatures. Once more, would it not be strange indeed if the everlasting patience of these innocents had not been planned by an Infallible Wisdom, with a view to counterbalancing, in the most secret scales of the Lord, the savage restlessness of humanity ? "

The voice of this counsel for the tigers had taken on a vibrant, majestic tone. The wild beasts were gazing curiously at him from all directions in the dim gallery, and even the Canadian bear seemed attentive.

Clotilde, in deep amazement, was relinquishing her whole mind to this discourse, which was like nothing else she had ever heard. From head to foot she was all listening—incapable of finding fault, moulding her thought, as best she could, to the thought of that moving pleader.

Finally, nevertheless, she risked a remark.

" I should imagine, Monsieur, that you are very seldom understood, for your words go far beyond ordinary ideas. The things you say seem to come from some strange world that nobody, surely, knows. So I find it very difficult to follow you—and I must admit that the essential point seems still obscure to me. You declare that the animals share the fate of man, who dragged them down in his own fall. Very well, then! You add that, being without moral consciousness, and not having to suffer on their own account, since they were incapable of disobedience, they necessarily suffer because of us and *for* us. That I can't understand so well. All the same, I can still accept it as a mystery that is in no way repugnant to my reason. I quite realise that pain can never be useless. But, in Heaven's name, must it not be of some help to the being that does the suffering ? Doesn't even involuntary sacrifice call for a recompense ? "

" In a word, you want to know what their recompense or payment is. If I knew and could tell you, I should be God, Mademoiselle, for in that case I should know what animals are *in themselves* and not merely in relation to man. Haven't you perceived that we can never know animate or inanimate things or creatures except in their relation to other beings or things, never in their essence and substance ? There isn't one man on earth with the right to say, with complete assurance, that any discernible form is indelible, carries within itself the mark of eternity. We are, according to the holy Word, as those who sleep, and the external world is in our dreams, as in a glass darkly. We shall not comprehend this 'groaning universe' until all hidden things are revealed to us, in fulfilment of the promise of our Lord Jesus Christ. Till then we have to accept, with the ignorance of lambs, the universal spectacle of immolations, and remind ourselves that if pain were not enveloped in mystery it would neither have power nor beauty to recruit martyrs and would not even be worthy of the endurance of the lower animals.

"In this connection, I should like to tell you a strange story, a very strange and sad story—but I see Gacougnol beckoning to us. If he will honour me with the same attentive hearing as you do, I think it will be good for myself to tell it."

CHAPTER XIII

"WAITER!—One madeira and two absinthes," ordered Gacougnol, when he, Clotilde and Marchenoir had taken their seats in a café near the main entrance of the Gardens.

The quick nightfall of December had come over beasts and men, and the visitors had decided to settle down in that prosaic place for the hearing of Marchenoir's narrative.

"But first," said the painter again, "let me write a few words, if you don't mind. Waiter! You've a telegraph office close here. I want you to take a telegram there at once. Bring me some paper."

Then, hiding the sheet with his left hand, he hastily scribbled the simple words, *"Clotilde not returning—*

Gacougnol." This telegram, addressed to "Madame Chapuis", was dispatched forthwith.

"And now I am all ears. You know, Marchenoir, you're almost the only one among our contemporaries whom I can listen to for long with any pleasure. Even when I don't quite know what you are talking about, I can still feel your *power*, and that is quite enough for me to enjoy hearing you."

"My dear Gacougnol," replied Marchenoir, "don't flatter me, please—and don't flatter yourself, either! It is for Mademoiselle, in particular, that I am going to speak."

Then, looking at Clotilde,

"I hardly know if what I am going to venture to offer you rightly deserves to be called a story. It is rather a travel-memory, an old impression, which has remained very vivid and very profound, that I want you to share with me. You will see how it bears on our conversation about animals.

"You must have heard of La Salette, of the Pilgrimage to Our Lady of La Salette. As you know, about fifty years ago the Virgin Mary appeared on that mountain to two poor children. Naturally, people did all they could to discredit that phenomenal happening by ridicule or calumny. This is not the moment to explain to you just how excellent are my reasons for feeling compelled to regard it as the most overwhelming Divine manifestation since the Transfiguration of Our Lord—which Raphaël, with his profane decorator's imagination, so little understood—that is one for you, Pélopidas!"

"I know it is," said the other, "but I am not a Raphaël fanatic. I'll admire him as anything you like—except as a religious painter. His only tolerable Virgin is the Dresden

one—and even that's a rosary. As to his ' Transfiguration ',
in all the three hundred years it has been in existence, has
any solitary man ever found he could *pray* before that
picture ? At the view of those three wrapper-clad gymnasts
rising symmetrically over the springboard of the clouds, I
declare it would be utterly impossible for me to mumble the
slightest prayer."

"And do you know why ? " retorted Marchenoir.
" Because Raphaël, in the teeth of the Church—which
has never uttered a word to such an effect—insists on making
his three luminous figures *float*, in obedience to a painting
tradition of the ecstatic state that is definitely misplaced in
this case. The famous ancestor of our modern St. Sulpice
school of religiosity was far more familiar with the baker-
woman's sheets than the leaves of the sacred volume, and
he never realised how utterly indispensable it is that the
feet of Jesus should be touching the earth, so that the
Transfiguration should be a terrestrial one, and Simon
Peter's words offering three tabernacles should not be an
absurdity. You talk of prayer. Ah, there's the point! A
work of art that claims to be religious and does not inspire
prayer is as much of a monstrosity as a beautiful woman
who stirs nobody's senses. If we weren't hypnotised by
traditions of compulsory admiration, we could never dream
of imagining—why, we should be appalled at the idea of
—a Madonna or a Christ that lacked the power to bring
us down on our knees.

"And now, here is their punishment, a more dire one
than anybody would imagine. The sublime image-sculptors
and eikon-painters of the Middle Ages often asked, at the
bottom of their works, very humbly, to be prayed for,
hoping thus that they would be included in the murmured

ecstasies that their simple-souled representations stimulated. On the other hand, the despairing soul of Raphaël has been hovering vainly for three centuries before his canvases of immortality. The throng of the generations admiring him will never give him any alms but the empty suffrage he asked for. . . . Perhaps one day we shall be allowed to say that the so-called religious painting of the Renaissance was as calamitous for Christianity as Luther himself; I am waiting for the poet with real *vision* who will sing the ' Paradise Lost ' of our aesthetic innocence. But let's close this parenthesis and return to my subject.

" Well, one day I made the pilgrimage to La Salette. I wanted to see that glorious mountain which had been touched by the feet of the Queen of Prophets, and where the Holy Spirit spoke through her lips the most redoubtable canticle that mankind has heard since the *Magnificat*. One stormy day I had climbed to that whirlpool of light, in the wild downpour of the rain, in the midst of the strife of the maddened winds, in the tempest of my hope and the whirlwind of my thoughts, with my ears dinned by the roar of the rushing river—I have made up my mind that I won't die without having first perpetuated in some book of love the superhuman memory of that climb during which I offered my whole soul to God on the hundred thousand hands of my desire. Wallowing as I have for twenty years in all the muck of Paris, I have never managed to discover what amalgams of sebaceous residue, what filthy sweepings from the foetid sewage of the cesspools, could ever have generated the foul scions of the bourgeoisie who were scandalised by the Salette phenomenon, and invented any old dirty lies to discredit it. But I bear testimony that at the very spot where the might of the

Spirit was manifested, I felt the most indisputably real disturbance, the most overwhelming shock that could ever bring a man to his knees. On my word of honour, it still makes me tremble."

" Well, certainly," said Gacougnol, " if, as I suppose, you are going to tell us of a caress from on high—it must have been with the whole five fingers of the Divine hand, for you're the thick-skinned sort of rhinoceros that it would take a lot to make any impression on. Besides, if I am rightly informed, you must be pretty hardened to all the ordinary emotions——"

" Yes, I ought to be—that journey to Salette was not long after the inexplicable death of my poor little André. . . ."

At this point the narrator's voice seemed choked to silence. Clotilde, who for over an hour had been hanging on this stranger's words, which appeared to exercise an extraordinary influence over her, involuntarily put out a hand, as if she had seen a child falling down. But the gesture was abruptly checked by another gesture of Marchenoir's, followed by the resounding summons of his saucer banged on the marble table.

" Waiter! " he cried. " Some more! To continue. You can guess that I may have been in a pretty condition of soul. I had gone there on the long-standing advice of a sublime priest, dead for years, who had said to me, 'When you fancy that God has abandoned you, go and confide your plaint to His Mother on that mountain.' 'Turris Davidica!' I thought. All I needed was the ' thousand shields hung up, and all the armoury of the heroes ' of which Solomon spoke. I could never be sufficiently armed against the shafts of my lamentable distress. And there I was, already, on that road onto which I had flung off, despite storm and counsel, unspeakably transported!

"How can I make you see it? When I got to the top, and saw the Mother seated on a stone, weeping, her face in her hands, with that little fountain that looks as if it flowed from her eyes, I went up to the railings and threw myself down, and spent myself in tears and sobs, praying for the compassion of her who was named *omnipotentia supplex*. How long did that prostration last, that flood of Cocytus? I can't tell you. When I first got there twilight had barely set in; when I rose to my feet, weak as a convalescent centenarian, the night was completely dark, and I could have fancied those were my tears sparkling in the black skies, for I felt as if my roots had been transplanted to the heights.

"Oh, my friends, what a divine impression that was! Around me, the human silence, not a sound but that miraculous fountain harmonising with the music of Paradise composed by the rustlings of the mountain, and occasionally, too, at a vast distance, the tinklings of a few flocks and herds. I cannot express it to you. I was like a man without sin who has just died, so completely free was I from any suffering now! I was athrill with the joy of those ' robbers of Heaven ' of whom the Saviour Jesus spoke. An angel, without doubt, some very patient seraph, had unwound from me, strand by strand, the whole tangle of my despair, and I was exulting in the intoxication of the sacred Madness, when I went and knocked at the monastery door, where they take in travellers."

CHAPTER XIV

MARCHENOIR, everlastingly vanquished by life, had been ironically endowed with the eloquence of a conqueror. He was not simply one of those Raiders of the Gospel to whom he had alluded, whom the Heavenly Legions cannot resist, but also, and far more, one of those Meek to whom was assigned the inheritance of the Earth.

Whatever the occasion of his speech or the theme with which it dealt, it was generally looked on as a hard thing to resist this new Judge in Israel who fought with both hands. He struck straight at your heart at the very outset.

The continuous, effortless, flow of his imagery was rendered clear-cut in its precision by intonation or gesture, with a spontaneous vigour that routed the defensive.

Like most of the great orators, he would spring forthwith into the press of battle, looming up mightily in his wrath against invisible foes, and all the time he was speaking, you could see his soul surging within him—as if it were some great imprisoned Infanta peering through the windows of a burning Escorial.

Clotilde, enthralled, thought what an irresistibly powerful preacher he might have made, and Pélopidas, dazed, gazed at him as at some sanguinary, fuliginous fresco of remote antiquity, in which the adorations or furies of an age long dead were miraculously alive once more.

The narrator had paused a moment. The worthy painter took advantage of the chance to speak a little, in hope of masking some of his confusion.

"Don't you think, Marchenoir, that, to feel religious emotions like that, either at La Salette or anywhere else, one must be just in the state of mind you were in that day? —have passed through just such anguish?"

"My friend, that is just the objection I was waiting for. Here is my reply—a very simple one. We are all creatures of misery and desolation, but few of us are capable of looking into the abyss of ourselves.—Well, yes! I had passed through some blessed sorrows," he declaimed, in a deep voice that stirred the depths of both his hearers, "I knew *real* despair, and had given myself up to the kneading of its iron hands. But you must not do me so much honour as to consider me as exceptional as all that. My case only seems surprising because it was given to me to feel a little more clearly than others do the unspeakable desolation of love. You yourselves, you don't know your own hell. One must be, or have once been, devout, to be well acquainted with one's own abandonment, and take full count of the silent troops of devils we all carry about within us.

"But until such time as you attain that vision of dread, beware of imagining that succour is to be had indifferently in this place or in that. 'At La Salette or anywhere else,' you said. Well, I can assure you personally that that spot is especially frequented by the Thunders of the Apocalypse, and that there is no other spot on earth where those can go who are interested in the final culmination of the Redemption. At La Salette and nowhere else can you be fortified if you are aware that *all things are not fulfilled* and that the High Mass of the Comforter has not yet begun.

"Once more, this is not the time to enter on such unaccustomed speculations. Listen to my anecdote. I need hardly tell you, Gacougnol, how far I .was from

expecting to find any powerful stimulants for my ardour
in that hostelry, built by industrious piety a few yards from
the scene of the apparition. I am one of those people whose
voices have no echo, especially among reasonable Christians
who are not troubled by the Supernatural. The Salette
pilgrimage is served by practical missionaries, who don't
lose themselves in any mystical labyrinths, I can tell you.
They provide plain bread and butter for travellers for
Heaven, and billets for unextravagant virtue. Their pious
exercises and verbal exhortations, drawn up with prudence,
never interfere with the concurrent service of the table-
d'hôte and the lodgings. Making up the accounts for the
meals and 'extras' mingles with the canticles and litanies,
on that mountain, a mountain as dread as Horeb, where
Our Lady of Swords manifested herself in the burning bush
of her Sorrows. It is an awesome thought, that that
marvellous Congregation has not the faintest understanding
of what really took place, and probably the utmost reach of
those neat-herds of the Priesthood is to imagine that the
Divine Power was demonstrated simply so that they should
come into existence! You ought to hear their accounts
of the miracle, that identical patter that they serve out
every day, beside the Spring, in the rest-hour after dinner!

"So there I was, at table, at that table-d'hôte I mentioned, along with about a score of miscellaneous pilgrims.
The female pilgrims are received in the opposite wing of
the building, the two sexes being thus separated, on the
two sides of the sanctuary.

"Two or three priests, not much marked with the
strain of apostolic toil, and goodness knows what other
faces, hands, bellies! All eating and drinking without
apparently caring what. In short, the ordinary tableful of

any provincial hostelry. I even fancy there was a little loud-voiced talk.

' I had scarcely crossed the threshold when I heard Marseilles mentioned. This geographical allusion emanated from a fat bearded man, with a bloated face, evidently bent on not letting anybody be unaware of his origin, which his beastly accent proclaimed anyhow. But such ringing trumpet notes still sounded in my heart, that I scarcely heard anything, and did not even start wondering what those people were after in such a place. Automatically, I ate whatever was set before me, my fellow-guests separated from me as if by the foaming waters of an ocean. True, my hiker's get-up, dripping wet and covered with mud, could hardly have struck a powerful chord of sympathy in those diners. None of them had spoken to me, and the chatter had not slackened for a moment at my entry, since contemporary vulgarity does not allow of deference for the Stranger.

"I was actually thinking of the Third Divine Person, when a hand touched my shoulder. I turned, and saw a sad-faced figure, in rustic costume, who said :

" ' Sir, your clothes are wet, and you must be very cold. Will you take my place ? It is nearer the stove. *I pray you, take it.*'

" There was such sincere prayer in his expression, his eyes told me so plainly that he would think himself guilty of whatever catarrh I might fall victim to, I at once accepted his place as simply as he had offered it. This exchange won me a little attention. The obese man from Marseilles, who was now facing me, vouchsafed to look at me with his big elf eyes, rimmed with moisture from the luxurious pleasure of swallowing.

" ' Hi, you there, the man with the cattle! ' he shouted, addressing my unknown friend, ' is that how you go and desert us ? Really! That's not very polite of you! '

" I had exactly the same sensation as if somebody had suddenly opened the door of a latrine. That tradesman's tone had something so nauseous about it, his well-breeched coarseness seemed so ingrained in the fat of his hoggish prosperity, that I all at once felt suffocated. The blue birds of rapture took wing and left me plunged back into base reality, very malodorous and accursed reality.

" The man addressed made no reply. So, bending over towards his neighbour, who was one of the clerics I had caught sight of as I came in, the fat man said :

" ' Really, Monsieur l'Abbé, if that ain't a bit thick, him changing places, just when it was getting to be a bit o' fun, like.' Then, once more raising his hateful voice with its intolerable accent :

" ' Eh, my lad, maybe you don't know I'm from Marseilles, I am. If you'd had the good fortune to frequent that " metropolis " you'd have learned to give a civil answer to a civil question. I asked you why you went and left us as if we was dirt. This gentleman that's taken your place looks very nice and all that, I don't say nothing to the contrary, but we'd got accustomed to your dial, and it puts us out not having it to look at.'

" The whole company remained silent, bent on getting some fun at the expense of one poor wretch.

" ' Monsieur,' replied the latter, eventually, ' I am sorry to have deprived you of my *mug*, to use your own word. But the pilgrim who has taken my place was cold, and, as I have had plenty of time to get warm while you have been doing me the honour of amusing yourselves with me, I thought it my duty to give him my seat.'

" This was all said without irony or bitterness, in an extraordinarily humble manner, with an almost grotesque mildness of tone, that I could never hope to give you any idea of. For instance, if I asked you to try and imagine a dying child heard talking through the thickness of a wall, that would sound absurd—and yet I can't find a better comparison. In short, I instinctively sensed the presence of something very rare, and I became more attentive.

" I will spare you the facetious clerical-outfitter grimaces with which the individual facing me was at pains to treat us, to the great enjoyment of the munching jaws, both sacerdotal and lay. Here is the reason of that joyous mirth : the poor creature who served as butt to those beasts was a sort of apostolic vegetarian, labouring under the perpetual necessity of explaining his abstinence. He would not allow animals to be killed on any pretext whatever, and, in consequence, he debarred himself from eating their flesh, refusing to be involved in complicity in their murder. He would explain this to whoever would listen to him, undeterred by any mockery, and it was apparent that he would have given his own life for this idea.

" Eventually one of the priests, a lank ecclesiastic, who looked as if he might have been a teacher of logic in some college of the Higher Rationalism, took the floor with these words :—

" ' I would like to ask you, as a favour, to answer one simple question I will put to you. You wear leather shoes, a felt hat, probably braces, you are using at the present moment a knife with a bone handle. How can you reconcile such abuses with the *brotherly* sentiments you have been expressing? Do you realise that innocent quadrupeds have had to be slain to provide you with this criminal luxury?'

"I will make no attempt to depict the audience's enthusiasm. It was a delirious riot of acclamation! They clapped, they stamped, they shouted, they did imitations of animal noises. Exactly the success of a star cabaret turn. When a little quiet had been restored in that pen of beasts, the first articulate word that could be heard came from the comical, flippant snout of the man opposite me. He roared:

"'Ah! You've got your licking this time, my lad! No getting away from it this time, my fine friend! It's a theologian putting you through it now; a minister of the altar. How are you going to answer him, Jackanapes?'

"The answer was such that there ensued a general silence. With the exception of the last rascal who had spoken, everybody's eyes were cast down to their food, obviously uncomfortable at the length to which the joke had gone. I stretched my head round to see the victim. He was weeping, his face cupped in his hands.

"You know, Gacougnol, whether I am a man to see the weak persecuted in my presence. So I got up amidst a stupefied silence, and walking round the table I brought the flat of my hand down on the mastodon's shoulder with a pretty substantial degree of force that almost threw him off his balance.

"'Up you get!' I cried. He turned right round, bellowing like a bull; but if he had some idea of displaying indignation, I assure you that the moment he had had a look at me he lost any impulse to indulge in any such big-hearted sentiment. I forced him to his feet, dragged him towards his victim, who was still weeping and had not raised his head, and said to him again:

" 'You have basely and vilely insulted a Christian who was doing you no harm. Now you are going to beg his pardon, are you not? Perhaps it will be a salutary lesson for some of the cowards who are listening!' As he seemed inclined to protest, I set my hand against the back of his neck again with such commanding fury that he fell to his knees at the feet of the worthy fellow, who was frozen with stupefaction.

" ' Now,' I added, ' in a loud and distinct voice you will proceed to humble yourself before the man whose offender you are, or I swear before God that I will tear your skin off you before we leave this den. As to *you*, sir, you must not interfere with what I am doing. I am accomplishing an act of justice, not for your sake but for the honour of Mary, to which just a little too much violence is here done.'

"I proved once more on this occasion the amazing power of a single man who displays his real soul, and the matchless cowardice of scoffers. That fellow begged pardon on his knees, as I had insisted he should, adding, to save some draggled remnant of his dignity as a wit, that he was no ' Cossack ' and had no intention of hurting anybody's feelings. The other raised him to his feet, and threw his arms about him in an embrace, and I went to bed. That is the first instalment of my adventure, which, if you will allow me, shall be a diptych."

CHAPTER XV

" Do you like our narrator of stories ? " Gacougnol asked of Clotilde.

By way of sole answer, she made the universal gesture —drawing a smile from Marchenoir—of animatedly clasping both hands and pressing them against her heart, drawing up her shoulders.

In truth, the metamorphosed woman was experiencing something extraordinarily powerful. Meeting Marchenoir was a revelation for her, like emerging from a void. It was not exactly the things he said, but his " big " way of saying them, that thrilled her.

Till now, she had been utterly unaware that there were such men. The very concept of this type of superiority was something unknown to her. And now, never having had the least suspicion of her own intellectual faculties, she suddenly found herself under the sway of the master best able to cause their instantaneous development. This effect upon her was so dominating that the man who so stimulated her mind had only to say anything, no matter what, for her to be carried away altogether. She was no longer astonished at having been able to find some more or less valid counter-arguments when he and she had been talking alone together in the Gardens. Obviously, even if it were only for an hour, he inevitably raised to his own level anybody who listened to him with attention.

In short, that charming girl had, by her own nature, been so preserved from the contagious, trivialising influence of the Paris streets, that at thirty she still had the fine flower of enthusiasm of the most idealistic-minded adolescence.

"Isn't it touching," went on Pélopidas, "to see her listening like this? Would God my own poor masterpieces were gazed at with as much affection! But it is an exasperating reflection, my poor Tongue-o'-Gold, that the wretched tripe-hounds who envy your gift actually get some comfort from your contempt for them. For it is said that you don't waste yourself on everybody. Everybody knows that."

"Let's not go into that, please. You know my views. I try not to write more idiotically than I can help, and to write what I think this emetic generation of ours should be informed of. As to the eloquence of the political or lecture platform, bah! Even if it were true that my words were as powerful as certain pioneers of destruction have declared, and were capable of ' changing the shape of the mountains ', like the word of fire that breathed against Sodom, I would not exchange my solitary meditation for the rostrum of some toadying demagogue. I prefer talking to the animals. This evening, I am talking to you, and still more to Mademoiselle, with the utmost pleasure."

Gacougnol burst out laughing, and said, turning to Clotilde, who had remained serious:

"My child, if you knew the barbarian who favours us with this madrigal, you would know that he's the only man living who possesses the secret of saying to his friends anything he chooses to say without offending them."

The remark seemed to surprise Clotilde.

"But how could Monsieur Marchenoir offend us? I can quite see that he is not to be measured with other men,

and when he is talking to animals I fully realise that he is
speaking to God."

"Mademoiselle," interposed Marchenoir. "If I had
entertained any doubts, that last remark of yours would
suffice to convince me that you are worthy to hear the end
of the story.

"The day after the little drama of which I have been
telling you, the first person I saw near the Spring was
the man whose part I had taken. He was praying with
great absorption and I had an opportunity of studying
him. He was a man of commonplace appearance, dressed
almost like a tramp. He must have been the wrong side
of fifty, and already showed signs of approaching baldness.
It was easy to see that he had been battered with all the
storms of calamity. His shy, resignedly sorrowful face
would have been utterly insignificant, but for a peculiar
expression of joy which seemed to be the effect of some
inward colloquy. I noticed his lips moving slightly, and,
occasionally, smiling with that mild, pale smile that some
idiots have, and some rational beings whose souls are
plunged into that phase of meditation called by the
mystical saints ' delectation '.

"His eyes, above all, amazed me. Fixed on the mourning Virgin, they were speaking to her as a hundred tongues
might have spoken, as a whole nation of supplicatory or
laudatory tongues ! I imagined—on that Divine register
where the vibrations of the heart will one day be transposed
into ringing waves of music—a whole peal of praises, of
raptures of love, of thanksgivings and aspirations. It even
seemed to me—and the impression has remained with
me through the years—that from the midst of the encircling hills, girdled just then with shimmering clouds,

there shot innumerable beams of light, of infinite tenuity and sweetness, converging on the calamity-scored face of that worshipper, round whom I seemed to see a faint, vague emanation floating like an aura . . . the simple Hodge of the night before had, as you will perceive, rather grown in importance.

"When his prayer was finished, his eyes met mine, and, baring his head, he advanced to me:

"'Monsieur,' he said, 'I should be happy to speak with you a moment. Would you do me the honour of walking a little way with me?'

"'With pleasure,' I replied.

"We went and sat down behind the church, at the edge of the plateau, facing towards Obiou, whose snowy summit was at the moment flashing with the radiance of the sun, which was hidden still from us by the mists.

"'You grieved me greatly yesterday evening,' he began. 'Unfortunately, I could not stop you, and it has caused me great sorrow. You do not know me. I am not an individual to be defended. Formerly, when I did not yet know myself, I used to defend myself unaided. I was a hero. I killed a friend in a duel because of a joke. Yes, Monsieur, I killed a being formed in the image of God, who had not even wronged me. That is what is called an affair of honour. I ran him through the chest, and he died with his eyes fixed on me, without saying a word. That gaze has never left me during twenty-five years, and now, while I am speaking to you, he is up there, right before me, on that ancient pinnacle of the firmament! . . . Whenever I recall the picture of that moment, I am capable of enduring anything. My only consolation and my only hope is to be mocked, to be insulted, to have my face rubbed in filth. Those who use me thus I love, and bless them, " with all the blessings of this world ", because, you see, that is justice, the *true* Justice. You gave way to anger and misused your strength against a poor man whose shoes I am certainly not worthy to clean. You compelled me to pray for him all through the night, stretched out in front of his door like a corpse, and this morning I begged him, in the name of the Five Wounds of Our Saviour, to walk on my face. You saw me weep, and that is what moved you, because you have nobility. I was wrong, but I cannot help it when it is a priest who is speaking to me, because in him I see a judge who reminds me that I am a murderer and the lowest of all vile creatures. . . .

" ' Oh, Monsieur, don't try to excuse me! *Give me no human counsel,* I beg you, for the sake of God's Love which walked on this mountain! Whatever can be said in mitigation of an infamous act, do you imagine I have not said, to myself, and had said to me by others, until the day when it was vouchsafed to me to know that I am an abomination ? That man whom I murdered had a wife and two children. His wife died of grief, do you understand that ? *I* gave a million francs for the children. If I did not give all I had, that was because there were family reasons against it. But I promised the gentle Virgin that I would live, to my last hour, after the fashion of a beggar. I hoped that in this way peace would return to me—as if the life of a Member of the Mystical Body of Christ could be paid for with francs! It was the High Priests' money that I gave to those poor children, treated as little Judases by their father's murderer. Ah, yes, indeed—that Divine Peace has never returned, and I am crucified every day!

" ' I have told you this, Monsieur, because you had

compassion, and you might have entertained esteem. I
am still too cowardly to tell my life story to everybody,
as perhaps I should, and as the great penitents of the middle
ages used to. I wanted to become a Trappist, then a
Carthusian. I was told that I had no vocation. Then I
married, in order to have my fill of suffering. I took an
old prostitute of the lower sort, whom the sailors would
no longer have. She rains blows on me, and drenches me
with ridicule and abuse—I do not let her lack for anything,
but I have put the remnant of my fortune, which was pretty
considerable, in safety beyond her reach. That is the
property of the poor, and from it I take the slight amounts
necessary for my travels. Last year I went to the Holy
Land. To-day I am at La Salette for the thirtieth time.
I must be known here. This is where I have received the
most help, and I would prescribe this pilgrimage for all
who are unhappy. It is the Sinai of penitence, the Paradise
of Pain ; those who do not realise it are much to be pitied.
For myself, I am beginning to realise it, and sometimes I
am set free for an hour——'

"He stopped, and I was careful not to break in on his
thoughts. In any case, I should have been hard put to it
to utter a single word that would not have seemed an
absurdity in the presence of this voluntary convict-slave,
this stupendous Stylites of Expiation.

"When he resumed speaking, after a moment, I was
taken by surprise, by an extraordinary transformation.
Instead of that terrible figure of pathos who had plucked
at all my heart-strings, instead of that surge of remorse,
that volcano of lamentations, shooting forth its lava of
anguish in all directions, there was the humble, mysteriously
placid voice that I had heard the night before.

" ' I am often twitted on the matter of the animals. As you saw for yourself. I think I am right in sensing that you are a man of imagination. Consequently, you might suspect—crediting me, possibly, with an admirable if rather indiscreet zeal—that I *chose* to bring this mockery upon myself. Nothing of the kind. I am really made that way. I love animals, of whatever kind, almost as much as it is either possible or lawful to love humans, though I am fully aware of their inferiority. I have sometimes longed, I will confess, to be a genuine imbecile, so that I could escape altogether from the sophistries of pride, but, that longing not yet having been fulfilled, I am far from unaware of what there is that may be a ground for scorn in this attitude of mind, which amounts with me to a passion, and has been rebuked by men of great wisdom. But is there not some misconception? Can it be that most men have forgotten that they themselves are *creatures*, and therefore have no right to scorn the other side of creation? St. Francis of Assisi, whom not the most impious can help admiring, declared that he was a very close kinsman, not only of the animals, but of the stones, and the water in the springs, and the righteous Job was not blamed for saying to corruption, " Thou art my brother! "

" ' I love animals because I love God, and profoundly revere what He has made. When I speak affectionately to a wretched animal, rest assured that I am trying to bind myself more closely, in that way, to the Cross of the Redeemer, Whose Blood, you know, flowed on the earth, before flowing in the hearts of men. And the earth, that common mother of all animal life, was greatly cursed. And I know, too, that God gave us the animals for our meat—but he did not command us to devour them in a material sense, and for scores of centuries the experiences of the ascetic life have proved that the strength of the human species does not consist in that food. People do not know Love, because they do not see the reality beneath the symbols. How can one slay a lamb, for example, or an ox, without remembering then and there that those poor creatures had the privilege of prophesying, congruously to their nature, the Universal Sacrifice of Our Lord Jesus Christ ? . . .'

" He talked to me in this way for a long time, with great faith, great love, and, do please believe this, with great knowledge—or, rather, a marvellous intuition of the symbolism of Christianity, such as I never for one instant expected from him. Would God I were able to reproduce all his words exactly for you!

" I owe a great deal to that simple man who, in a few conversations, gave me the luminous key to an unknown world. You remember, Mademoiselle, the whole of this story rose out of the subject of animals. Well! I assure you, he was a wonderful being when he was talking of them. Gone were the great, rending outbursts of his first confidence, gone the tempest and the mournful falling star. Divine calm—and a transparent sincerity! Placidly he kindled like a small, small night-light by the side of some sleeper whose dwelling angels watched. As I listened, I thought of those Blessed who were the first companions of the Seraphic Doctor, their hands filled with flowers that have perfumed the Occident ; I could see again, too, all those other Saints of olden times whose pathetic feet have left us a few grains of the sands of Heaven.

" What little I have repeated of all he said will have served to show you that it was not a matter of those idiotic raptures that are, perhaps, the most disgusting form of idolatry. Animals were, for him, the alphabetic signs of Ecstasy. In them he could read—as could those elect I mentioned—the only story in which he was interested, the sempiternal story of the Trinity; and he taught me to spell it out in the symbolic characters of nature. My delight was beyond words. As he saw it, the Empire of the World, lost by man's first disobedience, could only be regained by *plenary* restitution of the whole ancient Order of Things that had been outraged.

" ' Animals,' he said to me, ' are held by us as hostages for the Celestial beauty we have vanquished.'

"A strange saying, whose full content I have not even yet plumbed! Precisely because it is animals that have been the most scorned and the most oppressed by man, he believed that it would be through them that God would work something ineffable when the moment should come for Him to make His Glory manifest. That is why his tenderness for these created beings was accompanied by a kind of mystic reverence that is very difficult to describe in words. He saw in them the unconscious guardians of a sublime Secret, lost by mankind beneath the leafy boughs of Eden; a secret which their sad eyes, veiled in darkness, have been unable to divulge since the awful Betrayal. . . ."

Marchenoir said nothing more. Leaning on the table, his finger-tips pressed against his temples, in one of his familiar attitudes, he was gazing vaguely before him, as if seeking to discern in the distance some great bird of prey, in despair at finding no catch, that reflected his melancholy.

Shyly, Clotilde asked him the question that could be seen trembling on the lips of Pélopidas.

"What became of the man?"

"Ah, yes! I was leaving my story unfinished. I never saw him again, and only heard of his death through a compatriot of mine who had settled in the little town where *he* lived, in Brittany, by the sea. He died in the ghastliest fashion—and, consequently, in the fashion he desired most—that is, in his home, under the eyes of the vile Xantippe whom he had purposely chosen to torture him. He had a paralytic stroke shortly after our meeting, and refused to let himself be removed to some nursing home, where he might have run the risk of expiring in peace. Having lived as a penitent, he elected to agonise and die as a penitent. It seems, his wife made him lie in filth. The details are dreadful. For a little while it was even thought that she had poisoned him. What is certain, is that she was impatient for his death, expecting to be his heiress. But he had taken his precautions long before, as he had told me, and the remainder of his patrimony went to the poor. The woman whose function was to serve up his diet of agony, naturally lost her appointment when he passed away.

"Now my story *is* finished. You see, it was not a very complex one. I simply wanted to make you see, just as I saw him myself—incompletely, alas!—an absolutely unique human being, whose counterpart I am convinced does not exist anywhere on earth. But for my Breton correspondent's letter, which was too circumstantial, I should sometimes be tempted to wonder whether the whole thing had been quite real, whether indeed that meeting had been anything but a mental mirage on my part, a sort of interior refraction of the picture of the Miracle of La Salette, modified as it was by its free passage through my own mind. The poor man remained, in my mind, as a likeness and parable of that mighty Christianity of the olden time that our degenerate modern generations will have nothing to do with. For me, he presents the supernatural combination of being as a little child in respect of love, while attaining a mature profundity of sacrifice, which was the whole spirit of the early Christians, when the tempest of a God's sufferings had raged around them. Mocked by fools and hypocrites, in voluntary poverty, in deadly sadness whenever he contemplated himself, his troth plighted to all tortures, the contented companion of all contempt, this firebrand of the Cross is, in my eyes, the image and faithfully accurate miniature of those dead centuries when the earth was like a great ship upon the deeps of Paradise! "

CHAPTER XVI

THEY decided to dine where they were. Gacougnol asked nothing better than to prolong the gathering, with a simple-minded, frank pleasure at meeting on the same day, and confronting together, two characters as unusual as Clotilde and Marchenoir.

The latter, stimulated by the young woman's presence and sensing her exquisite temperament, gave of his intellectual best, and spent more eloquence than it would cost to emancipate a nation. He even astonished Gacougnol by displaying a robust gaiety that was known only to his most intimate friends, and which the painter had never dreamed that the scourger of society possessed.

" I have several months' silence to make up for," he said,
" several months that have been given up to the most
unrighteous toil ; I have just given birth to an extraordinarily
futile work. Now I am suffering from puerperal fever.
Anybody who comes my way must make the best of it."

To Clotilde it seemed a heavenly evening, and she would
have liked it to last indefinitely, and end only when, at a
very advanced age, she was ready to take her departure in
a narrow coffin.

But it was getting late. Night had long fallen, and it
was with a sudden shock of despair that she realised that
she must return " home ". Go back to Grenelle, to that
horrible room, where she had so often thought she must
die! She would have to undergo the venomous question-
ings of her mother, and—unless he was dead drunk and
vomiting—the imaginings of that scoundrel, more filthily
defiling than his drunkenness—the way she was dressed
would in any case have to be explained, and how could
those base souls, as narrow as sin, be expected to believe
in her innocence ?

All that, however, was nothing by comparison. There
was that bed, that terrible bed, that mattress of corruption
and horror! Was she to sleep on that again, now ? Not
that, never! This morning that had been possible, quite
an easy matter, for she herself had been but filth belonging
to the sewers. But after a day like this it was impossible!

She was only too well aware that this charming costume
and toilet had made a difference to her inner self. One
cannot make a transformation confined to one's exterior.
It was folly to pretend one could. Besides, that M. Marchenoir, whom her benevolent protector himself seemed to
admire, whose words, words such as she had never heard

before, filled her being as with light and perfumes, had done her the incredible honour, had he not ? of talking to her as a friend, treating her as an equal. For the three hours they had been together, had he not been doing exactly the same thing for her mind that M. Gacougnol had done for that poor, ragged, starved, despairing beggar's body of hers ? . . . Her dread and disgust were so immense that she thought of not going back at all, of walking about all night, every night, and begging Gacougnol (since she was going to his place every day) to let her sleep for an hour in some corner.

She had reached that point in her thoughts, when some new customers came in. The unhappy girl could scarcely forbear a cry of fear.

The new arrivals stamped their feet on the threshold, and shook out their clothes, covered with snow. It was the first night of that agonising Parisian winter when the municipal street-sweepers find they have to pile the snow up on the boulevards to the height of a first-floor window.

Gacougnol, attentively watching his trembling friend, had, with a smile, gauged the cause of her anxiety, and hastened to reassure her.

" My dear Clotilde," he said, " please don't upset yourself. That snow is nothing for you to be afraid of. Are you imagining for a moment that I am going to desert you ? Take a little glass of this excellent Chartreuse, instead. It's the best thing there is as a protection against snow. Which way are you going, Marchenoir ? "

" Oh, don't bother about me! I only live a few yards from here, at the end of the Rue de Buffon. Let's part here. I'll come and see you soon, now that I have got rid of my book at last. Shall I see you again, Mademoiselle ? "

"I hope so, Monsieur," answered Clotilde, who, especially just then, was hardly capable of speaking with non-committal conventionality. "I expect you will see me again at M. Gacougnol's. You have made me very happy this evening. That is all I can say. I shall think of you a lot."

"She is delicious!" mused Marchenoir, as he went away. "Where has she sprung from? She can't possibly be the mistress of that great Tommy Atkins, Pélopidas. He would certain have made no secret of it with me. . . . How she listened to me! So there are still souls left on earth!"

CHAPTER XVII

"My dear child," said Gacougnol, as he took his seat beside Clotilde in another cab that carried them silently over the snow, "it is time to let you know what I mean to do. I have sent a wire to your mother."

"Ah!——"

"Yes. She must have had that wire at least two hours ago. It told her that you were not going back—— Silence! Good Heavens! Give me a chance to explain! You know perfectly well, my dear girl, that I didn't make you tell your story just for my amusement. It was necessary for me to *know* you. Now, I have made up my mind to concern myself with you very seriously. To begin with, you can't go back to that pigsty. I have my reasons for considering that you deserve to have somebody take an interest in you, and, unless you categorically insist on it, I shall certainly not allow you to return to Grenelle, along with M. Chapuis, to die of disgust and cold there. Look at this snow. A terrible winter has been forecast for us, and here is the beginning of it. Now listen. I know of a decent house where I will take you. It's in the Avenue Des Ternes, not far from my studio. A respectable boarding-house run by a lady who is an old friend of mine, a rather absurd but quite bearable governess, and I think that she will make you very welcome when she sees that you are brought to her and recommended by me. Her boarders are foreign young ladies from all parts of the world, to whom she teaches a little French, while she scours their imaginations. You'll have nothing to do with that school. You will have your room, as at an hotel, and take your meals at the common table, and we shall work together in the afternoons. Suit you ? "

She made no answer, but he could hear her crying.

"*Now* what's the matter ? Look here, can't I speak to you without your bursting into tears ? "

" Monsieur," she said at last, " I am too happy. That is why I am crying. You guessed quite right. I was in despair at the idea of going back to Grenelle. After the exquisite day I've spent with you, after hearing M. Marchenoir, the thought of that horrible Chapuis was driving me mad. Just imagine! I am not used to all this, you know. I hear nothing but curses or dirt. I had almost decided to walk about all night, thinking of that poor man whose story your friend told us. But I don't know if I should have had the strength to do it. Now you offer me a shelter, after giving me so many things. How could I refuse ? Only—"

" Only you have one objection, haven't you ? And it is this : you don't know what right or authority I have to meddle in your affairs. Really, my friend, it's very simple. I am a Christian. A pretty sort of Christian, granted, but still a Christian. And since it is perfectly obvious to me that you are in danger of death if you continue your existence with your good mother and her charming companion, I should be a bad lot if I didn't get you away. My means render it practicable. Have no fears on that score. I am no millionaire, thank God! But I have enough to help people when opportunity presents itself, and you won't be the first. Then again, remember that I am not giving you charity. Don't forget we are to work together.

" On the other hand, there are certain constructions that might be put on it which you may be afraid of. Well, my dear child, take with all simplicity the good fortune that comes your way, and don't bother about anything else. If only you knew the world! I know it, all right, and for donkey's years now I haven't given two pins what people say about me—always provided they don't come up and tickle me in the ribs, because then I go raging mad. But people know me, and they don't bother me. Look here, in a minute I'll introduce you to Mademoiselle Séchoir. I shall tell her you are a young friend I have undertaken to see settled somewhere. Just one point. She has no right to ask you for any further information. They'll try to pump you. Don't be having any."

Clotilde could think of no answer to make. She simply took Pélopidas's hand, as she had in the morning, and raised it to her lips with an instinctive gesture reminiscent of some innocent captive incredibly set free by a generous Mussulman.

It was nearly ten o'clock when Gacougnol rang the bell

at Mlle. Virginie Séchoir's door, on the third floor of one of the finest houses in the Avenue Des Ternes.

" Why, if it isn't you, M. Gacougnol, and at this hour of night! What good wind blows you here ? " exclaimed the mistress of the premises from the back of a room near at hand as she ran forward on hearing the painter's voice in speech with the maid.

The figure which now appeared had once been compared by him, with more accuracy than respect, to a sack of potatoes half empty. She looked like it, and, if one may say so, walked like it.

One became immediately aware of one of those characters of armoured virtue which never forgive. There were certain aged men who declared that she had once been pretty, but impregnable, and there emanated from her such a treacly plenitude of maidenly modesty that one must be a Pélopidas to doubt it.

She did not seem to be much over forty, but her face, dry-cured by experience, and finished off with the caustic enamel of professional dignity, suggested a maturity beyond computation.

All the same, she greeted Gacougnol with the utmost cordiality, with some of the exuberance of a frigate bellying its sails to bound forward and meet the commodore. Obviously, the artist held a lofty position in her estimation.

" My dear lady," said he, " I do hope you will forgive my turning up so late, when you know what has brought me. First of all, allow me to present Mlle. Clotilde Maréchal a young lady in whom I take a very active interest, whom I would commend to your good care. Can you give her your hospitality right away this evening ? "

At the sight of Clotilde, stepping forward shyly, Mlle. Séchoir took up her supreme pose, which consisted in straightening up her torso, while drawing in her train from behind, to support the pivotal movement of her cervical vertebrae, and gazed at this unknown young woman with lifeless eyes that were calculated to put out all the wise virgins' lamps.

Her eyes, the colour of scullery slops, had a fainting languor characteristic of the soulful " lady teachers " of the north. One would have had to be blind not to read in them a lofty habit of saturating all the trivialities of life in the intimate delights of transcendental speculation and sublime sentiments.

So, after majestically waving them to seats, she eventually deigned to speak, with that blend of friendly frankness for Gacougnol and polar condescension for Clotilde.

" You are very welcome, Mademoiselle. . . . Upon my word, my very dear sir, you could not have come at a better time. I just happen to have a vacant room all prepared, intended for an American boarder whom I was expecting, and who has just telegraphed from Nice that she will not be coming till the Spring. Our Parisian winter frightens her. The snow! This evening—Well! And now, you naughty man, why do we never see you these days ? How are the masterpieces getting on ? Are you ever going to publish those adorable poems ?—Alas, I only know two or three of them! And your music ? And your painting ? And your sculpture ? For you are such a *universal* genius, like ' our ' Renaissance masters. If I were not afraid of running into some of the odd people one does meet at an artist's place, I should certainly come along and see your studio. It must be full of marvels."

As she cooed these last words, her dove-like eyes seemed
to wander in the direction of her newest boarder. But
if this glance implied the very faintest hint of pointing the
allusion, it was so vague and remote that not the tenderest
susceptibilities could have taken umbrage.

Need we add that her voice was in keeping with her
physiognomy? She had the gobbling articulation of
certain table-birds that only cook well by green wood;
but every now and then she would soar with merry abandon
into the twittering arpeggios of an aeolian harp, when
it seemed appropriate to demonstrate a spirited enthusiasm;
then drop back flatly down the tonic scale to burrow in
the sombre caverns of sound of a melodious contralto.

Overwhelmed with this spate of questions, Pélopidas
contented himself with the reply that such a visit would
certainly be the most intoxicating favour that he could
desire, but that it really would, alas! be impossible for him
to guarantee absolutely the modesty of such persons as
she might risk encountering if she called on him.

" Well, well! " she sighed, " that is another treat I must
forego! But I must not forget that Mademoiselle is sure to
want to rest, especially if she has had *a long journey*—would
you care for a cup of tea? No? Then would you come
with me? I will show you your room. Monsieur Gacougnol, I really don't know if I ought to allow you to come
with us. But perhaps you would like to see your protégée
installed, so long as Mademoiselle does not think it would
be, er, *not quite nice*——"

" But, Madame," said Clotilde, who had not yet opened
her mouth, " that would surely be quite natural. In fact,
I should very much like M. Gacougnol to know how I
am settled in your house."

The three of them eventually arrived at a most comfortable room.

"I hope you will be quite happy here," said the landlady who constituted the other half of the governess's personality. "You have a simply delightful view. The sun sets just over your bed, and the little birds greet it with their song all round the house, even in the bitterest months. There is actually a swallows' nest on the upper balcony, almost within arm's reach of you. Being a friend of M. Gacougnol you must have a *poetical soul*."

The last remark, inappropriately reminiscent of Mother Isidore, was pointed with the significant smile of an intellectual who knows just how to discount all the nonsense that is indulged in by the common herd.

Pélopidas, losing patience, drew out his watch and, in his turn, remarked that the newcomer must want her sleep.

"Good night, my dear," he said, shaking Clotilde's hand, "sleep well, and may the angels of God be with you. Don't forget, I shall depend on your being punctual to-morrow. And perhaps you, Mademoiselle, will be kind enough to see me out."

Clotilde, left alone, wondered, for the first time in her life, just what was meant by the "angels of God"....

CHAPTER XVIII

"Monsieur, you are angelically handsome—Madame, you are diabolically witty."

If there were ever a field of manœuvres in which the fullest possible scope was given to those instincts of prostitution that are peculiar to the human race, it must be the kingdom of Heavenly Intelligences, or the gloomy empire of reprobate spirits.

The confined abode of the Archangel of Disobedience has been so well understood to be filled with invisible companions, that in all ages these have been insistently associated in some way with the visible acts performed in the different cabins of the world.

And so people have always called one another, " My little cherub!—My little imp! " And all the vile doings under the moon, as well as the most exultant idiocies, have been practised under arbitrary invocations insulting alike to Heaven and Hell.

Those are Seven—Oh, tender love of mine!—who gaze curiously at you from the seven recesses of Eternity! They would seem to be on the point of putting their lips to the dread Trumpets that are to call up the dead, and their ineffable hands, beyond the invention of delirium, are already clasped around the seven Vials of Wrath.

Let a signal be given them by the little lamp that burns before the humblest altar in Christendom, and the inhabitants of the world would be fain to escape to the planets from the rending of the earth, the rending of the ocean, the rending of the great rivers, from the enmity of the sun, from the terrible invasions of the Abyss, from the awful Horsemen spreading fire and havoc, and, above all, from the ubiquitous gaze of the Judge!

In truth, these are the " Seven who stand before the face of God ", as the Apocalypse tells us, and that is all that is knowable of them. But it is permissible to imagine —as in the case of the stars—that there are millions of others, the least of whom is capable of exterminating, in a

single night, the eighty-five thousand Assyrians of Senna-
cherib; to say nothing of those who are specifically
called the demons, and who, deep down in the chasms of
chaos, are the inverted reflections of the roaring firebrands
of Heaven.

If life be a banquet, those are our guests; if it be a
comedy, *they* are our supers; and such are the redoubtable
Visitants of our sleep, if that be but a dream!

If some baritone impresario of romance sings of the
" angelic " glories of Celimène, witness is borne to his
folly by an audience of the Nine Hosts, the Nine spiritual
cataracts unknown to Plato: Seraphim, Cherubim, Thrones,
Dominations, Virtues, Powers, Principalities, Archangels,
and Angels, from which perhaps he should make his
selection; if it be *Hell* that is invoked, then—at the
opposite pole—there is precisely the same choice.

And yet they are our very near neighbours, those who
come and go perpetually by the luminous Ladder seen by
the Patriarch, and we have been warned that each one of
us is jealously watched over by one of them, as an inestimable treasure to be guarded against the marauding raids
of the opposite abyss—which gives us a most confusing
notion of the human race.

The most sordid rascal is so precious that, solely to
tend his person, there is allotted to him one comparable
to the Being who went ahead of the host of Israel in a
pillar of cloud, and a pillar of fire, and the Seraph who
turned as flame upon the tongue of the mightiest of all
the prophets may be a convoy, as great as all the worlds
of this universe, charged with the duty of escorting such
an unworthy cargo as the soul of some old pedagogue or
magistrate.

An angel comforted Elijah in his famous terror; another accompanied the Hebrew Children into their furnace; yet another sealed the jaws of the lions of Daniel; a fourth, called the " Great Prince ", in disputation with the Devil, found himself not yet immense enough to curse him, and the Holy Spirit is represented as the only mirror in which those unimaginable acolytes of humanity can wish to contemplate themselves.

Who then are we *in reality*, for such defenders to be offered us, and, above all, who are they, themselves, those beings chained to our destiny, of whom it *is not stated* that God made them in His image, and who have no bodily form or countenance?

It was in reference to them that it was written that we should never " be unmindful of hospitality ", for fear there should be one of these hidden among the necessitous strangers.

If any such wandering tramp were suddenly to cry out, " I am Raphael! I seemed to eat and drink with you, but my nutriment is invisible, and that which I drink could not be shown to man," who knows whether the poor householder's terror might not spread to the very constellations?

Reeking with fear, he would discover that everybody lived gropingly in his little cell of shadow, knowing nothing of those at his right hand or at his left, unable to guess the real " name " of those who weep on high, nor of those who suffer beneath, without realising *what he is himself*, without ever comprehending the whispers and the great roar of voices that echo in endless reverberations through the sounding corridors. . . .

CHAPTER XIX

CLOTILDE'S awakening was as delightful as her sleep had been. The poor girl was born for well-being and that comfortable life which had for long been beyond her hopes.

She at once understood that it would take much more than a day for her to grow used to her good fortune, to realise it in the depths of her mind. What an inconceivable difference between yesterday and to-day! Oh, the joy of knowing sound sleep, warmth, one's own possessions around one, not to be conscious of that horrible propinquity, not to have to begin the blessed day with a long, silent sob!

She laved in the thought, immersed herself in it as in a lustral spring, capable of purifying her, even to her memories. Barely emerged—and by what a miracle!—from the forest of sighs in which her cruel fate had led her and lost her, how obvious that elementary truth seemed to her, so completely unrecognised by the Rich, that the heart of the poor is a black dungeon which must be taken by silver weapons, which only ammunition of money can forge!

And this does not for a moment mean that poverty is degrading. It could not be, since it was the mantle of Jesus Christ. But, more certainly than any torture, it has the power to make human beings feel the burden of the flesh and the deplorable enslavement of the mind. It is a Pharisaic atrocity to demand from slaves a mental detachment that is only possible to the free.

Clotilde could indeed have testified what had been wrought in her by one good man's money, just his money, alas! That mysterious, execrable, divine Money that in a twinkling of an eye had metamorphosed her life and her soul.

There already dawned within her a tenderness, almost as of one in love, for that painter who had rescued her from the dragon, and whose most compassionately sympathetic words could have produced no such result had he not been armed with the strange force represented by that *metal.*

She certainly did not dream of thinking that her intense emotional gratitude towards Gacougnol could ever become love, and seeing them together was quite enough to make such a thing, in fact, seem very improbable. If the wild bells of passion could ever threaten to shake the foundations of her tower, the grandiloquent Marchenoir would assuredly have been much better able to set them ringing.

All the same, her liberator could depend upon a rare friendship, and this, once more, was the work of that terrifying power, Money, more formidable than Prayer, more conquering than Fire, since it needed so little a sum of money to purchase the betrayal of the Second Person of the Deity, and perhaps it will need even a smaller sum to trap the great Love when that descends upon the earth!

She was amazed to find that it did not upset her at all to think of Grenelle. She knew perfectly well that her being away for the night would be interpreted in the most insulting way, and that her new life would not fail to be attributed by her mother to the foulest shamelessness. But knowing, also, that the saintly old woman would

immediately try to make a profit on her alleged improprie-
ties, she admitted to herself, without shrinking, that it left
her totally unconcerned.

Within the innermost depths of her dormant self there
had been taking place, since the day before, such a complete
revolution; so many vaguely realised ideas, so many old,
old yearnings, comparable to the thirst that is felt in
dreams, had been awakened in her; that she could not
find, now, the false equilibrium of her former hopelessness.

Coolly, she resolved to have finished with that. In what
way? That she did not know. But she must; and, with a
complete assurance that for the future she must regard
this sudden change as a gift from Heaven, she felt herself
filled with the strength to defend her independence.

As she finished dressing, the maid came to tell her that
breakfast was waiting for her. Having, through ignorance
of the time, come down late, she had the satisfaction of
being alone at table and free to muse at her ease as she
enjoyed the "correct, subtle, and potent" coffee that
Parisian women make—too often, alas, disguised by
treacherous chicory—the coffee that "builds upon the
bosom of darkness, out of the materials of their imagination, cities fairer than Babylon or Hecatompylos."

The beverage toned up her system and did her good.
Her sensations were almost those of a bride as she gazed
round the dining-room, far from palatial, but fairly spacious,
and bearing witness to a certain mastery of that life of
material plenty which she had never known; the sudden
revelation of which always produces in the real poor a
kind of nervous disorder that is pretty well similar to the
effect of an abrupt initiation into physical love.

This shock, so common, but so little noticed by the

greatest analysts, went right through her like the shock of lightning, and was done with. She was too clear headed not soon to realise the nullity of that pretentious eating room obviously designed for the attraction of exotic boarders.

It had something of a railway buffet, of the custodian's lodge in a block of flats, of the reading room of a Turkish Bath. On the walls were the everlasting chromolithographs to evoke the delights of the table by displaying rare game and the fruits of Canaan, thrilling photographs of various Transatlantic liners speeding through green waves towards azure gulfs ; a few medallions, a few plaster casts or composition statuettes to remind all comers that " art is long even if life is short ", and that it would be a grievous error to imagine that this was any abode of the uncultured Philistine. And, as a finishing touch, the imitation stained-glass windows with which café proprietors delight to honour the archaic. That was about all, and there was nothing, really, to perturb for two minutes the veriest little princess of the infirmary or work-house.

Accordingly, she saw there just what there was there to see, that is to say, simply a place of no particular character in which she was to be allowed to eat, and, in all humility, she wondered what Providence would demand in return for this favourable migration.

About noon Mlle Séchoir herself came to her in her room. But, to Clotilde's unbounded surprise, a porter accompanied her, bearing a trunk which he had said had been sent by M. Gacougnol.

She had the presence of mind not to show her excitement, which was intense, and, notwithstanding her impatience to take stock, went down to the common room, replying mechanically to the mechanical verbal courtesies of the proprietress, while the blood pulsed in her-ears and there was a burning lump in her throat.

After some emphatic introductions, which left in her memory no trace of the outlandish names she had been told, she found herself at table, along with half a dozen strange damsels, of indeterminate virginal status, perched on varying steps of the ladder of time.

Mlle Séchoir had arrived with dignity at the age of forty. The youngest, a rosy Swedish girl who snuffled, sat at Clotilde's right, and never opened her mouth except to eat. The rest, scattered in Curiatian formation, were anything from twenty-five to thirty, and demonstrated a greater loquacity. Rich and plain, as befitted studious passengers on the allegorical vessel of Paris, they made the poor girl from a garret who was among them seem like a work of art that has been overlooked in a rubbish-yard.

Naturally, even before she sat down, she had already given offence. At the very outset it was felt that the new boarder was branded with the Great Anathema—she was *not quite like everybody else*, and possibly the amiable Mlle Séchoir had hinted as much during the morning to her brood.

One of these ladies, a little, round, vapid Englishwoman, whom one might have fancied stuffed by some insane cook, such was the oily shine of her, soon undertook to question her.

"Mademoiselle, do you mind my asking whether you are a painter ? "

"No, Mademoiselle," replied Clotilde, who, having decided in her turn how little sympathy her presence was inspiring, and mindful of Gacougnol's advice, was resolved to give away no information whatever about herself.

"Ow! How disappointing. But perhaps you are studying painting?"

"No, Mademoiselle, I am not studying painting."

"Miss Penelope," intervened Mlle Séchoir at this point, "is passionately devoted to the arts, and I took the liberty of telling her you knew M. Gacougnol, who sometimes calls here, so she inferred that you were a pupil of his."

Clotilde bowed, without speaking, wishing from the bottom of her heart that they would consent to forget her altogether. But the plump English girl, encouraged by a surreptitious wink from the mistress of the establishment, would not acknowledge defeat, and returned to the charge in her English French—which it would be useless trying to represent.

"Oh, yes, Mademoiselle! I love art! If you only knew! You *are* lucky to be associated with M. Gacougnol. I do envy you, being allowed in his studio; it's so difficult to get into. That is why I should like to be friends with you. I should beg you to introduce me."

"Really, my dear young lady, you are going a little too fast." This was the reasonable Virginie speaking once more. "I told you that Mademoiselle was on very good terms with our great artist, but I did not say she had permission to penetrate into his sanctum—and still less, to take other people there."

Clotilde, for the sake of peace, declared that being addicted to a solitary way of life, she feared she would not be able to make a worthy return for the precious friendship the other was kind enough to offer her, adding that Gacougnol's studio was actually open to her, but that she had no authority to take anybody there.

That was the end of any direct questioning. Only, the

little flock's chatter revolved around the painter-sculptor and poet-musician, with contradictory opinions expressed about him, in the vain hope of catching the young woman off her guard, but she forced herself to think of other things. That day she learned to appreciate rather better than before the invincible power of silence.

Her fellow-guests had to confess that they had got no further in trying to sound her, and even Mlle Séchoir was mildly disconcerted by the trenchant precision and strange firmness of somebody whom she would have expected to find so timid!

The meal was a second warning to Clotilde to be most carefully on her guard in defence of the inestimable treasure of her independence against possible entanglements of her fancy for strangers of either sex who were not *obviously* —as in the case of the artist whom they had had the audacity to criticise in her presence—the plenipotentiary ministers of her destiny.

She left the table as soon as she could, and rushed off to her room to examine the box sent her by Gacougnol. It contained every variety of drapery needed by a woman, various toilet articles, and a few books. The good man had gone out early, it was evident, and ransacked the shops so that she should have that surprise before she called on him.

Could such attention, such rare solicitude, be accounted for wholly by the Christian charity to which the artist had appealed the night before in justification of his munificence? No divine would have ventured to commit himself to such an assurance. Clotilde was a girl as simple of heart as the sky-line, and, in consequence, perfectly capable of discerning or divining the slightest deviation from a

similar simple directness; but she was still under the
influence of the thrill of yesterday, and any fleeting
suspicion that may have fluttered for a moment around her
little head was victoriously repulsed by the generous
currents of her enthusiasm, and failed to penetrate. Upright souls are reserved for rectilinear torments.

Hearing a clock strike one, she hurried off at last towards
her rescuer's studio, arriving there a few minutes after her
mother had left.

CHAPTER XX

HERE a parenthesis is necessary. Those worthy people
who dislike " digressions ", or look upon the Infinite as
a trifling irrelevance to whet the appetite, are humbly
prayed not to read this chapter, which will modify nothing
and nobody, and will probably be regarded as the most
futile thing that could be written.

Take it all round, in fact, and those gracious readers
might do even better by not opening the present volume
at all, for it is itself a long digression on the evil of living,
the infernal misfortune of existence, hogs lacking any
snout with which to root for tit-bits, in a society without
God.

The author never promised that he would entertain
anybody. He has sometimes even promised the opposite—
and kept his word. No judge has any right to ask any
more of him than that. The end of this " story ", moreover,
is so gloomy—though lit up with some strange and vivid
gleams—that it will, in any case, come quite soon enough,

to rouse pity or horror in those horrid sentimentalists who are interested in love-stories.

It is beyond cavil that the fact of receiving gifts, and especially what are called, conventionally, " *useful* gifts ", is in the eyes of the world an obvious evidence of monstrous depravity, when the woman who accepts such gifts is of marriageable age, and the man, whether a bachelor or not, who has the audacity to offer them, is neither her near relative nor her betrothed. But the depravity, instead of being simply monstrous, becomes positively extreme and outrageous if the articles given on the one side and frankly accepted on the other are articles of intimate personal use, and, consequently, significant of turpitude. The oblation of an under-vest, for instance, cries aloud to Heaven for vengeance. . . . .

From this point of view the indefensible Clotilde would have incurred almost super-humanly violent rebuke from economic moralists. Among women, all the same, even the strictest prudes would have been forced to acknowledge, while they pronounced their anathemas, that Gacougnol had only done his bare duty, and that the gifts he made, be they what they might, ay, even though they had the magnificence of many caliphs, could never be aught but a deficient and inadequate offering.

There is a universal persuasion among women that *all things are their due.* This belief is imbedded in their nature as the triangle is inscribed in the circle which it determines. Beautiful or plain, slave or empress, every female is entitled to regard herself as WOMAN, and therefore not one of them escapes from that marvellous instinct for the preservation of that sceptre of which the Titulary Holder is forever looked for by the human race.

That awful pedant, Schopenhauer, who spent his life studying the horizon from the bottom of a well, was assuredly quite incapable of suspecting the *supernatural* source of the ideal of domination which casts the strongest men down beneath women's feet, and the beastliness of the modern mind has unhesitatingly glorified that blasphemer against love.

Against Love, surely, for woman can never be nor believe herself anything but Love personified, and the Earthly Paradise, sought for so many centuries, by Don Juans of every grade, is her Miraculous Image.

So for woman, a being who is *temporarily*, provisionally, man's inferior, there can only be two aspects, two modes of existence, to which it is essential that the Infinite should accommodate itself : Beatitude, or Pleasure. Between these two, there is nothing but the " respectable woman ", that is to say, the female of the Commonplace Man, the unconditionally reprobated, whom no holocaust can redeem.

A female Saint may fall into the mire, or a prostitute raise herself to the Heavens, but neither of the two can ever become a " respectable woman "—because the terrible barren, futile creature called a respectable woman, who of old refused the hospitality of Bethlehem to the Infant God, is eternally impotent to escape from her nothingness by any fall or any ascent.

But all women have one point in common—the preconceived assurance of their dignity and office as Dispensers of Joy. *Causa nostrae laetitiae ! Janua coeli !* God alone knows in what way, sometimes, these sacred formulae cause that which women's mysterious physiology suggests to be mingled with the meditations of the purest among them!

All women—wittingly or unwittingly—are persuaded that their bodies are Paradise. *Plantaverat autem Dominus Deus paradisum voluptatis a principio : in quo posuit hominem quem formaverat.* Consequently, no prayer, no penitence, no martyrdom, have an adequate efficacy as conferring a rightful claim for possession of that inestimable jewel, whose price could never be paid with the weight of the starry firmament in diamonds.

Judge, therefore, of the immensity of the gift when they give themselves, of the immensity of the sacrilege when they sell themselves !

And here is the conclusion to be drawn from the prophets : woman is RIGHT to hold such a belief, to make such a claim. She is infinitely right, since her body—since that part of her body !—was the tabernacle of the Living God, and no one, nay, not an archangel, can determine the limits of the *collective unity* of that baffling Mystery!

CHAPTER XXI

It has been seen above that Gacougnol had gone out first thing in the morning and expended an unusual amount of activity on Clotilde's behalf.

On his return, he found in front of his door an old woman whom from a distance, since he was rather short-sighted, he mistook for a very long and lanky priest, withered up with apostolic toil, and bowed down with the plague of human hearts.

Mother Chapuis, actually, was wearing black, and sheltered beneath the shadow of a huge, round, flat-brimmed hat, of fabulous antiquity, which she had found on a rubbish dump, and was actively engaged in mopping her eyes with a dirty check handkerchief that would have been much more at home in a street gutter.

In tones of labouring agony, she introduced herself to the artist, whose first impulse was to send her packing. He thought better of this, however, in view of the way in which her vile mother might have destroyed all possibility of peace of mind for Clotilde.

He resigned himself, accordingly, to the necessity of asking the woman in, bethinking himself that, after all, such a bundle of foulness as she would not take up a lot of room, and so it would be a simple matter to burn a little perfumed incense afterwards where she had been.

The impressive, mincing entry she made proved, moreover, to be a sufficient reward for his unselfishness. She seemed to slide into the room, leaning against the walls as she moved, as if she could not support the weight of her burden any longer, at the same time releasing the sluice-gates on a spate of gurgling moans calculated to give the whole world the impression that one poor mother's powers of endurance were definitely exhausted, that it had at last become impossible to carry such a heavy cross, and that if succour from on high should be any longer delayed, she must inevitably succumb within a few moments.

At any other time the supreme disgust inspired by such a creature's presence would have been too strong even for his sense of the ridiculous, and Pélopidas would certainly have been anything but gentle with her. But his heart was happy, because he had done precisely what he pleased, and the caricaturist in him won the day.

" Madam," he said, " I am infinitely delighted to see you.

Unhappily, my work will not allow of my giving myself up for more than five minutes to the charms, as I am sure they will be, of your conversation, so I should be infinitely obliged if you would be good enough to put your business into a few words."

Mother Chapuis advanced to the centre of the spacious room, and there stood, holding both hands, open, palms outwards, straight down at arms' length and close against her hips, in the carefully studied pose of a noble Christian facing a savage proconsul.

At the same time her chin, with two skilful oscillations, described a re-entrant curve on the ancient hypocrite's withered throat, raising to left and right the gasping visage of Cynodocée[1] of the pavements of old, aspiring towards her celestial home.

" My daughter ? " she breathed, at last. " What have you done with my poor daughter ? " And this maternal demand sounded like the ultimate supreme sigh emanating from a Parthenian flute.

Pélopidas, inspired for the moment with ribald humour by the mummified old crone, experienced a transient temptation to address her with the same words that produced such a startling effect twenty-four hours earlier, and was on the point of shouting at her, " Get undressed! "— but he suddenly conceived a horrid fear that he might be taken at his word, so he contented himself with replying :

" Your daughter is probably at home where she's living. I shall want her to pose for me pretty often, and your neighbourhood is a deuce of a way away, so I advised her to stay somewhere not quite so far off, now. Hence the telegram I sent you last night."

[1] " Cynodocée "—see *Les Martyres*, Chateaubriand. *Translator.*

At these words, the martyr seemed to totter. Gripping
her brow with both hands, she uttered this pathetic cry :
"Oh, God, this is the final blow ! This time it is the
end. You are punishing me, dear Saviour, for loving my
child too much. Oh, my poor heart! "

That precious organ had apparently become too heavy
a burden for her feeble strength, so she cast about with
wild eyes, and when no charitable soul brought her a
chair, she reeled towards the sofa, her gait an excellent
imitation of the locomotor ataxy suggested in such
movements by the exponents of melodrama on the
stage.

The painter's alarm was extreme, at the idea of that
nightmare houri sprawling on the couch that was the
confidant of his sublimest meditations. He rushed at her
and grabbed her by one scythe-sharp elbow, steering her
back towards the door.

"My dear madam, do you think you are at the mortuary ?
I had the honour of expressing, as respectfully as I could,
my deep distress at not being at liberty to give you my most
concentrated attention. And I can spare less time still to
admire your grimaces of despair, though they are performed
with great skill, I admit. So if you have nothing more thrilling to communicate to me, I must beg you to be good
enough to be gone."

Realising that she was about to be turned out, and that
here was a man with whom it was in vain to rely exclusively
on effects of pathos, the old woman decided to speak out.

"Sir," she moaned. "Give me back my daughter !
She is the only consolation of my declining years. You
have no right to separate a mother from her child. She
must be hidden in your house, since she has no money

to stay at a boarding house. God knows, I shouldn't see
so much harm in it, even if the precious darling had found
a nice friend. I can see that you're a good, honourable
gentleman, and a man of the world, and you wouldn't like
to do anybody a wrong, would you? Only, you see, she is
just an inexperienced child, and there is nothing like the
advice of a loving mother. Heaven is my witness that I
have brought her up holily!—You wouldn't want to betray
her, you are too scrupulous for that. I can see you are an
honourable artist. Well, one can always come to an
understanding, when both parties are educated people.
I have known adversity, I have, you see, Sir, but you
understand I am not just a nobody. I am of very good
birth, you know! You can tell I am not a woman of the
people. I am a woman of the world, and a lady of good
breeding. It was my misfortune to marry a man beneath
me, who has been the sorrow of my life and crowned
me with thorns. But everybody can tell you how nobly I
endured hardship. I have nothing to reproach myself
with, I have always gone straight and set my daughter a
good example——

"Look here!" she exclaimed, suddenly carried away,
like a woman unable to hold out any longer against the
impulses of her heart, opening her arms to Pélopidas, who
recoiled in fright. "If you liked, we could be so happy
together! None of us need ever be separated—I could
come *with my darling man* and live with you; we should be
just one holy, happy family!"

This was a direct hit, and landed right on its mark, on
the man whose patience was just then pretty well on the
point of proving unequal to the demands made on it.
All the same, the unexpected offer of Old Man Chapuis,

viewed as the future companion of his domestic life, revived
his mirth for a moment.

"Really," he said, gravely, "that is a prospect. No
doubt the darling man you speak of is that nice boy who
was here yesterday? Allow me to congratulate you.
You have excellent taste for a lady of breeding—you
and he are a well-matched pair. He knocks you down
and kicks you, doesn't he?"

"Oh, Sir! How could you say such a thing? Such a
noble soul! And he loves *our* dear Clotilde so!"

"Yes, so that he would like to sleep with her, wouldn't
he? While her virtuous mother would hold the candle——
Why, you old witch," he cried, letting himself go at last,
"you've come here, trying to sell me your daughter—
whom you probably stole to start with, because it's incredible that she should have ever been born in your verminous
bed. It's enough to disconcert the thunders of God!
And you hoped you were going to do me for money—
didn't you?—my fine lady. You worked out the whole
pretty business with your bully—that your daughter had
become my mistress, and that you could touch me for
unlimited cash by making scenes at my house. You must
think I've just come up! Listen to me, once for all. I
am not going to waste my time trying to make you understand that Mlle. Clotilde is not and is never likely to be
anything to me but a friend. You couldn't understand
how any girl brought up by *you* could be anything but a
harlot. But since you imagine you have some rights over
her, which is richly funny, I warn you, in your own interest,
that there is nothing doing with me, absolutely nothing.
And I am not a man who allows people to make themselves
a nuisance. Your daughter will go and visit you if she

wants to. That's her business. As for me, I *forbid* you to set foot here again. My studio isn't a trollops' assembly-room, and I am not patient every day. As to your black-guard of a man, I warn him to lie low, if he values his carcase. Enough said. Clear off, and quick march, or I'll have you picked up by the police. Off you go! "

The door closed, and Isidore's female companion, transported magically to the pavement, fled, weeping and raging, but vanquished with a salutary fear instilled by that diabolical man with the voice that sounded like the cymbals of Jehoshaphat.

CHAPTER XXII

FROM that day there fell about Clotilde a great peace. Her life flowed onward like a sweet river, without breakers or cross-currents. She accepted this peaceful life in the same spirit in which she had accepted her sufferings, with a placid, firm resolution of will not to let herself be robbed of her treasure. Even if such happiness was to be a mere transient respite, she intended to enjoy it to the full, and to provision herself with courage, at least, for future possible tribulations.

Every day she spent some hours at Gacougnol's studio, inspiring in him an ever-growing wonder. He had under-taken her education with incredible zeal. Her posing for " Saint Philomena " could not be prolonged for more than a few sittings, but he displayed a perfect genius for giving his delightful comrade the illusion of being indispensable.

He had the original notion of utilising her services as " reader ", while he worked at his easel, on the specious pretext that the verse of Victor Hugo or the Prose of Barbey D'Aurévilly sustained his inspiration, as if he had been hearing the melodies richest in suggestion of Chopin or Beethoven.

Being, like most cultured Frenchmen of the south, rather a virtuoso at reading aloud, he utilised this ability to teach her that difficult art, so completely despised by the twitterers of the Comédie-Française and the diphthong-liquidators of the Conservatoire—thus revealing to her the loftiest works of creative literature, at the same time as he imparted the secret of expressing its substance " The Sublime and How to Use It! " he used to say.

One day he had made her read *Britannicus* in its entirety, lightening the terrible wearisomeness of that masterpiece by frequent interruptions, and that day he took her to the Théatre Français, where they were then performing the same tragedy that was still echoing in her brain.

To his pupil's extreme stupefaction, he drew her attention to the fact that not a single line of the poet's work, not a single word, is *pronounced*, but that the famous actors, brought up in the traditional ranting convention, superimposed on the text a sort of declamatory counterpoint, absolutely foreign to it, which does not permit the emergence of a single atom of the living poem they presume to claim that they are interpreting.

He showed her how the public, raised to the Third Heaven of the Trite, hypnotised by such terms as " Diction ", " Phonetic Syntax ", " emotional intonation ", as if they were the branded corks in a restaurant, sincerely imagine they are listening to what the even more sincere actors believe themselves to be serving out to them—Racine.

This remarkable painter now discovered that he possessed marvellous pedagogic abilities hitherto unsuspected. He more or less knew a rather great number of subjects, but when his lore was deficient, the lucid explanations of his ignorance that he would offer seemed more valuable than the very facts of which he proclaimed his lack.

He said, for example, that he had never really understood what is commonly called Philosophy, because he had never been able to attain to the preliminary conception of the bee in the bonnet of those pedantic dolts who dare to attempt balancing conjectures on hypotheses, and deductions on postulates. In this connection he was copious in imprecations against the Germans, whom he accused, with justice, of attempting, with their cumbrous domestic mentality, the destruction of the good sense of the Latin races, who, after all, were designed from eternity for domination over such riff-raff.

"Let me alone!" he exclaimed to Clotilde, who certainly was not bothering him in any way. "There are only two philosophies—if you're going to insist on using that vile word: Christian speculative, that is to say, the philosophy of the Pope, and *torcheculative*.[1] The former for the South, the latter for the North. Would you like me to put the story of this abomination in a nutshell for you? Before your Luther, there was none too much brilliance as it was, in the Teutonic world. When I say ' your ' Luther, I mean that beastly nation's Luther. It

---

[1] So-named by Gacougnol from the French word, *torche-cul*, whose nearest (printable) English equivalent is perhaps " tripe ". *Trans.*

was an ungovernable bear-garden of five or six hundred States, each State representing a huddle of obscure nobodies, impermeable to enlightenment, whose descendants can only be directed or disciplined by whacking them with a cudgel. Spiritual authority over them was like a bee over a dung-heap. Luther had the supreme advantage of being just the Blackguard whose advent the patriarchs of Northern raggamuffindom were awaiting. He was a perfect incarnation of bestiality, incomprehension of anything profound, and the strutting pride of all lick-spittles. Naturally, they worshipped him, and all Northern Europe rushed to forget Mother Church and wallow in that pig's vomit. The movement has continued for about four hundred years, and German philosophy, as accurately defined by me just now, is the most copious ordure that has issued from Protestantism. They call it the Critical Spirit, and the infection can be caught before birth, like syphilis, and you can find little Frenchmen of such cesspool begetting that they write about it as altogether superior to the intuitive genius of our nation."

This summary method was admirably suited to the young woman's direct, quick intelligence, so that she at once assimilated, in the happiest way, all the essential notions, whether transcendental or elementary. In fine, the sympathetic Pélopidas gave her real *pabulum*, despite the sometimes heroically disordered nature of his views.

For her, the instruction imparted by such a master was like bread that has been made by a journeyman baker walking in his sleep, that might contain pebbles, nails, bits of paper, patches from old pants, bits of string, pipe-stems, fish scales, and beetle legs—but, for all that, real wheaten bread that would build up strength.

"What are the 'Middle Ages'?" she asked him once, after reading a famous sonnet of Paul Verlaine's.

That evening Gacougnol came right out of himself, and was magnificent. He got up from his stool, laid aside his palette, his brushes, his cutty pipe, everything that might get in a man's way when he was settling down to the diapason of the sublime; and then, rising to his feet in the middle of the studio, he enunciated these words, worthy of the Marquis de Valdegamas :—

"The Middle Ages, my child, are a vast church such as we shall never more see till God returns upon earth— a house of prayer as vast as the whole western world, built with ten centuries of ecstasy that recall the Ten Commandments of Sabaoth! It was the Genuflection of the whole universe, in adoration or in awe. Even the very blasphemers and the men of blood were on their knees, because no other attitude was possible in the presence of the dread Crucified Christ who was to judge all men. Outside, was nothing but shadows filled with dragons and infernal rites. It was still the time of the Death of Christ, and the sun was not seen. The poor folk in the fields tilled the soil, trembling, as if they feared to awaken the dead before their hour. The knights and their thanes rode silently afar, over the horizons, into the twilight. All mankind wept, imploring mercy. Now and then a sudden squall would fling open the doors, letting in a rush of sinister beings from outside, right into the very Sanctuary, and its candles would go out, and you would hear nothing but one long cry of dread that echoed through the worlds of both the holy and the fallen angels, until such time as the Redeemer's Vicar on earth should have raised his awful Hands of Power in exorcism. The thousand years of the Middle Ages were the great Christian period of mourning, from your patron Saint Clotilde to Christopher Columbus, who carried the ardour of supernatural charity away with him in his coffin—for none but the Saints or the adversaries of the Saints can set the boundaries of history.

"One day, many years ago, I witnessed one of the great floods of the Loire. I was very young, and therefore a fool, and as sceptical as anybody could be, who has been stung by the scorpions of fantasy. I had been travelling for twenty-four hours through the happy countryside of Touraine, filled with the vibrations of the tocsin. As far as my eyes could see; on all the highways and byways, throughout the vineyards and the woods, I had been the beholder of a population's panic, as they fled in despair before the great mad slayer, that swallowed up villages, tore away bridges, carried off stretches of forest, mountains of debris, barns filled with the harvest, herds of cattle with their sheds, wrenching aside all obstacles, roaring like an army of hippopotamuses. All this beneath a gold and crimson sky, for all the world like another angry river, proclaiming a supplementary destruction of all life. At last I reached a little isolated town, and followed a pallid crowd thronging into a church of ancient days, whose bells were all leaping together.

"I shall never forget the spectacle. In the middle of the dim nave an old, dilapidated reliquary, fished out from somewhere under an altar, had been placed on the floor, and eight red, glowing fires, lit in braziers or chafing dishes, illuminated it by way of candles, from ground level. All round, men, women, and children—an entire populace —prostrated, sprawling on the stone slabs of the floor, were imploring the saint whose bones were there to deliver them from the scourge. The volume of lamentation was enormous, and growing every minute, like the soughing of the sea. Already much stirred by all that had gone before, I began crying and praying in union of hearts with that multitude of the poor, and then I knew, by the eyes of the spirit, by the ears of the soul, what the Middle Ages must have been.

" A sudden recoil of my imagination carried me back to the midst of those distant days when people only paused in their suffering in order to supplicate. The scene that was before my eyes was for me the undoubted type of a hundred thousand similar scenes spread through the thirty unhappy generations whose astonishing misery is barely mentioned in the histories. From Attila to the Mussulman encroachments, from the famous ' fury of the Norsemen ' to the English rage that lasted for a Hundred Years, I reckoned up the millions of unfortunates who had thus everywhere thronged to kneel before sacred relics of martyrs or confessors who were said to be the sole friends of the poor and distressed.

" We of the common crowd are the offspring of that marvellous patience, and, when, after Luther and his following of reasoners, we repudiated the great Lords of Paradise who had been the consolation of our ancestors, it was just that we should be excluded, like the dogs, from the feast of poetry at which simple souls had for so long been guests. For those men of prayer, those ignorant, unmurmuringly oppressed men, whom we in our idiotic complacency despise, carried the Heavenly Jerusalem within their hearts and minds. Their ecstasies they translated as best they could into the stone-work of Cathedrals, into the glowing stained glass of their chapels, into the illuminated vellum of their Books of Hours, and our whole endeavour, when we have some scrap of genius, is to get back to that radiant fountain-head. . . .

" Marchenoir, who is a sort of man of the Middle Ages, would tell you these things much better than I can, Clotilde. He has the thoughts and feelings of the eleventh century, and I can well picture him at the First Crusade, in the company of Peter the Hermit, or of Gautier Have-Nought. Question him one day.'

As will have been seen, Gacougnol's teaching was primarily aesthetic. Finding in his disciple an extraordinary thirst for Beauty in all things, he directed all his zeal to that end, and never held up to her any other objective, assured that her virginal mind, shimmering like dragon-flies in the light, would always comprehend whatever was inscribed for her on the golden beam.

Needless to say the poor girl had barely the rudiments of intellectual culture. She had received a grade of education belonging to the humblest working class, and the Isidore couple's propinquity was not calculated to develop it. A few wretchedly poor novels from circulating libraries had been her only resources, and the fineness of her nature had done the rest.

Conformably to Gacougnol's unexpressed desire, a strong wish to improve her mind had risen in her on coming into contact with the artist and his friends, for the only visitors he had were three or four remarkable characters, including Marchenoir, and these visitors' growing interest in the new unit that had been added to their number was undisguised. She found herself admitted to a circle of a rare order, which was rendered enormously illustrious in her eyes by the mere presence of the "Inquisitor".

She therefore within the first few days begged her delighted teacher to get her the elementary manuals she needed for the acquisition of grammar, geography, and general history—the three branches of knowledge that, as Marchenoir had told her, should be enough, along with the catechism, for a superior woman—and set to work zealously, giving to her studies all the time not required by Gacougnol, to whom at first she had a simple-minded dread of being a useless burden. She was wrong in that respect. He had got to the point where he could not do without her, and had made no effort to conceal the fact.

"My dear friend," he had replied to an anxious, worried question of hers one day when her function as a model had come to an end and he had just promoted her to the higher office of reader, "do get it well into your head that I am a man of tenacious purpose, and I'm not going to let you go, unless my company is repulsive to you, which, alas, is quite possible! I don't flatter myself that I am always a charming companion. But if you can stand me, I swear to you on my word of honour that you are more than useful to me.

"For one thing, you read books I love to me, which is most important to me, I assure you, since you have the almost unique talent of not being ordinary. And for another thing, if, even, you were not rendering me any specific active service, for which the dictionary had any exact name, is it nothing to save me from the boredom of my existence, which is anything but jolly? I am somehow a great-man-who-might-have-been, and isn't; I know that better than anybody else, and don't need telling it.

Later on, you will understand better how bitter a thing that is to say.

" So I need a ' companion-help '. That's an eccentric thing to want. It isn't done. All the more reason. I have spent my life doing, from choice, things that aren't done. So you see, in my estimation you are in the most unexceptionable position.

" Besides, I expect you have realised, poor child, the guesses and gossip that are likely to prevail at Grenelle. Whatever you might really be doing at my house, your lady mother and her worthy companion would still say that you were my mistress. I did not conceal from you that she came here, the first day, to look for her lost drachma in my sheets.

" So just don't bother, as I have already advised you ; and if it is my privilege to represent for you a more or less comic image of Providence, rest assured that I receive what is perhaps a good deal more than I give, and don't worry me with your scruples."

Clotilde's position in regard to her mother had been settled the day after the memorable visit, to which Gacougnol had referred. On his advice, she had written her, expressing without heat her decision to live alone, for the future, and her definite refusal to have any interview with her mother till the latter had dismissed Chapuis for good. The delightful couple, evidently heart-broken at such black ingratitude, had not answered, and the fugitive's peace seemed, from that point of view, to be assured for an indefinite period.

CHAPTER XXIII

Stories true to life have become not worth telling. Naturalism has decried them until there has been engendered among all intellectuals a habitual craving for literary hallucinations.

Nobody will dispute that Gacougnol is an impossible artist, and Clotilde a young woman such as is never seen. The pedagogy and mutually Platonic nature of their ways is an obvious outrage against public psychology. Marchenoir, who was introduced to the reader long ago, has never seemed very plausible, and it is highly probable that the characters which are to come will be appreciated only with great difficulty. Such a narrative, consequently, appeals to the suffrages of those people—growing ever scarcer—who are insubordinate to the accepted canons, and claim rights of pasturage outside the fields marked out by the legislators of Fiction.

In contempt of all passionate molecules, there was still, after two months, nothing to suggest that the patron and the protégée would soon be in one another's arms and duly sleep together.

If Gacougnol entertained any designs, he never breathed a word of them nor made the faintest allusion to anything of the sort. On her side, Clotilde was moving in an orbit a million miles from the sun of desire, happily content to be a small moon innocently reflecting a little light.

The decisive test that happiness constituted, moreover, proved entirely favourable to her, making no difference at all to her deportment, that of a respectful lamb. Indifferent to the surprise she caused in the boarding-house, she went every morning to spend an hour in the Church of Les Ternes, begging God to preserve her fleece from the shearer a little longer, and to infuse her with courage for all the future vicissitudes that she anticipated. For she could not believe that the present condition of things could be anything but a refreshing halt, a transient whim of her fate, which paused for a moment in its task of tormenting her while it sharpened its handy little implements of torture.

She recalled with anguish the Missionary's mysterious words, which she had got into the habit of considering a prophetic warning, and which seemed to foreshadow extraordinary sufferings, different, surely, from the commonplace tribulations of her past:

"'When you are in the flames'," she wondered. "What do those words mean? Why did the good Father say that? My God, Thou knowest I have not the heart of a Martyr; I am very frightened of those flames that are promised for me."

Then she bowed her head, and made herself very small beneath the burning breath of the wilderness of fire which she pictured as being between herself and Paradise.

She remembered Eve, also, that "mother of all living", whom the Bishop of the Heathen had counselled her to supplicate fervently, assuring her that the First Woman was her true mother and that she alone possessed the power to succour her.

Such then was the *child's prayer* she prayed; and of a surety it would have horrified the litany-makers in the devotional factories which do so flourishing a trade.

"My dearly loved Mother, deceived by the Serpent in the beautiful Garden, I pray You make me love the Image of God that is in myself, so that I shall not be too unhappy when I find myself suffering.

"If there is some dangerous little reptile round about me, be pitiful and warn me. Place upon its head a crown of burning coals, so that I may recognise it by the way I shall be afraid of it.

"Do not let me be deceived in my turn as to the nature of a humble joy that is so new to me. It goes to my head, and may not last, perhaps, for as many days as it would take to get me out of the habit of being used to humiliation.

"I know quite well, poor Mother, that You are not much loved in this world that was lost through Your curiosity, and I mourn bitterly that Your magnificent name is so seldom invoked.

"Men forget that You must have suffered in advance all the repentances of all mankind, and what a terrible thing it is to have so many ungrateful children.

"But ever since You were shown to me by that good old man, I have ever spoken with affection of You, and have felt Your companionship in the unhappiest hours.

"I remember that while I slept You used to take me by the hand and lead me to an adorable land where the lions and the nightingales languished in deadly sadness.

"You would tell me that it was the lost Garden, and Your great tears, that were like light, were so heavy that they crushed me as they fell upon me.

"Yet that used to console me, and I used to wake up feeling that I *lived*. Will You desert me to-day, because others have taken pity on Your child?"

Certainly the devout housewives in the neighbourhood must have formed peculiar and unpleasant theories about this stranger, who never spoke to anybody, and was so unlike the edifying plump females commonly seen pilfering in the sacristies.

All the same, she got in nobody's way, and in no way laid herself out to attract attention. But an offensively transparent sincerity eradiated from her pretty, immobile face, and it annoyed their consciences. She was so eccentric as to pray with her arms folded, after the style of sailors or convicts, thus leaving her face completely unhidden, and one could see religious enthusiasm carrying its flaming light across that face.

At such times she was so charming, and occasionally beautiful, that the five or six withered ladies of the parish who saw her in the same place every day, charitably adopted the explanatory hypothesis that she was " some streetwalker who came from Andalusia and was superstitious ".

Clotilde was completely unconscious of this popular interest. She went there for her meditations before the Blessed Sacrament, and took back with her to Pélopidas's studio, as well as to the Séchoir boarding house where she was nested and fed, a soul that was tempered and made supple in its own radiance, as difficult to break as those superb sword-blades of Mozarabia, forged under the Magnanimous, with which one might slay an Asturian bull.

CHAPTER XXIV

HOWEVER much Marchenoir might be a friend of Gacougnol, there had never existed between them any real intimacy. Their relations, though thoroughly cordial, lacked the true hall-mark—they did not gravitate in harmony.

The ruthless writer whom Gacougnol called the " Grand Inquisitor of France " had the airs of a soldier-priest, or Teutonic knight, which doubtless delighted the imagination of an artist so much in love with the Middle Ages. He had even enthusiastically espoused most of his ideas, and nobly defended him whenever his reputation was attacked in his hearing.

But that excellent man, the artist, had a spirit of aesthetic vagabondage and incessant whim, that found oppressive the *absolutism* constantly sensed in Marchenoir's rectangularity. This scourge of others had never been scourged himself by anybody, in spite of certain influences which at one time had seemed likely to change his course, and one could always be sure of finding him in the same place, his true centre being outside all circumferences.

The real basis of the interest Gacougnol found in him was his lack of resemblance to anybody else, and the fact that a terrible injustice had foully robbed him of the attention of his contemporaries. But there was too little given in return, for the eloquent rebel had never taken quite seriously the lucubrations, taking such a multiplicity of forms, of the fatherly good fellow who had not grown up.

Fortunately, a third person established perfect equilibrium of feeling between them. A stranger character,
this, and one not easy to explain.

Léopold—he was known by no other name—practised
the forgotten art of illuminating manuscripts, and looked
like a corsair. Nothing was known of his past, except
that he had taken part in an ill-starred expedition in Africa,
in which two hundred men had been massacred, around
Tanganyika, and that he had brought back the wretched
handful of survivors through four hundred leagues of
deadly perils and privations beyond human endurance.
This had left him with a certain melancholy, livid tint
which became accentuated to the pallid hue of a ghost
when some strong emotion tensed his features.

The way he would speak of this pilgrimage of agony, and
also certain vague expressions, gave the impression that
he was a privileged dare-devil who had plunged deliberately into the most appalling adventures, not so much as
a mere escape from the humdrum life of our day, which
exasperated him, as in the hope of escaping from *himself*.

Misfortune or crime—anything might be conjectured
as lying at the root of the known vicissitudes of his sealed
life. If he had not left his bones in the Central African
bush, that was only thanks to the fact of having to save
the men with him, his instinct as their responsible leader
proving stronger than his despair, at the time or antecedent,
so that he had won through to safety by almost impossible
struggles as the one way of saving his comrades.

His every gesture struck the eye of the beholder like a
blazoned motto, " *I Will* ". To adopt the words of a
popular novelist, the author of forty volumes, who never
encountered any characteristic but this one, " he was one

of those men who always seem to have their hands filled with the forelock of opportunity ". Seeing him, one thought of those legendary filibusters of the Honduras who, with three sloops, spread terror in a Spanish fleet. Of middle height, he had the leanness of the highly strung, which made him seem tall. Gracefully built, with supple limbs and easy gait, his gestures had at times a tempestuous swiftness that was all the more disturbing because every fibre of his body, to his very finger-tips, seemed to be bounding in pursuit, though all his muscles preserved the immobility of perfect discipline. One felt that his long, strangler's hands might at any moment become the vehicle of his whole being, as if into them he was wont to project all his power ; one felt that at some time those hands must have clasped, with a terrible grip, about some piratical or knightly weapon. He was forever vibrating, with a wild force forever hovering about him.

When he entered a room anywhere and said " Good morning ", in his distinct voice, with the utmost friendliness, his calm eyes, the palest blue, glancing all round, you could almost fancy you heard him say, " Let no one leave ", or " shoot the first man who moves ". And when he took a cab, though he instinctively always chose the burliest-looking driver he could find, in the everlastingly disappointed hope of having to repay some insolence, the poor trembling wretch would fancy that in his carriage he was driving all the repressive authority of potentates. An ambition to reduce that class of citizens to slavery was almost a feature of his character.

No hot-head crazed with passion could have been more completely indifferent to the consequences of any-

thing he did than was the enigmatic Léopold, in placid
cold blood, with a lucky star that had never failed.

Nobody knew what was in this man's inner mind.

One day, to his utter stupefaction, Gacougnol had
seen a cab shoot past, with the speed of a projectile, hurled
along by two maddened horses whom a foaming Auto-
medon, standing up in front of the driving-seat, was lashing with the handle of his whip ; while Gacougnol's friend,
comfortably installed in the passenger's seat, and as cool
as boredom personified, watched the public fleeing out of
their way. At the risk of running a dozen people down,
he had conjured all the demons of his own will into possession of the first cabman he happened to find, invincibly
resolved not to miss a train for Versailles that was almost
due to start—a dangerous feat rendered almost impossible
by the outrageous nature of the course. He had the
incredible luck not to kill anybody, and to escape any
embargo on the part of the police entrusted with the
protection of the public roads, and to be able to leap
onto the train, not without jostling a number of
railway employees, one second after it had got under
way.

He could not be called handsome. There were times
when one would have thought he had been cut down
from some gibbet. The imperious line of the aquiline
nose, with its constantly twitching nostrils, did nothing
to temper the hard expression of the eyes, while his mouth,
always closed and compressed until the lips were drawn
inwards, was inflexible. At the same time, his really lofty
brow was well worthy of its position, as dominating characteristic of a commanding face that seemed to control the
thunderbolt.

Such a countenance, fascinating in its intensity, was inevitably bound to impress less forceful souls, and it was said by those around him that women could not long resist a conqueror incapable of softening to tenderness or stooping to implore.

What was quite bewildering was that such a pacific and meticulous art as Illuminating should be the occupation of such an unfettered freebooter to whom Marchenoir had applied an adaptation of the historian Matthieu's words about Le Téméraire, " Whoever inherited his bed ought to hire it out to cure insomnia, since in it such a restless prince had been able to sleep." The contrast between his personality and his work was so striking that the statement of the latter had to be repeatedly reaffirmed whenever he was introduced to strangers.

Moreover, he was not only an illuminator, but a renovator of illuminated work, and one of the most indisputably real artists of the day.

He used to relate how, after he had worked hard at the study of drawing in his early youth, this singular vocation was revealed to him much later, when he had come back from his expeditions and his patrimony had disappeared, leaving him in the most stringent penury so that he was compelled to look for some means of earning his living.

At all periods of his life this man of action, chained to the grid of his talents, had automatically sought to cheat them by applying his hand to whimsical ornamentations, with which he would cover in his hours of burdensome leisure the surprisingly laconic notes he wrote to his friends or mistresses.

People used to show one another messages from him consisting of only three words, making an appointment, but in those letters amorous elaboration of the text was replaced by a network tracery of arabesques, of impossible foliage, of inextricable scroll-work, of eccentrically tinted monstrous faces, among which the few words that expressed his royal pleasure were forcibly impinged on the reader's eye by Carlovingian-style uncials, or Anglo-Saxon characters, the two most virile scripts since the rectilineal capital letters of the Consular *ephemeridae*.

A Gothic contempt for all the intrigues of the day had given him a real need, a passionate love, of those venerable forms in which he dressed his thoughts, as he would have dressed his body in armour.

Little by little, ornamental lettering had inspired him with an ambition for *storied* initials, then for the miniature separated from the text, with all that it led to—analogously to the progress of that primordial art, parent of the other arts, that began with the poor transcription of the Merovingian monks, and was to culminate, after half a dozen centuries, in Van Eyck, Cimabue, and Orcagna, who continued on canvas, in more substantial pigments (which were to be abused by the Renaissance), the aesthetic traditions of the intellectual Middle Ages.

His skill became extraordinary as soon as he decided to make practical use of it, and he became a wonderful artist, of the most unexpected originality.

He had carefully studied and constantly consulted the beloved treasures of the past preserved at the Bibliothèque Nationale, or in the Archives, such as the Evangelaries of Charlemagne, Charles the Bald, Lotharius, the Psaltery of St. Louis, the Sacramentary of Drogon of Metz, the famous Books of Hours of Réné of Anjou and Anne of

Britanny, and the exquisite miniatures of Johan Fouquet, Royal Painter to Louis XI.

He had stooped almost to ignominious depths to get the permission of the mean Duc d'Aumale, a millionaire thirty times over, to copy without payment a few Biblical scenes and a few landscapes from the magnificent Hours of Charles V's brother, in the unworthy possession of the miserly Member of the Académie at Chantilly.

And finally one day he had managed to make the expensive pilgrimage to Venice, solely in order to study there the marvellous Breviary of Grimani, in which Memling is supposed to have collaborated, and which inspired Dürer.

At the same time he never produced, even in recombined elements, the work of his precursors in the Middle Ages. His compositions, always strange and unexpected, whether Flemish, Irish, Byzantine, or even Slavonic, were wholly his own, and had no style but his, the " Léopold Style ", as Barbey D'Aurevilly had accurately called it, in a remarkable article which was the beginning of the illuminator's reputaion.

Disdaining the jejune effects of water-colour, his exclusive technique consisted in painting in gouache, body-colours, without any thinning down of their dough-like consistency, intensifying the solidity of his colour-reliefs by means of a certain varnish of his own invention which he allowed nobody to analyse.

In consequence, his illuminations had the brilliancy and luminous consistency of enamels. They feasted the eyes, while at the same time providing a powerful meditational ferment, for those whose imaginations were equal to the tack of reining back the phantasm of the grotesque and revivifying dead centuries.

This extraordinary individual, an old friend of Pélopidas, was an enthusiastic devotee of Marchenoir, whom he frequently consulted, yielding a sort of reverential homage to his slightest counsels. It would not have been safe to speak disrespectfully of Marchenoir in the presence of Léopold, who was so incomparably eccentric as to regard in the light of an insult any commission, however profitable, that was not given by a professed admirer of that outlaw. Accounts of the oddest scenes circulated.

Only through him had Gacougnol, deemed by a way of special exception to be worthy of the honour, got to know him.

A magazine article some years before had been the rather unusual occasion of Léopold's first meeting with Marchenoir. The redoubtable critic, writing in the name of the ordinary man-in-the-street, had demanded grim tortures for that fellow Léopold, who was threatening to revive a dead art of which business men had never heard. Everybody thought this particular art was shrouded in the crypts of the Middle Ages, and now was it really to come to life again at the insolent will of a man who knew nothing of the achievements of modern progress, and be added to all the other chimaeras in which the ragged apostles of enthusiasm are fools enough to glory? The urgency of steps to suppress it was manifest; so Marchenoir enumerated, with the precision of a butcher from Djarbekir or Samarkand, the subtle and superfine tortures that ought to satisfy the claims of retributive justice and be proportionate to the enormity of the attempted outrage.

Irony of this sort, so often practised by the pamphleteer,

was carried to such a pitch of exasperated fury that it grew into a soaring crescendo of sarcasm, contumely, and gnashings of teeth, so overwhelming in its savagery that Léopold, hitherto more or less indifferent to literature, received, as it were, a revelation of the power of human words.

He persuaded himself that his strange defender's art had a mysterious affinity with his own. The writer's use of violent colouring, his caustic, elaborated savagery, his whirling, reiterational emphasis, his obstinate unfolding of certain cruel pictures that persistently recurred, writhing in endless combination like convolvulatious plants; the unparalleled audacity of his form, multiple as a raiding host, and as swift, though so heavily armed; the methodically tumultuous crowding of his vocabulary, with its mingling of flames and lava, like Vesuvius in the last days of Pompeii, studded, encrusted, crenellated with antique gems, like a martyr's reliquary, but, above all, the enormous degree to which such a style expanded the scope of the humblest theme, the most trifling and tritest postulate—all these things made for Léopold a magic mirror in which, with a start of admiration, he soon saw his own likeness.

" You are a much abler illuminator than I am," he had said, simply, to Marchenoir, "and I invite your counsels."

" Why not ? " replied the other. " Am I not a contemporary of the last men of the Byzantine Empire ? "

CHAPTER XXV

HE had explained what he meant.

" People always forget that the Middle Ages lasted a thousand years. From Clovis and Anastasia up to Christophorus, by way of Joan of Arc and the last Constantine, the measure is filled full. A thousand years! Is it not inconceivable ?

" When we are told that the sun is fourteen hundred thousand times larger than the earth, and that a gulf of twenty-eight million leagues separates us from it, these figures seem absolutely meaningless to us. The same thing applies to the duration of this or that historical era. Man is so supernatural, that what he is least able to comprehend are the notions of space and time.

" Ten centuries! One hundred and sixty popes, not counting the barbarian princes, thirty or forty dynasties and almost as many revolutions as battles! Well, try and imagine it, even if you were an archangel!

" Massacres, devastations, cities in flames, cities at prayer, populations clinging to the fringes of miracle-workers' robes, peals and tocsins, plagues and famines, interdictions and earthquakes, cyclones of enthusiasm and anticyclones of terror ; no halting-place—even at the foot of the throne—no certain refuge—even in the house of God! Among the ruins, indeed, there spring up the Saints, and do what is possible ' that the days may be shortened ', but they are days of twenty-five years, alas! And no fewer than forty of them will serve.

" A Lent unparalleled in duration, even more so than

in severity, routs the reasoning faculty. One can imagine that some men, despairingly, may well ask whether this incomparable penitential period was simply intended to culminate in the derisive Hallelujahs of the Renaissance, and the brutishness of Christendom in this latter century!

" Myself, Marchenoir, I cannot formulate such a question, since, as I have just had the honour to tell you, I am a contemporary of the last men of the Byzantine Empire, and, in consequence, completely ignorant of what followed the fall of Constantinople. Sufficient for me, the belief that all those sufferings were endured in order that there should one day appear that marvellous passion-flower in the Middle Ages, Joan of Arc—after whom, indeed, the Middle Ages might just as well have died out.

" They lingered on, nevertheless, till the time of Christophorus, who was to lay them in the grave ; and then, and only then, was the abject modern era allowed to appear. But the sack of Constantinople is the real line of demarcation.

" The Middle Ages without Constantinople at once seemed like a great tree whose roots had been cut away. Consider how it was the Reliquary of the world, the Ecumenical Golden Casket, and how the dispersed bones of its olden Martyrs, wherein the Holy Spirit had for so many ungrateful centuries abided, were able to cover the whole Western World with a dust of light!

" Schismatical she might be, and utterly perfidious, polluted with deeds of baseness, weltering in spilled blood and gouged-out eyes ; she might be an abomination to the Popes and the Knights ; but none the less Constantinople was the gateway of Jerusalem, where all good sinners aspired to die of love; a gateway so beautiful that she dazzled Christians as far off as Britanny, as distant as the farthest fjords of Scandinavia! Something, in short, like a Sun that never set!

"Remember, Monsieur Illuminator, that the sumptuous applications of gold that are the glory of the missals of the oldest periods are nothing but the reflection of that unimaginable Byzantium in the twilight of those Irish and Gothic monasteries, around whose walls the starving wolves howled an accompaniment to the supplications intoned by the monks for those on pilgrimage to the Holy Sepulchre. Thus speaks Orderic Vitalis, a narrator of sublime ability.

"From the day when the Emperor Anastasius had decked Clovis out with all the insignia of Consular dignity, it is beyond dispute that everything in Europe wherein was the least echo of poetry had turned towards that strange City, the *only one* in the world that had not been engulfed in the flood of barbarianism.

"Rome, needless to say, still remained the Mother. There dwelled the Gaoler of Beatitude, holding in his hands the Keys, with power to bind and to loose; yes, unquestionably, but that Seat of the incontestable Primacy had, by dint of repeated outrages, lost all its adornment, while the other, the Eternal City's rival, had simply had to stretch out her hands a little way beyond the confines of her impregnable walls to draw towards her all the splendour of the earth. How could nations so young have been proof against the seductions of that prostitute city that bewitched the Caliphs, and the Kings of Persia, and of which the very mirage had been enough to make the Queen of the Adriatic rise from the bosom of the waters?

"The art of illumination, as I have already said, was a photogenic eradiation, a diffusion of light from Byzantium into the brooding soul of the West; the inverted mirror, miraculously softened and sweetened by a child-like faith, of the Byzantine mosaics, marbles, painted domes, palaces, Golden Horn, Propentide, and sky. It was the perfect type of the Art of the Middle Ages, and bound to come to an end when it did. When the Eastern Empire became the pigsty of the Mussulman, the prestige which had given it birth disappeared, and in their despair, the dreamers plunged into the indelible printing ink of Guthenberg, or the thick oil-paint of the Renaissance.

"That was bound to be the end of all things for such a one as I, and for the half-dozen lunatics whose brother I am. You are privileged to be one of these, my dear M. Léopold, if you have understood me; we can hold hands lovingly as we wait for the General Judgment."

CHAPTER XXVI

A BIG evening party at Gacougnol's. Except for Clotilde, all present are men. A half-score of men, counting as man a certain half-fledged snake of the most venomous type who crawled habitually in the spittoons of various editorial offices, and had achieved fame by his ferocious tongue. He is designated only by the descriptive epithet or nick-name of Apimanthus. He was once given a crippling cudgelling with a walking-stick—and ever since had trailed himself round. He devoted himself to studied insolence, for all the world like a still in which deadly poisons were prepared.

A queer gathering, if without superficiality one can call anything queer. It was sometimes Gacougnol's whim thus to group together the most ill-assorted individuals.

For instance, who would not gaze in wonder at the droll exterior of the old engraver, Klatz, when he was seen in the company of Léopold and Marchenoir—a dirty and ill-smelling Jew, but incurably untalented, whose babble of apophthegms, like the chattering of an Alsatian second-hand dealer, was valued as an unrivalled medicine against all forms of melancholia?

He was once handsome, people said. When, in Heaven's name? For he looked every minute of a hundred years old! The first time of meeting him, one could fancy one was looking at Ahasuerus, the Wandering Jew. His long beard, of an earthy, dingy white, that outvied the ashes of the dead, looked as if it had dragged for nineteen centuries through all the highways and tombs of the world. Despite their obvious vivacity, his eyes seemed so far off that a telescope, one might almost think, would have been useful for studying them. With that, possibly, one might have discerned, far back in their depths, the morose countenance of the " good " Titus watching the destruction of Jerusalem.

Of a surety such eyes must once have bewitched the foolish daughters of Tyre or Mesopotamia, who came to play upon the citherum or the tympanon beneath the very walls of the impregnable tower of Hippicos, for the damnation of God's people. But since those distant ages how many layers of dust! How many rains upon that dust! How many winds, burning or frozen, all-withering, all-dispersing, all-destroying!

In fine, this personage, with an air of being still in search of the Ark of the Covenant carried away by the Philistines, whenever he entered any place, was for keen ethnologists the definitive result of the most irrefutable Jewish selective breeding.

His Levitical nose in itself implied, inevitably, the *Ve'elle Shemoth*, the *Shophetim*, the *Shir-Hashirim*, or the Lamentations of the Prophet; and the decay of sixty venerable generations, pulverised by planetary ruins, clung to him.

Zéphyrin Delumière was not excluded. A mystagogue bearing no malice, he had certainly forgotten the ungracious welcome accorded to him by Pélopidas on an occasion described earlier in these pages. The magi have memories that lack the knack of retaining anything not occult. This one, moreover, had for some time been clinging closely to the coat-tails of old man Klatz, whose semitic scent fascinated him, and from whom, too, he had picked up a few Hebrew words.

But Gacougnol's eclecticism was especially demonstrated by the presence of Folantin, the naturalist and futurist painter, whose success, long withheld, had just come to him.

It would be difficult to find anything more instructive than the chronological catalogue of his works.

After an initiatory series of unpleasant little landscapes laboriously scratched in the sterile suburbs, after the semi-triumph of a " genre-picture " in which the indecisive love-making of a young mason and a crafty-eyed sempstress, in the privacy of a " furnished bed-sitting room ", coagulated beneath the eyes of the spectator into livid mastic, like a cheese that has been cut into—Folantin, wearying of not appearing as a Thinker, decided to dispense a modicum of philosophical moralising in his output.

Then there rose on the horizon, to the inexpressible discouragement of a number of manikins of the mahlstick, the startling picture of a complaisant or betrayed husband, made of sugar, carrying a candlestick, and showing out, with the most frigid politeness, a dried-up looking creature whom he has surprised in the arms of his wife. This was entitled, " Domestic Life! " But it evoked less praise than the furnished bed-sitting-room, the vogue of which, alas, was beginning to be threatened, and it became necessary to think of something else.

With a complete change of weapons, he painted, with emphasis, a Great Gentleman, a Scion of lofty lineage, whose type he studied in the person of a genuine specimen of the Gentry who had adopted the career of collecting the unlabelled cigar-ends of modern poetry.

The aristocrat was depicted, entirely without his own consent, straddled on a bidet, reading verses with twenty-five feet in the line. And, contrary to all possible human expectation, it so happened that this allegorical portrait became a minor sort of masterpiece, and the nobility of France—once the foremost in the world—once more proved themselves so low that the caricature conceived by Folantin, when confronted with the original, created for a moment an illusion of strength.

The fortunate painter held his head high among the stars, and managed to annex a few disciples. There was no getting away from it. However much opposed one might be to Folantin and his hateful painting documented like a novel of the Moron School, his personality surmounted its pillory, which had become a pedestal, with something of the grandeur of an equestrian statue.

From that moment the new Master spurned small frames, and plunged into huge canvases on the heroic scale.

Crowds jostled one another round his *Black Mass* and his *Trappists at Prayer*—enormous rough-cast compositions, daubed with little niggling brushes, that had to be scrutinised by the square centimetre, with a geologist's or numismatist's magnifying-glass, with no hope of ever attaining the beatific vision of any general whole.

The first of these monstrosities was apparently calculated for the moving and firing of a recent brood of Philistines consumed with a longing for the lubricities of Hell. Nevertheless since our great man felt that in spite of everything it was his mission to instruct his contemporaries, it is at the same time a supreme achievement in a sort of clowning in paint, elaborated and fine-drawn till it becomes a whirlpool of detail—but a black whirlpool, unspeakably foetid and profaning!

The Trappists at Prayer aimed at being an antithesis, the obverse of the preceding revelation. Folantin, more triumphantly and blatantly complacent every day, set out to demonstrate how an artist daring enough to kiss the Devil's saddle, was able on the other hand to exploit spiritual ecstasies.

Folantin, with sudden wizardry, discovered Catholicism!

His vision was but poorly rewarded. The bigoted religiosity of St. Sulpice, challenged to a duel, pierced his heart with its aspergillum. Once more, however, he profited by the revival of credit which religious interests seemed to be enjoying, towards the end of the century, and his mantle as an innovator did not shrink to the humble jacket one might have supposed after such an achievement.

The outward appearance of this pontiff might have been compared to one of those very poor trees, the American Walnut, or the Japanese Gum, that bear poisonous or illusory fruit, and give but a pallid shadow. He was specially proud of his hands, which he regarded as extraordinary, " the hands of a very thin baby, with thin, tapering fingers," was how he described them, in his kindly way—for he bore himself no grudge.

" I see myself," he declared, to a reporter, " as a courteous cat, very polite, almost affectionate, but touchy— ready to bare my claws at the least word."

The cat, indeed, seemed to be *his animal*, but without its gracefulness. He was capable of lying in wait for his prey, indefinitely ; and even for the prey of others. And this with a ferocious gentleness that no insult could disconcert. He welcomed all with a feigned half-smile just showing, letting fall, every now and then, a few delicate, metallic, wire-drawn sentences that sometimes left his hearers wondering if they were listening to a living being.

He was the man who " never got worked up ". The scornful tilt of his upper lip was assured, for everlasting, against all lyricism, all enthusiasm, all vehemence of the emotions, and his most apparent passion was to seem like a razor-sharp current beneath a flooded river.

"That fellow is Envy Personified!" Barbey D'Aurévilly one day exclaimed, with precision, and with that word slew him.

All the same, his malignancy was not without circumspection. Exceedingly careful of his celebrity, which he cultivated in secret as if it had been a rare and sensitive cactus, he lost no opportunity of mingling with journalists whom he considered himself entitled to despise, or with certain fellow-painters of frank unreticence, whose ideas he refined on. The nasty story about the original sketch for the *Black Mass* is considered to be authentic—how he got it for a few *louis* from an artist dying of want—a superb rough outline which he lost no time in debasing with the brush, after ignominiously dismissing the wretched man who had presented him with such a godsend.

It will seem difficult to believe that the independent Gacougnol should have received at his home a character so perfectly calculated to exasperate him. But, as we have seen, this good man recognised no rule but his good pleasure, and it was undoubtedly in the hope of some clash occurring that he had drawn together under the same roof those whose antagonisms were so inevitable.

In any case, apart from Léopold, Marchenoir, or himself, were there not present Bohémond de l' Isle-de-France, and Lazare Druide, and could the extreme repulsion inspired by Folantin fail to be outweighed by these two radiantly sympathetic personalities?

The former was known all over the world, that is to say, known by the few hundred scattered contemplatives, for whom a true poet sings, and Bohémond, named among the greatest, scarcely sang even for himself. Persuaded that silence was his real spiritual home, he liked to borrow the cry of the eagle, sometimes even the rumble of the wounded rhinoceros, to tell all the stars that he was in exile.

Accoutred, for the derision of the literary public, with a lofty name in which he was dying, his whole efforts were strained to project himself out of the ghastly world in which a savage fate had imprisoned him.

One might liken him to one of those brilliant insects, the brighter coloured dipterans, shut in, as it were, by the bed of a river of light, dashing itself to death with a quivering, undying optimism, against the clear, pitiless glass that separated it from its heaven. A woodlouse, surely, would have found some other way out. *He* did not even look for one. He strove wildly for the one impossible way of escape, precisely because he knew its impossibility, and because it was against the law of his nature to attempt anything not out of all reason.

One knew his Arch-angel-like hatred for the Philistine, the Knight-Templar ferocity that he held in reserve for the confusion, when opportunity arose, of that respectable member of the Reprobated, that " slayer of swans ", as he dubbed him, for whom Satan himself in his Hell must blush. It went so far that he could imagine no other way of sanctifying himself.

" Ah! I am compelled to endure your propinquity," he told himself, " I am condemned to listen to your riff-raff's voice, the absurd expression of your debased ideas, your miser's mottoes and the sententious baseness of your loathsome astuteness! Well, then, let's have some fun! You won't get away from my sarcasm! "

So he made himself, for the moment, the Philistine's friend, his dear friend, his nearest of kin, his disciple, his admirer. Affectionately he invited him to open up his heart, to display his innermost emotions before him, Bohémond ; led him step by step to full confession and self-revelation, then, unmasking his glittering armoury, he would transfix with one avenging word.

The white-hot mockery of this collateral descendant of the fallen Principalities and Powers sometimes reached such depths of subtlety that his victims were not even aware of it. No matter, it sufficed that it should be recorded by the Unseen Witnesses.

Another painter, Lazare Druide, accompanied him. But Druide was still very little known to fame, and as different from Folantin as a censor swung before the altar is different from a pot of mustard powder in a tradesman's dining-room.

Here was one who was a painter as he might have been a lion or a shark, an earthquake or a flood—because it was absolutely inevitable to be what God made one and to be naught else. Only, it would need more than any human language to express how unarguably God had willed him to be a painter, poor man! For it seemed that all that was in him was calculated to rebel against that vocation.

Ah, let him do what he would—let him rouse to a frenzy of admiration or of terror a whole host of intellectuals or devotees; it might well happen that one day soon he would burst upon the notice of the general public by some tremendous discovery; let him! That would still not be *he*.

One could picture him as a vagabond, a brigand chief, an incendiary, a merciless pirate—fighting with both hands, like that night-mare filibuster who never bounded over the decks of the galleys of Vera Cruz or Maracaibo till he had lit a burning brand in every lock of his infinitely abundant swarthy hair. It is even easier to imagine him placidly guarding the herds of swine beneath the oaks of some ancient monastery, in a stained-glass landscape, his head crowned with the halo of the shepherd-saints, for his was a soul of lovable simplicity.

But painting—or, if you prefer it, the laws of that idiom that consists in the painter's technique—its rules, its methods, its syntax, its canons, its rubrics, its dogmas, its liturgy, its traditions—were never able to cross his threshold.

And in reality, might that not be a truly lofty way of conceiving and practising the art of painting, comparable to the Evangelical perfection which consisted in stripping oneself of all things?

He was, like Delacroix, reproached for the poverty of his drawing, the frenzy of his colouring. Above all, he was reproved for existing—for he existed too intensely, indeed. Those of his fellow-painters, whose imagination was a muddy and slow-welling spring, could not understand so impetuous a bubbling forth of vitality. How could he tarry for a rigorous accuracy, even if it were really necessary, in the execution of his pictures? Could they not see that he would imperil his chance of ever catching up with his soul, which sped for ever ahead of him, like an unharnessed steed?

Ay, exactly! He had only that—his soul; the noblest and most princely of souls! He seized it, plunged it, saturated it, in a subject worthy of it, and flung it, all shimmering, upon the canvas. Therein lay the whole of his "art", the whole of his "method", his only "trick"; but it was so powerful that it made men cry aloud, and weep, and sob, and raise defensive hands, and flee!

Did we not see this miracle come true at the exhibition of his *Andronicus Delivered to the Populace of Byzantium*? Such a work can never be forgotten, once it has been seen, even though a man should drag his body for a hundred years through all the miry highways beneath the sun!

Here is the outline of this picture, the work that made him known. Andronicus, the brutal tyrant of the Empire, suddenly hurled from his throne, is abandoned to the mercy of the rabble of Constantinople. And what a rabble! All the scum of the Mediterranean: bandits drawn from Carthage, from Syracusa, from Thessaly, from Alexandria, from Ascalon, from Caesarea, from Antioch; sailors from Genoa or Pisa; Cypriot, Cretan, Armenian, Cilician and Turkoman adventurers; not to speak of the mongrel horde of barbarians, from that delta valley of the Danube, which made Greece stink even to the confines of Bulgaria.

The infamous prince has been thrown into the midst of this chaos, this terrible confusion of savagery, like a worm thrown into an ant-heap. The populace were told, "Here is your emperor—devour him, but share fairly. Every cur must have his morsel." And that foul populace, executioners of a justice of which they knew nothing, tore their emperor to pieces and gnawed at him for a space of three days.

Andronicus, it is said, suffered quietly to the end, content to sigh, every now and then, "*Lord have pity upon me. Why wilt thou break the bruised reed yet further?*"

The misery of this man steeped in cruelties, the gouging out of eyes, parricide, and sacrilege, is so intense, his *solitude* so perfect, that one would really think that, as if he were a Redeemer, he was taking upon himself the abominations of the multitude who were rending him. The monster is so alone that he suggests the picture of a dying God. His blood-filled countenance provides an orientation for the insults and outrages of a whole world, and he is draped with the pain of the universe as with a mantle.

Let the crowd, their work finished, find their eyes dazzled with the sun of torture that has left history amazed! Doubtless, the expiatory sublimity of such a horror was needed, that the collapse of the ancient empire should be delayed for another three hundred years.

What is to be said of a painter able to suggest such thoughts? And the suggestion once more, is so powerful, so spontaneous, so triumphantly irresistible in its force, that the composition, vast as its scale is, bursts with its content, and the breathless drama overflows it, and surges out, like a dragon, into the midst of the terrified spectators themselves.

The man's appearance, still youthful, was as vehement as his work. There was never an artist who expressed more completely than he did every trait of his art in his features. In them could he read a sustained, a continuous, enthusiasm, such an enthusiasm as is a rare thing; a marvellous nobility of mind, a devouring zeal for Beauty, which —to his vision—was the raiment worn by holy Justice; intuition flashing lightning-like over the pomps and trappings of Pain; an indignation like that of a river against the folly that obstructs its rolling flood; and all in soaring, tower-like capitals.

As swift as a volcano, and no less sonorous, when some boor was disrespectful, his fury, instantly pathetic, would

burst forth, to the confusion of the Philistine, from the
heart of a politeness so exquisite that, by comparison with
him, the Master of Ceremonies of the Escurial would have
fallen at once to the level of a dock laborer.

CHAPTER XXVII

THE ostensible pretext for this strange gathering, this
fantastic synod organised by Clotilde's patron, was the
exhibition of Rollon Crozant, the musician, who has since
become famous but who at that time still needed to be
" discovered ".

Pélopidas's real intention was to treat the young woman
to the unusual entertainment of a combination of wild
animals, picked out by himself with all the cunning of a
Venetian.

She, innocent of the conspiracy, had very gracefully
helped the company to some preliminary refreshments,
and the incense of many cigars was already scenting the
room, when Crozant sat down at the piano, not without
a careful study of his seat, like a passenger installing himself for an all-night journey in a non-stop train.

For a long time he sang, in a voice as supple as a clown's
body, a variety of melodic interpretations of some of
Baudelaire's gloomiest poems. He proved himself a
passionate and insidiously infectious virtuoso of the
melancholy that stifles, the blackest pessimism, the madness that devils brew for men. He made one hear the
cries of damned souls, the plaints of spectres, the moan-

ings of ghouls. There was no escape from the grip of the evilly dead and the basest terror. Incompetent to discover the Christian spirituality of the great poet whose work he imagined he was translating into music, endowing that poet with his, Crozant's, own soul, he soon produced an effect of paralysis on an audience which did not really want searing plasters of oblivion.

Despite certain bravura rhythms hammered out with a certain power, in spite even of incontestable flashes of simplicity, that music, all vertigo and tetanus, which was to ensure for its producer the suffrages of all the neurotics of our day, seemed, that evening, very childish ; in fact, to some of his hearers the singer's virtuosity seemed a species of acrobatics worthy of no forgiveness.

In any case, the performance had not succeeded in lasting as long as it had, without criticisms, though the minstrel remained unaware of them. Folantin, bored stiff, but with a stronger interest than anybody else in not allowing his discomfort to be perceived, had breathed half-inaudibly, in a fit of cold-blooded fury, that he preferred reading the *Fleurs de Mal* in silence by his own fireside.

" By the side of your own stewed steak, you mean," had promptly retorted Apemanthus, who for a moment chose to pretend admiration for the mournful crooner.

" This is all very nice," lisped old Klatz thickly to Delumière, fondling his verminous beard. " But I can't see quite why this young man does music at decent people's houses. I once knew a handsome young fellow who would dig up corpses in the graveyards and eat them. Ha-ha! That was much funnier."

The taciturn Léopold had not opened his mouth, and Marchenoir had eventually picked up a portfolio and, concealed by Gacougnol's body, was turning over its contents.

Gacougnol himself, exclusively occupied in watching Clotilde, was watching the varying emotions sailing across the limpid sea of her face—surprise, first, then terror, then melancholy, then disgust, and gradually at last something that looked like humiliation.

Questioned, she replied, "*I am ashamed for Death*— your singer profanes and debases it so."

Thereupon the master of the house got up and, going towards the piano:

"My dear Monsieur Crozant," he said, "you behold us almost dead, slain by delight. You must be wanting to rest. Moreover, I simply must be frank with you—we are avid to learn from your own lips the genesis of an art so extraordinary as yours. I imagine that you have a few things to explain it up your sleeve that will be anything but commonplace."

"Ah, yes—anything but commonplace! You may well say that!" the musician at once exclaimed, swinging round on his stool, and throwing back, with a bull-like gesture, his abundant mane. He blinked his eyes rapidly three or four times, made the little finger of his left hand do a furious dance in the entrance of his ear, drew a Gallican-style snuff-box from his waist-coat pocket and helped himself from it copiously with full ritual—to the alarmed surprise of the onlookers, who were disconcerted to see so much black powder drawn up into so young a nose; and eventually took up a suitable pose for one of those pulpits of aestheticism to which he had become addicted in the dens of the Latin Quarter, where he was looked on as a fine orator.

"I was brought up," he began, "on the knees of Madame George Sand——"

At this moment Bohémond de L'Isle-de-France, who had been fidgeting on his chair for the past half-hour, and making unintelligible signs to his neighbour Druide, and who, by some miracle, had not yet uttered a single syllable, suddenly struck his forehead with his clenched hand, like an Archimedes on the point of being delivered of a new discovery :—

"Now I understand!" he declared, roundly, accompanying his words with one of those formidable smiles with which he masked his normal Vulcan expression whenever he was pricked on by a spirit of mischief—"I understand it all! No doubt Monsieur Crozant is privileged to be possessed by a number of demons. My sincerest congratulations! I know of nothing to equal it for passing the time. How often have I not myself dreamed of being the abode of several Archangels formerly hurled down from Heaven, and thus being able to pass through the frog-marshes of this valley of tears, to the confusion of the glowering priestcraft that seems to have lost the secret of driving them out! The good lady who brought you up on her knees, my dear sir, naturally encouraged your first efforts at black music?"

"Don't you believe it!" replied the other, unconscious of the hidden barb of caustic mockery. "No, on the contrary; I could show you letters in which she advised me, if you please, to bring a fresh note into the melodic repertory of young ladies making their First Communions! '*My Beloved Tarrieth Long*', '*Youth Fadeth Away As A Flower*', '*Thus is it Ended! Farewell, Fleeting Pleasures!*'—or else to work at sentimental love-songs for the use of poor working girls, whose virtue was in danger, and who needed the consolations of music."

Bohémond seemed touched, almost on the point of bursting into tears.

" Ah, isn't that just she! How like her! What a heart! What a brain! Not content to have enriched all our libraries with ' Little Fadette ', and the ' Sin Of Monsieur Antoine ', and any number of other poems that dressmakers' assistants are never tired of reading, she wanted to go further and to raise up in our hard-working nation the musician needed to go with that admirable literary school! You tried, no doubt?"

" Against my own inclinations, I admit, and without success. Undoubtedly I was not entitled to despise the advice of Mme. Sand, in whom I saw a friend, the twin-soul of our beloved Chopin, his last love; but I was driven on by a different inspiration. I needed the fantastic, the macabre, deep shadows, pallid fear, and I soon learned that it was not for me to echo aught but the howlings of damnation."

" Of course!" decided Gacougnol. " A man must do what he can do. Please, my dear Bohémond, don't stop Monsieur Crozant again."

" Oh, I shan't take long," replied the latter. " I only mentioned the illustrious and pellucid writer in whose lap I am proud to have spent some of my infancy, so as to make it quite clear just what method one may expect to look for in my demoniac fury. Monsieur de L'Isle-de-France touched on the hub of the matter, when he spoke of possession—I actually am one who is *possessed*. My usual obsessing entities are the Demon of Grim Apparitions, the Demon of False Burials, and of fists gnawed in the tombs,

the Demon of the Mouldering Crypts and of the Black
Pits, and, especially, the Demon of Panic, of the Immeasur-
able and Unending Terror that nothing can allay."

"He might have added, the Devil of Idiocy!" Druide
whispered into Bohémond's ear.

CHAPTER XXVIII

"This mode of existence, not so rare as people imagine,
is due, beyond all doubt, to what I will take leave to call
the *Conspiracy of the Ambiances*. Yes, Monsieur," the
orator insisted, addressing Druide, who had suddenly
slumped in his chair, with his eyes stretched open to their
widest, "I must adhere to that word. We are surrounded
with things that are apparently inanimate but are, in reality,
hostile or friendly towards us. The majority of discoveries
or catastrophes have been produced by the benignant or
malevolent will of inert objects, mysteriously banded
together around us. As far as I myself am concerned,
I am convinced that a complete understanding of my music
is impossible to any artist, however profoundly intuitive,
who is unaware in what an extraordinary environment I
received my initial and decisive determining impulses.

"So I am going to attempt to describe to you, in a few
words, my father's house, in a sleepy country district of
Berry, not far from the evil and untamed Creuse, on whose
banks I have often fancied, in the dusk of evening, that I
could see terrible fishermen angling, who looked like the
dead.

" From the main road, along which no one passes, ever, the house can be seen in the depths of a garden so funereal that one day a stranger, wearied of life, rang the bell at the gate and asked that he might be buried. And yet there are no cypress or weeping willow trees. But that is the general effect. Melancholy vegetables, drooping flowers, grow there, in the shade of a few grudging fruit-trees, ' in a soil of turgid texture, wherein snails abound ', whence emanate exhalations of certain decay and putrefaction; and the dank humidity of this garden is such that the hottest summers do not affect it.

" Among the peasantry is preserved a tradition of some vague but ghastly crime committed of old in that spot, long before the house existed, somewhere in the dark ages of Bertrand de Got and Philip the Fair. In brief, the house itself is supposed to be *haunted*.

" As you can well imagine, gentlemen, if ever there was bound to be a reader of Poe and Hoffman, it was I. Well! They never invented anything more sinister. I venture to say that I lived there, in uninterrupted intercourse with the shades of the damned, and the darkest spirits of Hell !

" I knew to a nicety just what phases of the moon, just what hours, would inevitably produce a given disturbance, a given horror, a given visual phenomenon—and it was my exquisite delight to be deadly frightened in advance.

" Around me everything conspired to soak my soul in a delicious terror; everything was grim, sinister, queer, monstrous, or unnatural. The walls, the floors, the furniture, the utensils, had voices, unexpected shapes, that thrilled me voluptuously with dread.

" But how can I express my joy, my rapture, when I felt stirring within me for the first time the evil angels who had elected to make in me their abode! How can I put it? It was as if I felt the very jubilation of budding maternity! I even received the faculty of discerning, by a sort of affinity or sympathy, the presence of the Devil in some other persons, for, as I have said, my case is not particularly rare," he added, staring hard at Folantin, who looked uncomfortable.

" And there, Monsieur Gacougnol, you have the whole genesis of my art. To speak with precise accuracy, you know now what I've got inside me. My music comes from Below, I assure you, and when I seem to be myself singing, be assured it is *another* who sings in me! "

" Mademoiselle, would you like me to throw him out of window? "

This question was asked, almost aloud, by Léopold, who had not yet spoken, and who now came across to Clotilde specially to ask it.

The astonished girl hastened to reply that she wished nothing of the sort, and that the gentleman seemed to her rather to need treating kindly. But the filibusterer of illuminated manuscripts denied the efficacy of any such treatment, declaring that the safest and surest form of exorcism for that type of rascal was a good pummelling, and he could not understand Gacougnol's having inflicted such a mountebank on them. All the same, he consented to behave himself.

" Monsieur Crozant," said Gacougnol, " I am much obliged to you for the trouble you have taken to explain your case to us. Personally, I have no difficulty in believing that you are fully entitled to proclaim boldly that your name is 'Legion', just like the savage demoniac in the Gospel story. But I had no idea that I was inviting such a number, and I am afraid you find me rather embarrassed. I really am surprised, however, I must admit, to find you are so highly pleased at having such a garrison. They are usually considered rather a nuisance, and I remember reading, in the Roman Ritual, in the Rubric for Exorcisms, a number of epithets that give anything but a gracious idea of your lodgers."

"Not to mention," remarked Apemanthus, "that pigs must be rather scared of you. It's an impossible life, that's what it is."

"Our good friend Apemanthus is right," rejoined Bohémond, determined not to let go of his bone, "I did not think of that. The swine must remember the dirty trick that was played on them in the land of the Gadarenes. St. Mark assures us it needed no fewer than two thousand porkers to house the unclean spirits from one possessed man. That's a big number, y'know! One cannot help thinking that the tragic end of those four thousand hams in Galilee must have left an indelible impression, and that in spite of the length of the centuries that have elapsed, the whole breed must have preserved the tradition. Even the pork-butchers seem to have retained some dim fear in the murky convolutions of their brains, and I am sure that must be why they insist on cutting and re-cutting and mincing the flesh of those animals, and mixing it carefully with other meats, under the pretext of *assorting* it, as if they were afraid of some sudden panic that might ravage their tills.

"But not all the swine are in the hands of these honest traders. We meet pigs everywhere that are not *dealt in*,

and cannot be, on account of the numberless legal regula-
tions.   It is only too obvious that these must be liable to
get into trouble, when Monsieur Crozant is anywhere
about.   I am wondering whether the detail of music is
not just the very thing to make their jitters worse.   Ah!
We shall never know just what pigs think——"

"If we are to use that word at all," said Marchenoir, in
his turn, "I suppose they '*think*' exactly what lions
themselves '*think*'.   It has been proved that animals are
aware of the presence of the Devil, all animals; so much
so, that rats and even bugs remove precipitately from a
house that is haunted.   I don't believe there is any instance
of a demoniac torn by wild beasts in the desert places where
the Evil Spirit led those unfortunates.   The poor lunatics,
without knowing it, revived in themselves the lot of Cain,
whom the Lord, with a mysterious solicitude, had marked
with an unknown *sign*, that his carcase might be spared.
The carnivora and the vermin, alike, flee from the face
of the Prince of this world.   I say, from his *face*, because
the lower animals, being without sin, have not, as we have,
lost the gift of being able to *see* what seems invisible.   At
the opposite pole of mysticism the history of the Martyrs
and Hermits is filled with instances of famished beasts of
prey who refused to hurt them, and, instead, humbly
licked their feet.   Say 'Miracles', if you like.   For my
part, I simply see in these incidents an unsophisticated
revival of the Earthly Paradise, which no longer exists
except within the eyes, the frightened, sorrowful eyes, of
those unwitting animals.   It is from those eyes, we may
be sure, that God will be compelled to bring that Paradise
forth again, when the hour strikes for a return to absolute
Order.   It must have been in an infinite solitude that our

first parents expiated the dread Disobedience. The presence of the Demon must have put the animals to flight, I imagine, to such an extent that the exiled rebels would have to go three or four times round the earth to find them again in their wild state."

"Dare I venture to ask, Monsieur Folantin," queried the excellent Apemanthus, "if you have any objection to such a recrudescence of Eden as Marchenoir promises us ?"

"Not in the least," the man addressed replied, sourly. "Marchenoir is a man of genius. That is unquestionable. Consequently, he cannot be making any mistake. Anyhow, I am not at all particular about Paradises. I should call any place a Paradise where I was served, in suitable dishes, with tender steaks just cooked to a turn."

"You would even dispense with Muhammad's houris ?" interposed Druide.

"Oh! Very easily, I assure you!"

"If he was fat," growled old man Klatz, who was thinking of the obese eunuchs in cartoons, "the terrestrial Globe could not support him !"

The Paradise of Steaks had been a little too much for Clotilde.

"If you absolutely must have a victim," she said suddenly to Léopold, who still seemed to be in search of a holocaust, "I will willingly give that gentleman up to you. Execute *him*, if it amuses you; but without any violence, please."

CHAPTER XXIX

" WITHOUT any violence." That was not exactly in the
Illuminator's line. However, a fellow could only do his
best.

Léopold had nothing of the orator about him. Useless,
expecting from him the serene amplitude, the forceful
texture, of Marchenoir's style, any more than the slick
chatter of the worthy Gacougnol. His speech was dry,
sentences clipped off and flung out, short and brittle, and
sharp as a scythe; the speech of a man accustomed to
driving animals and slaves.

" You do not appear to have the qualities of an explorer,"
he began, abruptly, addressing Folantin.

" An explorer? Oh, dear me, no! Central Africa,
and all that? An indigo sky, a vile sun that eats into your
brain, a hundred and forty degrees centigrade in the shade,
and a bath inside your clothes the whole time; mosquitoes,
snakes, crocodiles, and negroes—no, thank you! I
should prefer Greenland or the North Pole, if one could
get there without having to move. There, at any rate,
you could be sure of not being pestered by the sun or any
over-emphatic vegetation.

" Besides, everybody knows what I think of the South
as a whole. I hate, above all, things that are exaggerated
and people who are exuberant. Now, all Southerners
shout, their accent sets my teeth on edge, and, worse
than anything else, they gesticulate. No, if I have to
choose between the people who have astrakhan curls on
their heads and ebony palissades along their cheeks, and the

phlegmatic, silent Teutons, I shouldn't hesitate. I shall always feel more affinity with a man from Leipzig than with a man from Marseilles. Naturally, I am only speaking of the Southerners of France—I don't know anything about those of the tropical zones. But I am only too ready to believe they must get more and more loathsome as one gets closer to the abominable sun."

" The way that cad talks about the sun! " whispered the impulsive Druide suddenly, to Bohémond. Druide was for the time being a worshipper of the luminary in question, and his patience was always on a hair-trigger.

" Just look at his hands! " said the poet, already lapsing into musings, by way of response. " A child's hands, those! Why, my dear fellow, those are a dwarf's hands! "

" Really! " broke in Gacougnol, at this point. " Then, if I may draw an inference from your Teutonic sympathies, in 1870 you must have kept at a certain distance from the battlefields ? "

" As far from them as possible, you can be sure. I make no secret of having had diarrhoea—or the wind up, if you like—all the time ; I was the best-known figure in all the hospitals. ' *Marching Kit !* ' I would undertake to provide all the material he needed for any bold disciple of Zola who would not be above writing my epic experiences. I give you my word, the result would do nothing to rekindle enthusiasm for fighting. Moreover, if everybody had been of the same way of thinking, the war would have finished at once, and, I should imagine, cost a lot less."

" A great deal less, certainly," agreed Apemanthus. " Ha-ha ! That is one way of looking at it ! We could have bought sanitational installations, and astringents, instead of the ruinous expenditure on big guns. It would have been a less heroic but more enlightened kind of patriotism. Then again, we should not have had the fresh opportunity for devotion that is provided by the mere idea of a return-match."

" Patriotism! " retorted Folantin, who was definitely in his stride now, " that's another fine, romantic farce for you! It's—like the ' gold of the corn ', which I have always seen the colour of rust or of donkeys' slops—or like the gentle Virgil's bees, those ' chaste sippers of dew ', who are said really to settle on dung or carrion—an old poetic leg-pull repeated over and over again by the rhymsters and novelists of the present day.

" Would you like to know what my patriotism is ? Right you are! So far from crying over the loss of Alsace and Lorraine, all I grieve over is not seeing the Prussians at Saint Denis or at Grand Montrougae, where, without any expensive removal, I could drink German beer—in Germany."

Druide and Marchenoir were both preparing to take up this base sally, when Léopold, with a gesture, checked them.

" Monsieur Folantin," he declared, " you disarm me. When I said, a few minutes ago, that you did not seem to be an explorer, just for the sake of saying something, I'll admit I was a bit worked up over your steaks. I wanted to draw you out. Well, upon my word, I have succeeded so well that you've put me back into the good temper I was nearly losing! I have even gained some light on your painting, which I imperfectly understood till I learned of your attitude during the war. All the same, I should advise you to reserve the expression of your patriotic ideas for a strictly limited number of the elect. There's no telling whose ears it might drift to, and I have known lovers of Terpsichore with whom your German beer would hardly have agreed!

"However, to get back to our steaks. Do you know what sort of meat men eat—men who *are* men, mark you—in a vast, desolate region to the south-west of Tanganyika? These unfortunates, perpetual nomads, are constantly watching the sky, on the look-out for low-flying vultures, in order to share with them the carrion those birds settle on. I don't know whether that hyaena-like pittance is a suggestion or reminder to them of Paradise, but I have tasted it, and I can give you my word, Monsieur Folantin, that you would have found it as delicious as I did. I expect that is a result of being forced to remember, at such moments, that one is oneself a little lower than the vermin."

This speech, listened to by Folantin with a smile, with that patience spoken of in the Common of Bishop-Martyrs, was so different from Léopold's usual manner, and seemed to Gacougnol so supernaturally inspired by the desire to please Clotilde, that he became very thoughtful.

CHAPTER XXX

THE evening went on and on. Everything that could be said, in a few hours, by such a group, was said by those odd men, two or three of whom were men calculated to start commotion and lamentation in the belfries of all the alarum bells and church bells of the land, if they had been

less strictly confined in the deepest dungeons of an inarticu-
late democracy.   The singer of death had been forgotten,
thrown into the discard.

After innumerable digressions and bewildering, maze-
like side-turnings, after many paradoxical doublings in
their tracks, in which they seemed to be unanimously
agreed in one thing only—the routing of all the rules of
logic or of elementary coherence in discourse ; after
Bohémond, in reply to lawless audacities of speech, had
spat forth a certain number of those famous " parables "
whose acrimonious incoherence had been the evergreen
amaze of literature for the past twenty years; after half the
band had been overwhelmed, cowed, paralysed for a few
minutes ; when, finally, there were only watch-dogs left,
Marchenoir took his seat, with lighted taper, on the open
powder-barrel of Jean Bart.

" What do you take me for ? " he was saying.   " Oh,
Bohémond!   Am I an artist for your Wagnerian music
to throw me off my balance and get me down ?   I fear,
Heaven forgive me, that you can't even pronounce his
name without risking the loss of your own, you idolise
him so!   And why ?   In Heaven's name, why ?   Will
you tell us it's because he was the greatest or the only
musician of a century that heard Beethoven ?   Really, I
find that hard to believe.   Would you have the impudence
to claim, to my face, that those unbearable poems of his
can be read by anybody who avails himself at all of the
right not to die of boredom ?

" You've been maintaining in your dissertations, for
quite a while, that the monstrous amalgum of Christianity
and Scandinavian mythology, dished up by this German of
yours, is nothing less than the rending of the veils of

Heaven. The resplendence of Divinity was unknown on earth before *Tannhäuser* and *Lohengrin*—that's agreed on, eh? And that ancient stirring of the Holy Spirit among the bones of the dead, which was the whole religious music of the Middle Ages, must, of course, give up its place to the deafening counterpoint of your charmer. . . . People assure us, my dear poet, that you are endowed with a marvellous understanding of music, as well as of all those other spells by which men in all ages will hope to recapture some pale reflection of the True Substance. Ignorant as I am of all the magic jargon of art, and still more ignorant, if it were possible, of any of the ritual of controversy, I should be ill-advised to engage you in single combat on the field of aesthetics. But I must confess that it is more than I can stand when I hear that lyrical dramaturgist the present generation is going mad over, being ' tempted ' by you, like the Son of God Himself when Satan carried Him up to a high mountain and showed him all the kingdoms of this world and the glory thereof."

"Many considerations render your person dear to me, Marchenoir," retorted Bohémond, borrowing that "precious" expression from the older Balzac; "I am not unaware that you are a Christian of extraordinary verbal potency. But you are misusing your strength now. Please believe me, I haven't forgotten my catechism yet. It is well-known that, about the intellectual time of the Popular Vote, I did not shrink from standing as a candidate ' for the clerical party ', in a constituency of ponces in the Piscina of La Villette; and for about an hour I harangued that scum, magnificently though not without peril. What makes you think I am trying to make a four-some out of the Blessed Trinity by adding Richard

Wagner ?   Since when is it an act of idolatry to admire an artist ?

" You yourself say you know nothing of art ; which is a very strange saying, and singularly contradicted by your work as a writer.   But will you at least agree with me that a mortal may have appeared, even in this century, solely by the inflowing of the Divine Will, in whose case there has been a sufficient *economy* of the clipping of the Seraphic wings for him to give us—by one of those spells you so despise—some valid foreshadowing of the Glory Beyond ?   ' *Man is only the sum of his thoughts* '—I have spent my life saying that——"

" Rather overdoing it, perhaps," interposed Marchenoir.

"——So if Wagner *thought* Beauty in its True Substance," continued the fanatic, ignoring the interruption, " if he *thought* God, he was himself God, as far as it is possible for a created being to be so.

" But—did I not speak, just now, of ' admiring ' ? Where on earth were my wits ?   Wool-gathering, I should think.   Really, Marchenoir, it is you who put me off my balance.   I, yes, *I*, I am supposed to ' admire ' Wagner, as a solicitor would ' admire ' Boieldieu!   Ha-ha! Very pretty!——

" I am on my knees," he cried, suddenly stirred, like a fire, to a leaping of lambent flames, bristling like a porcupine, his eyes unimaginably dilated in his pale face, " quartered " with the eight or ten centuries of his lineage—" Do you hear ?   I crawl on my two knees, with my heart pierced, like Amfortas, in the sacred dust of Mount Salvatus, in the saving shadow of the sacred lance of Parsifal, and, with the angelic children, I sing:

" ' The bread and the wine of the Last Supper, God

hath changed, by the loving power of His Mercy, into the Blood that He did shed, the Body of which He did make oblation——' "

He had hurled himself at the piano, jostling Crozant on his way, and was, in fact, singing, accompanying himself with a few chords, in a tremulous, sepulchral voice, but a voice so impregnated with the wine of love, with adoration, with tears, that Wagner's hymn became a wailing sigh of preternatural tenderness and sweetness.

It was so beautiful that, for a moment, everyone was startled into attention, except for Folantin. His upper teeth were bared in a malicious smile; he had heard, all right, the remark about his hands, and now chuckled, fancying he saw the chance of being revenged.

" The brandy is alight—this is going to be fun! "

As to Marchenoir, however deeply affected he might be by this sublime *Benedicite*, that was something that was powerless to alter his previous and old-standing hostile prepossessions. This was not his first dispute with L'Isle-de-France. The poet's mental locomotor ataxy, so to speak, and the perpetual, infinite stampede, away from all order and discipline, of his mercurial imagination, were too familiar to him for him to be taken aback. Besides, he was fond of him, as far as such a rectilinear temperament as Marchenoir's could be fond of one who was the incarnation of chaotic asymmetry.

" He is one of the Innocents of Bethlehem, not properly slain by Herod's murderers," he would tell himself; and he always found a boundless pity welling up in him afresh for that aged infant's unparalleled unhappiness.

When the crisis was past, Bohémond turned back to Marchenoir, as a wave returns to its reef.

"When that foretaste of the banquets of Paradise that is called *Tannhäuser*," he said, in a deep, remote voice, "was given to the dogs of the Opera House and the suburbs, some twenty years ago, there was no insult spared or overlooked—as perhaps you know, though you are younger than I (in more senses than one). But I was there, and I declare to you that never was all the scurrility of Hell more abundantly drawn on to vilify an ineffable Celestial Visitation. How can I help feeling disconcerted, when I find you, Marchenoir, you who profess to trample on the rabble, among the Hyrcanian herds of dogs baying their insults! Would you like to hear a little parable?"

He found himself a chair, and took his seat exactly facing his opponent, both feet close together, elbows on hips, hands clasped between his knees, in the devotional attitude of a gardener with a clear conscience listening to a sermon. He seemed to spend a moment, thus, in recollection, then, abruptly raising his head, he clucked with his tongue, rubbed his hands together, flung back, once more, the refractory lock from his forehead, and, with the mysterious manner of a Buddhist Priest about to unveil some sacred secret, began extempore:

CHAPTER XXXI

"THERE was, at the Marriage Feast at Cana, in Galilee— the Evangelists, I fancy, omitted this detail—a little Jew, a horrible reptile-like fellow, of the Tribe of Issachar, who travelled for a well-known wine-grower at Sarepta, and who was present when the master of the house drank the miraculous wine.

" This young man, a man of great genius, and probably a spy, saw, at a single glance, the terrible danger to the wholesale wine trade that was involved in such manifestations of Divine Power.

" Consequently, after a swift but careful consideration of the case, urged also, I have no doubt, by some diabolic impulsion, he got the master of the house, who was delighted at such a bargain, to agree, in return for twenty or thirty *ephas* of the finest vintage of Saron, to let him have whatever might be left over in the bottoms of the vessels used for the miracle, of the *Blood of Christ.*

" You understand, Marchenoir?—The BLOOD OF CHRIST!

" Now, this ' good wine ' had been saved up for the end of the nuptial banquet, when the guests had already drunk enough of the ordinary wine—as is positively deposed to by a Historian who was put to the test in boiling oil, sixty years later, by the Emperor Domitian—and there is good ground for believing that there must have been a reasonable quantity left, which was dispatched, that same evening, to Jerusalem, with a very circumstantial report, that it might be analysed in the laboratories of the Sanhedrin.

" There is no excuse for anybody to be unaware that the priests and doctors of the Law who constituted the Supreme Council were blackguards who had a simply terribly erudite knowledge of Talmudic lore at their finger-tips, completely conversant with all the Messianic traditions and all the signs by which the advent of the Son of God was to be recognised. When they demanded His death, they were fully cognisant of what they were doing, preferring the most thorough damnation in a distant hereafter to the more immediate ill of having to humble their Pharisaical, pedantic beards before Him.

"In the absence of positive documentary records, it would be difficult, not merely to *know*, but even to *imagine*, the sacrilegious abominations and the incalculably unspeakable *blendings* and *compoundings*, that were, in the upshot, perpetrated within the heart of the Pan-Diabolic College. But here is what I have been enabled to glimpse, in a lifetime that has already been long and up to now entirely devoted to iniquity.

"This Wine, identical, according to an irresistible and convincing theory, with what was to be caught in the mystic cup of the Holy Graal, was preserved by the Rabbis and handed down, from century to century, to all the foul Cohens or Priests of the Tribe of Levi, who guarded it carefully in the recesses of their ghettos, as an infallible and *inexhaustible* electuary or magic potion for causing the demon to enter into the bodies of men who should drink a single drop of it, mixed with no matter what beverage.

"It seems highly probable that a great goblet of it was given to Judas to drink, and that the maddened populace who howled for the death of Christ on Good Friday were foaming with the drugged frenzy of that terrible adulterated wine made from the wine of the symbolic Bridal. . . .

"So I venture to presume that this poison from the blackest dispensary of Hell is always administered without fail whenever it is expedient to stir men up to riot against God, or, if you prefer, against a Man whose scandalous Presence makes manifest, once for all, the worse than

awful hideousness of a world whose denizens have ceased
to be in the likeness of their Creator. I have spoken."
He stopped dead, as motionless as a ship caught in ice
of the Antarctic, his hands held out tensely half an inch
above the threadbare material of his poor trousers, worn
and wearied with many autumns, his mouth snapped shut
as if responsible for the keeping of some secret that must
never be revealed, and with the blue flame of his pale eyes
hypnotically focused on the other man.

CHAPTER XXXII

ACCUSTOMED though his hearers were to the poet's
imaginative divagations, this seemed rather extreme, and
there was a silence. Everybody, even Folantin, gazed
curiously at Marchenoir, who had sat very quiet and
apparently unmoved. They wondered what this formidable
man would say. Clotilde, especially, whom he had so
astonished the first day, and who, moreover, had scarcely
understood the parable, was on tenterhooks, fancying that
something big was about to happen.

"Marchenoir," said Léopold, "you are the only one
capable of replying to what we have just heard."

The man they called the Inquisitor lit a cigarette, and,
addressing L'Isle-de-France, said :

" *When music is not blessed by the Church* "—it was with
an immense calm that he uttered the words—" *it is like
water—very evil and inhabited by demons.* If I were speaking
to intelligences untrammelled by anything of matter, and,

therefore, comparable to the angelic intelligences, that sentence would be sufficient to dispose of Wagner. Unfortunately, something more is wanted.

" First, as to your Jewish poison, that is nothing to do with me, my dear Bohémond. Nobody has ever seen me indulging in any collective emotion or commotion. I am one who stands scornfully aloof, hermit-like, as you very well know. I know nothing, and wish to know nothing, of whatever may have been chirped or croaked or roared about the German who has begun, he and his vainglorious operatic scores, the conquest that was dreamed of in 1870 by old Wilhelm, when he thought to score over us with a million soldiers.

" It is, for me, enough, to know that he invented a religion. Prostrate yourself to your heart's content at the threshold of the Venusberg or Valhalla, go and follow along the marches of the Graal, which is simply their poetical extension in the ' Twilight of the Gods ' ; *omnes dii gentium daemonia*—' all the gods of the gentiles are demons '. Reconcile the whole thing with the readings of your catechism, which seem to have left you only a dim, confused recollection. My knees will not bend with yours. They belong, exclusively, to Holy Church, the Church that is Catholic, Apostolic, and Roman.

" ' Whatever is foreign to Her emanates from Hell, *inevitably, absolutely*, without further examination, without any vain compromise, for whatever disturbs bewilders is the foe of the Peace of God.' That is what you wrote yourself, on one of your lucid days. Can you have forgotten it already ? Though one were the greatest artist the world had ever seen, it would not be permissible to touch the Sacred Forms, and what is seething in the chalice

of Mount Salvatus, I greatly fear me, may it not be that
terrible elixir itself, described in your poetical effort to
us just now? Beethoven never undertook to bring nations
and kings to their knees, and he needed no strength save
that of his own genius. Wagner, in his impatience to
subjugate the world, has had the impudence to make the
very Liturgy an accessory in the concoction of his would-
be masterpieces. *That is the difference between legitimate
and bastard art.* Why should you expect me to follow
devoutly on my knees in procession behind this noisy
turmoil? Could it seem like an array of luminiferous
nebulae, except to the coarse imagination of a Teuton?"

These words, emphatically approved by Gacougnol,
seemed to exasperate Bohémond. For a moment they all
thought he was going to give way to some verbal outburst
of violence. Fortunately, he remembered some earlier
altercations of the same sort in which he had felt in his
antagonist an unscalable, cold impregnability, like that of
the loftiest peak of the Himalayas, and he managed to
confine himself to saying, with a sort of stormy good-
humour:

" You are perhaps actually the *only* man, as Léopold
judiciously remarked, who enjoys a plenary and Papal
dispensation from any admiration of Wagner. All the
same, are you quite sure that the Church, *our* holy Church,
is necessarily as severe as you are?"

" That, L'Isle-de-France, is a sentimental platitude.
The Church, here, stands in no need of severity in her
own defence. The nullity of those who insult her is super-
abundantly proved by her silent and indefectible presence.
She is, as God is, simply, uniquely, substantially, and
innovations are inimical to her. Now, it is a terrible

instance of such, when her Liturgy is prostituted. There exists no graver profanation, and whosoever dares to commit it, by his own initiative, makes himself anathema.

" One last word. I have read that Wagner loved plunging his audiences into darkness. It would seem that his work gains by being heard by people who cannot see one another and who could not take three steps without *falling*. Does it not seem to you that there is something rather disturbing about this idea of getting rid of light just when one is going to serve up a hash of ingredients from Heaven ? "

" A puerile comment, a rotten sophistry ! " roared the foaming man addressed. " Why not say right out—as some filthy-minded cads from the theological colleges of Geneva and St. Sulpice hinted—that the darkness you speak of was deliberately meant to serve as a facility to the erotic fumblers and degenerates who got over-excited by the 'cellos ? "

" Ha-ha-ha ! " from Marchenoir.

" Oh, yes, I've no doubt that idea appeals to you. Well! I call it disgraceful to begrudge a great man the means by which he effects his work. In such a matter he is entitled to be the sole judge, and the frog-like babble and petty clamour of a pack of ephemeral humans aren't worth the few seconds one would waste gasping at them. As to the Liturgy——"

" Let's drop that, Bohémond," replied Marchenoir, interrupting him abruptly. " We should never reach any agreement, in any case. And you would say things, insulting things, to me that your big-heartedness would soon impel you to apologise for, and we should both be miserable about it. What's the good of so many words? Our lines are divergent. You knew in advance that it was impossible to make me an adherent of your sect, and I long ago gave up the attempt to make you understand anything. Your genius has laid waste your reason. It is a cherub with a flaming sword, forbidding your intellect to regain Paradise, and, on top of that, you are hampered by the sticky Hegelian formula—— And, anyhow, why Wagner? Why this artist or that, when art itself is at the bar of the court?"

The lion-tamer had risen, as if to shake off the annoying intrusion of frivolous thoughts. Bohémond, who had kept his seat, his hand clasped about his chin, in the lithographic pose of the Mayor of Strasburg listening to Rouget de L'Isle mouthing the *Marseillaise*, was eyeing him from head to foot, with the same air as a tiger, half conquered but with undiminished courage, might gaze at a mammoth resurrected from the Deluge.

"Modern art is a maidservant who has rebelled and usurped the position of her employers," dogmatised the apostle of the Absolute. "I have sometimes denounced —with a bitterness that seemed excessive—the amazing imbecility of our Christians, and the vile hatred with which they invariably reward the Beautiful. You will agree with me, gentlemen, that it is impossible to speak too strongly on that head. For three or four centuries, Catholics and Dissentients alike, of no matter what brand, have done all they could to degrade the human imagination. On this one point, heretics and orthodox have been consistently unanimous.

"The order issued to both alike by the Almighty Lord of the Lower Regions was *to obliterate the memory of the*

Fall. And so, with the ostensible pretext of reinstating man, they have *revived afresh* the ancient Food of the Flesh, with all its consequences. Cathedrals fell into ruin, sacred nude figures gave way to the nudities of Venus, and all the rhythms became the servants of Lust. The rigid lines assigned by the straight, rectilinear righteousness of the Middle Ages to their extra-corporeal representations of the Martyrs, once they were broken, followed the inexorable law of the worlds, a law that the sublime spirit of a child-like age had for a moment conquered, and became curves, became the scroll-work of the altar of Pan. That, I think, is what we have finally arrived at.

" What would have happened to Christianity, had even the holiest pictures been more than the accidents associated with its substance ?—marks recognisable to the senses, but not themselves of the essence of its being ? Our Lord Jesus Christ did not entrust His ship to magnificos. The world was conquered by folk who knew not their right hand from their left, and there were whole nations governed wisely and well by Men of Vision who had never seen anything of all the teeming life that stirs upon the surface of the earth. To speak only of music, the most glorious melody is less than silence when there comes the *Custodiat animam meam* of the Priest's Communion. The essential thing is walking upon the waves, and restoring the dead to life. The rest, *what is too difficult,* is just to amuse the children and put them to sleep in the twilight.

" All the same, the Church, with her perfect knowledge of man, has allowed and willed pictures and statuary, in all ages, to such a degree that she has raised to her altars those who gave their lives for that traditional framework of her cult, but subject to the absolute reservation of a supernatural veneration that is strictly relative, and having reference to the unseen originals which those pictures and statues represent to the sight. That is the pronouncement of the Council of Trent.

" Assuredly, the contempt or horror of modern Christians for all the manifestations of the higher orders of art is intolerable, and even seems to be a new, and more diabolical, variety of the Iconoclastic Heresy. Instead of ripping paintings, or smashing coloured statues, as the Isaurians made a practice of doing, they suffocate luminous souls in the sentimental slime of a stupid piety, which is the most monstrous form of the corruption of the innocent——"

" Well! " exclaimed Druide, turning to Folantin. " Isn't that what you prophesied for me, a few days ago ? ' *Do you expect to end in the gutter ?* ' We were talking about my poor painting, and you were charitably trying to discourage me from it. I beg your pardon, for this interruption, but I couldn't keep it back ; for those last few words revived so strongly in me a feeling of gratitude that will last as long as I do—and end in the same place, in all probability. . . ."

Folantin confined his reply to a smile—as mysterious as he could make it—and Marchenoir went on :

" All the same, I repeat, Art has nothing to do with the *essence* of the Church, plays no part in her real life, and those who practice it have not even any right to exist if they are not her very humble servants. They are entitled to her tenderest motherly protection, because in them she sees her unhappiest and frailest children, but if they grow up big and handsome, all she can do is to point them out to the crowd, at a distance, explaining that they are like wild animals that it is dangerous to go too near.

"At the present day, that same Church, of whom I have to keep talking, because she is the only bosom for the feeding of mankind, has been abandoned by all nations, without exception. Those that have not expressly, officially, repudiated her, look on her as very old, and are getting ready, like pious sons, to bury her with their own hands. Surrounded with a family council, and an army of sick-nurses, in pretty well every country that still imagines itself to be in obedience to the Papacy, how much influence can she exercise over the vagabond throng of dreamers? One may come across a few rare and aristocratic individuals who are both artists and Christians—which Wagner most certainly was not—but such a thing as *Christian Art* is bound to be impossible. Some of you probably remember that I was bitterly rebuked for this statement by the same thinkers, I venture to believe, who rebuke Joseph de Maistre for a brutal tyrant.

"If there existed such a thing as Christian Art, one could say that a gate had been opened to the lost Eden, and, consequently, Original Sin and the whole of Christianity were mere fables. But as such an art does not exist, any more than that Infused Light of Deity on our planet, which for the last six thousand years has been barely illuminated (instead) by the last lingering beams of a Sun that was extinguished by the Disobedience of our first parents, it was inevitable that artists or poets, in their impatience to re-kindle that blazing light, should have drifted away from the old Mother who had nothing to propose to them except the catacombs and Penitence.

"Now, when Art is anything but on its knees—not, as my dear friend Bohémond claims, in the dust of the Graal, close by, I am told, to an old theatre built by Voltaire,

but at the feet of a very humble priest—it is inevitable
that it should be either on its back or sprawling face downwards—and that is what is named ' *Passionate Art* ', the
only kind that is able, nowadays, to give any semblance
of a palpitation to human hearts hung up like offal in the
butcher's shop of the Devil ! "

CHAPTER XXXIII

THE vigour of this harangue seemed to have given Bohémond a distaste for any fresh sally against an intractable
opponent, whom he admired, in any case, for his uncom-
promising ruthlessness and " catapultuosity "—a monstrosity of a word that he had picked up in Flaubert's
once far too well-known " Brawlery ".

" Poor Bohémond ! " murmured that good old good-for-
nothing, Apemanthus. " Ever since one night when he
was drunk, and sold his ' reflection ' to Catulla Mendes
for a few coppers, like the fellow in the German story,
he's been unable to find himself, even going on all fours ! "

The others, whom Marchenoir had led up paths they
were unused to treading, pulled themselves together and
got their bearings again as best they could. Gacougnol,
very well pleased with such a fine defence of what he
imagined were his ideas, congratulated the eloquent orator
loudly, and passed round drinks.

Clotilde, all the same, was still hungry for intellectual
emotions ; it seemed to her that there must be more to
come. The primitive creature she was, the new disciple

who wished her hero to be utterly sublime, found something lacking, she could not have said what, and was waiting, instinctively, for a thunderbolt.

So her mental pulse quickened when Druide, obviously
scared since Marchenoir had stricken Bohémond dumb,
tackled him with these words, which allowed of no evasion :

" Out of all you've just said, Marchenoir, I cannot, and
do not wish to, remember more than one word, which I
am bound to confess, plunged me into stupefied bewilderment. ' Am I an artist!' you exclaimed, just now, like
a corsair threatened with the chains of a galley-ship. Our
friend expressed his astonishment—which could not have
been slight! May I ask you a question? If you are not
an artist, what are you, then?"

" I am a Pilgrim of the Holy Sepulchre!" replied Marchenoir, with that fine, grave, clear voice of his that usually
set all the crests and wattles shaking; " I am just that—
and nothing else. Life has no other objective, and the
' folly' of the Crusades is precisely what has done the
greatest honour to human reason.

" Before the rise of scientific moronism, the very children knew that the Sepulchre of the Saviour is the Centre
of the Universe, the pivot and heart of all worlds. The
earth can go turning round the sun as much as you choose.
I will agree to that—on one condition, that the sun, being
uninformed as to our astronomical laws, shall go on quietly
with its own rotation about that invisible point, and that
all the myriads of solar systems that form the wheel of
the Milky Way shall carry on the movement. The inconceivable immensities of the heavens have no other use,
save to mark the position of an old stone where Jesus slept
for three days.

" Born, for my inexpressible grief, in a freak century in which this conception has been utterly forgotten, could I do better than take up the staff of those ancient travellers who believed in the infallible fulfilment of the Word of God ?

" Sufficient for me to believe with them—that the Holy Place must become once more, at the appointed time, the Episcopal and Royal See of that Word Made Flesh by Whom all words shall be judged. Thus will be solved the precious worry that our politicians idiotically call ' the Eastern question '.

" So what do you expect me to say ? If I carry Art in my pack, so much the worse for me ! All that is left for me to do, in that case, is to place at the service of Truth what has *been given me by UNTRUTH*. A dangerous and precarious last resort, for the true function of art is to manufacture its Gods!

"——We ought to be horribly unhappy," added this strange prophet, as if speaking to himself, " *Behold, the day dyeth, and night cometh, when no man shall work*. We are very old, and those who follow us are still older. Our decrepitude is so advanced that we do not even know that we are IDOLATERS.

" When Jesus comes, those of us who are still ' watching ', by the light of a tiny lamp, will have lost the strength to turn towards His Face, so intent will they be on interrogating the ' Signs ' that cannot give life. The Light will have to strike their backs—they will have to be judged from behind! "

CHAPTER XXXIV

CLOTILDE got home at three in the morning, escorted by
her friends Gacougnol, Marchenoir, and Léopold, who
had insisted on seeing her to her door, in that neighbourhood, one of the most formidable in Paris, filled with salted
provision dealers from the Pacific and white-slavers from
Pentapolis.

Intoxicated with the singular party she had been in,
that any other woman would no doubt have found un-
endurable, where there had been such a decisive demon-
stration of Man's superiority to the animals that have no
grammar; moreover, accustomed as she was to paying
no attention to anything that passed at Mademoiselle
Séchoir's, it did not occur to her to be surprised at the
fact that the inmates were still up, and she refused even to
notice the sudden whispering of many voices in the large
drawing-room as she crossed the hall on her way to her
room.   It was only later that she was to remember that;
but she felt a vague uneasiness, and shot the bolt on her
door the moment she got in.

With her usual courage, however, she was not long in
recovering herself entirely, and laughing at her momentary
nervousness.   A short prayer, undressed rapidly, and
asleep.   And these were the phantoms that now crossed
the field of view of the open eyes of her soul :—

Dressed with a splendour more gorgeous than any queen,
she beheld herself seated in some place deep, deep down.
She was cold, she was hungry, but not for the salvation
of the world could she have moved a finger.

The silence and darkness were monstrous, a few yards away; so solid, so congealed, so oppressive, that in that thick darkness the sun would have been extinguished.

The thoughts and feelings that, when she was alive and strong, she used to send stepping out ahead of her, were engulfed in that dim blackness.

Her powerful desire to live had disappeared. It seemed as if her heart was empty, as if God was infinitely far away, as if her inert body was a sad little hillock alone in the depths of an immense abyss.

Everything upon the earth must certainly have been destroyed. And yet she had not seen the Fiery Cross that was to appear when Jesus should come in His Glory, to judge the living and the dead. She had seen nothing, had heard nothing.

" Have I then been judged while I slept ? " she mused.

At last the silence stirred and rippled, like a leaden sheet of water in which strange creatures were awakening. She heard a sound. . . .

Such a still, small sound, so far off; one might have thought it the voice of one of those poor dead folk who have scarcely the right even to appeal for help, and to whom the living in their cruelty never listen.

The pathetic girl's heart was beating in great hammer-beats against the walls of her bosom, a deep, muted bell whose despairing clamour would never disturb as much as one atom. . . .

The external sound grew louder. For a moment, a knocking, a reverberating outcry, and then silence again.

Now the darkness had gone. The shadows had taken flight, like a black horde scattered by a swift panic.

Clotilde saw a sad, pale expanse, "a desert land, without

path and without water," according to the words of the
Prophet, and the kindly Gacougnol appeared to her.

He was dead; a knife protruded from his heart, his
chest streamed with blood. He did not walk—he glided
like a weightless substance drifting in the wind. He
passed quite close to her, gazed at her with his spark-
quenched eyes, in melancholy compassion, and said to her :
" You are naked, my poor girl! Take my cloak! "

She discovered then that she was completely naked. But
already the spectre had no cloak to give her, had ceased to
have face, or hands, and the gesture he had attempted to
make had been sufficient to disintegrate him.

Then Marchenoir came into sight. He, at least, seemed
to be alive. But you could not distinguish his features,
so bent was he as he walked, and the load—God of mercy,
the terrible load!—that he carried on his shoulders!

And then that was all. No one else came by. An
impenetrable forest had sprung up from the ground, one
of those tropical forests where the lightning kindles great
fires. There, even now, was a forest fire breaking out.
Terrifying and magnificent spectacle!

Oh, Jesus in Agony, was not that Léopold she could
see, in the heart of that furnace, his lofty and scornful
face ravaged with inconceivable torture ? He must have
been trapped, unhappy man! She could see him fighting
against those cascading floods of flame, as he would have
fought against a horde of angry hippopotamus. But his
hair was on fire ; he folded his arms, and burned, with an
impassive immobility, like a torch. . . .

The sleeping woman contrived, at last, to utter a loud
cry. Suddenly awake, she jumped out of bed, tore down
the burning curtains with a firm hand, rolled them up in

a rug, and opened the window to let out the suffocating fumes.

She must really have been extraordinarily disturbed, or extraordinarily exhausted, to have forgotten to put out her candle before going to sleep. She pressed both hands to her heart, to suppress its palpitation.

" You did not pray enough to God, this night, Desdemona! " she said, recalling the readings in the studio. " What a ghastly nightmare! "

Once more she remembered the mysterious prediction of the Missionary : " *When you are in the flames*——" She always thought of that very often, by day ; must she now think of it continuously by night, as well ? . . .

But why that man Léopold, whom she had scarcely seen, who was a stranger to her ? Why was *he* shown to her in so tragic a fashion, and in a way, too, that corresponded so exactly to her own secret, ever-present thoughts?

Sleep, which enchains the human body, has the power of restoring to the soul, for a flash of time, that *simplicity* of vision which is the privilege of *Innocence.* That is why the impressions of horror or joy received in dreams have an intensity of which consciousness is ashamed when the mechanism of sensuality has resumed its reign.

The pirate- or brigand-like countenance of Léopold had seemed to Clotilde so supernormal that, in the scenery of her dream, she thought that enigmatic person had been *revealed* to her. She saw in him one of those heroes that have gone out of fashion, obscured and humiliated by a debased world, who can show themselves for what they really are only when some sudden and inconceivable conflagration provides the opportunity.

And forthwith that became for her a different dream of such impressiveness that all else was obliterated. The picture, terrible as it was, of her benefactor stabbed, and the picture of Marchenoir crushed beneath the burden of a life as heavy as the ramparts of Heaven, disappeared. She marvelled mildly at the versatility of her sympathies, which she could not hold in check, which went out spontaneously towards a stranger.

" Oh, I am a fool! " she exclaimed, to herself, as she closed the window again (it was letting in an Arctic draught), " a dreaming fool, and an ungrateful little beast!"

She knelt by her bed for a prayer, and fell asleep again in that position, sobbing.

CHAPTER XXXV

" You sleep very soundly, Mademoiselle," her hostess remarked to her, at breakfast. " Here is a letter for you that the bearer asked me to let you have immediately. As I had heard you come in at three this morning, I thought I had better knock you up. But you were so sound asleep, I couldn't wake you. When I see M. Gacougnol I shall scold him for keeping you so long. The dear man isn't reasonable. *He should be moderate with you.*"

Clotilde, who had taken the letter and recognised her mother's writing, was suddenly motionless, arrested by those concluding words ; they might have been wafted on the wings of a gentle zephyr, and there could be no mistaking their intention. She saw clearly the infernal petty spite with which the nasty woman was trying to insult her, and could sense the high delight of the boarders, whose innermost recesses were voluptuously titillated by that bit of insolence. For a moment she was on the point of an explosion.

But, even then, she remembered her resolution, taken on her first day there, to place a dragon on guard at each of the three portals through which her tormentors could penetrate the defences of her spirit. For a number of months, since she had been boarding there, she had said nothing, seen nothing, heard nothing. She had shut herself up in the stronghold of her will as in a tower.

Why then should she not have borne with the conjectures and degrading suspicions, so long as the low hatred she felt encircling her was not incompatible with her interior peace? Especially as she had as little self-esteem as a woman could have, and deemed it absolutely natural that she should not inspire esteem in others. To the frequent questions put to her by Gacougnol, she had invariably replied, in an assured manner, that nothing was lacking to her welfare and comfort—and, indeed, she really thought that.

This time, all the same, the insult was so flagrant, that she found it difficult to swallow, and it needed a little heroism for her to limit herself to replying that Gacougnol had done her the honour of admitting her to an artist's party in which there figured no less personages than Folantin and Bohémond and L'Isle-de-France.

An infallible revenge; the governess despoiled of her glory and mad for celebrity—unable to attract to her home anybody more important than reporters, and poets whose work appeared only in competitions, would have performed acts of heroic sanctity to obtain such a favour.

Clotilde could not make up her mind to open her letter till she had retreated to her own room. She did not hope for any consolation from the reading of it, and the terrible night that had left its shadow upon her did not predispose her to joyful anticipations.

Chapuis's woman had, it was true, left her alone so far, without even trying to get money out of her, which was something of a miracle. But for her dread of meeting her mother's horrible " protector ", Clotilde would have been tempted to see her again, for the delightful peace that had swallowed up the memory of past tribulations inclined her to a sort of pity for her wretched mother. But at that moment she felt nothing but anxiety and fright. This is what Isidore's companion wrote :

" MY DEAR CHILD,

" Your loving mother, who carried you under her heart and endured agony to bring you into the world, is about to terminate her earthly pilgrimage. My darling Clo-Clo, I should like to give you my blessing for the last time, before returning to my Heavenly Home. A mother's benediction brings good luck. I do not wish to reproach you for anything, at this moment when I am on the point of donning my white raiment to appear before my Bridegroom. I know that everything in life cannot be beautiful, and I do not blame you for having secured yourself an establishment, but you have not been kind to your old parents, who worship you. When your M. Gacougnol threw me out, it gave me a fever, and that is what is causing my death. You would be sorry for Zizi. The poor lamb is like a soul in torment since you left us. I shall go to Heaven to await him there, where he will not be long in following me, the cherub! Still, we forgive you with all our hearts. Come to our arms, come and close the eyes of the saintly creature who has sacrificed everything for you. Come quickly, my child, but do not forget to bring a little money to bury me, for we have nothing now at all.

"Your poor mother, who will have soon ceased to suffer,
"ROSALIE."

"*It is a lie!*" said Clotilde, laying down the letter, which was filthily dirty and ill-smelling, though written in fine copper-plate with a firm hand, and even spelled with meticulous artistry and grammar. A whole childhood of tears and a whole adolescence of Hell were in that brief comment.

Nevertheless she decided to go to Grenelle. But she could not help feeling she must tell Gacougnol, and so first hurried to the studio.

"Good heavens—my dear girl!" cried the painter, when he caught sight of her. "Why, you look as if you'd been *dug up!* Are you ill?"

She told him of her bad night, and her curtains burning, but without saying anything about her nightmare; then, spontaneously, she handed him her mother's letter.

"But, my poor Clotilde, they're just setting a trap for you. *Your mother is no more dying than I am*, the good woman. They are so noble-hearted as to imagine that I shower wealth on you, and they're simply dying to extract it from your purse! All the same, I quite realise that you are anxious to make sure. Look here—I am far more interested in your circumstances than in the idiotic jobs I'm doing here. Don't you know that? We'll go together. I shall park you at the nearest church to the 'cherub's' residence, and go by myself to see how the 'saintly creature' is. Needless to say, I shall not loiter in that charming place. Whatever happens, you will see me back quickly, and if your presence is really necessary you shall know it from me without any doubt about it."

The proposal seemed to be rather a wild one. Clotilde hesitated a minute, but only a minute, just long enough for her will, already so completely surrendered to this man, to submit—and that minute settled their destiny.

PART II

FLOTSAM OF THE LIGHT

Libera me, Domine, de morte aeterna,
dum veneris judicare saeculum per ignem.

Officium Defunctorum.

CHAPTER XXXVI

"THE poor you have always with you." In the whole abyss of time since that Word no man has ever been able to say what poverty is.

The Saints who wedded Poverty from love of her, and begot many children by her, assure us that she is infinitely lovely. Those who will have none of such a mate, die sometimes from terror or despair, at her kiss, and the multitude pass "from the womb to the grave" without knowing what to make of such an anomalous entity.

When we inquire of God, He replies that it is He who is the Poor One—*Ego sum pauper*. When we inquire not of Him, He displays the glory of His riches.

Creation appears as a flower of Infinite Poverty; and the supreme work of Him Who is called the Almighty was to cause Himself to be crucified like a thief in the most absolute and ignominious destitution.

The Angels are silent, and the trembling Devils tear out their tongues rather than speak. Only the idiots of our own generation have taken upon themselves to elucidate this mystery. Meanwhile, till the deep shall swallow them up, Poverty walks tranquilly in her mask, bearing her *sieve*.

How aptly these words of the Gospel according to St. John apply to *her!* "That was the true light which illumines every man that cometh into the world. It[1] was in the world, and the world was made by It, and the world did not know It. It came into Its Kingdom, and its own received It not."

" *Its own!* " Yes, certainly. Does not mankind belong to Poverty ? There is no beast of the field so naked as man, and it should be a commonplace to declare that the rich are " bad poor ".

When the chaos of this fallen world is sorted out, when the stars are begging their bread, and only the most despised dust of the earth is permitted to reflect the Glory ; when men know that *nothing was in its place*, and that the rational species lived only on enigmas and illusions ; it may well be that the torments of unhappy, unfortunate man, may reveal and display the wretched poverty of soul of a millionaire, corresponding with his rags, on the mysterious Register of Redistribution of Universal Solidarity.

" I don't give a rap for the poor! " cries a Mandarin.

" Very well then, my fine fellow! " says Poverty, under her veil, " then come home with me—I have a good fire, and a good bed——" And she leads him in, to sleep in a charnel-house.

Indeed, it would be enough to disgust one with the idea of immortality, were it not for the surprises there are, even *before* what is conventionally called " death ", and if the pastry that Duchess feeds her dogs with, which they vomit

---

"*It* " : In English versions of the Gospel the pronoun is usually rendered " He ", as referring to the Word made Flesh ; but the French feminine gender of "*parole* ", " Word ", used for the Greek *Logos* in French versions of the Bible, and corresponding feminine pronoun referring to " the Word " facilitates the quotation, in the French edition of this novel, of the Gospel text with the French feminine pronoun, here rendered " it ", that could refer equally to " the Word " or to " Poverty ".—*Translator.*

up again, were not destined one day to be the only hope of her eternally famished stomach!

"I am your Father Abraham, Lazarus, my dear dead child, my little child whom I nurse in my Bosom till the joyful Day of Resurrection. You see that great Chaos there, that stretches between us and the cruel rich man. It is the Abyss that cannot be crossed—the misunderstandings, the illusions, the invincible ignorances. None knows his own *name*, none is acquainted with his own *features*. All faces and all hearts are veiled, like the brow of the parricide, beneath the impenetrable tissue of the elaborate scheme of Penitence. The sufferer knows not for whom he suffers, the happy knows not on whose account he is in joy. The pitiless man whose crumbs you envied, and who is now imploring a drop of Water from the tip of your finger, could not perceive his destitution, except by the illuminating light of the flames in which he is tortured; but it was necessary that I should take you from the hands of the Angels in order that your own wealth might be revealed to you in the eternal mirror of that front of fire. The permanent joys on which that cursed man had counted will, in fact, really never cease, and neither will your poverty ever come to an end. Only, now that Order has been restored, you have changed places. For between you and him there was an affinity so hidden, so completely unknown, that there was none but the Holy Ghost, Who visits the bones of the dead, able to make it spring forth thus into manifest light while you and he are made to confront one another endlessly!"

The rich have a horror of Poverty because they have a dim premonition of the expiatory compact implied by her existence. She terrifies them like the gloomy visage of a creditor who knows no forgiveness of debtors. It seems to them, and not groundlessly, that the terrible poverty they conceal within themselves might well suddenly break through its shackles of gold and its wrappings of iniquity, and run weeping to Her who was the chosen Bride of the Son of God!

At the same time, an instinct inspired from Below warns them against *contagion*. These detestable creatures sense the fact that Poverty is the very Face of Christ, the Face that was spat upon, that put to flight the Prince of this world, and in the presence of which it is not possible to devour the hearts of the poor to the sound of flutes and oboes. They feel that the propinquity of Poverty is dangerous, that the lamps smoke when she draws near, that the candles on their banqueting tables take on the appearance of funeral tapers, and that all pleasure succumbs —that is the contagion of the Divine Sorrows. . . .

To use a trite platitude disconcerting in its profundity, the poor *bring bad luck*, in the same sense in which the King of the Poor declared that He came " to bring a sword ". An imminent and inevitably terrible tribulation is incurred by the man of pleasure the fringe of whose garment a poor man has touched, who has looked into a poor man's eye, face to face.

That is why the world is so filled with walls, from the Tower in the Bible that was to have reached up to Heaven —a Tower so famous that the Lord " came down " to see it more closely—and which was doubtless being built to keep away, to all eternity, those naked and homeless Angels who were already wandering about on the earth.

CHAPTER XXXVII

FIVE years have passed. Clotilde is now Léopold's wife.
Gacougnol is dead. Marchenoir is dead. A little child
is dead. And what horrible deaths!

While she waits for her husband, her dear husband whom
she reproaches herself for loving as much as God, she is
reading the Lives of the Saints. Her preference is for
those who shed their blood, who endured horrible tortures.
These stories of martyrs overcome her with power and
sadness, especially when she has the luck to light upon
some of those candid fragments of their *True Acts*, such
as the narrative of St. Perpetua, or the famous letter from
the Churches of Vienna and Lyon, preserved by miracle
from the diabolical confectionery-factory of the abridg-
ment-mongers.

Then she feels as if supported by a column, and able
to look back.

At this moment she is just closing her book, blinded
with weeping, her face all tears. No—she has not
changed. Still the same " autumn sky " as of old, with
the beginning of twilight, a sky of rain and a dying sun.
But she is more *like herself*. By dint of suffering she has
so conquered her *identity* that, sometimes, in the street,
very small children and young babies will stretch out
their arms to her, as if they recognised her as somebody
they knew. . . .

How many things have happened in so little time!

There is one terrible minute which will always press on
her heart, to the moment when the holy words of the

death-bed are recited to her, which deliver the soul from the weight of minutes and of hours that presses upon it : *Profiscere, anima Christiana, de hoc mundo!* Unceasingly, she sees poor Gacougnol dying, brutally slain by her mother's abominable companion.

From the Church at Grenelle, where she was waiting for his return, a premonition had suddenly driven her out into the street, as if dragged by the hair by the Angel who came to Habbacuc. In a few moments she had reached the murderer's dwelling, before which there was a crowd already milling, and her benefactor had appeared before her, carried out by two men, with a knife right through his chest, and with the same face as in her dream. They had not yet dared to pull out the weapon, which had been driven very deeply in.

All that had followed after this seemed to her like another dream. The four days the wounded man's death-agony had lasted, his death, his burial ; then the trial of Chapuis and of his woman, at which Clotilde had had to appear as a witness, though she was almost totally unable to articulate a word, such was the paralysing effect of seeing her mother more alive and more audaciously sanctimonious than ever. She could remember, how, as long as the legal arguments had gone on, she could hear, like a bell ringing in her ear, the victim's words, " *Your mother is no more dying than I am——*"

The blood-stained toper had escaped the Guillotine only by the sense of equity possessed by certain jurors who were wine-shop keepers, and who had admitted the extenuating circumstance of alcoholism, pleaded by a counsel of Polish extraction, and he had been sent to sober up in a life-long sentence at the galleys.

As to the canting woman, she was now consummating her martyrdom in the claustral, " dim, religious light " of a gaol cell, not far away from the dignified and poetical Mlle. Séchoir, who had been betrayed by letters found among the old harpy's rags, and had been convicted of conspiring against her boarder in preparing the trap into which Gacougnol had fallen.

The preliminary hearing of the case had brought to light the devilish, almost incredible plot for a *rape*, which the scale-maker, in his vaunted gallantry, had undertaken to effect himself, with an incomparable virtuosity.

There was no other obvious design. They simply aimed at overwhelming the unhappy girl in the deepest despair, killing her with horror, relying on their assurance that she would not dare to denounce her mother.

For three weeks the papers had let loose this torrent of filth. Clotilde, broken down with grief, had seen herself compelled to submit (by way of overweight) to the wounding pity of the journalists, who wept, by the banks of Parisian News's Nile, over the misfortunes of the " exquisite mistress " of Pélopidas Gacougnol, who was at last described as " the celebrated ".

His poor, ridiculous name, which for her alone was a synonym for the Infinite Mercy, had been profaned on *her* account by those unclean dogs.

But, since it was necessary that all things should be exceptional in the case of a poor woman consecrated to the flames, there had been something else, also.

About two hours before his death, Gacougnol, awakening from a long coma, during which Extreme Unction had been administered to him, had suddenly inquired about her. Léopold and Marchenoir, who never left his room, had told him, in reply, that the Examining Magistrate had summoned her before him in haste.

" Poor girl! " said Gacougnol. " I should have liked her saintly face here at the last. But I don't want to leave her unprovided for. Give me some paper, dear friends— I'm going to write a bit of a will."

And he had actually found the strength to write for a few minutes, then, indifferent henceforth to terrestrial things, he had begun gently forcing his way through the pallid portals. . . .

The will had been adjudged INDECIPHERABLE!

A hitherto unknown brother, a virtuous magistrate who had arrived from Toulouse to take charge of the funeral, had grabbed everything, and not all the pathetic exhortations of the two friends, who informed him eloquently of the dead man's last wishes, had any power to make him relinquish a halfpenny.

The detailed steps in this drama had been filled with the uttermost bitterness, and now Clotilde found the whole sequence of events deep in her heart, lodged there as in a cave, whenever she might choose to look inwards into the depths. Nothing had been able to slay that dragon, not even her other sufferings. Sometimes it seemed to be swallowing *them* up, so alive was it!

From time to time her benefactor would appear in her dreams, as she had beheld him on the eve of the crime. Always with the same gaze of sad compassion, but without speech ; and the spectre would vanish immediately.

All she could do was to pray for the suffering soul, but, to her last day, she accused herself of having caused the death of the man who had saved her from despair.

And for what? Good Heaven! For what? Because

she had been afraid ; just that.   Because she was a coward,
an unpardonable coward!

She got up, flung her book down on the table, and looked
round unhappily. She saw the large ancient figure of
Christ in painted wood, a relic of the fourteenth century,
given her by her husband. There, only, would it be well
with her. She pressed her forehead against the hard steps
of the base of the image, and said, weeping :

" Lord Jesus, have pity upon me! It is written in your
Book, that in your Agony you were *afraid*, when your
soul was sick unto death, and you were afraid even to the
sweating of blood. You could descend no lower. Even
the very cowards had to be redeemed—and you let yourself
sink even to that level. Oh, Son of God who was afraid
in the darkness, I implore you to pardon me! I am not
a rebel. You have taken my child from me, my sweet
little son with his blue eyes, and I have offered up to you
my desolation ; I said, as in the Sacrifice of the Mass, that
it was ' just and reasonable, equitable and salutary '——
You know that I have no vain conceit of myself, that I
do truly look upon myself as a slight thing, feeble and
wretched. Heal me, fortify me, remove from me, if it
be thy will, the Cup of this bitterness—that Water, my
Saviour, that Living Water that you promised to the
Samaritan prostitute, give to me, that I may be of the
number of those who shall live for 'ever, that I may drink
of it, that I may lave in it, that I may be washed in it, that
I may be a little less unworthy of the noble husband you
have chosen for me, whose courage is sapped by my unhappiness! "

Léopold had just come in, and Clotilde had thrown
herself into his arms.

"My dear comrade! My beloved! Don't be sad to see me crying. These are just tears of tenderness. It grieves me so to be a bad wife for you! I was asking God to make me better. How pale you are, my Léopold! How worn out you look!"

One might, indeed, have fancied it was a ghost she held in her arms. This was not the filibusterer, the terrible bandit, the close-lipped fascinator before whom people used to tremble. All that was long ago. Something of great power has tamed this wild creature. Suffering, undoubtedly, and some *specific* suffering, in particular. Only it had to be that this potion, this magic philtre, should be given him by the hands of the compassionate mistress of spells whose captive he had become.

Unlike Clotilde, he had aged much, though he was scarcely forty. His hair had turned grey, and his eyes, strained with his work as an illuminator, had lost that disturbing fixity that made them resemble the eyes of a tiger. His countenance had preserved its energy, but had sloughed the " mask " of that cruel hard immobility, which had made it suggest the picture of a soul choked by despair.

" Don't worry, my Clotilde; thanks to God and to your prayers, I have nothing fresh to trouble me," he said, in a tone of voice that his old friends would not have recognised, so tender was it, so broken now and then by emotion, when he pronounced his wife's name.

He pressed her to him, as a shipwrecked man might cling to a piece of flotsam rendered luminous by the shimmer of the milky way. After a pause he said :

" On my way home, after going my rounds, I went in and kneeled at St. Pierre, then visited our tombs, and I have the feeling that we shall not be abandoned," he added, looking round the poverty-stricken room in which they had lived, nobody knew how, for some months. For they were very poor.

CHAPTER XXXVIII

THEIR marriage had been a strange and pathetic poem. From the day after her rescuer's death, Clotilde had fallen back into poverty.

A famous psychologist has pronounced his infallible decision that the sufferings of the poor cannot be compared with those of the rich, whose sensitivities are *finer* and who, in consequence, feel their sufferings much more intensely.

There is no disputing the importance of this valuation, worthy of a gentleman's gentleman. It is obvious to the meanest intelligence that the coarse soul of a penniless man, who has just lost his wife, is plenteously consoled, nay, let us rather say, is *providentially* succoured, by the urgent need to scrape together, somehow and somewhere, the wherewithal to pay for the funeral. It is equally obvious that a mother without refined sensibilities receives powerful consolation from the fact that she can't provide a coffin for her dead child, after she has had the encouragement, the marvellously efficacious encouragement, of watching (while herself dying of hunger) the successive phases of an illness which costly treatment would have cured.

Such instances could be multiplied indefinitely, and it is unhappily only too certain that the subtly sensitive wives of bankers and the ultra-refined dowagers of high finance, who are gorged on shoulder of lamb and delicately saturated with rare wines, while they read the analyses of Paul Bourget, lack the resources of such a spur.[1]

Clotilde knew nothing about psychology, and a long apprenticeship to poverty ought to have indurated her against all emotional afflictions, which are the exclusive prerogative of elegance, and yet she had the incredible presumption to suffer just as deeply as if she had been possessed of numerous packs of hounds and several castles. There was even, in her case, the monstrous anomaly of the fact that the pangs of destitution, so far from alleviating her grief, actually aggravated it to a ghastly extent.

Bravely, she set out to earn her living. But the poor girl was ill equipped for the undertaking. Her name, moreover, was scarcely a recommendation. She had become a " heroine of the criminal courts ", an appointed victim for prowling sadism. Moreover, she carried so clearly limned in her face the scar of her life, the massacre of her feelings, the wound in her soul's side——!

No possible or acceptable help from among her friends. At about the same time, Marchenoir was himself more hard-pressed than ever, struggling with the claws of the Sphynx whose breasts are of bronze and her ribs lean, whose riddle he could never solve, and who finally devoured him.

[1] " Paul Bourget! Alas, poor, starving strumpets! The unhappy girls who are ironically said to have gone ' gay ', wandering wearily about the pavements, seeking your food in the filth of the dogs! You who, at least, surrender nothing but your ravaged *bodies* to the wantonness of the ' respectable ', and who, some-times, have preserved some soul, some remnant of soul, to love with and to hate with—what would *you* have to say, to that paramour of unrepentant Folly's, when that dread Day comes, on which the Hecubas of the flaming earth shall cry aloud to Jesus their terrible miseries ? " Léon Bloy, *Belluaires et Porchers.*

As to Léopold, a shyness that she did not understand herself forbade her to take any kind of help from him, despite his most pressing and respectful supplications. So much so, that she deliberately disappeared together, and the two faithful friends lost all trace of her for more than a month.

A terrible month, that—she thought it had been the wretchedest month of suffering of her whole life! Wearied of ever-vain approaches to uniformly vile employers, who never had anything but insults to offer her, she spent her days in the Churches or on the tomb of the unhappy Gacougnol.

Her face resting against the marble slab, and flooding it with her tears, she told herself, with a depth of feeling that could not but have seemed superstitious, that it was terrifying that the first man who had ever loved her as a Christian should have been doomed to pay with his life for that charity, and that undoubtedly anybody else would suffer the same fate.

That was why she had been so determined to fly from Léopold. In a confused way, she felt that there are some human beings, especially in the camp of the poor, about whom influences of evil accumulate and focus, by some unknown and unfathomable secret law of commutative justice, just as there are trees which invariably draw the lightning. She, perhaps, was one of these beings—deserving of love, or of hatred ? That only God knows—and she divined readily that the hard corsair enveloped in flames, whom she had seen in her vision, was only too disposed to make " contact ".

One day, eventually—it was July 14th, 1880—she sat down, exhausted, on a bench in the Luxembourg Gardens.

The night before she had paid her last few coppers away to the keeper of a lodging house of the lowest grade, and she had no longer the means to buy the piece of bread she commonly ate in the street. Scarcely clothed; for she had retained nothing but the merest necessities from the two or three outfits given her by her dead friend; without, now, any shelter; and without food—she saw herself now delivered up into the hands of God alone—like a Christian given to a lion.

She had just been at the Church of St. Sulpice, taking part in one of those Low Masses which, that day, were hurried through at feverish speed in all the Parish Churches, for they were impatient to lock and bolt their doors.

It was about ten a.m. The Gardens were almost deserted, the sky wonderfully soft.

The sun appeared as if dissolving, as if melting away into the soft golden-blue haze, that, towards the horizon, shaded into an opalescent milkiness.

The powers of the air seemed to be in league with the rabble whose Jubilee day that was. The summer Solstice tempered its heat, that six million hooligans might get drunk in comfort in the middle of every street, streets that had been transformed into drinking shops; the rose of the winds sheathed its pistils, letting forth only a gentle breath sufficient to flutter the banners and streamers; clouds and thunder had withdrawn, routed, chased away beyond the distant mountains, to the lands of nations who knew not " liberty ", so that the bombs and petards of the firework celebrations for the Assassins' Anniversary might be the only things heard within the territory of the Republic.

This Holiday—truly National, like the idiocy and degradation of France—has nothing to vie with it in the folly of mankind, and will certainly never be surpassed by any other hysterical madness.

The lamentable annual hullabaloos that have succeeded to that first anniversary can give no idea what it was like. They lack the blessing of the Infernal Powers. They have ceased to be activated, energised and motived, by that power *foreign to mankind* which God occasionally, for a brief space, releases onto a nation, and which might be called the Enthusiasm of Baseness.

Let us just recollect that hysteria, that frenzy, naked and shameless, that lasted all that week ; that raging mania of illuminations and flags, even to the very garrets where famine crouched ; those fathers and mothers making their children kneel to the plaster-pallid bust of a hussy in a Phrygian bonnet, which was to be seen everywhere ; and the loathsome tyranny of a mob threatened by no forces of discipline or repression.

On other occasions of public rejoicing, at the reception offered to an emperor, for instance, with the proudest republicans throwing themselves under the chariot wheels of the potentate, it is easy to note how everybody lies, lies horribly, for all he is worth, to other people and to himself.

But on this occasion we were confronted with the ghastliest universal candour. While they glorified, with such apotheoses as had hitherto been unheard of, the foulest of unclean victories, that newly conquered multitude persuaded themselves, actually, that they were accomplishing a great thing, and the rare protests were so mute, so indistinct, so drowned in the torrent, that doubtless there was none who could hear them, save the great Archangel leaning on his sword, the Protector, despite everything, of the parricide Child of Kings!

Clotilde gazed at these things, as a dying animal might gaze at a halo round the moon. In the state of torpor to which she was reduced by the exhaustion of her body and mind, she began day-dreaming of a religious joyousness suddenly precipitated on the vast city. Those flags and streamers, floral decorations, triumphal arches, fountains of coloured fire, lighting up the twilight, everything, *all in honour of Mary!*

Certainly, at that time in the ecclesiastical year, there was no liturgical solemnity of the first rank. No matter, that morning the whole of France had awakened utterly holy, mindful, for the first time, that of old she had been genuinely, royally, given to the King of Heaven by one who had the power to do so; and at that instant, two hundred years later, France was compelled suddenly to give expression in a great blaze of light and sound to her delayed Hallelujahs!

Then, dismayed, with nothing within reach but the tokens of the Revolution, tokens of madness, tokens of idolatry, she had cast them at the feet of the Virgin of Consolations, just as ancient Christendom had been wont to cast down the overturned altars of the Pagan Gods at the feet of Jesus.

The Church would bless all these things when she could, and in whatever way she could. But the aged Mother's step is slow, and Love was so tumultuous in the hearts of those who *could* not wait, for that day had but twenty-four hours, and would never return, that unparalleled day on which a whole dead, corrupted nation was rising from its grave——!

A shadow passed over her dream, and the vagrant raised her head. Léopold stood before her.

CHAPTER XXXIX

Two cries, two human beings in one another's arms. Just an involuntary, instinctive movement, that could never have been foreseen, that could never have been prevented. Contrary to what one might have expected, it was the man who first regained control.

"Mademoiselle," he stammered, "forgive me—you can see, I have gone completely mad."

"Then so have I," replied Clotilde, letting her arms drop gently back. "No, though; neither of us is mad, and we have nothing to apologise for—we just embraced as two very unfortunate friends. Let me sit down again, please—I am tired. I was not looking for you, Monsieur Léopold—God Himself must have willed that we should meet like this."

Léopold sat down beside her. His face was more than a little ravaged by hardship, and, just at that moment, he seemed carried away from himself. He studied her for a little while, his lips trembling, simultaneously delighted and haggard—as if he were inhaling her like a perilous perfume. Finally, he came to a decision:

"You have not been looking for me—I know that only too well. You are in distress, I can see that, obviously—but why do you say we are *two* unfortunates?"

"Unhappily, I only had to look at you. And I was overwhelmed with sympathy, at once, and wanted to take you into my heart!"

She raised her eyes to his face, eyes transfigured with a glory. Then her lids drooped—her head sagged forward, as if it had become too heavy for her, onto the man's appalled chest. In a voice so faint it was barely a sigh, she whispered :

"*I am dying of hunger, my Léopold—give me something to eat.*"

To him who loved her it was as if all the azure and gold of the heavens had come showering down upon him. The gravel of the gardens seemed like a carpet of fire-shot diamonds strewn at his feet, overwhelming him. For a moment the mingled tumult of Love's Desire, of the Compassion that rends, of the infinite tenderness of Affection, blent into one intense focus, paralysed him, as by the striking of lightning.

But the fierce man who had vanquished the desert leaped to his feet in the midst of the lightning shock, and, with one bound, lifted the fragile form into a passing cab.

"Montparnasse Station!" he ordered, with so despotic a ring in his voice, so fierce a gaze, that the trembling driver, imagining a planetary conflagration, started off at a gallop.

An hour later they were lunching alone together, far from all the noises of that day, beneath a canopy of verdure. Thus there began again for Clotilde the sequence of incidents that had marked the commencement of her association with Gacougnol—but how changed the circumstances!

There was no need to say it—she had betrayed her own feelings spontaneously, and felt nothing but joy, a vast joy, a joy intense enough to slay!

Could it be real ? It had been sufficient for her just to meet Léopold, to know that she would never again belong

entirely to herself, for her to lose the fears, the premoni-
tions of evil, the pitiless phantoms that had so long obsessed
her. . . .

There was only one point, one vital, essential point, that
was common to the two adventures. A man, in both
cases, had taken pity on her distress. Only this time, here
in this pleasant, secluded spot, she was with one who
worshipped her, one whom she worshipped. For the
first time she was able to remember Gacougnol without
too greatly suffering. " My child," he had said to her,
" take with all simplicity whatever good fortune comes to
you." Those words, with many others, had lodged in
her memory. They shot through her mind like a flash
of light, while she looked at her companion, and it seemed
to her as if the subtlest essence of the things God has made
was flooding over her, to caress her, to intoxicate her.

As to Léopold, happiness had made him like a child.

" *You* are *my* National Holiday," he said, still using the
pronoun of formal speech—he dare not, yet, use the
familiar " thou " of French intimate address! " You
are the illumination of my eyes ; you are my ' colours '
of victory, for which I would die ; and your dear voice is
a flourish of trumpets that would raise me from among
the dead ; you are my Bastille——" and so on, and so forth.

" Blessed be poverty," he added, " the holy poverty of
Christ and his angels, which has thrown you in the path
of this tiger, hungering for you, which has compelled you
to surrender to me, without my doing or willing to do
anything to put you at my mercy! "

Clotilde answered more sanely, but with such a tenderness of love, such a pure, touching tone of joyous content,
that he trembled as he listened.

When the meal was ended, however, he seemed to come back to himself. Ever deepening shades of melancholy accumulated over his face. Very anxiously she questioned him.

" The moment has come," he said, " to tell you all that *my wife* is entitled to know."

With simple pathos she took one of his formidable hands—the hands that had perhaps killed men—and turned it over on the table; she buried her face in that hand, and bathed it with her tears, as if, without altering her position, she were offering herself as a ripe fruit for him to crush.

" Your wife! " she said.   " Oh, my friend—I was so happy, for a moment, just forgetting the past!   But don't you know, yourself, that the woman of the poor has nothing—*nothing*, do you understand?—to give you? "

With a placid, slow movement, he raised the weeping face, kissed her on the forehead, and said :

" That woman of the poor is all I ask, my beloved.   You have no confessions to make to me.   The day our souls first began to know one another, you bravely insisted that our friend should tell me all the story you had told him yourself, and he obeyed you.   You are my wife, I have said it, once for all.   But before we are blessed by a priest, you must hear *my* story.   If it seems to you too abominable, you will just tell me so, very simply, won't you ?   And I shall be only too happy to have had these few heavenly hours! "

Clotilde, her face cupped in her clasped hands, her eyes moist, her beauty like that of earth's first day, was already listening.

CHAPTER XL

"I AM almost famous—and *nobody knows my name*. I mean, my family name, the name that is *printed* on the individual soul, but is left to others when one dies. My friends do not know it, and Marchenoir himself is unaware of it.

"That name, a name that 'belongs to history', a name that is a horror to me, I shall be compelled, if we marry, to reveal it to the municipal authorities; they will inscribe it on their register, between the name of some poultry dealer and the name of some undertaker's man, and stick it up on the door of the town-hall. Thus the curious will learn that you have been crowned by me with one of the most ancient ducal coronets of France. I hope they'll have forgotten all about it within a week. Let that pass.

"Here is my story, or my romance ; I will put it briefly, without trimmings—there are memories I can't bear.

"My father was a brutal man, with a terrible pride. I cannot remember ever receiving a caress or an affectionate word from him ; his death came to me as a deliverance.

"As to my mother, whose features I cannot remember, I was told that she had been murdered by my father— kicked in the abdomen till she died.

"I had an illegitimate sister, a little older than myself, brought up from birth away in the provinces. I never knew her till I was already fully grown up. She was never mentioned to me. Our father, who could have acknowledged her, had taken it upon himself to deprive me of that affection.

"I lived, therefore, as lonely as an orphan, left to servants, at first, and then sent to a college where I was left to stew for years. Inclined by nature towards melancholy, such an upbringing was not calculated to give me a happier disposition; I doubt if there was ever a gloomier child.

"When I reached adolescence, I started on the razzle—the most idiotic, futile, joyless course of 'gay' dissipation imaginable, I assure you, till one day, marked out by a ghastly fate, I made the acquaintance of a girl I will call—well! 'Antoinette', if you like.

"Don't ask me to describe her. I believe she was very beautiful. But in her (and she was innocent, though encountered for my damnation) there was a perverted strength, a mysterious *affinity*, something that was irresistible, that mastered me completely.

"From the first glance that passed between us, I felt my feet fettered, my hands manacled, an iron yoke pressing down on my shoulders. It was a black, devouring love, torrentially overwhelming as a burst of lava in eruption—and almost instantly reciprocated.

"She became my mistress. Do you understand, Clotilde? My *mistress!*" the narrator went on, his face convulsed with agony, as of a seaman hearing the sullen menace of the maelstrom.

"Circumstances of a very singular kind, doubtless calculated by a demon, did not permit of our minds or consciences being troubled for a single moment by any thought but what belonged to our delirium; and that was really something unique, a frenzy of the damned.

"However improbable it may sound, we scarcely knew anything about each other. We had seen each other, for the first time, in a public place, where I had the opportunity of rendering her some insignificant service which I seized on as a pretext for introducing myself to her.

" Living almost independently with an old lady in her dotage, who called herself her maternal aunt, we had every opportunity to poison one another, and we knew no other interest.

" One day, all the same, the duenna seemed to wake up, and asked me, in a queer tone, to be good enough to let her know the purpose of my continual visits.

" ' Why, Madame,' I said, ' surely you know ? It is my formal intention, as well as my deepest wish, to marry your niece as soon as possible. I believe I know that she shares my feelings, and I have the honour to ask you officially for her hand.'

" The proposal was belated, ridiculous, and, from every point of view, highly irregular. All the same, I was telling the truth.

" At my words, she gave a great shriek, and fled, crossing herself over and over again, as if she had just caught sight of the devil.

" Antoinette was not there to give me any explanation, or to share my amazement, and I had to withdraw.

" I never saw her again, poor Antoinette! That was twenty years ago, and I have no idea to-day whether she is alive or dead——"

He broke off again, without strength to speak.

Clotilde came round the table, and sat down beside him.

" Dear friend," she said, laying her hand on his shoulder, " dear husband, always and in all events—don't go on. I do not need your confidences, when it hurts you to recall things, and I am not a priest, to hear your confession.

Didn't I say we were *two* unfortunates? I implore you, don't spoil our joy."

"I still have," went on the man, with authoritative insistence, "to tell you of the terrible scene the next day.

"My father sent for me. All my life I shall see the vile face with which he greeted me. He was a tall old man, with a complexion like beef-tea, in the sixties, still amazingly virile, and famous for prowesses of many kinds, some of them, I fancy, anything but reputable.

"He had fought in wars, for his own pleasure, in various countries of the world, especially in Asia, and was considered the most ferocious brigand left to us from the Middle Ages.

"The most salient feature of his character was a chronic impatience, a perpetual discontent, which became fury at the slightest opposition. As incapable of bearing with anybody as of forgiving anybody, he was covered with the blood of many duels, in which he had been horribly, and scandalously, fortunate. The evil brute should have been hunted down with dogs and slain in an unclean place. He displayed, too, a revolting Sadism. It would seem that ours is a bastard race, which has produced not a few monsters.

"All the same, I ought to acknowledge that in 1870 he died in a way that may have atoned for some part of his crimes. He got himself killed in the Vosges, at the head of a company of volunteers whom he led like a daredevil, and he is said to have sold his life dearly.

"'Sir,' he exclaimed, as soon as he saw me, 'I have the honour to inform you that you are a perfect jackass.'

"At that time, I was quite a fiery, dignified young cockerel

and such an insult seemed to me to be one that could not
be tolerated. So I retorted instantly:

" 'Did you send for me to pay me compliments of that
kind, Father?'

" ' I ought to give you a good thrashing for your insolence,' he said; 'I'll settle that account with you another
time. Yesterday you declared to a worthy person, who
deemed it her duty to inform me of the fact, your intention
of marrying, very shortly—and with or without my consent,
of course—a certain young lady. Is that correct?'

" ' Perfectly correct.'

" ' Charming! You would have the impudence, also,
to assert that this young lady shares your very pure sentiments?'

" ' I do not know to what extent my sentiments may be
called pure, but I certainly think I have positive assurance
of their not being scorned.'

" ' Ha-ha! Positive assurance, eh? Still, I was just
as big a fool as you, when I was your age. Well, my boy
—I regret to have to inform you that that particular tit-
bit is not for you. Here is a letter which you will, if you
please, deliver in person to an old friend of mine who lives
at Constantinople. I am asking him to do me the favour
of completing your education. You will pack quickly,
and start in an hour.'

" A spasm of rage choked me at hearing the object of
my passion thus spoken of; besides, though I could not
guess at that monster's real idea, I knew him too well
not to feel that the sarcastic tone he affected concealed something horrible, something unspeakably horrible—God!
How *could* I have guessed it? I snatched the letter and
tore it to shreds.

" ' Start in an hour! ' I exclaimed, roaring like a savage. ' There! That's how much I think of your orders—that's how much I respect your correspondence! Oh! You can murder me, like you murdered my mother, and have murdered so many others. It will be easier than taming me——'

" ' You son of a——! ' he growled, rushing at me.

" I had not time to run away, and thought of myself as already as good as dead, when he pulled up. Here are his exact words, his impious, accursed words, words from the Abyss :

" ' Do you know who Antoinette is ? You don't, do you ? You haven't the least idea, nor she, either. I AM HER FATHER, AND YOU ARE HER BROTHER ! '

" Clotilde, keep away from me, please—I snatched down from the wall a loaded pistol, and fired on that devil, but missed him. I was on the point of firing again, when a manservant, who had rushed in at the sound, grappled with me, and, at the same time, I was dealt a violent blow on the head, and lost consciousness.

" This story terrifies you, Clotilde. It is commonplace, all the same. The world is like those caverns in Algeria where the rebel populations crowded in with their cattle, and were smoked in with fires, so that man and beast, suffocating and maddened, should massacre one another in the dark. Such dramas as this are not so rare. They are more successfully concealed, that is all. Parricide and incest, to say nothing of other abominations, prosper in the present world, God knows! provided that they are discreet and that they wear a handsomer seeming than virtue.

" But *we* were unreserved in our frenzy, and the scandalised world condemned us, for our quarrel had had ear-witnesses, who spread it around. But what cared I for the blame of a world of criminals of both sexes, with whose hypocrisy I was well acquainted?

" Two days later, I enlisted for service in the colonies, and no more was heard of me. Would God I had been able to forget *myself!*

" I learned that the unhappy girl, whose real name I have resolved not to utter, escaped into a Cistercian Convent following the strictest rigour of the Rule, and, despite everything, had been allowed to take the Veil there. Deprived at one blow of my sister and my lover, ghastly in their *inseparability*, there was nothing left for me to look forward to but an existence of torment.

" Turned soldier, I solicited all the most dangerous duties, in the hope of getting killed, and so being through with it quickly, and I fought like a wild creature. I only succeeded in getting promotion.

" One day, when that gnawing cancer was making me suffer more than ordinarily, I rushed off and hid in the depths of a wood, and, with a firm hand, the revolver barrel at my temple, I fired as one would fire at a mad beast. You can see the scar here—anything but a glorious one. Well, death wouldn't have me, would never have me. But I assure you that no wretch ever courted it more assiduously.

" About the beginning of that loathsome Franco-German campaign, I was made an officer by way of reward for an act of insanity. It was like this :

" A very deadly battery was wiping us out. With incredible, incomprehensible alacrity, I harnessed four

horses to an ambulance-tender that was waiting for a
load of stretcher-cases ; and then, with the help of a couple
of men spurred on by my own madness, I made each of the
terrified animals swallow, forcibly, a huge quantity of
spirits, and then, leaping up on the driving seat, and lashing
at their quarters with my sword, within a few minutes I
had reached the Bavarian ammunition waggons and
succeeded in blowing them up.   There was a sort of earthquake, in which sixty Germans left their carcases.   And
I, who should have been the first man to be blown to bits,
was found, that evening, just slightly concussed, under a
nightmare heap of horses' entrails, men's brains, and
bleeding or burning fragments.

" When the war was over and my father dead, I realised
his damned fortune, and spent the whole of it, without
keeping back a halfpenny, on organising a caravan expedition to the heart of Central Africa, in a region till then
unexplored, an especially dare-devil exploit that I had
long had in mind.

" What little you have been told of this, at Gacougnol's
—he always loved drawing me out about it—may have
been enough to give you an inkling of the whole epic.
Most of my companions never returned.   Once more,
Death, taken by force, with a fury of rape, mocked and
made game of it, just said, ' No! ' and turned away, grin-
ning at me.

" When I got back, penniless, I tried to cheat my vulture.
From an adventurer, I became an artist.   Such a trans-
position of my active faculties seemed radical enough, but
instead of evading the vulture, had apparently only aggravated its rage, when you, Clotilde, at last appeared on my
terrible path. . . .

"I don't know what your heart will decide, after what you have heard now, but if I lose you *now*, my condition will be a hundredfold more awful. Don't abandon me! You alone can save me!"

Clotilde had drawn closer to the unhappy man, and taken him in her arms. He slipped down to the floor, laid his head on the simple-hearted girl's knees, and his eyes, eyes that one might have imagined more parched than the dried up water-holes spoken of in Lamentations, welled over like fountains. Sobs followed—sobs hoarse and heavy, forced from the depths, that shook him through and through.

The woman of the poor, very gently, and without speech, stroked the tormented lion's mane, and waited for the first tumult of his weeping to die down, then she leaned over him, bending right down, like flowers whose drooping stems have become unequal to their weight, imprisoning his head in both her hands, and whispered :

" Cry, my darling ; cry all you can, cry your fill. Cry, dear one, *at home* with me, in the depths of *my* being, so that you will never, never want to cry again, except with love. Nobody shall see you, Léopold mine ; I hide you, I shelter you. . . .

"You asked me what was my answer—Listen : I cannot live without you, and I cannot die without you. This evening, let us go back, filled with happiness, into this dazzling Paris. It is illuminated for *us*, flagged and decorated for *us*. For us alone, I tell you, for there is no joy like our joy, and no Feast-Day like our Feast-Day. That is what I did not realise, fool that I was! when we met, a few hours ago, in that happy garden. . . ."

Unlike Léopold's formal French " you ", Clotilde had

used throughout the intimate "thou" of lovers. She
went on :

"And now listen, my love. To-morrow you are going
to see a poor priest I will direct you to. He has the power
to draw out from your body the old heart that has made
you suffer so, and give you a new heart in its place. And
after that, if you are very energetic, perhaps we shall
receive the Sacrament of matrimony before the last of the
banners have disappeared, before the last illuminations
are extinguished. . . ."

The couple, in fact—two whose likes are not seen—
were married a week later.

CHAPTER XLI

THE first three years were happier than can ever be told or
sung to any common instrument of music.

Léopold and Clotilde fused so utterly into one another
that they seemed no longer to have any separate personalities.

A melancholy joy, miraculously gentle and placid,
arrived, every morning, for them alone, from a strange
and unknown bourne. Leaving on their doorstep all the
dust of the highways, all the dew of the woods and plains,
all the scents of the distant hills, this joy would gravely
awaken them to the work and burden of the day.

Then would the soul of each one of them quiver, at
the other's glance, as an ephemeris may be seen to shimmer
and quiver in a beam of golden light. A wordless, almost

cloistral, felicity was this, by dint of its very intensity.
What was there they could have said? To what purpose?
They saw hardly anybody. Marchenoir yes, decisively,
giving battle for the last time to a poverty that had become
wildly savage through his many years of resistance, that,
after months of dire struggle, was destined to slay him
treacherously by the bank of a rushing river whose foul,
miasmic waves tumbled the carcases of those monsters
he had overcome.

Sometimes he would come and see Clotilde and Léopold,
his face ravaged with calamity after calamity, pallid and
dank, his head white with the spray of the cataracts of
modern Turpitude, but more intrepid, more indomitable,
more unbowed, than ever—filling their quiet home with
the roar of his wrath.

"Peter has once more denied his Master!" cried the
prophet, the day after the expulsion of the religious orders.
"Peter, 'warming himself in the courtyard' of God,
and sitting 'in full light', refuses to know anything of
Jesus when the 'maidservant' questions him. He is too
much afraid that he, too, will be buffeted, his face spat
upon!

"Oh, if only this Pope had the soul of a Gregory or
an Innocent! What a beautiful thing it would be!

"Can you see Leo XIII hurling an Interdict upon the
eighty dioceses of France, an absolute Interdict, *omni
appelatione remota*, until such time as this whole nation
should beg, with sobs, for pardon?

"Listen—it is midnight. Those bells are tolling, the
Church bells that will not ring again after this. The
Cardinal-Archbishop, accompanied by his clergy, steps
silently into the Cathedral. With mournful voice, the

canons intone, for the last time, the *Miserere*. A black
veil hides the figure of Christ, the relics of the Saints have
been carried away into the crypts. The flames have consumed the last fragments of the sacred Bread. Then
the Legate, wearing his purple stole, as on the day of the
Passion of our Redeemer, pronounces, in a loud voice,
in the name of Jesus Christ, the Interdict upon the Republic
of France. . . .

"From that moment, no more Masses, no more Body
and Blood of the Son of God, no more solemn chants, no
more Benedictions. The images of the Martyrs and Confessors have been laid in the ground. The instruction
of the populace will cease, the proclamation of the truths
of Salvation. Stones thrown down from the pulpit, a
little before the closing of the doors, notify the multitude
that in this manner the Almighty drives them from His
presence. No more baptisms, save in haste and in darkness, without candles, without flowers ; no more marriages
unless the union be consecrated on the tombs ; no more
Absolution, no more Extreme Unction, no more burial
rites! . . .

"I will tell you, from all France there would rise but one
single cry! Swooning with mortal fear, the nation would
realise that its very entrails were being torn from it, would
awaken from its abominations as from a nightmare, and
the canticle of penitence of the ancient Cock of the Gauls
would restore the universe to life! . . ."

His two friends poured the "oil and wine" of their
perfect peace over the ghastly wounds of the smitten man,
and he would go away blessing them. Clotilde kissed
him like a brother, and Léopold, anything but rich, helped
him a little with money.

Léopold would have given much to be able to withdraw Marchenoir from the unequal and deadly fight he was waging—the outcome of which could be only too clearly foreseen! But what could he do? He realised that ordinary considerations are valueless when applied as critical standards to the conduct of anybody so exceptional ; and his own path was too widely divergent from the other's for him to join himself in his destiny.

One day, one of the last few times they met, Marchenoir said :

" Nothing can save me. God Himself, for the sake of the poor quarters in His Heaven, must not permit me to be saved. It is necessary that I should perish in that ignominy which is the lot of those who blaspheme against the Gods of greed and impurity. *I shall enter into Paradise with a crown of dung!* "[1]

Amazing words, but they were a life-size portrait of the speaker, of that orator of mud and flames, and one that, of a surety, none but himself could have so presented!

A noteworthy thing was the complete and incredible transformation that Léopold had undergone since his marriage. His manner, ways, poses, his very face, had changed.

---

[1] Léon Bloy quotes this remark—which is historically accurate, by the way—for the sake of heartening a considerable number of his contemporaries who reproach him with being unable to write two lines without introducing a little " dirt ". Certain critics have even had the penetration to discover some in the *Chevaliere de la Mort* "—(*Author's Note*).

This seems an appropriate place for me (since the translator is to the author of any work as the jackal is to the lion, and should not be expected to be his equal in courage) to mention that, rather than be false to my author, or obscure the issue as between him and his critics, I have minimised, as far as my timidity permitted, the " Bowdlerisation " that suggested itself from time to time—but " as far as my timidity permitted " is a reservation which has prevented my being *completely* faithful throughout, even in the translation of the above footnote and of the word to which it is appended !—*Translator's Note.*

He had entered upon conjugal life as a corsair weighed down with his loot might have entered a money-changer's shop. He had tumbled out on the counter all his load of heterogeneous, ill-assorted foreign currency, coin disfigured by rust, other coin stained with blood, and had received, in exchange, the weight of gold that it all represented, a little rivulet of very pure gold, reflecting but one image.

A passionate compelling instinct to mould himself on his wife, and, no doubt, some interior conflict of his own for which she had been the cue, had led him to adopt spontaneously the pious practices of the Watchful Woman of the Holy Book with ever-kindled lamp, whom he had married, and, little by little, he had become a man of prayer.

Let who will or can be surprised. Léopold was primarily a soldier, of the order of those whom no man can kill. So God has to deal with them Himself, and He has His own way of dispatching them.

CHAPTER XLII

His own way. Assuredly it was no human way, and the word " miracle " might have been used without extravagance.

Léopold had been very far removed from anything of the sort. It is true that the proud exaltation of his disposition had removed him equally far from the antichamber or the stable of scepticism. He " believed "—believed naturally, spontaneously, without inductive reasoning, like all human beings created to command. His unreserved admiration for Marchenoir, incidentally, would otherwise have been inexplicable.

But the furious passions that had made him their stronghold from adolescence onwards, had only to show themselves on the battlements of his formidable countenance, to rout in disorder every impulse of contemplative recollection or compunction that might have tried to seek admission.

Delivered once for all by Clotilde from everything that could form an obstacle to God, he needed but to leave the door wide open, that door which had remained closed for so long but by which she had made her victorious entrance into his heart. Then, everything that could melt down the brazen images of the olden idols rushed into his heart with her.

It is related of the holy Pope Deusdedit that he healed a leper with a kiss. Clotilde had repeated this miracle, with the difference that she herself had been healed at the same time as her leper, and, from thence forward, they both of them had but one task—the giving of endless thanks, in the twilight of a little chapel of love, warmed by a stained-glass window of purple and gold, painted with the Passion of Christ.

As in the case of the Sacrament for the sick, a remedy, as the Ritual says, for soul and body, Léopold, blessed by the priest, *juxta ritum sanctae Matris Ecclesiae*, had been visited in all his senses, touched as by an Unction : on his cruel eyes that had not seen the countenance of Pardon ; on his inattentive ears, which had not heard the " groaning of the Holy Spirit " ; on his wild-beast nostrils, which had not perceived the fragrant odour of the Divine Rapture; on the "Sepulchre" of his mouth, which had not eaten the Living Bread; on his violent hands, which had not helped to carry the Saviour's Cross; on his impatient feet, which had hastened in all directions, except towards the Holy Sepulchre.

That word "conversion", so often prostituted, if applied to him, did not altogether explain the catastrophic change wrought in him. He had been grasped by the throat, by the hands of One stronger than himself, carried off into a dwelling of fire. His soul had been rent out of him, his bones broken; he had been flayed, trepanned, burned up; he had been made putty, made into something malleable as soft clay, which a Potter gentle as light itself, had remodelled. Then he had been thrown head first into an old confessional whose floor-boards had creaked beneath his weight. And the whole work had been wrought in one single moment.

"——Unknown glories, the light of the Eyes of Jesus, miraculous voices, harmonies that have no name!" says the Admirable Ruysbroeck.

Literature and art had played no part in this scaling of his defences. No, indeed! Léopold was not of the "precious" who suddenly discover Catholicism in a stained-glass masterpiece, or a stave of plain-chant, who go, like Folantin, to the Trappists to be "documented" on the Aesthetics of Prayer and the Beauty of Renunciation. He would never have said, like that idiot, that a funeral service had more grandeur than a nuptial Mass, for he was persuaded, in the deepest intimacies of his reason, that all the forms of the Liturgy are equally holy and equally powerful. Neither did he imagine that a particular archi-

tectural type was indispensable to the springs of devotion ;
when he was kneeling before an altar he would not for one
moment have dreamed of wondering whether the arch
over his head was Semi-Circular or Gothic.

He even believed, with Marchenoir, that Art had not a
word to say in any matter whatever, once God had manifested Himself, and his *natural* inclination was towards
a profound humility, as has been found to be the case
in the historical study of most men of action trained for
despotism.

CHAPTER XLIII

THE long awaited birth of a son marked an epoch significant for more than the definite abolition of durational
time, for our two tipplers of ecstasy.   They felt as if they
had only been married a few hours, and were amazed to
discover that they had never known what Love was.   In
the depths of both, new and deeper depths opened, which
seemed to them cousin-germain to the vasty deeps of the
firmament.

An analytical study of such intoxications of bliss must be
left to those young slippered pantaloons of literature whose
function it is to make impotent revelations of the human
soul to inattentive panders.   These two, greater, of a
surety, than it is permitted to be, in a state of society subse-
quent to so many deluges, seemed robbed of all breath,
pallid with solicitude, as they bent over a little pauper.

They named him Lazare, after the Lazare Druide who
has already been met with, whom Léopold selected to be

godfather, rather than Marchenoir, who seemed to him, after all, to be rather a gloomy tree to spread its shade over a cradle.

Clotilde, like a true daughter of a nation that was once Christian, refused to have anything to do with the idea of a wet-nurse, intuitively certain that a mercenary, along with her milk, gives a little of her dark or contaminated soul to the Innocents abandoned to her, when she is kind enough not to let them die.

Little Lazare, exceptionally vigorous and beautiful, was a glowing flower on his mother's bosom, and Léopold, who liked to work by their side, was convinced that an infinitely tender reflection of some unknown luminosity emanated from their presence and spread over his painting like a peach-down of light. . . .

The great artist's works, at this period of his life—his last works, alas!—showed the influence of his revolution of feeling, losing the violent hues, the savage clashes of tones, the sudden warring of colours, that had contributed such a striking originality to his more than strange illuminations.

Little by little, the whole dissolved, melted into a sort of tacky acqua-tinta, bounded by a rigid outline. Druide, one evening, turned aside from a leaf that the unfortunate man was showing him, pretended to be flabbergasted, and looked at Clotilde with eyes so haggard that she realised that calamity was knocking at their door.

Léopold was going blind; at the least, he was threatened with blindness.

Some time before, compelled to work through one night, he had suddenly found he could not see, as if the two large lamps by which he was painting had abruptly been extinguished. Attributing the phenomenon to the exhaustion of fatigue, he groped his way to bed, and, the next morning, clear sight restored, had just spoken lightly of the incident, affecting to regard it as a trivial matter not worth bothering about. In silence, Clotilde prepared for suffering.

And very soon, similar troubles recurred. A specialist who was consulted gave it as his verdict that all work at illuminating must be dropped, must in fact be given up altogether, under pain of total blindness.

This was a very hard blow. Léopold had a passionate love for his art, the art that he had created, had resuscitated, had forced to make its appearance again alive and young, when men had thought it so dead that its very memory was becoming obliterated. It was so completely his own, this painting that went back through the centuries and was like the dreaming of an infant sage!

What was he going to do now? For many years he had lived solely by his brush, and had never for a moment given a thought to " putting something by ". Ah, yes, " putting by! " The lower Powers, the drab and implacable Powers, of which the uniform baseness of the Many boasts itself against the lonely of heart, are unforgiving. They exact sure and deadly reprisals. When Léopold stopped painting, Poverty flung herself upon him, like a ravenous beast on a ripe fruit torn by the wind from its stem.

It became an almost immediate necessity to find another means of livelihood. A terrible search began. No more of that sweet seclusion and cloistral peace. This was the end of the pale blue velvet canopy, in the silent glade where the emerald and coral of the vegetation in a Book of Hours stood out with languishing sweetness against the gold of a Byzantine sky. Everything like that was done with, done with for all time. The soul must be plunged into the mire of monetary anxiety, into the purulence of egoism of those who had to be applied to, in the filth of hand-shakes.

The former Gentleman-Pirate airs of the undisciplined man who, in the past, had always seemed to be holding off his fellows with a pair of tongs when he spoke to them, had not been such as to gain him a large circle of friends. When they saw him down, he was met with grins or spiteful condolences. Certainly his manners had changed in a way that could only be called miraculous, since he had found happiness; but at the same time he so completely disappeared from sight that few people had any idea of the change. Moreover, like most famous people, he was endowed with a special " legend "—a sort of engraved picture so deeply bitten in by the acid of Envy that no transfiguration or transformation of the original could alter it.

For another thing, his marriage had scandalised the rotten birds and the fishes hall-marked with yellow fever, who, in Paris, promulgate the decrees of a festering society, whose ancient morality—driven out with horror from the lowest dens of prostitution—seeks its nutriment in the dirt.

He had been credited with taking the unfortunate Gacougnol's " left-overs ". A few amusing witticisms, in the style of " *sauce Léopold* ", had even brightened the gossip columns of certain papers that the recluse did .not read—very fortunately for the jesters, who were shivering in their shoes, even though they had carefully disguised themselves with borrowed pen-names.

The little family was put to all those shifts that one shudders at in the life of the poor; the sale, one after another, of loved possessions that they had thought they could never part with; the changing of some habits that had seemed to be inseparable from the very mainsprings of emotion; the gradual, painful demolition of all the barriers of intimate privacy, which the poor can never maintain. Above all, they had to move. That was the hardest thing of all.

Their pretty nest, peaceful and bright, near the Luxembourg Gardens, had been to Clotilde and Léopold a unique spot, a privileged place, the only address they had given to Happiness. They had furnished it with their emotions of love, their hopes, their dreams, their prayers. Even the mementoes of gloom had not been excluded. Worn away thread by thread, by a benediction that had come so late, the unhappy times gone by had there been interwoven with the new joys, like dream-faces seen floating over a wall in the faded tints of a tapestry.

And their child had been born there. He had lived eleven months there, the months during which their tribulations had begun, and his gracious face smiled at them from every corner.

When the moment came to abandon that retreat, the unhappy pair felt as if exiled from the Peace of God. An uprooting all the more cruel, in that the new shelter to which necessity transplanted them struck an ominous, as well as sordid, note. They had inspected it on a warm sunny autumn day, and had deemed it habitable. But the cold rain and black sky of the day on which they moved in transformed it, in their disconcerted eyes, to a damp, gloomy, poisonous hovel, that inspired horror.

It was a tiny out-house at the end of a blind alley in the Petit Montrouge quarter. They had taken it, in their hatred of the small flats available, hoping thus to escape from the vile promiscuities of a tenement house. Two or three other tiny shells of the same sort, inhabited by miscellaneous Saturnian, ill-starred clerks, at a few yards distance, displayed hypochondriac fronts " whitewashed " (in more senses than one) with blinding lime distemper, and separated from one another by the dusty vegetation of a suburban cemetery, its odour fouled by the vicinity of a goods station or candle factory.

A little middle-class township, with a pretension to the possession of gardens, such as are to be found in the quarters colonised by eccentrics, where murderous landlords hold out the bait of horticulture to trap those condemned to die.

These were welcomed on the threshold by every shudder the place could afford. Clotilde, trembling and appalled, promptly rolled her little Lazare up in a heap of blankets and shawls, with no thought save to protect him against the glacial dampness, the *peculiar* moist cold, and waited, in such anguish as she had not hitherto known, for the removal men to be finished with their work.

Alas! They were never to be finished with it, in the sense that to the last moment of her life the poor woman was to retain the impression of melancholy, sordid disorder belonging to those few hours.

CHAPTER XLIV

MISFORTUNE is a larva that clings to damp places. The two exiles of Joy felt as if floating in a limbo of viscosity and twilight. The hottest fires failed to dry the walls, chillier indoors than out, as in the case of catacombs and tombs, on which a horrible paper mouldered.

From a loathsome little cellar, that had certainly never been chosen for any generous wine, there seemed to rise at night black creatures, the ant-like life of the dark, spreading themselves along all the crevices and cracks of the geographical parquet of the floor-boards.

The evidence of a monstrous filth was obtrusively blatant. The house, deceptively rinsed out with a few buckets of water, when visitors were expected, was actually foul almost throughout with terrible unknown sediments that would have necessitated endless toil to obliterate. The Gorgon of nausea squatted permanently in its kitchen, a kitchen that only arson could have purified. From the very first, it had been necessary to install a cooking stove in a different room. At the bottom of the garden (and what a garden!) there persisted a heap of refuse that was terrifying. The landlord had undertaken to have it cleared away, but this was a promise never to be fulfilled.

Then, suddenly, the abomination. An indefinable smell, something half-way between the effluvium of a subterranean store of corpses, and the alkaline noisesomeness of a latrine ditch, assaulted the nostrils of the despairing tenants.

This smell did not come exactly from the latrines, which in any case were almost unusable, nor from any other precisely determinable spot. It surged throughout the confined space, uncoiling itself like a riband of smoke, describing circles, ovals, spirals, patterns. It floated over the furniture, rose to the ceiling, flowed down again by the door, escaped onto the staircase, wandered from bedroom to bedroom, leaving everywhere a sort of reek of putrefaction and excrement.

Occasionally, it would seem to disappear. Then it would be rediscovered in the garden, that garden on the banks of Cocytus, enclosed with a prison wall that was calculated to arouse a paranoiac obsession for escape in a bandy-legged Dervish who had become a knacker for plague-stricken camels.

None but the angel entrusted with the flagellation of souls could have told what existence was like for the stranded couple during the first few days.

An evil-smelling miasma is one of the harbingers of the cruel larvae of the Pit, when it is permitted to them to issue forth from their abyss, and a chill of dread accompanies it. Certain attendant incidents too terrible not to be real—followed, as they were, too, by such an orgy of horror!—made it impossible for Clotilde, in the first instance, and, after that, for her husband, to doubt that their courage was being supernaturally tempered by their falling into one of those accursed places, not designated as such by any fiscal survey, that are bestridden by the Enemy of Man, who takes his pleasance in them.

Little Lazare had seemed indisposed ever since the miserable upset of moving, so his mother slept alone, by his cot, in a room on the ground floor that had appeared less sinister than the other rooms. Léopold carefully closed all the exits and betook himself to a fetid cell of a room in the upper storey. Starting with their second night there, Clotilde was snatched from sleep by knocking, knocking of extreme violence, on the outer door, as if some criminal were trying to break it down. The child was asleep, and its father, whose even and sonorous breathing she could hear from the distance of his room, did not seem to have been disturbed. The terrifying noise, therefore, had existed *for her alone*. Frozen with terror, not daring to move, she invoked the pious souls of the dead who are said to be powerful for the warding off of dark spirits. The next day she said nothing about this, but that first visitation of Fear left on her a heavy load of anxiety, a trance from the catacombs, that gripped at her heart.

Similar " warnings " were given to her during the succeeding nights. She heard a panic voice crying aloud of death. Mysterious knockings, angry and impatient, resounded in the partitions and the very framework of her bed. Distracted, haggard, with the sensation of claws dragging at her hair, but dreading to share this first course of agony with her afflicted man, she got a priest of the parish to come and bless the house.

" *Pax huic domui, et omnibus habitantibus in ea.* . . . Lord, Thou shalt lave me with hyssop and I shall be clean. . . . Hear us, Holy Lord, Father Almighty, Eternal God, and vouchsafe to send from Thy Heavens a holy angel that he may guard, warm in his bosom, protect, visit, and defend, those who dwell in this habitation. By Christ our Lord."

The night that followed this benediction was peaceable.

But the night that followed that—— Oh, Jesus of exemplary obedience, Who didst rise from death and from the tomb, what a night of terror!

An inhuman cry, a moaning outburst of a soul tortured by the demons, brought the poor woman stark upright in bed, with dilated eyes, chattering teeth, limbs palsied to impotence, and her heart compressed, like the hammer of an alarm clock, against her ribs, beneath which she had carried a child of God. She flung herself upon her child's cot. The innocent had not roused from his sleep, and by the pale rays of the nightlight he was so white that she had to make sure he was breathing.

Then she was suddenly struck by the fact that for a week he had been sleeping too much—that he had been sleeping almost continuously, and that his feet were always cold. Stifling a burst of sobs, she took him very gently up in her arms and carried him over by the fire.

What time could this have been? She never knew. About her dripped a vast silence, one of those silences which render audible the tiny cataracts of the arteries. . . .

The child whimpered, a feeble whine. The mother tried in vain to make him drink ; he struggled, suddenly seemed startled and alarmed, threw out his tiny arms to ward off the Invisible, as do the mighty ones when dying, and his death-rattle commenced.

Clotilde, wild with fright, but not yet realising that this was the end, pillowed the dear sufferer's head on her shoulder, in a position that had more than once soothed him, and walked up and down for a long time, weeping, imploring him not to leave her, calling to her aid the Virgin Martyrs whose entrails lions and crocodiles had devoured for the amusement of the populace.

She would have liked her husband with her, but she dared not raise her voice, and the stairs were so difficult, especially with the baby to carry, in the dark! Finally, the little creature fell from her shoulder to her breast—and she understood.

"Léopold! Our child is dying!" she cried out, in a terrible voice.

Léopold said afterwards that the clamour of her voice had fallen upon him in the depths of his sleep, as a block of marble falls upon a diver in a bottomless gulf. Rushing down to her, like a projectile, he was barely in time to receive the last breath of that budding new life, the last unillumined glance of those beautiful eyes, their clear azure clouding over, glazing with a milky opacity that quenched their light. . . .

In the presence of a little child's death, Art and Poetry indeed seem like great helpless poverties. A few dreamers, who deemed themselves as great as all the Poverty and Misery of the World, have done what they could. But the moanings of mothers, and, above all, the silent surging in the breasts of fathers, have a power very different from that of words or colours, so completely does man's sorrow belong to the invisible world.

It is not exactly contact with death that makes men suffer so—for that punishment has been so sanctified by Him who said He was the Life. It is the totality of past joy that rises up and growls like a tiger, storms like the hurricane. It is, to be more precise, the memory, glorious and desolating, of the *sight of God*, for all the nations are idolators, Thou hast said it often, Lord! The unhappy beings made in Thy likeness can adore nothing but what they fancy they can see, ever since that distant day when

they ceased to see Thee, and for them their children
are the Paradise of Pleasure.

Moreover, there is no sorrow save what is told of in
Thy Book. *In capite Libri scriptum est de me.* Search
as one will, there is no suffering to be found outside the
scope of the circle of flame of the whirling sword guarding
the lost Garden. Every affliction of the body or the soul
is one of the pains of Exile, and the heart-rending pity, the
devastating compassion, that bend above tiny little coffins
is, surely, the most powerful of all the reminders we have
of that famous Banishing for which a humanity without
innocence has never been able to find any consolation.

CHAPTER XLV

THEY dressed him with their own hands for the final Cradle,
which the Word of God rocks gently among the constellations. Then they sat, facing one another, waiting for the
day-break. For two or three hours they experienced that
salutary paralysis of thought and feeling which is the first
phase of a great sorrow.

There was but one word uttered—the word " Blessing ",
which fell from the mother's lips. Léopold understood,
perfectly. " These are those whose raiment is not soiled
. . . they follow the Lamb Without Blemish whereso-
ever He goeth," says the Liturgy. Christians have the
consoling comfort of knowing that, above all, there are
little ones in the Kingdom, and that the voice of the Innocents who have died " makes the earth to resound ". . . .

Let them suffer what they would, henceforth, let them go crawling on all fours in search of their souls throughout the worst by-ways beneath the skies, nevertheless they had always the certitude that something of theirs, something of themselves, was shining in blissful glory beyond the worlds.

Day broke—a pallid, livid daylight that seemed equally to be of the dead, and showed them their loneliness. Nobody, up to that moment, had yet been to see them in their new home, and the few friends who had remained loyal were scattered far afield.

The sharpest anxiety of all that can pierce a father's heart suddenly struck Léopold.

" How shall I find means to bury our child ? "

In the whole house they could not have raked together five francs. He rushed off and begged the caretaker to take his place with his wife, and then sped away, running like a madman. Some hours later, furnished with a trivial sum, obtained at what a cost! he got back just in time to miss the comforting opportunity of assaulting and battering the Medical Inspector of Deaths.

This grotesque functionary, conjured up by his absence, was on the point of leaving. In him could be studied one of those dangerous, inexcusable failures, who would be too incompetent to diagnose a simple case of indigestion, but to whom the municipal authorities delegate the responsibility of legally establishing the decease of their citizens, who are thus sometimes doomed to awaken to a renewal of their agonies six feet beneath the ground. The undertakers, always ready with a jolly quip, had nicknamed him the " Executioner of the Fourteenth Borough ".

Clotilde had had the sudden vision of some sort of lawyer

or undertaker's mute, with yellow fat and rusty side-
whiskers, on whose ignoble snout a greyish wart, for all
the world like a huge woodlouse, quivered continually.

This bully, finding himself in a home of the poor, had
come in bawling, and, without even raising his hat, had
for a moment felt, turned over, with his defiling hand, that
pitiful little corpse, then looked at the mother—overwhelmed as she was by all the sordid horror—and uttered,
with a grin, these unthinkable words:

" *Ha-ha!   You're crying, now it's all over!* "

Yes, it was certainly a stroke of luck, if the dog valued
his skin, that Léopold was not there to hear that !

Immediately after this, with the authoritative air of a
convict-prison warder, he demanded to see the " pre-
scriptions ", doubtless guessing that no such documents
existed.   Clotilde, whose heart was right up between her
lips, managed somehow to summon up enough voice to
reply that as a matter of fact the child had seemed pining
for some days, but having herself several times cured him
of this or that similar indisposition, it had never even
occurred to her to secure the dangerous intervention of a
doctor, and, moreover, the final crisis had come in the
middle of the night, as such a sudden blow that it would
have been impossible to call on any human aid.

The man seemed irritated with this answer, and appeared
to have adopted the manner of the Devil's barrack-room ;
he spluttered various vague, but more definitely insolent,
nothings, that tended to imply warning of a horrible suspicion, and was careful to make play with such words as
criminal negligence, grave responsibility, etc.

"Enough of this, Monsieur!" cried the Christian,
emphatically ; " nothing has happened but what God

has willed, and I have nothing to do with your insulting speeches. If my husband were here, you would not speak to me like that."

At that moment Léopold came in. One glance was sufficient. Without speaking a word, or making a single gesture, he turned on the ruffian a countenance so eloquent with dismissal that the latter rolled towards the door like a dirty bit of paper blown along by the wind.

At the Town Hall the Clerk to the Registrar of Deaths assured Léopold that the time of burial could not be fixed, as the Medical Inspector's report rendered an " inquest " necessary; another blackguard would be sent to hold this inquiry; he even hinted gracefully at the likelihood of an AUTOPSY! . . .

The second learned man, implored almost on their knees, proved a little yielding, and the poor wretches were spared that culminating horror. But, with that reservation, their cup was filled up.

For two days and nights they were able to eat and drink of their torment, and they were given that viaticum to keep for all the rest of their days.

Of the two so crushed with affliction, Clotilde seemed to have the more fortitude, and to be compelled to succour her comrade. The gloomy artist, the adventurer who had dared death in all its forms, the dare-devil among dare-devils, whose heart had never been known to fail him, had to lean upon his wife lest he should fall.

He remembered one gesture, just one gesture. The evening before their calamity, just when he was about to go up to his room, the child had turned away from its mother and held out one of its hands to caress him, as was its wont. But Clotilde, who had only just succeeded,

with some difficulty, in making the little one feed at her
breast, and was afraid of having his attention distracted,
had made a sign with her head to her poor husband, so
that he had gone away; and now the memory of that
childish gesture, of that last caress he had lost, tortured
him in a way that was terrible. For the human soul is a
gong of pain, on which the slightest percussion sets up
vibrations that continually grow, waves that spread outwards in limitless circles of dread. . . .

Pauper funeral—Bagneux cemetery—a common grave—
all this, and in the snow——! Only Marchenoir was
present. Druide, informed too late, was not to be found
till they were coming back. The four anomalous beings
wept together in the desolate, abominable, house.

Then, what we dare to call Life quietly resumed its
course.

CHAPTER XLVI

LÉOPOLD and Clotilde had been happy for three years.
Three years! That had to be paid for, and they soon
realised that their child's death was not enough. Reflecting that their share of joy in the unhappy world might well
have represented the delights of ten million men, they
wondered whether *anything* could ever be enough.

To begin with, there was that loathsome dwelling-place,
that den of plague and fear from which they were unable
to flee at once, where poverty condemned them to the
unspeakable atrocity of a *mourning of smell*.

Let us try to picture the demoniac horror of this thing.

At the moment when the undertaker's men were about to lay him in his bier, Clotilde had wished to give a last kiss to her little Lazare, whom no God's tears would restore to life; and the foul stench which had killed him, wafting just then over that sweet brow, had almost choked her.

Why, why, that hideous suffering? *Why* that affliction of the reprobate? Dear Lord! We would not refuse to suffer—but to suffer in just such a way as *that!* Could it be possible?

The inexplicable fetidity seemed to grow denser, heavier, more clinging, more intense. They found it everywhere at once. It impregnated their clothes, and followed them all over Paris, and neither rain nor frost could dissipate it. They began at last to suspect a corpse concealed somewhere in the thickness of the masonry, a conjecture rendered singularly plausible by the nature of the visions or nightmares by which Clotilde continued to be ceaselessly harried, when she was awake as well as during sleep. There seemed reason to think a crime had been committed there, the traces of which could be discovered by a search.

Léopold wrote a forcible letter to the landlord; the only result of which was the appearance of an extraordinarily repulsive rascal of the lowest type.

This man was a second-hand clothes-dealer and dry-cleaner; a lout with smarmed hair, who might easily be taken for a synthetic product made with quarters of Jewish meat, or refuse from a soap factory, that had been monstrously built up onto the foundation of a Parisian white-slaver. A horse-coper's huge, crusted, bull-dog pipe, and a whole boulevard pavement-stall of jewellery, completed his personal appearance.

This fellow found Clotilde alone, gave her a patronising little nod, without removing his hat, or his pipe, and rubbed his muddy boots on the floor, took a few steps into the rooms, puffed out gusts of smoke, and spat, gave the understanding wink and reticent smile of a cunning gaoler who knows all the ropes, and finally cut short the complaints that the poor woman, almost paralysed with disgust, was trying to thrust forward into the anteroom of his attention, with a peremptorily pronounced declaration that no tenant up to date had ever complained of that hovel, and, moreover, they had been given every opportunity of inspecting it before they signed the agreement, and that, for his own part, with all the good will in the world, he did not see what he could do.

A few days later, when threatened with an official inquiry, he condescended to send an architect, an impressive and polished personage who instantly cut short all questions and uttered a decision confirmatory of that of the employer who had sent him.

An application to the Public Health authorities, where his patience was tried by a score of office-stool dignitaries, distributed among a number of inaccessible departments, gave Léopold at least the satisfaction of knowing that he had nothing to hope for from that administration. He had to write to the Prefect of the Department of the Seine, on government-stamped paper, setting out to this exalted lord his grievance in lucid and respectful manner, and then wait, possessing his soul in patience—but paying his rent regularly and promptly in the meanwhile—until such time as it seemed good to the Prefect's staff to take some notice or other of the petition, after the lapse of an uncertain number of months.

The victims of the poisoning addressed themselves next to the Commissioner of Police, without obtaining any more consolation. The emissary sent declared that the smell of a corpse was a delusion. Possibly, indeed, it was not there on the particular day of the visit. Or possibly the infernal miasma floated very carefully round, and away from, this inspector, without affecting his olfactory nerves, as had been noticed on various occasions. In fine, there was nothing to be done, as the amiable landlord had pointed out, absolutely nothing, especially for poor people. Society is exceedingly well organised and subtle, and Landed Property is admirably protected.

An incontestable truth is that a Christian, a real, poor Christian, is the most defenceless of all creatures. Having neither the right nor the wish to sacrifice to idols, what can he do? If his soul is lofty and strong, the other Christians, bowing down to all the false gods, turn from him in horror. The infamous deities stare at him with their brazen faces, and the renegades, humiliated by his constancy, clamour for him to be thrown to the beasts. If he stretch out a hand to beg an alms, that hand is plunged into the furnace. . . .

Léopold, fallen from the pedestal of his art, could not escape the sewer into which that fall precipitated him. People thrust him deeper and deeper down into it. As he tried to get onto his knees, to suffer better, former friends would trample on him, heap up the filth over him, and triumphal chariots were driven past him, wherein the pimps and prostitutes of society rode in their glory. Then they accused him of idleness, of " scatology ", of— ingratitude.

He found by experience the truth of that law, always

unbelievable and always proclaimed, that an artist is invariably hated in exact proportion to his greatness, and that if his strength gives out, when the baying pack are hunting him, he won't even find a plough-boy generous enough to refrain from stretching out his plough-share to trip him up. The Great Holiday of mankind is to see the death of whatever does not seem mortal.

He tried innumerable occupations—an unhappy man in whose soul all the luminaries of the Middle Ages still scintillated! The Unseen Ones who give to drink to those left to die alone, were witnesses to his endless search.

He realised, then, exactly what the famous tribulation of Marchenoir might have been. Marchenoir's whole life had been spent pulling on the oars of that galley, and he, one of the loftiest writers of his century, was to die without having received or solicited from his boldest contemporaries the restorative tonic of a single teaspoonful of justice.

The illuminator had been indebted to the writer for a few of his finest inspirations. Above all, it was largely he whom he had to thank for his becoming deeply Christian, and because he tried to see God face to face, he desired to be moulded into the likeness of that martyr.

On her side, Clotilde had found some life-destroying needlework to do, filthily underpaid, and so, with each other's help, they managed to subsist, with no prospects, in a life of rigorous austerity.

" The foxes have their lairs," said the Word ; the lowest depth of poverty, undoubtedly, is the having no place that can be regarded as a domicile. When the burden of the day has been too crushingly heavy, when the spirit and the flesh are exhausted, and by dint of suffering one has perceived the *real* abomination of this world, the

spectacle of the horrified Seraphim, then how sweet a
refreshment it is to withdraw into some place where one
is truly at home, truly alone, truly isolated, where one
can take off the suffocating mask required by the world's
indifference, close one's door, and clasp the hand of one's
sorrow, hug it long to one's breast, sheltered by those
kindly walls which hide one's tears! This consolation
of the poorest was forbidden to our two wretched ones.

"My dear," said Léopold, one evening, to his wife,
who had been unable to suppress a fit of sobbing. "I
can read your thoughts. Don't deny it. A few words
you have let fall have shown me what was in your mind,
long ago. You are blaming yourself as one who is fatal
to all who love you, are you not? I do not know whether
such a fear is lawful for a Christian who daily receives the
Body of her Judge; no, really, I do not know; and
possibly the wisest do not know, either. But, for a
moment, I am going to suppose it permissible. So there
you are, somebody terrible. Your presence attracts the
buzzing bees of death, your footfall awakens misfortune
from its sleep, your gentle voice encourages the asp and
the basilisk to join forces. On your account, men are
murdered, or go blind, or die of grief, or are prisoners
in foul dungeons—what does that prove, except that your
importance is great, your path a very special one? Why
should you not be, in virtue of some decree promulgated
before your birth, one who stimulates the action of God,
a poor little person who sets in motion His Justice or His
Mercy? There are such beings, and the Church has listed
a few of them in her Diptychs. They have the power,
unknown to themselves, to *mark out instantly the bounds of
destiny*, to focus and condense, with the pressure of a

hand, with a kiss, all the coming events, all the possible events, that lie scattered along the road of the individual who is responsible, so that the flowering of that thorn-bush of dolours comes in one sudden burst of unfoldment. Before I knew you, my Clotilde, I thought I was alive, because it seemed to me as if my passions were something. I was an animal, nothing more. You have filled me full to congestion with the higher life, and our thirty months of happiness comprised what would not be found in a whole century. Do you call that being fatal? To-day we are called on to rise to a height that is above happiness. Do not fear—I am equipped to follow you."

Clotilde closed his mouth with her lips.

"You must be right, my love. I am ashamed to be so little a thing in your presence; but since you dare to claim that I have this power, I gladly imprison you in eternal life."

CHAPTER XLVII

THEY had to endure six months of it. First came the spring, reviving and expanding the pestilence, then the summer, making it bubble up and soar. An unclean, scabby, sickly vegetation made its malignant appearance in the garden, which swarmed with legions of black insects. Flowers, sown long ago by hands that were insensible to any valid blessing, hands that would have baffled the scent of a mastiff, swung over the narrow path blooms in which repulsive parasites crawled.

And then, as if all this were not enough, there rose up a

colossal, Babel-like building, suddenly, almost next-door. An army of masons who knew not any Holy Day sprinkled plaster all over the scene, in lieu of the disinfectant that would have been such a boon.

During the last couple of months eighty windows in course of construction, gaping in the impious walls by which the pitifully narrow strip of Heaven was daily more affronted, made themselves the insistent sieve for the spraying of suffocation and despair. Lime dust invaded furniture, clothes, linen, powdered their heads and their hands, smarted in their eyes. They ate and drank it. Any attempt to seal themselves in from it, whenever they felt for a brief time the strength to face the rushing ferment of decay indoors, was futile—that implacable tooth-powder slipped in by every crack and crevice, like the famous ashes that smothered Pompeii, and spread itself invincibly through the shuttered rooms.

The heat—extreme, that year—made their nights even more atrocious than their days. " Snow " lice—whitish, starchy lice that realised the ultimate apotheosis of horror and disgust—were now to be seen scurrying everywhere.

No cure for any of these ills, no complaint that it was any use making, no remedy or compensation to be looked for. That was common knowledge. The heroes who are producing buildings are, if anything, even more worthy of worship than the demi-gods who have already built, and the indigent man is a negligible bit of dirt between the two majesties.

The Deuteronomy of the Conquering Philistines, that Civil and bloodthirsty Code promulgated by Napoleon, simply does not condescend to notice his existence, and that explains everything.

Léopold and Clotilde fled as often as they could. They went into the churches, the only caves still left where hunted beasts with bleeding hearts can still take refuge. They walked in the sublime peace of the cemeteries, kneeling, here and there, at the ruined tombs of the most ancient dead, a few of whom, doubtless, had of yore crucified their brethren. Then, to delay as long as possible the hateful moment of returning " home ", they would sit in front of a café, and watch the ghosts go by.

More rarely, when a little money came their way, they would hurry off to the country, chatting and reading, for a whole day, in the most isolated corners of the woods. But it was soon time to get back to the stench, the suffocation, the sleeplessness, the terror, the nausea, the bitter grief and pain in the depths of a black pit, and their souls, garbed in patience, drifted in the shadows. . . .

Often alone in the house, Clotilde would dream daydreams of her buried child; with all the strength of her heart, she would strive to banish the exact picture, the terrible picture, but the obsession was too strong.

It would begin as a speck, a mere point, on the horizon of her heart, suddenly clutching at her breath; then, in a little while, her needle would slip from her fingers, her pretty head sink backwards as if in the last gasp of death, her hands would clasp and clench over her face; " *Fiat voluntas tua!* " she would moan—and her distress would be infinite.

If she roused in Him who watches the revolution of the worlds enough compassion for a flood of tears to be sent to aid her, and assuage her torment, it left her dazed, stupefied, hallucinated.

" No—don't go in that dark corner, baby darling !—

Don't touch that big knife, it might stab you to the heart!
—Mind those wicked men, who might carry you off!—
Come and go bye-bye on my lap, dear, sick, little love! "

Was she really pronouncing such words, or were they
but the recurrent echo of by-gone torments ? She could
never have said, but they struck on her ear like sounds
uttered by her own mouth, and the memory of that life
extinguished at eleven months was so inextricably blended
in her mind with the *lustral* conception of Poverty, that
she would see him about her, again, *five years* old—the
soul's capacity for suffering is something of which we
know nothing.

In the earliest days it used to be recommended, for those
undergoing torture, to invoke the Good Thief, and to
remain motionless, not to stir, not to move the lips, however great the anguish. But that, O God! is the secret
of Thy martyrs, the sacred method which is not easy for
Christians lacking miracles. The lot of the multitude,
surely, is to die of thirst by the banks of Thy rivers! . . .

At last, they were able to leave that ghastly place, to
leave the foul, fetid borough ward—onto which, by the
way, there had swooped down a colony of prostitutes,
attracted by the smell of death, to the great delight of the
landlord. This was the last straw, and the trial of their
fortitude had become impossible by reason of its very
excess.

An unlooked for payment of an old debt gave them just
sufficient money to enable the couple orphaned of their
own child to move out of Paris, and set up home in a
very modest cottage in Parc-La-Vallière, where for some
days they could breathe in peace.

CHAPTER XLVIII

So now their life was changed. No more nightmares, no more infection, no more vermin. They had come out from the cloud of plaster. But what still remained was quite enough for anybody to succumb.

At the point of this only too truthful narrative where, a little while back, it took up their lives once more, when Clotilde, on her knees, was waiting for her dear husband, and weeping at the feet of the great crucifix, the only object of any value that they still possessed, she had doubtless been seeing again in the torrential, synoptic, illumination of thought, what has been here told in so many words. She had even seen the whole sequence, we may be sure, in a more poignant and more detailed way.

But the bitterness of it might not have been entirely without a certain sweetness, if the present condition had been less hard, and the immediate future less terrifying. Instead of which, every peril threatened them. Léopold's sight became dimmer from day to day, and the Sphynx's riddle of their daily bread was becoming more and more unguessable.

On the advice of a publisher who made him tiny advances, he had just begun a literary revelation of his mysterious and tragic pilgrimage in Central Africa. There was reasonable ground for hoping for some success for this effort, but what a task for a poor man who had never done any writing!

His amazing wife helped him with all her might, with all the intuition of her soul, writing from his dictation, helping him to collate and order his material, sometimes pointing out to him luminous inter-relations of detail that amplified the episodes and gave them a general human interest, and showing an unbelievable quickness in establishing the line of thought by the expression, showing the narrator himself the suggestive effulgence of certain pictures he had himself conceived.

As far as possible, it was, after a new fashion, a continuation of his work as an illuminator, for Léopold ; he never ceased to bless and admire his wife. Unhappily, this labour of two children building a Pyramid proceeded with extreme slowness. Too often it had to be dropped altogether owing to the necessity of getting a scrap of bread somewhere.

They thought of consulting Marchenoir, who for some time had not shown up. They had, in fact, just written to him, when Druide came, in despair, to announce his death.

It was a tremendous calamity, an overwhelming blow for them both. And the pathos of his death, the pathos of it!

Alone, utterly destitute, without even having been able to get a priest, this Christian of the Catacombs had had nothing but a miracle to look to for any chance of being fortified in his last moments.

Nobody had had any idea of his danger, and nobody reached him till too late. There was none to catch his last words, his who had spoken so magnificently in life, to whom men had so obstinately refused to listen!

Slain by the direst poverty, he found his rest in the same graveyard as Léopold's little son, who had preceded him only by a few months, and the two graves were but a small distance apart. The hard couch of those who slept there was not disturbed by the footfalls of those who brought the new sleeper. Nay, for they were few indeed, but they wept in all sincerity.

That lofty, supernatural compassion, which assumes the remorse of the implacable ones, seems to be the most agonising sword in the human heart. Half a dozen prostrated souls, in silence, felt that day, with an extraordinarily deep realisation, that the only excuse for living was the fact of waiting for the " resurrection of the dead ", sung of in the Creed, and that it is indeed a vanity of vanities to go to and fro " under the sun ".

Where could the world find an intellect more omnivorous, more formidably balanced, competent to crush and round off all the angles in the table of Pythagoras, more fitted to vanquish what seems invincible, than the unhappy man whom they were carrying to his grave?

That strength which might have been imagined more than sufficient to tame all the monsters of folly, and the cetaceans of obstinate perversity, had been worn out by the sandbag-defences of filth and human offal!

Condemned to live apart from the world, he had lived outside it like the Turks outside Constantinople, a permanent and terrible menace to a decaying and foul society.

And now they had all been delivered from him, from this menace! What joy for those who were sold, for those who sold them, for the exploiters and capitalisers of the fortifications of conscience, for the " dogs who return to their own vomit, and the swine who, being washed, plunge again into their uncleanness " ; for the emasculated beasts of burden and transport-camels laden with

the goods of a nation migrating to the Pit, letting down
their laws and customs carefully by the snail-staircase of
the Abyss!

Doubtless, there would be illuminations. Why not?
He could at least be assured of a " good press ", at all
events, for the first and last time, that bold writer who
had been silenced by the coward silence of all, from the
proudest downwards! The rag-tag and bob-tail of the
popular rags would be able to rush at him and tear him
apart. Nothing more to be feared from *him!* The
archers shoot not their deadly arrows from the depths of
the grave, *they* have no use for the booming of publicity.

Léopold, mad with grief as he was, still reflected that it
really *was* amazing that there had not been found one
solitary man, among all who ran gossip columns, who
would spit back that injustice in the face of the rabble!
Not one—it was bewildering. Of the three or four around
whom there still fluttered a semblance of a something—
not one, not even one emboldened by drink or a crazy
bet, had exclaimed :

" For my part, I don't intend to be an accomplice in
this dirty conspiracy. I don't care if this or that rascal
may have been more or less fraternally gone for by the
man Cain, whom nobody could ever accuse of any baseness with his pen ; he was, after all, and beyond dispute,
one of the great writers in the history of French literature.
However much of a literary prostitute I may be, it makes
me sick, when you come to think of it, to hear nothing
but people whispering that a noble fellow who wouldn't
reverence our brothels must be stabbed in the back by
velvet-footed gangsters and trembling ponces! So I'm
going to give myself the heroic treat of speaking for

the man that our paladins and gladiators dare scarcely name under their breath! I'll even blush, if I have the power of blushing; and I'm hanged if I'll have it said that I waited for him to starve to death before I'd dance ostentatiously round his corpse, like the Papuan cannibals, who can at last pluck up their courage because he's gone!"

Druide, who laboured under the same distress as Léopold, suddenly recalled—there is no explaining how these things come to one!—a poem of Victor Hugo's that had once left him marvelling:

An astronomer forecasts a mighty comet which nobody will be able to see until, amid great anguish, it is seen by a distant generation of posterity. Mocking fingers point at the prophet as a dangerous lunatic, and soon afterwards he dies in ignominy. Many years shower onto his tomb. The poor man is now but a little mouldering heap of bones that nobody remembers. His name, carved in the stone, has been obliterated by the succession of the seasons. The worthy people whom he had scared, and who struck him down like a beast, now enjoy a profound peace, for most of them are themselves laid to rest near him.

But the hour, the minute, the very second, have arrived, that were calculated so long ago by that thing of dust, and, behold, the firmament is lit up, and there appears that monster of fire, trailing a tail of many billions of miles across the skies. . . .

If man is nobler than the universe, "because he is aware of his mortality", the sidereal analogy conceived in the brain of the glorious painter of the Byzantine populace is not exaggerated.

Certain works of Marchenoir's, given forth of yore in the chilly void, and deemed by the criminal lunacy of the times to be interred with his bones, were certain to blaze one day, and for many a day thereafter, into splendour in the startled eyes of a new generation, with the air of a formidable prophecy announcing the end of the latter days.

Only, when that time comes, it will not be within the power of any mortal to console the victim, to grasp in friendship that hand consumed by worms, to tender the electuary, the restorative draught, of kindness to those starving, golden lips forever silenced, to let those sad eyes look on the face of fraternal sympathy, for their very sockets will have decayed.

" Not do justice to the living! " wrote Hello. " Men say, ' Oh, well, of course he is a great man. But posterity will do him justice.'

" And they forget that the great man knows hunger and thirst during his life; when he is dead he will not know hunger nor thirst, at least not for our bread or our life.

" Ye forget that it is to-day that this great man has need of you; that when he has departed to his eternal home, the things that you refuse him to-day and that you will then be ready to offer him will be then useless to him, forever useless.

" Ye forget the tortures which you cause him to undergo, during the only brief span for which you are responsible for him!

" And ye postpone his reward, ye postpone his joy, ye postpone his glory, to the time when he will no longer be in your midst.

" Ye postpone his happiness until the day when he will be beyond the reach of your thrusts.

"Ye postpone justice until the time when it will be beyond your power to render it. Ye postpone the doing of justice until such time as he himself will be incapable of receiving it at your hands.

"For we are speaking now of the justice of men; and the justice of men cannot reach him, for reward or for chastisement, at the time for which you promise it.

"At the time for which you promise him reward and vengeance, men will not be able to be either the ministers of reward or the ministers of vengeance to the Great Man.

"And ye forget that he, before being a man of genius, is first and foremost a *man*.

"And the more he is a man of genius, the more he is a man.

"As man, he is subject to suffering. As man of genius, he is, a thousand times more than are other men, subject to suffering. . . .

"And the sword with which your puny hands are furnished makes atrocious wounds in a flesh that is more living, more sensitive, than your own; your blows, falling again and again on those gaping wounds, have an abnormal power of cruelty. His blood, when it flows, flows not as the blood of others.

"It flows with pains, with bitterness, with sorrows, with rendings, that are peculiar. It watches itself flow, it feels itself flow, and that vision, that awareness, have potentialities of cruelty of which you do not dream——

"When we contemplate this crime, from the point of view of heaven or of earth, we are confronted with the Incommensurable. . . ."

"*Et exspecto resurrectionem mortuorum!*" murmured

Druide, his cheeks streaming with tears. "Indeed and indeed, that is all there is."

Clotilde, remembering her first conversation with the friend of captive tigers, wondered whether the wild beasts might not be admitted to testify on behalf of their dead advocate against the terrible malice of man.

Such were the varying thoughts of the group, by the side of the grave where that madman, L'Isle De France, tried to say something—nobody ever knew what—and was choked with sobs.

CHAPTER XLIX

PARC-LA-VALLIERE is one of the dullest suburbs of Paris, dull and sordid beyond expression. Louis XIV's famous mistress really had a Park there, it is said; and it still existed as late as the middle of the nineteenth century; but by the 'nineties had left not a vestige or trace. The mangled estate was sold in innumerable lots to the eligible posterity of all the lackeys belonging to all the King's light women, a thick-skulled and money-grubbing lineage whom it would be futile to submit to an examination on the Attributes of the Three Divine Persons.

The obese village that has replaced the sumptuous droves of yore had become a nest of small landowners, packed like sardines, jostling each other so closely that it seemed impossible for them to make any use of their eggs and dairy produce.

Former servants who had become capitalists by dint of pandering to their masters, or petty tradesmen who had managed to retire after selling by false weights the goods they had hoarded up for half a century, they set, for the most part, an example of white hair and a few virtues to which they clung because from experience they had learned that they paid.

The remainder of the leading inhabitants were recruited from the clerks in the different Parisian offices, idolatrously devoted to nature, and finding an elevating influence in the odour of farm manure, who indulged in country rambles as a prophylactic against the painful afflictions induced by sedentary occupations.

Except for the acacias and parched plane trees in the main street, one would search in vain for an honest tree in this district that was once a woodland. One of the most characteristic signs of the lower middle class and the minor capitalist is their hatred of trees. A furious and watchful hatred, unsurpassed by aught but their well-known detestation for stars and the imperfect subjunctive.

The most they will tolerate, quivering with rage, are fruit-trees—trees that *bring in something;* but only on condition that these unhappy growths will creep humbly along the walls, and not have the insolence to invade the kitchen-garden. For your " petit bourgeois " loves the sun. It is the only one of the stars he will patronise.

Léopold and Clotilde were there, very close to the Cemetery at Bagneux, and in front of their house they had a few yards of cultivatable land. Those were the two factors that had decided their choice. Though deprived of shade, and roasted for most of the day, they rejoiced in getting a little fresh air and a semblance of quietude.

Just a semblance, alas, and one that was not to last long ;

for they had not reached the end of their troubles. They
still felt the weight of the Hand that bruised them.

At first, the neighbourhood was not hostile. True,
they certainly seemed to be very small fry, which is what
no community of lackeys and shopkeepers will tolerate;
but, after all, that might well prove to be no more than an
artifice, a refinement of cunning; the new tenants might,
in fact, have more " brass " than they " let on ". Then
the high and mighty ways of them both seemed to relegate
all those nice people, by comparison, to the dirt, and
disconcerted their judges, who did not quite know where
they were with them. They must find out something
about this couple, eh ? That was the first thing to do.
There would always be plenty of time to crush them. A
minute and cautious watch was organised.

It was under these circumstances that they made the
acquaintance of Monsieur and Madame Poulot. They
were the tenants of the house immediately facing them,
which looked on their garden, and from which their very
bedrooms were overlooked. Just nondescript mamma-
lians, Clotilde and Léopold imagined, who demonstrated,
however, from the first day, a kindliness of sorts, declaring that people must help one another, that union was
strength, that one often needed something from lesser
folks than oneself; that such were their principles. And
they did actually render little services which the confusion
of the removal made it impossible not to accept.

The two mourners, not in a condition to be dis-
criminatingly observant, were far from taking any alarm
at these attentions, which seemed to them very innocent
and simple, and at first failed to recognise the base vulgarity of their obsequious neighbours, whom they good-

naturedly credited with the possession of some slight but appreciable superiority over the dumb animals. And the neighbours so manœuvred that they contrived to invade, and to be admitted into, the home, even after the necessity of seeing no more of them had begun to make itself very pressingly felt.

The man Poulot had a " business office ", and confessed, not without pride, to a former position as Sheriff's Officer, in a town not far from Marseilles ; but without explaining the premature abdication which had ended that department of his services. For he had not grown old in the service, and was not now more than about fifty.

This good man was phlegmatic and heavy, with about as much joviality as a tapeworm in a chemist's shop. Still, when he had drunk a few glasses of absinthe, with his wife, as they soon learned, his high-boned cheeks would glow like a couple of light-houses on a stormy sea. And then, from the centre of a face whose tint oddly reminded one of a Tartar camel in the moulting season, there jutted out a bugle of a nose whose tip, usually veined with purplish streaks, would at such times display a sudden rosy hue and glow like an altar lamp.

Beneath it there shrank from sight a weak, flaccid mouth, shaded with one of those bristly moustaches favoured by certain bailiff's men, to give an air of military ferocity to the professional cowardice of their calling.

There is little to be said about his eyes ; at the best, their expression might be compared to that in the eyes of a sated seal, when it has gorged its fill and is giving itself up to the raptures of digestion.

The whole man gave an impression of pusillanimous humility, accustomed to tremble before his wife, and so acclimatised to the background that he seemed to be casting his own shadow on himself.

His presence would have been unperceived and unperceivable, but for a voice like all the outfalls of the Rhône. It sounded like a bugle on the first syllable of each word, and lingered over the last syllables with a kind of nasal bellowing that would have set a guitar on edge. When the one-time functionary of the civil power elected to vociferate in his own house some indisputable axiom or other bearing on the caprices of the weather, passers-by might easily have supposed him to be orating in an empty hall—or in the echoing hollows of a cavern—so infectious was the void and emptiness of his personality!

But, by the side of his wife, M. Poulot was nothing, nothing at all.

She seemed to embody a reincarnation of the most estimable "hot stuff" of the last century. Not that she was charming or witty, or in the habit of tending, with a lascivious grace, flower-decked sheep by any riverbank. On the contrary, she rather inclined towards the coarse and dull, and her profound and hen-like stupidity suggested a less bucolic flock. But there was something about her face and her movements that had an extraordinary power of lewdly provoking the imagination.

Fame credited her, as if in metempsychosis, with a previous existence in which she had been kept very busy, a career wherein she was much sought after, and it was said, in smoking-rooms and wine-shops, that she was still very well preserved, in spite of her forty years, for a woman who had gone the pace so.

It had needed nothing less than her meeting with the sheriff's officer to produce the sudden change in her habits which had been so mourned in all the houses of assignation and produced so many tears in the pleasure-resorts of the Rue Cambronne.

She went to earth for a few months with her conqueror in a den in the Rue des Canettes, not far from the last mortal remains of the illustrious Nicolardot, and then ended up by getting married at St. Sulpice, to terminate a delightful but illicit " regular " association, of which the transports were inconsistent with the religious principles of both parties.

Thus purified of their stains, and laden with a hypothetical bag of gold, they enjoyed at Parc-la-Vallière, a precarious and impersonal degree of respectful consideration, when they moved there a little later to extract all the honey from their honeymoon.

Such local consideration as they enjoyed, however, did not go so far as to secure them the entry into any respectable household. Mme Poulot could never get over the wonder of having *married* somebody, but no matter how constantly she might declaim " My Husband ", in season and out, on any or no pretext, as if those three syllables had been an " Open Sesame ", everybody still visualised her on her former beat, and her spouse's unsavoury profession was all the more remembered from the fact that every now and then he would be mixed up in some petty little bit of shady business.

With little vocation for the solitary life of a cenobite, the festering process-server's lady was therefore compelled, willy nilly, to make shift with the society of servant girls and cooks and the undertaker's concubines of the neighbourhood, more or less addicted to the glass ; and these she would generously invite to her place for drinks, with a view to flaunting for their admiration her "alliance" and dazzling them with the 25,00 francs her husband had settled on her.

Often, the Ex-Empress of the Bed would condescend, like a good housewife, to conferences in the street, with fish or fruit hawkers, whose mercantile ideals soared to the sublime heights of patting her on the haunches. That was her way of demonstrating to the proud her independence and breadth of mind.

With her hair down, her bosom open, bundled into a red skirt slit up at the back and flapping fanwise, negligently leaning on the costermonger's van, or even astride on the shaft, her stockings collapsing in spirals round her down-at-heel slippers, she would abandon herself, at such times, squalid and proud, to the exploring eyes of the populace.

Her conversation, moreover, lacked any veils of mystery; for she bellowed, if the comparison may be permitted, like a cow that has been forgotten in a railway truck.

The husband, much less on his dignity, did the rooms, did the cooking, blacked the shoes, ironed the clothes—washed them, if necessary—without prejudice to his disputable business, which fortunately left him plenty of leisure.

The newcomers, intent on healing the ghastly wounds in their hearts, remained for some time unaware of this idyll. They spoke to nobody, and had as yet met nobody but the Poulots, whom one would have had to walk *through* if one was to pretend not to see them. Then, like all fugitives, they imagined that they had left behind them the demon of their ill-fortune, and it had not occurred to them to foresee how he would hurry ahead of them like a courier.

The first thing you noticed about Madame Poulot was her moustaches. Not a virile, flourishing, triumphant bush like her husband's, but just a little smear on the upper lip, a suspicion of the delicate down of a newly littered bear-cub. It was understood that men had fought over it. The vigorous pigmentation of that hair was so well suited to the caper-sauce of her complexion, never washed save by the rains of Heaven, surmounted with a woodcock's nest of dark hair that defied the comb!

Her eyes, of indeterminate hue, and endowed with an amazing mobility, had a gaze which challenged all masculine modesty, and seemed to be forever offering mussels for sale in a stall of the Paris Fish-Market.

The precise shape of her mouth also eluded observation, owing to the extraordinary way that outlet for obscenity and shoutings would work and twist and contort itself to achieve those affected pursings of the lips and grimaces that characterised a public official's more attractive half.

She was, in her own eyes at least, the most exciting beauty queen on earth. Whenever she leaned out at her window, and gazed away into vacancy, gently stroking her plump arms the while, while her husband was washing up the crockery, she seemed to be saying to nature in general :

" Well! What do you think of me, you ? Where is that delicious little flower, that apple of love, that little imp of Venus ? Ha-ha! You don't know the half of it, you big ninnies, you clumsy brutes, you gherkin seeds, you! You just take a look at *me*, then! This is me, I'm telling you! This is the dainty bit of stuff, this is her boykin's little girlikins, this is the old boy's bit of fluff, this is! Yes, I can hear you, you naughty creatures. I can see, you'd

like a cutey like this! You could do with me, couldn't
you? Nothing doing! We're all respectable now, holy
little Virgins, now, my lads! That's hard luck for you,
I know. Just a wink of the other eye, and a little pat of the
handy-pandy, that's all you can have. Look, but don't
touch—that's the order of the day!"

Was she unfaithful to the happy Poulot or not? That
was a point that was never thoroughly cleared up. However
unlikely it might seem, the general impression was that
she reserved all her treasures for him. Such, at least, was
the opinion of the woman who kept the tripe-shop, and
the scavenger, well-informed authorities whose opinion
it would have been rash to controvert.

What was certain, was that the bailiff's absence, when
from time to time he was compelled to round up his
clientèle, caused her only a benignant sorrow that was by
no means incurable. She would sing at such times, with
complete assurance, certain sentimental ballads, such as
forlorn hearts usually delight in, in the shuttered " houses "
of their trade, such songs as, during the dull and idle
hours of the afternoon, the Ariadnes of such establishments
warble for the delectation of the passing valetudinarian.

With a great, generous, kind-hearted virtuosity, she
would open her windows wide and make the whole countryside a present of her nostalgic woodnotes. There was
doubtless a certain smell of the cooking-pot about " Love
Unrequited ", and a flavour of the dish-clout about " The
Pallid Pilgrim " ; and it must be confessed that there were
odd moments when some of her neighbours, in revolt
against the poetic, would get quite heated—but was that
any reason why other neighbours should be deprived of
it? A great heart is not to be muzzled, the gin-croak

knows its price, the blue bird will not permit its wings to
be clipped.

But whether she was alone or not, you could always
count on hearing her laugh. Everybody had heard it,
everybody knew it well, it was a laugh that was considered,
with good grounds, to be one of the curiosities of the
neighbourhood.

It burst forth so frequently, that obviously it required
less than nothing to provoke it—it was almost impossible
to imagine how such a cascade of noise could billow forth
from any merely human throat.

One day, for instance, the veterinary surgeon established
the fact, watch in hand, that the running down of the pulley
by which this remarkable cachinnation apparently worked
took a full one-hundred-and-thirty seconds, a phenomenon
almost incredible to any physiologist.

As to the effect on one's ears—who could say? Here,
all similes fail. It might possibly be compared to the roar
of a humming-top in a cauldron, but with an enormously
amplified resonance that it would be impossible to evaluate
accurately. It could be heard over the roofs of the houses,
many hundred yards away, and gave suburban thinkers
constant occasion to speculate on whether this exceptional
case of hysteria was a matter for cudgelling or for
exorcism.

As has been said, Clotilde and Léopold, scarcely settled
in, were unaware of all this. As if by magic, from the
moment of their arrival, the cry of that strange creature
became almost unheard in the land. All the same, the
Poulot couple, whom they had already had to stomach
several times, had begun to stink in their nostrils to a
remarkable degree. Léopold, especially, showed an

impatience that was almost tantamount to frenzied indignation.

" I've had more than my fill of that precious couple! " he said, one evening. " It's unbearable to have people one doesn't owe a penny to chasing one in one's own home in this way. I really think our last landlord was less foul, with his frank beastliness, than these accursed neighbours with their canting hypocrisy. Wasn't that trollop talking to you just now about her ' beads ' that she professes to be everlastingly reciting, because she saw a few religious pictures here ? I'd like to see those beads she's so devout over. Frankly, I can hardly picture them on that rascally frontage of hers. Why not just chuck the two of them out when they come here again ? What do you say, my dear ? "

" I say that that woman may not have been lying, and that you have never cured yourself of your violent ways, my Léopold. I grant you I am not particularly in love with those people. But who knows ? What do *we* really know about them ? "

Léopold made no reply, but it was at least obvious that the charitable doubt suggested by his wife had made no impression on him. She did not pursue the subject, but lapsed into a melancholy silence, as if she had witnessed the passing of gloomy visions.

CHAPTER L

THE next day, in response to a remarkably energetic ring, Léopold opened the garden door and beheld Mme Poulot, thoroughly drunk. There was no room for any uncertainty on that score. She reeked of alcohol, and clung to the gate-post not to fall. Without a word, he slammed the door to, at the risk of sending the tipsy woman rolling in the road, and returned to find Clotilde trembling. She had witnessed the scene from a distance, and was white of face.

"You did right," she said. "You could do nothing else. But aren't you afraid that these people will try to hurt us? They certainly could. We are so poor, so defenceless! It seems as if grief has deprived me of what little courage I ever had. I am terrified of that woman."

"What is there she can do? She is bound to realise that I renounce the honour of her visits. She will just not come again, and that's the end of it. If her sensitive soul is distressed, she can take refuge in booze, at home or anywhere else. I have nothing against it. So long as we are let alone. You can't imagine I am a man to let anybody pester us."

Vain confidence, vain words, to be belied in the ghastliest manner in the very near future.

From that moment, it was a one-sided fight. What could noble souls, yearning for beauty, do against the hatred of swine? Even the most decent people in the district—the very ones whose contempt the Poulot woman endured without putting herself out too much over it— because, in the words of a racy old market gardener, they were "up to their rumps in money", and the kind of good repute implicit in that posture was in exact ratio to her own ignominy—the pick of the citizenry of Parc-la-Vallière, would themselves have felt it an outrage for her to be defeated in such a contest.

Did not that drab of a Vestal, after her fashion, stand for "Universal Suffrage", for the righteous and sovereign

Will of the Rabble, the omnibus on the high-road, the sacred privileges of the Natural Man, the indisputable dictatorship of the Belly?

The instinctively sensed nobility of the new-comers was inevitably bound to revive the spirit of solidarity in the rabble scattered through all the varied stages of toggery; and the sympathy of persons wont to toss their hearts into the scales on their counters for the sake of giving fraudulently short weight in an ounce or two of offal or margarine, could naturally be ensured in advance for a draggle-tail snubbed by greater souls. They lifted their voices in one unanimous cry of denunciation against that empty-pocketed artist who was so brutal with women. From then on, Mme Poulot could do no wrong.

To begin with, she would watch for the times when Léopold was away, for his graceless roughness cramped her style. When she had made certain that poor Clotilde was alone, she would install herself at her window and lose no opportunity of insulting her. The poor woman could not venture into her garden, nor set foot in the street, without incurring some gust of abuse.

The bailiff's wife, with astute cunning, never risked any directly addressed insult. She would speak to passers-by, question them, consult them, spur them on to insolence by shouted allusions or insinuations. In the absence of any-body to call to, she would talk to herself, vomiting forth and regurgitating her filth to spew it out afresh and noisily, for as long as her victim was within earshot.

When the latter, determined to ignore it all, would bow her head, and, thinking of her dead child, pray for others who were "dead" without being buried yet, the creature would express her triumph in a fanfare of her maniacal laughter. A scandalous roar of cachinnation that awoke every echo and followed Clotilde all the way to the distant shops where she did her housekeeping—like a bellowing of cattle from some goitred valley colonised by murderers.

When she came back, carefully spied on, the shouting and jeering and laughing would be resumed with redoubled force, and it was a question for all the ruminating stomachs of the neighbourhood to chew over with the cud of their repasts, as to how long a defenceless being could hold out against those storms of uncleanness.

Sometimes some audacious street-arab would ring her bell and run away. What a treat, then, to watch the disappointment of the victim of the hoax, who would be disturbed in this way, as often as possible, when it was raining, and whose hurt face would reward the watchful cunning of the female tapir!

At first Léopold knew nothing of this persecution. His wife kept it all to herself, thinking he had quite enough to endure already, and fearing some outbreak of fury, some dangerous attempt at reprisals that would render the situation utterly impossible. But he guessed a little, and soon, too, the hostilities became so acute they *had* to be mentioned. There were now two female dogs of the pack baying at once.

Half of the Poulots' house was occupied by a sordid, repulsive old woman, threatened with general paralysis, who, in her Tour de Nesle, like another Margaret of Burgundy, regaled the appetites of journeyman-bakers and libidinous gardeners.

She was a widow, believed to be well enough off to be able to afford herself such tit-bits of the sort as she fancied, and habitually affected deep mourning in her attire. At the church she had a praying-stool inscribed with her name, and although she would express her disapprobation of such excesses of piety as were incompatible with the little consolations of the flesh that she permitted herself, she was a parishioner whom one could always count on seeing present at every solemnity.

Mme Grand, to give her her name, limped, like most of the women of Parc-la-Vallière, a local peculiarity which geographers and ethnologists have omitted to record.

She limped on an empty stomach ever since the day when, in the course of a violent drunken altercation, she fell from her window and broke a leg. But she limped more and better when she had been tippling in company with one of her chosen swains or alone with Mme Poulot. At such times she could be seen straddling frantically like a pontoon of rafts between cliffs; she looked as if dragging broken fragments of herself in her wake, mumbling the while muddled anathemas between her fangs. Impossible to imagine a more loathsome duenna, a helpless woman more calculated to estrange and stifle sympathy.

Madame Poulot and Madame Grand! Truly, the friendship of these two unclean creatures was never predicted by the Sybils. They had clawed at each other's faces in the past, and it was reasonable to suppose that their present interchange of smirks and drinks was only an armistice. Temporarily, the instinct to injure sufferers whose suspected superiority exasperated them, served as a strong cement to hold them together. The alliance of those two powers at once gave the vile warfare an absolutely demoniac intensity.

CHAPTER LI

On the old woman's advice, no time was lost in ferreting out information. A meticulous investigation revealed the whole past history of Léopold and his wife—that is to say, the whole of the legend that had long ago crystallised around them.

What a find, that criminal trial that seemed to have thrown them together, making them seem almost like accomplices! The entrails of savage janitors' wives thrilled to their innermost and foulest depths as they worked out the whole plot.

The bailiff got hold of the court records and the newspaper reports and comments ; caretakers and wine-shop keepers, grocers, fruiterers, charcoal and firewood merchants, were interrogated. Conversations were held with their last landlord—the man with the trousers—whom Léopold had often treated with very scant respect, so that *he* gave his former tenants a thoroughly discreditable testimonial.

Then the ruin of the illuminator was discovered, and heard opinions of his art were even canvassed, from which it appeared that he " lacked the talent necessary to make much money ". Without, most unfortunately, being able to probe his present means of livelihood, these were conjectured to be precarious and probably suspicious.

All this constituted a fine harvest, more than enough to kill them with. But what filled the Poulot woman's cup of contentment up to overflowing, what sent her back home one evening with the smile of a blessed soul who had glimpsed during an ecstasy the ramparts of Paradise, was the gathering of some particulars as to the death and burial of little Lazare.

All the rest was certainly not to be despised. But this was the tit-bit, the sweetest, most succulent morsel of all, the supreme goody goody of her vengeance!

In the most secret recesses of what it might be rather a daring figure of speech to call her " heart ", there writhed a horrid worm. The wretched woman, in whom was fulfilled that magnificent saying, " The grass never grows on a much-trodden road," could never get over not having a child to corrupt. Completely barren, she mourned the fact in secret, as much as any Jewess of the Old Dispensation could have mourned it.

Bedecked and bedizened with the utmost profusion of all those sentiments that are most in the mode for the rosaries of crocodiles, the very crown and apex of her good fortune, after having actually married a bailiff, would have been if she had been able to have by him—or by any other man capable of reproducing his species—any offspring to spoil and cram with food and doll up with gewgaws and dress up as a little soldier or a little canteen girl, to fill with all the moral infections and cankers of which she herself was full, and finally to hold up for the admiring envy of the multitude. The display of any such legitimate offshoot would have been, in her own eyes, the crowning, supreme, adornment of her status as a wife— a status which even custom had never succeeded in making credible.

Compelled to abandon this dream, she took comfort in a ghoulish counting of the tiny coffins of other people's children, and the bereavement of her unhappy neighbour was a Heaven-sent windfall for her. Then was accomplished a work of the Devil.

At the accursed window Clotilde witnessed the appearance of a tiny baby about the age of the one she had lost, held in the infamous woman's arms. Mme. Poulot was talking to it in the manner of a mother, prompting it to pronounce those words that grip at one's heart : " Come on! Say ' Dadda '! Say ' Mamma! ' " and ceaselessly defiling the child with resounding kisses.

Then the other window opened, the old woman's window, and she in turn showed herself, more hideous than ever.

" Good morning, Madame Poulot."

" Good morning, Madame Grand. Isn't my little boy pretty ? "

" He certainly is. You can see *his* parents aren't artists! Doesn't it make your hair stand up, to think of there being people that make them die, the little cherubs! "

" Oh, my dear Madame, don't talk to me about that! What horrible people there are in the world—you'd never believe! "

" Fortunately, there *is* a God! " remarked the old woman.

" A God ? Ha-ha, little they care for Him! They eat Him every morning, their sacred God! That doesn't stop them starving their children to death. I know some like that, not so far from here. The wife looks like a little plaster saint, and the husband's a penniless wastrel who looks down his nose at folks as if they were dirt. Well, would you believe it ? they strangled their little boy, between them, when they came back from Mass ; not so long ago, that was. There, my little angel, say ' Dadda! ' Say ' Mamma' ! "

"Ah, yes! I remember. Wasn't that at Petit Montrouge? People were talking about it in the neighbourhood. But the case was hushed up. The parish priest, who had a pull, made that his business, it seems. And I have heard say that the little woman used to sleep with the magistrate. The whole thing was pretty beastly."

"Ah, if that was all!" retorted the Poulot woman. "Has my husband ever let you see the old newspapers he has picked up when he's been cleaning out the offices? You know that painter who was murdered by his mistress —What! Didn't you hear of it! Why, that was the same creature, my dear Madame, with her ponce. They cut the poor gentleman up into pieces, and salted him in brine, like a pig, to send to Chicago, just like I'm telling you, my dear. They managed to make the judge believe somebody else did the job. A labourer was convicted in their place, a poor chap with five children who used to work himself to the bone all day to feed his family, and now he's at the galleys. What do you think of that? You're scratching me, you little darling! Now, say like me, ' Da-da-da-dadda! Ma-ma-ma-ma-mamma' !"

Though they were shouting at the top of their voices, Clotilde heard no more, that day. She only came to from a protracted swoon to find herself in her husband's arms. Shuddering with horror she reported to him the whole terrible dialogue.

Léopold went to the Commissioner of Police and made a complaint, and the commissioner sent for the two women, and then addressed Léopold as follows:

"Sir, I am forced to confess to you that I am powerless. You're dealing with a couple of hussies who are absolutely brazen—they are all out to attack you in every conceivable way they can, without putting themselves in the power of the law. I know all about the pair of them. I've got their records here—and they don't make pretty reading by any means. If we could once pinch them, they'd probably get it hot and strong. But first we'd have to convict them of some preconcerted offence. So try to get some witnesses and then lead them on to a well-defined slander. Then, we'll be able to get going. Failing that, I don't see what I can do, and these b—s are so sure of themselves that they don't care how cheekily they let me know it. It was all I could do not to have them chucked out by a few of the tough men I've got here. Ah, my dear sir, you're not the only man who complains, by a long way! Our duties are getting more impossible every day. We've gone a long way from the days when a magistrate could, within limits, make up for loop-holes in a legal system that does not take proper account of crimes other than those of a physical, material nature. The press watch every step we take— with how much justice, you know as well as I do. It's just asking for the sack to let them think we're overstepping the strict bounds of our authority by a hair's-breadth. I assure you, Sir, I have the utmost sympathy with your distress ; but I am just telling you how things stand. Bring me witnesses, that is all I can say."

Now, a witness is a tool that one must have always handy. Moreover, for lonely and destitute people, he is not easy to find. Druide was out of town, and L'Isle-de-France out of his mind. The two or three others on whom they might have counted were themselves in such distress, here and there, that it was better not to think of them.

Léopold bethought himself then of a poor man whom he had several times met at the church, and with whom

he had happened to exchange a few words. This was a
man with the absurd name of Hercule Joly, though a less
Herculean figure it would be difficult to find.

Extremely kind and extremely shy and even more
extremely bald, as long and lank and supple as a hair, he
spoke always in the most cautious terms, and the most tone-
less voice, as if forever whispering confidentially to himself. His eyes were a light blue, and not lacking in quickness
—but quicker, one would say, at expressing surprise than
perspicacity. He moved with tiny, quick, little steps, his
gestures had a certain fine bravery, his smile a touching
simplicity ; and sometimes he stirred abruptly like an
invalid enduring a sudden spasm of pain. Behind his
pointed beard he was for all the world like an old maid
hiding behind a horse-hair brush. Needless to say, he was
a bachelor, a minor civil servant, a native of Touraine.

The former explorer, who had a commander-in-chief's
quickness of observation, had at once spotted in him an
uprightness, a loyalty, and a kindness of heart, that were
unmistakable. So, the morning after his visit to the Commissioner of Police, Léopold took this man aside and briefly
explained the circumstances.

" I am applying to you," he said, in conclusion, " because
you strike me as having the characteristics of a Christian,
and I know nobody here. I must add that the foul and
criminal persecution which is likely to kill my wife, will
most probably fall upon any who help me with their
evidence."

" Sir," replied the other, without hesitation, " you may
count on me. I really think it is my duty to help you in
this emergency, as far as it may be put in my power to do
so. I should hardly be worthy of forgiveness if I shirked

it. As to the malice those two ladies may vent on me, I assure you it is no merit in me to brave the peril. I live alone, and any mockery or insults aimed at me behind my back have always affected me just as a favourable breeze filling my sails. Besides," he added with a laugh, as if to disguise a certain amount of feeling, " I am called Hercule, you must remember, and I owe a certain obligation to my mythological signature! So I shall have the pleasure of calling on you this evening."

On this assurance, he shook Léopold by the hand, and trotted off to his office.

CHAPTER LII

THE persecuted pair gained a friend, but the vile conspiracy was not foiled. Hercule, chained all day to the feet of the Omphalus of government, could only come in the evening, and there was no way he could arrive unperceived. It was impossible to ring Léopold's bell or stop at his door without Mesdames Grand and Poulot rushing to their windows. They immediately scented the purpose of his visits and carefully avoided any unconsidered word while he was there.

It was in this way that the worthy man earned the title of " copper's nark ", which at first seemed to amuse him, but which eventually compelled him to flee from Parc-la-Vallière, where this slander had been widely spread.

He turned up regularly for about a month, pricking up his ears like a hare, without obtaining material for a conclusive and effective deposition. Finally, realising the futility of his zeal, and fearing to become a nuisance, he stopped calling every day, and was naïvely happy to be sometimes welcomed as a friend. Anyhow, Léopold never met him without giving him a pressing invitation.

The lonely couple had taken to him from the first, and thanked God that He had put this simple-hearted man in their sad path. They found in him a certain spiritual and intellectual culture, that was very comforting in such a place; and especially, as Léopold had sensed, an upright, reliable goodness that seemed to shine like a diamond among the evil and malice of his environment.

This quality of goodness, almost as rare as genius nowadays, gave rise naturally to the most ingenious, the most resourceful, discretion. He had divined without difficulty the extreme poverty of the household, and, being a poor man himself, he exploited all the artful dodges of a Red-Skin Tracker to get them to accept, on various pretexts, little contributions of timely and useful help. The couple's table was often cunningly provisioned by him.

" M. Joly," Clotilde told him, " you are our ' Pelican of the desert '! "

He and they alike soon forgot how short a time they had known one another.

Still, the sluts' war continued, with even more unbearable virulence. The two women, enraged at their humiliating appearance in the office of the Police Commissioner, exhausted all the devices that a prudent fury could conceive.

Each day saw a resumption of the filthy play-acting at the two windows, a fresh dialogue, with strophe and antistrophe after the manner of the Classical Greek stage, and especially remarks shouted to passers-by, who rejoiced at the exciting opportunity of taking part in an attempted murder without exposing themselves to any risks.

Tiny little innocents, from three to five years of age, picked up here and there, came to learn from Mme Poulot the homicidal words presumed to have power to reopen and poison the terrible festering wound.

Whenever she got tired of the window, the barren wretch would make her appearance on the roof. This was arranged like a terrace, and decked out grotesquely with those wine-dreg coloured vases which a loathsome school of ceramic art chooses to multiply for the chastisement of mankind. There she would strut, dressed as already described, and often more than half naked, shouting to the four points of the compass that she was "on her own premises" and those who did not like it could just shut their eyes.

It was an excellent place for declaiming, for sounding her brazen trumpet, displaying those attitudes and postures bound to inflame the whole neighbourhood's concupiscence.

"That poor drab's case seems to me a very serious one," said Hercule Joly, one evening when she had made her laugh heard as he arrived at his friends' house. "She is a demoniac of a very special kind that must be on record in the treatises of specialists. Certainly, that sort of sardonic convulsion with which she is so often seized is expressive of something very different from any kind of joyous laughter. There seems good reason to think that the unseen entities who pestered you in your last home, must have taken possession of this bailiff's wife, to torture you *here*. The treatment for those affected in that way, I think, is indicated in the Book of Tobit—but it would need a more meet therapeutist than the wine-bibber she has for a husband. I am wondering whether a good drubbing administered to *him* might not be what is wanted to bring matters to a head with a very desirable reaction."

"I had thought of it," replied Léopold, who found it refreshing to hear such a suggestion put forward by a man so meek. "But the situation is such that I am bound to be afraid, in case it did not produce the desired result, of some abominable reprisals of which not I alone would be the victim."

Things had reached the point where Clotilde could not dare to step out of doors alone. Ruffians insulted her in the streets, and witty shopkeepers, standing in their doorways, greeted her passing by with whispers and sniggers. An oil-man with a gift for epigram and smut, distinguished himself especially in this direction. The poor woman could not walk past his verminous shop without his immediately embarking on a facetious conversation with his cronies. One day when Léopold was only a couple of yards behind her, the fellow was so imprudent as to display his brilliant humour without a preliminary survey of the horizon; and he was radically and swiftly cured of the habit. The "card" beheld the sudden apparition of such a disconcerting, nightmare-like, fierce Viking countenance, and heard a few words of such curt dryness, that he swayed and turned livid.

But the same thing would have had to happen at every door. Some incredible doom condemned these unhappy mortals, who asked nothing but solitude and a humble and secluded life, and sought for nothing from anybody, to be detested by the whole of the village in which they had hoped to find a refuge, and even the dirt between the cobble-stones rose up against them.

Clotilde went resolutely to see their landlady. This lady's dwelling backed on their own cottage, and one only had to open a wicket to be in her grounds. Consequently, there was nobody better situated to see and hear everything that passed.

Léopold and his wife barely knew her by sight, having had none but the most indispensable minimum of dealings with her in connection with their lease. They had retained but the vaguest impression of her as an incurably withered virginal vine-shoot.

Mlle Planude was a dried-up old maid who bore her sixty-five years of virtue with the utmost ease. She was as petulant as a turkey-hen and as bristly as a hedge-hog, with a voice like a sergeant-major's, and a habit of flinging her words out with the speed of a dried-fruit exporter terrified of missing the train. Slightly dwarfed, slightly hunch-backed, she was invariably in evidence at the church, where she would rush in as if fleeing from some wild monster, and whence she would dash out, every hour or so, to speed up a hired servant whom she was reducing to imbecility. She belonged to every Confraternity and Arch-Confraternity, meddled in every organised Good Work, took part in every propaganda movement, slipped little tracts into everybody's hands. But nobody remembered ever having seen her part with a halfpenny.

Her miserliness simply dazzled Parc-la-Vallière. Admiring voices would instance the strength of mind of this Wise Virgin—who certainly would never be caught squandering the oil of her lamp on sisters who had lost their way; she illuminated herself, exclusively, while awaiting the Bridegroom.

People gladly remember the lofty, affecting story of

that family of tenants—Léopold's and his wife's predecessors
—whom she had turned into the street with a vigour, a
serenity, a constancy, and an inflexibility, worthy of the
Martyrs. A sick and unemployed husband, four children
(of whom two died as a result) and a wife expecting a
fifth. The whole brood cleared out. She herself, on that
occasion, had likened herself to the " strong woman armed "
of Scripture. Undoubtedly, it would have been an easy
matter for her to be weakly sentimental, like some others
whom one must suppose, for the honour of landlords and
landladies in general, to be happily rare. She would have
been no poorer as a result. But such a course would have
been a breach of principle, and there are moments when
it is a duty to silence one's heart.

Mlle Planude would kneel at the Altar with a little
bag full of title-deeds, I.O.U.'s, and the like, suspended against her chaste person, along with medals and
scapulars.

Clotilde, who thought she had only an ordinary pietistic
woman to deal with, was pulled up sharply at her first
words :

" Ha, Madame! If you've come to bring me a lot of
scandal and tales, you're unlucky! I do not concern myself
with the affairs of my neighbours, and I don't wish to hear
anything of the sort. All I ask for is good tenants who
will pay their rents punctually to the minute, and not cause
any scandal in my house. If that doesn't suit you, you
are free to leave, on paying three months' rent in advance,
naturally."

Such was this damsel's first volley.

" But, Mademoiselle," exclaimed the caller, rather
taken aback, " I don't understand why you are receiving

me like this at all. I am no more fond of gossip and back-biting than you are, and it is precisely because I abominate everything of that kind that I am here. It is not possible that you haven't heard, that you should fail to hear every day, the horrible insults and continual provocations with which we are attacked. Naturally, I thought, being our landlady, you would not refuse us your intervention, or at least your evidence."

"My evidence? Ha! So that's it! You were depending on my evidence! Well, young lady, you can search yourself, if you wear pockets! Have me fetched before the Commissioner—me, as well—since that's your style, and you'll see what good *that* does you. If it is the people opposite you profess to have any complaint against, allow me to tell you, for your guidance, that they are reputable persons who have made some money, and don't owe anybody a penny. What have you to say to that? Besides, I know what I know. Your husband, I will take the liberty of mentioning, is a ruffian; he half killed that poor Madame Poulot. And it seems that your own tongue is anything but rusty, too. It's come back to me that you allowed yourself to use some very nasty words, not to mention that great eel of a man you have in to see you every day. He has a very queer reputation around here."

Clotilde got up and went—shaking off the dust of that accursed threshold from her feet by a purely instinctive gesture, as if the Counsel of Anathema in the Gospel were inscribed mysteriously in the hearts of mankind, along with the thousand and one other Words of the Lord " who killeth and maketh alive ". " Whosoever shall not receive you and will not hearken unto your words, on leaving his house, shake the dust thereof from off your feet."

"Oh, my dear," she exclaimed, when she got indoors again, "I have just seen the Devil!"

She fell ill and came near to dying.

The jubilation in the neighbourhood was enormous, and found expression like the programme of an ancient Triumph. Barbarian shouts, cannibal howlings, were to be heard all night long. Monstrous words, diabolical laughter, penetrated the walls and pursued the invalid into the darkest, farthest straits, frothing with giant breakers of despair, of the sea of her incipient death agony.

"Not dead yet in the Chapel there?" jeered a voice that might have escaped from the Pit.

"Waiter! A Pernod!" cried the bailiff's wife at the top of her voice, to her husband. "Come on, old Poulot. We're going to drink a toast to the baby-killers and tramps."

"Didn't I tell you there was a God!" croaked old woman Grand, in her turn. "Lord! When you've been killing little children, they sometimes come back at night to pull your hair——"

"Let's hope the corpses don't give us all the plague!" was the parting shot, in a resonant throaty chuckle, of the wife of a cemetery employee.

When a priest came, a little before dawn, to confess and anoint the sufferer and bring her the Viaticum, they did, it is true, refrain from any festive illuminations. It might even be said that the clamour was slightly modified. But as soon as he had taken his departure, the Poulot woman alarmingly drunk, began singing.

With the exception of M. Joly, who was present at the rites administered to Clotilde, and whose violent protests were greeted with sniggers and whistling, nobody thought to find the least fault nor notice any sacrilegious enormity about these outrages. Mlle Planude hurried off to be early at the first Mass, not without stopping on the way to inquire into the health of " that dear Madame Poulot ", who reciprocated her civilities, and the placid suburban sun rose once more upon happy vermin who asked nothing better than to fill their bodies.

Hers was a long convalescence, preceded and interrupted by frequent attacks of delirium. Clotilde had been very close to death, and the healing virtue—which people so completely forget!—of the Sacrament was all that had saved her. She related how she had seen pass before her eyes, in symbolic forms perceptible to the senses, and of the most terrifying kind, the vivid *malice* of her tormentors, whom she described—without explaining what she meant in any greater detail—as being infinitely wretched.

She avoided speaking, of them with bitterness, and ceased entirely to suffer from their insults, which, moreover, grew less and less at the same time as they lost their power to torture their victim, whose supernatural cure seemed to have disconcerted the slayers.

It was only now that Léopold, who had begun to look like a ghost, told her what he had ventured to do.

CHAPTER LIII

WHAT a position was this man's during those endless weeks!

A philosopher in Cambodia fed young tigers so that, when they grew up, they should not devour *him*. Reduced to destitution, he was compelled to give them pieces of his own flesh. When nothing but his bones was left, the noble lords of the jungle left him, abandoning him to baser carrion-beasts.

Léopold sometimes bethought himself of that pagan parable. He had decided that his former torments had been fickle and ungrateful indeed, not to have consumed him utterly, but to have left his sad carcase for vermin to prey on.

What did it profit him that he had had so bold a heart ? And what was there now that he could do ? Those days were far removed when a man could lay about him with a club ; there is no isolation like that of the noble of heart.

Everything beset them. Being " different ", what consideration, what respect, what protection, what compassion, could they look for ? Contrary to the Gospel precept about pearls, and about what the Crucified Word called " the bread of the children ", repressive laws are mainly for the profit of the swine and the dogs.

Ah! Had they been rich, all the paunches around them would have grovelled to the ground. The populace would have longed for more tongues to lick their shoes! Léopold, who had in the old days thrown away a million francs in the African deserts, spent twenty days and as many nights by the bedside of his wife, almost without sleep or food ; torn between the attentions that had to be given to his wife and the terrible anxiety of the shifts he had to think up to ensure that she would not lack for anything ; discerning with a fearful clarity, from under the billows that overwhelmed him, the clamour outside their house, and tempted, oh, how often! to rush out and exterminate that rabble.

Joly's devotion saved these two creatures so cruelly beloved of God. This excellent man did endless errands for Léopold, made endless journeys on his behalf, and often divided with him the killing fatigue of his day-and-night bedside watching. He contrived ways and means, almost impossibly ingenious shifts, incredible credit, seemed almost able to conjure money from the air. He was forever to be seen in the pawnshops. Not Providence itself could have done more. During one of her fits of delirium Clotilde saw his bald head among the faces of those children whom Jesus bade men suffer to come unto Him.

One evening, when the dear woman had managed to get to sleep, in spite of the incessant shoutings to which she had eventually become insensible, Léopold left the custody of the house to his loyal friend, and went out on an important errand which he could confide to nobody but himself.

A little short of the fortifications, though walking very swiftly and unbrokenly unaware of any external object, his eyes suddenly conveyed to him a disturbance that brought him to a sharp halt. Poulot, the bailiff, was before him.

Night was falling, and the spot was a completely deserted one. To beat the man up mercilessly would have been an easily indulged delight for the victim of persecution who was so close to despair, and at first he thought of doing so. But he retained sufficient command of himself to remember that he was dealing with a jackal of the police authorities, and that the wretch's revenge might definitely and finally cost Clotilde her life, by depriving her altogether of his presence and his care for an indeterminate period. So he choked down his rage, with an effort, that felt as if it would kill him, stepped up to the rascal, and said, with a voice that shook a little :

"Monsieur Poulot, I need hardly point out to you that we are very much alone, and that it merely rests with me to break your neck, if I were so disposed. Consequently, you are going to listen to me quietly and respectfully, I fancy. A few words will suffice. I am not in the habit of making long speeches to people of your sort. You are aware, I presume, of what takes place at your house. And you are not unaware that the imminent danger of death of somebody whom I will not do you the honour of naming before you is the work of your drunken wife. So here is my warning, given you for the first and last time, which I advise you to consider carefully. If the lady to whom I have referred should succumb, Monsieur Poulot, do you understand?—I should consider that I had no longer anything in this world to lose, and I swear to you that you would be in greater danger, you and your woman, than if your house were struck by lightning! . . ."

With those words, he turned away, having uttered them in a tone calculated to stab into the poltroon's vitals like a spear; indeed, the fellow was incapable of emitting the faintest sound.

Soon afterwards, however, an enormous melancholy had fallen upon Léopold. What good had that scene done? Was not that man beneath anything whatever? Even supposing he attempted to make his mate share his own cowardly fright, with which obviously he was inspired for at least a few days to come, it was all too likely that the female of the species would see in the incident a pretext for demonstrating the superiority of her own courage, and take a renewed pride in braving a peril that did not immediately menace her!

However much of a coward she might be in reality—

and although in her old days she had probably been beaten black and blue many a time—her brazenly shameless behaviour must have given her an obsession, of the sort which is so fixed in the basest of her kind, of the divine right of woman to immunity in respect of any insolence, or malice.

" And then," Léopold reflected, hopelessly, " they are so stupid, so abjectly ignorant! So utterly senseless! Apart from the sweating terror that an imminent trouncing might inspire, what is there that they are capable of understanding, how could they even vaguely sense the danger of driving such a one as myself to extremities ? "

Then did this man of courage, this partisan of the impossible, this leader of forlorn hopes, who had tamed fate, this artist in gold shot with flame, realise the depth of his humiliation.

He realised the nothingness of his strength, the vanity of heroism, the desperate futility of all faculties and talents. He saw himself the counterpart of one of those energetic insects that sup their fill of honey, then are tangled in the gummy threads of a spider's web. In vain do its most forceful efforts rend the unclean weft ; the loathsome foe, sure of its prey, leaps out of reach and promptly gathers up again the broken strands of the revolting snare, around the glittering armour of the victim.

The next morning, and daily thereafter, the defeated man went regularly to receive Holy Communion at the early morning Mass, and for eighteen days, two novenas of Masses, from a mouth filled with the Blood of Christ, uttered this cry :

" Lord Jesus! I crave, for Your justice' sake, for Your glory's sake, *for Your NAME'S sake*, that You bring to confusion those who outrage us in Your House, who hate us, who slay us, who aggravate so cruelly our penance.

" Since such appears to be the final form taken by the hostility of the Demon who so long sealed my lips, and from no man can I hope for anything, it is to You, Jesus, concealed under the species of the Eucharist, and hidden within myself, that I appeal for protection.

" Without circumlocution or periphrasis, I ask from You against these two women rigorous chastisement that may make Your Name shine forth, to wit, a very manifest chastisement, that will make their sin to be seen. And, finally, I ask that this chastisement may be soon.

" And I make this cry to You, Lord, from the very depths, by the mouth of Your Ancestor David, by the Patriarchs, and by the Judges, by Moses and by all Your Prophets, by Elijah and by Enoch, by St. John the Baptist, by St. Peter and by St. Paul, by the Blood of all Your Martyrs, and especially by Your Tabernacle in the Flesh of Your Mother!

" Note, Lord Jesus, that *I offer You no less than my life* in return for this justice, which I call upon with all the power given to human prayer by Your Passion! "

When Clotilde heard of this amazing prayer, she clasped her hands together, gently threw back her head, with tears running down her face, and said, simply, just this :

" The poor souls! The poor souls ! "

CHAPTER LIV

THEY started work again. The book that had been put
aside for three months—which was their sole resource
for the future, if it was God's will that such poor creatures
were to have a future on this earth—was resumed. As
before, this labour was constantly interrupted by poverty
or pain. But, owing to the good Joly continuing to play
Providence, they were able to plod on with it till its
completion began to be in sight.

Ever since the " eighteen days " of that terrible prayer,
the enmity of their neighbours seemed to be stricken with
some sort of paralysis, and Léopold, with a frightful assured-
ness, placidly awaited the catastrophe.

As a result of some kitchen squabble or other, the two
cats quarrelled and old woman Grand moved away. A
little while later, she was found dead in her room, at the
end of the village, with her entrails devoured by her dog,
a horrible, wall-eyed mastiff, pike-nosed, and with a
resemblance to its mistress.

" Now it's the other one's turn," Léopold remarked
quietly to the postman who told him the news.

This remark was overheard by Mme Poulot, who was
never far off; and for her it seemed to be the signal for
every kind of disaster. The Bailiff, discreditably involved
in some compromising fiasco, had to sell up his " recep-
tion-room "; even their most loved relics, the mirrored
wardrobe, and Madame's sofa—which she used to show
off with pride, like a veteran displaying his shield—disappeared, and the gracious couple departed to hide their
humiliation in Paris.

It took a week to disinfect their lair.

The persecution was finished with, more than finished with, for a sort of abject, superstitious terror spread round Léopold.

But the accuser still waited. He *knew* that there was more to come, that there must be more, and that not for merely that had he pledged the Body of Christ.

CHAPTER LV

" Woe unto the man who has divine thoughts, who is mindful of Thy Glory, while he dwells in the tents of the swine! " Druide said one day, on his return from a distant part of the world. In these words he summed up a whole course of inward lamentation on the subject of Marchenoir, and his host and hostess, who had just told him their story.

" Assuredly," said Léopold, " after our dear Cain, that was the lot of L'Isle-de-France. We've heard nothing of him, by the way, for a long time. What's become of him ? "

Across the open pages of the book that was the worthy Lazare's face there passed a gust of distress and rage.

" Become of him! Ah, my friends, anybody is lucky who can believe in a justice beyond that of men! I say that for all of us. But poor Bohémond! It is really too ghastly! Why, haven't you heard at all ? Of course— forgive me! I was forgetting that you have barely come up from the valley of the shadow! Well, here goes: He is passing peacefully away in the arms of—Folantin!

"Folantin! That leaden painter, that diarrhetic gris-aille merchant! That plagiarist of the null, that envious, sneering Philistine, who probably thinks the Himalayas are a low conception! Know what he did? Oh, ever so simple. Just made himself the custodian of the poet's last days, the sole, solitary watcher at his death-bed. Nobody allowed to see L'Isle-de-France without Folantin's orders or permission. Just that. Nobody who might have advised or warned him—Oh, I know it's hard to believe what I'm telling you. But it's only too true, unhappily. You behold in me one of the most amazing and amazed victims of that policy of excluding everybody who was a real friend of Bohémond's. I had been in Paris for two days and in those two days had made a dozen attempts to get in, at the hospital of the Brothers of St. Jean-de-Dieu, which seemed likely to be his last dwelling-place till the hour when he should be carried to the cemetery. Invincible obstacles, impassable doors! My cries of indignation almost got me thrown into the street."

"But, my dear Lazare," interrupted Léopold, "are you in your right senses? *Persons* can't be *confiscated* like that! Unlawful imprisonment! In a public institution!!! Come, come, old friend, try and explain a bit."

"Patience! You'll see it all clearly enough—if you're not blinded with tears. L'Isle-de-France was a voluntary prisoner, persuaded into solitary confinement. Oh! That was a story that went back a good many months. The last time we saw him together, a little while before I went away, you remember, he already felt seriously ill. It must have been about then that Folantin came on the scene. His pictures may be rotten, but his conquest of L'Isle-de-France was a veritable masterpiece, if you like.

"You know how our friend despised him, detested him ; some of the things he said about that botcher were enough to scare anyone. You couldn't think of two people more utterly opposite, more completely antipathetic to one another. But what's the good ? Bohémond was above all a man of *feeling*. He wasn't like Marchenoir, or like you, Léopold, with a rigid code of rules, a creed that not all the centuries could bend ; he was sophisticated with Hegelianism, undermined with the most perilous curiosities, sometimes unbelievably lacking in equilibrium ; it has always been obvious that he could never resist anybody clever enough to exploit hypocritically any real or pretended act of kindness."

"That's a true picture," said Léopold. "But it always seemed to me that there was in him an unusually watchful joker who wouldn't be easily caught napping."

"Certainly. But I think, towards the end, that faculty got a bit rusty. Whatever his disease was, he died mainly of sheer weariness. He was really not made to deal with the business of this world ; poverty—against which he was always defenceless—had three-quarters wiped him out. Remember his extraordinary fits of absent-minded-ness—how impossible it was to seize and retain his attention when he was communing with his phantoms—the sole realities, for him. Marchenoir was the only man I knew who could ever master his chimerical imagination, even for a moment or two, and even then——!

"Besides, and mark this, Folantin is a very subtle fowler—and managed to turn up just at the psychological moment. He began by getting hold of a poor boy who was particularly devoted to L'Isle-de-France and was con-stantly seeing him. This chap, a criminal unwittingly, was so imbecilically persevering in singing the praises of the painter, while putting up the best defence that he could manage for his absurdities and intellectual weaknesses, that Bohémond got to the point where he began to fancy he must have misjudged the man, and consented to welcome him. Folantin, who is not miserly, contrived to display infinite tact to get him to accept financial help that he knew was desperately needed, without waiting for the unhappy dreamer to confess or betray his difficulties, and going beyond the poor man's most secret desires, even, with a perfect geniality and suavity. The trick was infallible, and succeeded beyond all hopes.

"In short, taking advantage of his victim's double distress, material and mental, and appearing as his benefactor, he contrived, like a petty, jealous mistress, to drive all Bohémond's old friends away, do what they would, and succeeded—God knows how, or by what lies and treacheries!—in setting him against them. It was by Bohémond's expressed wish that I was refused admittance to him.

"But that's nothing, or next to nothing. Hear the rest of it.

"Naturally you can realise that I wasn't likely to accept such orders without a fight. Not to put too fine a point on it, I tried to *force* my way in. Then they called out the guard—to my unspeakable consternation, I was confronted with a vile drunken horror of a woman who proclaimed herself to be no less a personage than the Comtesse de L'Isle-de-France, the lawfully wedded, death-bed-marriage wife of the dying man. She was the woman who used to empty his slops, and one evening when he was drunk or mad he'd begotten a child on her.

"When he was practically at the end of his strength, and completely isolated from everybody who might have done his thinking for him, he had ended by giving in to the ' pious ' importunities of Folantin, who prevented his seeing any other way of legitimising his child—though it would have been perfectly easy to ' acknowledge ' the boy without prostituting his name by giving it to the mother. I contrived to find out that the almoner of the hospital, a religious of indisputable good faith, but who was on that occasion beautifully hoodwinked, himself undertook to remove the patient's last scruples. So I fled, and here I am, over my head in grief, choked with disgust."

An oppressive silence followed this narration.

At last Clotilde murmured, as if speaking to herself.

"Nothing happens in this world that is not willed or permitted by God for His glory. So we are compelled to believe that this ugly thing is a means to some unknown and assuredly adorable end. Who knows, but that the terrible passage of death will not be rendered easy to this poor man by such a sacrifice first of what was the mainspring of his earthly life ? But the liars are themselves deceived by themselves. I should not be surprised to learn that M. Folantin believed he was doing a praiseworthy act——"

At this point Hercule Joly, who up to now had been present but silent, interposed :

"Monsieur Druide, I know nothing whatever of the world of artists ; I know nothing of their passions, their feelings, their ways, their code. Will you forgive me asking you a question ? What could have been the motive of this M. Folantin, and what interest could he have had in thus darkening the last moments of M. de L'Isle-de-France? It would be unthinkable for him to have wished to play gratuitously the part of those devils whose function it is to drive the dying to despair."

Léopold got up abruptly.

" *I* will answer that," he said, " in the way Marchenoir would, if I can manage it. You are a Christian, M. Joly, and I think you are a prayerful man. So you do not need me to tell you the Catechism's sublime definition, ' Envy is being sorry for another's good and being glad of harm that happens to him.' Our psychologists can set out their analyses all the length of these walls, without making any impression on the bronze and granite of such a landmark.

" Some years ago, I called on Folantin one day—he was not then the illustrious personage he has become since! When I went in he had just finished reading a newspaper, and threw it down on a table, as if he were getting rid of an adder; with that air of supreme boredom, that smile that chills your blood, which you know so well in him, my dear Lazare. And here, in his own words, is what he felt called upon to say to me : ' When I get hold of one of these rags, I go straight to the obituary column, *and if I don't find the name of one of my friends there, I confess I am greatly disappointed.*'

" Ever since, I have been unable to see him or hear his name mentioned without recalling that epigram of his— a much ' cleverer ' one than he realised! For in it he lit up for me the whole cavernous recesses of his immortal mind and soul. I got a clear view of him, of his terrible soul, as it will be, under a ' new Heaven ', ten thousand centuries hence!

" It is very possible, as my wife has suggested, that in the case of Bohémond, Folantin thought he was doing a heroic act. He certainly took a great deal of pains, and his utter disinterestedness is beyond all question. Your genuinely envious person is the most disinterested, and sometimes the most generous, of mortals. There is no god so exacting as the Green-eyed Idol.

" Of all Folantin's contemporaries, there can be no doubt that L'Isle-de-France was the one man of whom he would be most mortally jealous. The discrepancies pointed out a few minutes ago by Druide constituted an infinite contrast between them. The lofty poet who is about to die—who may be dying at this instant—seemed to have been endowed with every gift—nobility, beauty, genius, absolute courage, expansive and invincible sympathy. Who is there who doesn't remember his sleeplessly active, imaginative and lyrical talents, reminiscent of the wandering fires of the Bible, and the Archangel-like readiness of his epigrams ? One can scarcely imagine how these things would cut up a man who was completely outclassed and whom circumstances incessantly confronted with his shining adversary.

" He took a hideous revenge, as was natural to his type ; and I really think he must have displayed a cunning assiduity that was of the Evil One. The result was worth the trouble. Just think of it! Bringing such a Black Swan as Bohémond—last representative of a proud race, a semiroyal line—to bestow his glorious name, if it were but in the dim twilight of his death-pangs, on a washerwoman! To force him to end up like a ruined libertine, trapped and conquered by his cook! What a revenge!

" You will see, my dear Lazare, we shan't even be able

to attend his funeral. But for you, I should not even have known the poor man was dying! Even if anybody condescended to inform us of the obsequies, which is at least improbable, we should have to go, don't you see? like the vanquished Sarmatians, in the conqueror's triumphal procession—to parade amid the tears of the Dowager, to listen, bursting with shame and rage, to the lachrymose speeches about the ' dear friend who consoled his last moments'. No, I'd far rather, even if it meant condemning myself to starvation, pay for humble Masses for a month, in our isolated church! "

CHAPTER LVI

AT that moment the bell rang, and Léopold stopped speaking to answer the door. But as he approached the garden door, he heard the footsteps of somebody in flight. At the same time, from the end of the street there burst forth the unnatural, monstrous laughter of the Poulot woman.

Had she, then, come purposely for that? It hardly seemed likely, and, after all, it hardly mattered whether she had come for that or any other purpose. But that unholy laugh, that neighing as of the horse of the Apocalypse, now that they had lost their accustomedness to it, caused many windows to fly up, as it went rolling grotesquely through the pilastered vastnesses of the night, in the resonant air.

It rose, fell, whirled, re-echoed, billowed to and fro, drew in like wire cable on a windlass, rushed forth again

with fresh vehemence, with gusts and starts and violent
bursts; then died slowly away, dragging itself out for
sometime with such lugubrious effect that the dogs of
the district fell a-howling.

All this—beneath a glorious sky, beneath tiered hosts
of stars, beneath the awe-inspiring pall of all the silences
of space—at the very moment when they were filled with
the thought of the imminent death of one of earth's noblest
beings—made an uncanny impression on all four listeners
in the ill-starred cottage.

" I have often heard that laugh," said Clotilde, " and it
has always filled me with horror.   But, to-night, there is
something about it I cannot define. . . . To me, it is
as if the unhappy woman were no longer one of the beings
made in the image of God, as if in chastisement for some
terrible crime—of which she sought to stifle the memory
by insulting us—she had become now a little lower than
those animals whom she terrifies.   Does it not seem to
you all as if that laughter were an expression of the direst
despair ? "

" It sounds to me chiefly like an expression of insanity,
which is certainly nothing comical or reassuring," remarked
Hercule Joly, simply.

" I am afraid you may think I am mad myself," said
Clotilde, " but I can't help telling you what I feel at this
moment.   It is undoubtedly true that for souls, space and
time do not exist.   We are utterly unaware of anything
and everything that occurs around us invisibly.   In my
delirium, when I was ill, I saw terrible beings who laughed
like that at the view of my sufferings, and cruelly pointed
out to me other sufferers without number, dying men and
women, some in ghastly agonies, to the farthest confines

of the earth, and I was told that there was connection between those unhappy souls and myself, a mysterious link. Well! I am thinking of that friend of ours who is fighting against death to-night, and I am wondering if what we have just heard is not a *warning*. Yes, my friends, I am terrified, wondering if that horrible laughter may not be a passing-bell—if there may not exist, stretching from M. de L'Isle-de-France to that creature down there, a spiritual bond comparable to the bond of flesh with which they have tried to strangle his last hours, and whether each of them may not be, at this moment, falling into the abyss each has chosen!"

The voice of Léopold's wife had *altered*, and her concluding words were pronounced as if she had been projected outside her own self.

Druide, a prey to an extraordinarily powerful emotion, remembered, then, that he had once heard the good Gacougnol say that she really had something of the prophetess about her.

They became silent, while their hearts took on the weight of a universe. The night by now was well advanced. They parted, and Clotilde, offering both her beautiful hands at once to her two guests, addressed them with this strange sentence, seeming to be a continuation of her vision:

"Life, dear friends, is the open hand—death, the same hand, closed. . . ."

Later, she prayed, for a long time, with a great love, for the living and the dead, and, when she slept, she beheld a loaf of bread which she shared out among the poor. That bread, instead of casting any shadow, cast a *light*. . . .

The next day, they learned that L'Isle-de-France had died during the night, and that Mme Poulot, completely insane, had been locked up at the St. Anne Asylum, in the " violent mania " section, whence she was to come out again only when carried feet foremost, with her neck twisted. . . .

Léopold quietly prepared to appear before God.

CHAPTER LVII

To-morrow will be the rent-day for October. Doubtless, the rent will be paid, as it has been in other months. With what money ? Only God knows. All that His creatures can know is that, ever since the foundation of Rome, where the savage Twelve Tables handed the debtor over to his creditor to be sold or cut to pieces, there has never been encountered a more savage beast than Léopold's and Clotilde's landlady.

Behold her, seated in her pew, a few rows in front of Léopold and his wife, who have come to hear the High Mass. She has no doubt already made many copious acts of thanksgiving, and expressed her gratitude to the Lord that she is not as the publicans.

At any rate, one thing that is sure and comforting, is that she cannot bite them then and there. " Sufficient unto the day is the evil thereof," says the Sermon on the Mount.

A priest has just ascended to the pulpit. This is not the rector, a personage of virtue, without indiscretion or wildness, who one day, when questioned by Léopold as to

the religious sentiments of his parish, made this reply:
"Oh, my dear Sir—there are none but very small estates
here!"—*he* did not once come to console the new members
of his flock when they were in the deepest shadows of
their torment.

No, it is not he.   It is a humble assistant-priest, the one
who administered the Rites to Clotilde.   She gazes at
him with very gentle eyes, and prepares to listen.   Who
knows but that this "unprofitable servant" may not be
about to give precisely the sermon that she needs?

And what an opportunity, that day, to speak to the
poor, to the suffering masses!   That Sunday is the twenty-
first after Pentecost.   The Gospel of the Two Debtors
has just been read.

"Therefore is the kingdom of Heaven likened unto a
certain king, which would take account of his servants.

"And when he had begun to reckon, one was brought
unto him, which owed him ten thousand talents.

"But forasmuch as he had not to pay, his lord com-
manded him to be sold, and his wife, and children, and all
that he had, and payment to be made.

"The servant therefore fell down, and worshipped him,
saying, 'Lord, have patience with me, and I will pay thee all.'

"Then the lord of that servant was moved with compassion, and loosed him, and forgave him the debt.

"But the same servant went out, and found one of his
fellow-servants, which owed him an hundred pence: and
he laid hands on him, and took him by the throat, saying,
'Pay me that thou owest.'

"And his fellow servant fell down at his feet, and
besought him, saying, 'Have patience with me, and I will
pay thee all.'

" And he would not : but went and cast him into prison, till he should pay the debt.

" So when his fellow-servants saw what was done, they were very sorry, and came and told unto their lord all that was done.

" Then his lord, after that he had called him, said unto him, ' Oh thou wicked servant, I forgave thee all that debt, because thou desiredst me :

" 'Shouldest thou not also have had compassion on thy fellow-servant, even as I had pity on thee ? '

" And his lord was wroth, and delivered him to the tormentors, till he should pay all that was due unto him."

What a text to paraphrase, on the eve of the date when so many poor beggars are " taken by the throat "! All the men and women who have been let off and set free, all the landlords and landladies, are there ; and it might not be absolutely impossible for just a few of their consciences to be touched. But the assistant priest is himself a poor beggar, and has general orders to humour the well-filled paunches, so he shies at the " taking by the throat ", and interprets the parable, a parable that is, after all, so explicit, so unequivocal, as a precept of indefinite elasticity for the forgiveness of injuries, thus overlaying with the sacerdotal confectionery of St. Sulpice that indiscreet and inconvenient lesson from the Son of God.

Then a cloud fell about Clotilde, and she slept. And now it is another priest who is speaking :

" There is the Gospel lesson, brethren, and here are your hearts. At least, I presume you have brought them with you. I should like to feel sure you have not left them at home, in the cash-drawers of your tills or under your counters, and that I am not just speaking to corpses. So I hope I may be allowed to ask those hearts of yours if they understood anything of the parable that has just been read.

"Nothing at all, did they? I suspected as much. Probably most of you had as much as you could do reckoning up the sums of money you will, or may, receive to-morrow from your tenants, which will probably be paid over with inward maledictions.

"At that passage where we read that the servant let off by his Lord took by the throat that other wretched man who owed *him* a trifling amount, some of your hands must have *clenched* instinctively and unawares, even here, before the Tabernacle of the Father of the poor. And when he sent him to prison, refusing to listen to his prayers, why, then I am sure you were unanimous in exclaiming within yourselves that he acted very properly, and that it is very vexing that there should be no prison of that sort nowadays.

"That, I think, is about all the fruits of this Sunday instruction to which only your Guardian Angels have listened, trembling. Your Guardian Angels, alas, your grave, invisible Angels, who are with you in this house, and who will still be with you to-morrow when your debtors bring you their children's bread or beg you in vain to have patience with them. And the poor, too, will be accompanied by *their* Guardians; there will take place ineffable conversations, while you are crushing those unfortunates with your wrath or your even crueller satisfaction.

"The remainder of the parable is not meant for you, is it? The contingency of a Lord who might in His turn

take *you* by the throats is just an invention of the priests.
You owe nothing to anybody—your books are in perfect order—your fortunes, big or small, have been most
honestly acquired, naturally—and all the laws are armed
in your favour, including even the Law of God.

" You have no idols at home—that is to say, you don't
burn incense in front of wooden or stone images and
adore them.   You don't blaspheme—in fact, the Name of
the Lord is so far from your thoughts that it would never
even occur to you to ' take it in vain '.   On Sundays, you
pay God the overwhelming honour of your presence at
His church; it is the respectable thing to do, and sets a
good example to the servants; and, after all, it doesn't
really affect *you* in any way.   You honour your fathers and
your mothers—in the sense that you don't fling handfuls
of filth at their faces from morning to night.   You do
not kill—with the sword or with poison.   That would be
displeasing to men and might scare away your customers.
Moreover, you don't indulge in debauchery in a too openly
scandalous way, you don't tell lies as palpable and big
as mountains;   you don't steal—not on the highways,
where one might so easily get hurt, nor by robbing banks,
which are always so admirably guarded.   So much for
the commandments of God.

" As to the commandments of the Church—well, when
one is ' in business ', as you put it, one has something else
to do besides being everlastingly looking up the ecclesiastical calendar;   and it is universally conceded that ' God
does not expect so much as that '.   That is one of your
most cherished maxims.   So, you are above reproach,
your souls are clean, you have nothing to be afraid of. . . .

" God, my brethren, is very terrible, when it pleases

Him to be terrible. There are here individuals who believe themselves to be among the Elect Souls, who frequent the Sacraments often, and who oppress their brothers with burdens heavier than death. The question is whether they will be precipitated to the feet of their Judge before they awaken from their awful sleep. . . .

"The irreligious think themselves heroes to put up a fight against the Almighty. They are proud men, some of them not inaccessible to compassion, but they would weep with shame could they but see the feebleness, the poverty, the infinite desolation and destitution of Him Whom they defy and insult. For God made Himself Poor when He made Himself Man, and, in a certain sense, He is for ever being crucified, for ever being abandoned, for ever expiring in torments. But what are we to think of these people, here, who are incapable of shedding a tear, and who do *not* consider themselves irreligious? And, above all, what are we to think of those who dream of eternal life, in shirt-sleeves and slippers, in the ingle-nook by the fire-side in Hell? . . .

"I have spoken to you of the poor tenants, with whom this parish is plentifully supplied, who are already trembling at the thought of the ill-treatment they may get from you to-morrow. Have I spoken to a single soul who is truly Christian? I do not venture to think so. . . .

"Oh, if I could but be a voice crying within yourselves! Could I ring the alarum in the depths of your fleshly hearts! Could I make you feel the salutary anxiety of a holy fear lest you might find your Redeemer among your victims! '*Ego sum Jesus quem tu persequeris!*' was what was said to St. Paul when he was fuming with rage against the Christians, who were then looked on like the 'tenants' in the Devil's City, and were driven out from one sheltering-place to another, with sword and fire, till they should pay, with their last blood, the rental of their eternal dwelling place in Heaven. 'I am Jesus, whom thou persecutest!'

" We know how often He, the Master, would hide Himself among the poor, and when we ill-treat a man afflicted with want, we know not which of the Members of the Saviour's Body we may be rending. We have learned, from that same St. Paul, that there is still something incomplete in the Sufferings of Jesus Christ, and that this something has to be made up in the living Members of His Body.

" ' What time is it, Father? ' His poor children cry to God, throughout the centuries, ' for we watch without knowing " the hour nor the day ". When will the suffering be finished ? What is the time by the clock of Your unending Passion ? What time is it ? '

" ' It is time to pay your rent, or to get out and die in the gutter, along with the children of the dogs ! ' replies the Landlord. . . .

" Ah, Lord, I am a very bad priest! You have entrusted me with this sleeping flock, and I know not how to awaken them. They are so vile, so horrible, their stench rises to Heaven, as they sleep!

" And here am I, falling asleep in my turn, through watching them sleeping! I am falling asleep as I speak to them, I fall asleep as I pray for them, I fall asleep by the bedside of the dying, by the biers of the dead ! I fall asleep, Lord, as I consecrate the Bread and the Wine of the dread Sacrifice! I sleep at Baptisms, I sleep in the Sacrament of Penance, I sleep at the administration of

Extreme Unction, I sleep at the celebration of the Sacrament of Matrimony! When I am joining, for Your
eternity, two beings made in Your Likeness, who are
stupefied with sleep, I am myself so heavy with slumber
that I bless them as from the depths of a dream, and almost
could I roll on the floor at the foot of Your Altar! . . ."

Clotilde "woke up" just as the humble priest was
leaving his pulpit. Their eyes met, and, because her face
was bathed with tears, he must have thought it was his
sermon that had set them flowing. Doubtless he was
right, for that woman with the gift of Vision had sunk
into a sleep so deep that she might very well have been
listening to the *real* words that he had not dared to pronounce save in his heart.

CHAPTER LVIII

LÉOPOLD and Clotilde are at the cemetery at Bagneux.
They always find peace walking there. They speak to the
dead, and, after their fashion, the dead speak to them.
Their son Lazare and their friend Marchenoir are there,
and the two graves are lovingly tended by them.

Sometimes they go and kneel in another cemetery where
are buried Gacougnol and L'Isle-de-France. But it is a
long journey, and often impossible, and the great garden
of sleep at Bagneux, not ten minutes from their home, is
their special delight, because it is the resting-place of the
poorest.

Grave-sites bought "in perpetuity" are rare, there,

and the guests it harbours, stripped every five years of their wooden casings, are then dropped indiscriminately into a nameless pit of bones. Other poor come pressing on their heels, impatient in their turn to find shelter beneath the soil.

The two visitors hope passionately that before that time has elapsed, before that other *rent-day* has fallen due, it will have become practicable for them to give a last home with more stability of tenure to those they so greatly loved. They themselves, it is true, may die, between now and then. The will of God be done. There will always be the Resurrection of the Dead which no by-laws can anticipate or prevent.

Moreover, the place is a lovable one. The municipal authorities of Paris, who have forbidden the ancient use of the monumental cross, while at the same time mockingly multiplying its *sign* in the systematic symmetrical design of their suburban burial grounds, has at least consented to the planting, along the avenues of the cemetery, of plenty of trees. At first, that geometrical, verdureless plain, was heart-breaking. Now that the trees are more vigorous in their growth, and have succeeded in thrusting their roots down into the hearts of the dead, there falls from them, along with their melancholy shadow, a grave sweetness.

How often, from the first moment the gates opened, Léopold had come there, and gone from the one to the other of the two graves, pulling up weeds, clearing away stones, binding up or trimming the young plants, and freeing them of insect pests, joying at the sight of a new rose, a nasturtium, or a just-flowering convolvulus, watering them with slow care, forgetting the world, and spending hours there, especially by his child's little white tomb, talking to the baby, and singing to it, under his breath, the *Magnificat* or *Ave Maris Stella*, as in the old days when he used to nurse it to sleep on his knees!   It stirs the hearts of passers-by to see that singing man, his face bedewed with tears, kneeling over the little cradle.   Clotilde came to join him, and found him in that attitude.

" Oh, my dear!   How lucky we are to be Christians! To know that death has so little real existence, that in reality it is only *something that people mistake for something else*, that the life of this great world is such a complete illusion!

" At the birth of Jesus, the angels announced to all men of good will peace ' *in terra* '—on *earth*—or ' *in earth* '.   It was you who yourself taught me that double meaning.   Look at these graves of Christians.   On almost all of them, these words—*Requiescat in pace*.   Don't you think this is how we may interpret the sacred Word ?   Is not rest, Rest, my beloved, the name of the Divine Life ?

" What are the doings of men by comparison with that powerful life which the Holy Spirit holds in reserve *beneath* the earth, along with the diamonds and the worms, for that unknown moment when all dust shall be awakened again ? "

" That moment is our sole hope.   Job invoked it, forty-six centuries ago.   The Martyrs invoked it, in their torments.   Death is sweet to those who are awaiting it."

Both of them went up and down among the graves. Many were untended, completely abandoned, arid as ashes.   These were the graves of the very poor, who had not left a single friend behind them among the living, and whom nobody remembered. They had been thrust away there, one day, because they had to be put somewhere. A brother, or a son, or sometimes a grandparent, had borne the expense of a cross, and then the three or four bearers had gone off to have a drink, and had parted with tipsy sententiousness. And that was all. The hole filled in, the grave-digger had planted the cross with a few strokes of his pick, and gone off to have *his* drink. No border ever had been or ever would be set there by anybody, to mark out the sleeping-place of a poor man who at that moment perhaps was seated at the right hand of Christ. . . . Beneath the onslaught of the rains, the loose earth had yielded and flattened out, and so many stones had come to the surface that not even weeds could grow there. Soon the cross would fall and rot in the ground, and the poor wretch's name be obliterated and exist no more except on a register of the dead.

Léopold and Clotilde had a great compassion for those forgotten ones, but what pierced them to the heart with loving pity was the crowd of tiny graves. One must visit the great necropolises around Paris to realise how great is the slaughter of children in the shambles of poverty. There, there are to be seen long rows and rows almost exclusively consisting of little white biers surmounted by absurd crowns of sham pearls, and cheap medals proclaiming illiterate sentimentalities.

But there are a few unsophisticated exceptions. Here and there, in a sort of niche attached to the cross, can be seen, exhibited along with the dead little one's photograph, the humble toys that had amused it for a brief few days. It was before one such grave that Léopold had often seen kneeling a desolate old woman. She was so old, she could no longer weep. But so grievous was her lamentation that strangers who heard it wept for her.

" The poor old woman is not there," he said. " I should have liked to see her again. I think I should have had the courage to speak to her to-day. . . . Perhaps, now, she herself is laid somewhere here, nearby. Last time we saw her, she seemed scarcely able to drag herself along."

" Happy those who suffer and weep, my dear! " replied his wife, her beautiful face lighting up. " Don't you sometimes hear the dead singing ? Just now, I was talking about the Noel angels, that heavenly host who sang ' Glory to God in the highest, and to men peace *in* the earth '. That sublime chant has never ceased, for nothing in the Gospel can ever cease. Only, since Jesus was placed in His Sepulchre, I think the canticle of the angels is continued beneath the earth, by the hosts of the dead to whom has been given peace. Many a time I have thought I could hear it, in the silence of created things that seem to be alive, and it is an inexpressibly sweet harmony. Oh! I can pick out distinctly the deep voices of the aged, the humble voices of men and women, the clear ringing voices of children. It is a triumphant concert of joy, that conquers the distant, despairing tumult of the lost souls.

" . . . Among all those voices there is one that sounds to me like that of a man of extreme age, a centenarian, carrying the burden of many centuries, and that voice has on me the effect of a placid beam of light reaching me from the remoteness of a forgotten world.

" This dreamer of a wife of yours has told you of this before, Léopold, mine, without being any too clear, herself what she was talking about. But I am certain

that I have seen him in my dreams, an old man, all broken
and withered by several thousand years of burial, and
although he did not speak to me, I sensed that he was a
man of my own blood, one who must have been great
among other men, in some nameless land long before
all the ages of history, and that he, rather than anyone else,
was mysteriously commissioned to watch over me. . . .

" And our Lazare's voice—how often I have recognised
that!

" . . . When I was suffering too much, when I felt
my heart slipping away into the abyss, he would whisper
to me, ' Why are you grieved ? I am close to you, and,
at the same time, close to Jesus, for spirits have no *place*.
I am within the Light, within the Beauty, the Love, the
Bliss, that is without limits. I am with the very pure,
and with the very meek, with the very poor, with those of
whom the world is not worthy, and when you have cried
too long over me, dear mother, you don't see that it is God
Himself, God the Father, who takes you in His arms,
and pillows your head on His bosom to sleep! . . ."

Léopold, shaken with emotion, had dropped onto a
seat, and was gazing at his inspired partner through a veil
of tears.

" You are right," he murmured, " we are lucky, happy, in
a Divine manner, happier, assuredly, than of old, when we
knew nothing better than the human way of happiness,
and it is in this vale of sorrows that we really feel our joy!

" Marchenoir often used to talk to me about the dead,
and he used to speak of them almost as you do, with that
terrific force of his. What do you think he said one
day ? Oh, you will think it beautiful! He said the lost
Paradise is the cemetery, and the only way to recover it

is to die. He had written a poem on that theme, but it
wasn't found among his papers, and was never published.
He read it to me two or three times, but as I only partially
understood it in those days, I have only an imperfect
memory of how it went. However, here is the beginning,
which fixed itself in my mind with an extraordinary clear-
cut definiteness. It deals with a pilgrim, such as there
were in the Middle Ages, who is searching throughout the
world for the ' Garden of Pleasure '. Listen :

" ' Never had man seen, nor ever again will man see,
so redoubtable a Pilgrim.

" ' From his childhood he had sought the Earthly Paradise, the lost Eden, the Garden of Pleasure—wherein is so
mystical a symbol of Woman—wherein the Lord God
talked with His Likeness after He had formed him from
the dust.

" ' This Pilgrim had been encountered upon all the
known highways and upon all the unknown highways,
by men, and by serpents, who drew away from before
him, for the Psalms issued from all his pores, and he was
made as a prodigy.

" ' His whole person was like to some ancient hymn of
impatience, and must have been conceived of yore amid
such sighs as cannot be revealed.

" ' The sun displeased him. Dazzled inwardly by the
hope he held, the cascades of light of the constellation of
Cancer or Capricorn seemed to him as they had come
from some sad expiring lamp, forgotten, in cavernous
catacombs of captive souls.

" ' Alone among all mankind did he remember the blazing
splendours whence their race was exiled, that Sorrows
might begin, and Time begin.

" ' Surely, somewhere, must yet be found that furnace of Beatitude which not the deluge could quench, since the Cherubim were ever there to hold back the charging battalions of the Floods?

" ' Of a surety, it needed but that one should warily search, for time has no licence to destroy that which belongs to it.

" ' And the Pilgrim trod the ways in ecstasies, reflecting that indeed that Garden had been the abode of those who were not to die, and that, the Nine Hundred and Thirty Years of the Father of fathers *could not reasonably begin to be counted till the same moment when he became a mortal,* wherefore the enduring of his sojourn in Paradise must have been absolutely unexpressible in human figures—dare one say millions of years of rapture, according to the wont of computation among the children of the dead! . . .'

" From there, my recollection is confused, at any rate as far as the actual words and images are concerned, but I remember the general outline.

" ' The Pilgrim searches thus throughout his life, continually disappointed, and continually ravished with hope, burning with faith and burning with love.

" ' His Faith is so great that the mountains move aside to let him pass, and his Love so intense that by night he might have been taken for that Pillar of Fire that went on ahead of the Hebrew nation.

" ' He did not know fatigue, and feared no manner of poverty or want. For more than a hundred years he searched and never knew one hour of unhappiness. On the contrary, the more he aged, the more he rejoiced, for he knew that he could not die without having found that which he sought.

" ' But at last the moment is undoubtedly approaching. He had so explored the globe that there was not one corner, not the vilest or the loathliest, that his Hope had not inspected. He had traversed the depths of the rivers and walked over all the beds of the seas.

" ' Deeming, then, that he had reached his goal, he stopped, for the first time, and died of love in a Leper's Cemetery, in the midst of which was the Tree of Life, where, among the graves, there walked, as we are walking, the Spirit of the Lord.' "

CHAPTER LIX

" . . . THEN it seemed unto His beloved as if there opened as it were a place of terror and of darkness, in the midst whereof was seen a fiery furnace. And that fire was fed by no other fuel save demons and living souls.

" Then above that furnace there appeared that soul whose Judgment had even then been heard on high. And the soul's feet were attached to the furnace, and the soul stood upright as it were an entire person. Nevertheless, it stood neither in the highest part, nor in the lowest part, but as it were in the side of the furnace. And the appearance of this soul was terrible and wonderful.

" And, Lo, the fire of that furnace seemed to be drawn upwards from beneath the feet of the soul, even as when water is drawn upward through pipes, and by reason of great pressure it leaped upwards beyond the soul's head, until the veins stood out as if flowing with glowing fire.

" And behold the ears of that soul were seen as it were an open bellows, for the whole brain seethed with a continual wind.

" And behold the eyes had the appearance of being sunk and dead, and seemed as if fixed interiorly to the base of the skull.

" The mouth also was open and the tongue, as if dragged outwards through the nostrils, hung down over the lips.

" And the teeth were like unto iron keys fixed into the palate.

" And behold, the arms were so long that they reached unto the feet.

" The hands also appeared to hold and clench a kind of needle with a burning point.

" Now the skin which was upon the soul was seen to have the appearance of an animal's hide upon the body, and was like unto a garment of linen soaked in moisture. And this garment was so cold that all who looked thereon shivered.

" And from it there issued forth such foulness and corruption of sores and unclean blood, and so evil an odour, that it could not be likened to any foulness of decay upon the earth.

" And when she had seen that tribulation, there was heard the voice of that soul, which said five times : ' Woe! ' crying with all its might aloud, with tears. . . . "
Revelationum Coelestium Sanctae Brigettae,
Liber Quartus Cap. VII.

The Spirit of the Lord does not walk only in the cemeteries. Those who know Him may meet Him everywhere, even in Hell, and He Himself has said, " fire goeth before His Face ".

CHAPTER LX

MAY 25TH, 1887.

Clotilde is alone in the house. Her husband left her some hours ago. The book they have been writing together is at last finished. It has even been printed, and is about to be put on sale. A probable success, and the probable end of poverty.

Léopold will be coming home very late. He had to dine at his publisher's, and then see some other people during the evening. Let him come back when he will, when he can, her beloved, and he will find his wife happy and unanxious.

A Tertiary of St. Francis, she has just finished reading the Office of Our Lady by the last declining rays of daylight, and now she is thinking of God and listening to " the sweet footfalls of night ".

She is filled with a sublime peace. Her spirit, agile, liberated, it seems, from the weight of the body, flits in one instant, without alarm or effort, through all the thirty-eight years of her life. All the terrible, torturing memories, she welcomes with kindliness, as the Martyrs welcomed their Torturers, and her strong composure deprives them of their power to rend her.

She thrusts herself against Heaven with a loving embrace, and gazes at herself *from afar*, as do those about to die.

" What have I done for You, my God ? Scarcely have I endured You to this day—and yet I know that You are as a father, and most of all when You chastise, and that it is more important to thank You for Your punishment than for Your boons. I knew, too, that You said that whoever does not renounce all that he has cannot be Your disciple. The little I knew was sufficient for me to have lost myself in You, if I had but chosen—Sovereign Jesus! Eternal Christ! Infinitely adorable Saviour! Make me a Saint! Make us Saints! Do not allow us who love You to go astray—' the highways are sorrowful, and the paths mourn, because they lead not where they should lead!' "

The church clock was striking nine. Clotilde was counting the strokes mechanically, and the final stroke seemed as beaten upon her own heart. Utter silence all round. It was now darkest night, and a scented, tepid rain was falling.

"Nine o'clock!" she said, in low tones, with a great shudder. "Why am I troubled? What is happening, then, at this moment?"

She made a great Sign of the Cross, and it reassured her, lit a lamp, carefully closed the doors and windows, in accordance with the oft-repeated exhortations of Léopold, who had said he was not sure of being able to get back before midnight.

Never had she so longed for him to be there. All the same, she was not anxious. She was far, even, from being unhappy. But she had a presentiment, almost, that the hour which had just struck was to be a momentous one.

Realising that she would not be able to sleep, she plunged once more into prayer.

First she invoked, with great inward cries, the Divine protection, and the protection of all the Saints, for her absent man. Every feeling and thought in her, all the precious things of her ravaged palace, all the enamels, all the mosaics, all the holy images, all the armour, trophies of victory, even the veil of her old remorse and penitence—assuredly of greater price than the famous Curtain of the sanctuary of St. Sophia, whose woven golden and silver were valued at ten thousand minae—all were flung into the depths of an infinite consecration and petition.

Then, suddenly, a change. She received, as in a flash of light, the certain assurance that she had been heard *most perfectly*. Streaming with tears, her Act of Thanksgiving went up from the depths.

"I have asked only one thing," she murmured. "It is, to dwell in the house of my Lord for ever, and to behold the Pleasure of the Lord!"

Was she unaware that these words came from a Psalm for the Dead? Or rather, does she sense that it must inevitably be so? At all events, the fact remains that it was at that moment that the fire broke out—the fire of the Holocaust of the Spirit.

Many times, ever since her childhood, and even in her most disturbed moments, she had felt the closeness of One who burned, but never had it touched her quite so nearly.

It began with swift, flying sparks, that turned her pale. Then there leaped out great flames. . . . It was already too late to flee, even if she had had the will to do so. Impossible to escape, to right or left, up or down. The courage of twenty lions would be vain, as would be the winged strength of the mightiest eagle. She must burn, she must be consumed. She sees herself in a Cathedral of Flame. It is the dwelling which she has asked, the Pleasure of God accorded to her.

For a long time the flames roared and surged about her, devouring all around, with the twinings and leaping

undulations of great reptiles. Sometimes they would
rear up, in a curving arc, with great bursts of sound, and
fall at her feet, coming no closer than to dart their angry
tongues at her face, at her eyes, at her bosom, melting like
wax.

Where are mankind? And what can men do? Realise,
poor Clotilde, this furnace is but a faint wafting of the
breath of thy Lord. . . . " It may be that the Holy Spirit
has marked you with His sign," the Missionary had said to
her, in the past.

The implacable flames, intense enough now to liquefy
the hardest metals, fell on her at last, all at once, with the
crash of a cosmic upheaval of the stars. . . .

" The children of men, Oh Lord, shall be drunken with
the plenteousness of Thy house, and thou shalt make
them to be drunken with the flood of thy pleasure."

.   .   .   .   .

The next morning, Paris and France learned with horror
of the terrible fire at the Opéra-Comique, where three or
four hundred corpses were still smouldering.

The first sparks had flown at *five minutes past nine*, to
the base music of M. Ambroise Thomas, and the asphyxia-
tion or cremation of the unholy rabble of the urban middle
class who had come to hear it, was beginning under the
" scented, tepid rain ".

That sweet May evening was the procuress or courtesan
of torture, cowardices, and heroisms, beyond description.
As always in such cases, it was unknown souls who came
to the fore.

In the nameless throng, in the crowded tumult of that
Hell's housewarming, desperate men were to be seen

forcing a passage for themselves with slashing knives, and there were to be seen, also, a few men exposing themselves to the most frightful of all deaths to save country solicitors, adulterous barristers, bridegrooms freshly blessed by some registrar complaisant to infidelities, virgins of commerce guaranteed as such by the vendors, or genuine straightforward prostitutes.

And finally some papers told the wildly epic story of an " unknown man " who had arrived on the scene along with fifty thousand sightseers, and had flung himself, none could say how often, into that volcano, dragging out chiefly women and children, snatching an incredible number of imbeciles from the hands of Eternal Justice, like a good pirate, or a demon for whom it was a refreshing bath to plunge in the heart of the flames ; and who, in the end, stayed there, as if " in the house of his God ".

Somebody claimed to have caught sight of him, the last time, in the centre of a whirl of fire, burning, motionless, *with his arms folded.* . . .

Thus was fulfilled, in a way that not even the subtlety of the angels could have foreseen, the amazing prediction of the old Missionary.

CHAPTER LXI

CLOTILDE is now forty-eight, and she looks as if she were at least a hundred. But she is more beautiful than before, and makes the beholder think of a column of prayers, the last column of a temple ruined by cataclysms.

Her hair has turned completely white. Her eyes, burned out with the tears that have furrowed ravines in her face, are almost quenched. Nevertheless, she has lost none of her strength.

She is scarcely ever seen seated. Always walking from one church to another, or from cemetery to cemetery, she stops only to go on her knees, and one would imagine she knows of no other posture.

Her head covered only with the hood of a large black cape, which reaches the ground, and her invisible feet bare in sandals, upheld for ten years by an energy that is much more than human, no cold and no storm can frighten her. Her dwelling is with the rain that falls.

She asks no alms. She is simply content to accept, with a very gentle smile, whatever is offered to her; and she gives it, secretly, to those in want.

When she meets a little child, she kneels before it, as was the custom of the great Cardinal de Bérulle, and guides its pure little hand to make the sign of the Cross on her forehead.

Those comfortable, well-dressed Christians, who are rendered uncomfortable by the supernatural, who " have said unto Wisdom, Thou art my sister ", regard her as mentally unhinged, but the common people treat her with respect, and in the churches there are a few women of the poor who consider her a saint.

Silent as the open spaces of the firmament, she seems, when she speaks, to be coming back from some happy world situated in some unknown universe; it seems to echo in her far-away voice, which age has deepened without marring its sweetness, and even more in her words themselves.

"*Everything that happens is something to be adored,*" she says, generally, with the ecstatic air of one whose cup is filled a thousandfold, and who, for all the stirrings of her mind and heart, can find no formula but that, were it on the occasion of a universal epidemic of plague, or at the moment of being devoured by wild beasts.

Although it is well known that she is a vagrant, even the police, bewildered themselves at her power, do not attempt to interfere with her.

After the death of Léopold, whose body could not be recovered from among the anonymous and ghastly remains, Clotilde had decided to conform to that Evangelical Precept whose observance is commonly considered more unbearable even than the torments of fire. She had sold all that she possessed, had given the money to the poorest of the poor, and had become overnight a mendicant.

What the first years of this new existence must have been like, only God knows! Marvels are related of her that are like those told of the Saints, but what seems really probable is that grace was vouchsafed her to have no need of *rest*.

"You must be very unhappy, my poor woman," a priest said to her, seeing her, dissolved in tears, in front of the Blessed Sacrament during an Exposition. It so happened that he was a true priest.

"I am completely happy," she replied. "One does not enter into Paradise to-morrow or the next day, or in ten years' time—but ' *this day* ', if one is poor and cruci-fied."

"*HODIE mecum eris in Paradiso,*" murmured the priest, and went his way dazed with Divine Love.

By dint of suffering, this woman, a living and strong, courageous Christian, has learned that there is only one way of making contact with God, and that this way, for a woman especially, is Poverty. Not that facile, interesting, *accommodating* poverty, that gives alms to the hypocrisy of this world, but the difficult, revolting, scandalous poverty that must be helped with no hope of glory and that has nothing to give in return.

She even learned to understand—and that is little short of the sublime—that woman only *exists*, in the truest sense, if she is without food, without shelter, without friends, without husband, without children ; that only thus can she compel her Saviour to come down.

Since her husband's death, the woman who was poor by her own choice had become even more than ever the wife of that extraordinary man who gave his life for Justice. Utterly gentle, and utterly implacable.

Naturalised to every form of want and destitution, she was able to see clearly the murderous horror of so-called public charity, and her continual prayer was for a torch flourished against the mighty. . . .

Lazare Druide is the only one who knew her in the past and still sometimes sees her. He is the only link she has not severed. The painter of Andronicus is too lofty to have been visited by Fortune, whose age-old practice is to reward only the unclean. That is why Clotilde can still go to see him, without exposing to the mire of worldly luxury her vagrant's rags, the rags of a " Pilgrim of the Holy Sepulchre ".

From time to time she comes and distils into the soul of the painter a little of her own peace, of her own mystical greatness, then she goes back to her vast solitude, to the streets crowded with common people.

"*There is only one misery,*" she said, the last time she saw him, "*and that is—NOT TO BE SAINTS.*"